The Land
of Angels

The Land of Angels

Fay Sampson

ROBERT HALE · LONDON

ISBN-10: 0-7090-8097-2
ISBN-13: 978-0-7090-8097-8

Robert Hale Limited
Clerkenwell House
Clerkenwell Green
London EC1R 0HT

2 4 6 8 10 9 7 5 3 1

Typeset in 10/12pt Sabon
by Derek Doyle & Associates, Shaw Heath
Printed in Great Britain by St Edmundsbury Press
Bury St Edmunds, Suffolk
Bound by Woolnough Bookbinding Limited

Chapter One

The tall Frankish girl sped across the palace courtyard. She felt the wind lift the ginger hair from her shoulders.

'Your Highness,' a chiding voice gasped behind her, 'a princess does not run.'

Bertha turned impatiently. Clotilda, chief of the ladies who attended the king's daughters, was hurrying herself. Her lined face was sharp with curiosity. It's not my royal dignity she's worrying about, Bertha thought. She wants me to slow down so that she won't miss hearing the news.

Charibert, King of Paris, did not ordinarily summon his daughters to a meeting about state affairs. It was not hard to guess the reason she had been sent for. The message had set her sisters and the palace women agog with squawks and flutterings, like finches when a magpie approaches their nest. An unmarried princess has only one value in political negotiations.

A single question was drumming in Bertha's head. 'Who? Who is it?'

She took a deep breath on the threshold of her father's hall. A guard stood on either side of the carved door – for ceremony, rather than security. She glanced at the ships moored on the River Seine. She had not been curious enough about whom they were bringing. The sentries lowered their spears and swung the doors open.

Bertha stepped from the sunshine of the island in mid-river into the shadows of the audience hall. Her father was seated at the far end in his royal chair, with her mother beside him. Her eyes flew to the strangers on his other side. A foreign delegation stood respectfully in the king's presence, watching her come with open curiosity.

They must be foreigners. Tall, blond men, though not as tall as most Franks. Their fair hair fell loose on their shoulders, like royalty. There was something shocking about that. Frankish warriors wore their hair combed forward over their heads, revealing the nape of their necks. This was unsettling. It made her feel the guards should seize these men and shear or scalp them.

'Bertha.' Her father's voice was kindly. 'These are ambassadors from the kingdom of Kent in Britain.'

She smiled automatically and curtseyed. Her pulses were racing. Kent? She knew the name, but little else. Britain, however, was unmistakable: the island across the Channel where the Empire ended. Barbarians.

'Come here.' Her mother held out a hand, inviting her to stand beside the queen's chair.

Charibert bent towards her. 'The Kentish folk are from old Germanic stock, like the Franks. Their king Aethelbert pays me tribute. Only a narrow channel separates his land from ours. We mean to bridge it.' He looked at his daughter, half-smiling. The smile meant nothing. He was not seeking her approval. He had already made up his mind.

She felt the blood mount in her cheeks. 'How, Father?' She knew, of course.

Her mother's hand grasped hers more firmly. 'Your father has offered you to King Aethelbert as his queen and these ambassadors have agreed to our terms for the contract.'

How much? Bertha wanted to ask. How much have you traded me for? What am I worth in tribute, territory, military service? She said nothing, but tried to keep the courteous smile on her face.

Charibert's own smile widened. 'Well? Does that suit you? I should tell you that Aethelbert is recognized as the greatest king in Britain, though that's small enough beer to the Frankish royal house. Still, you'll be a queen of some dignity.'

'Yes, Father.' A small bow of her head. She had always known this would happen one day. Yet now it had come, it was happening so fast, like a cup slipping from her hand which she could not catch before it shattered on the floor.

No. This was not breaking, but making. She would be a queen, with her own household, her own crown, her own throne beside her husband. A little queen compared to her mother, but still a queen.

The Kentish ambassador spoke, evidently welcoming her acceptance. Another shock. She could not understand him. The Latin translation passed almost unheard.

'I thought you said they were like us?' She turned on her father. 'Don't they speak Latin?'

'They're Germanic speakers, like our cousins beyond the Rhine. As we were ourselves before we became civilized. You'll pick up their English tongue.'

Some more debate, with the interpreters bending close to the principal parties. Charibert turned his beam back to Bertha. 'Of course, I shall give you your own Frankish household to escort you. Clotilda will head your ladies.' It was some satisfaction to see the older woman start. 'King Aethelbert agrees to respect your religion. That will be written into the marriage contract. I can appoint a bishop for you to take as your chaplain.

6

Your immortal soul will come to no harm.'

'He's not a Christian?' The question was jolted out of her.

'The English in Kent, I fear, are like many of the Germanic peoples. They worship gods of thunder and corn, of war and childbearing, as we did once.'

The narrow sea which separated the two lands ran suddenly cold and deep.

'I will have to marry a heathen? Share his bed?'

'You're a princess,' her mother told her sharply. 'Soon you'll be a queen. You have a duty. You're not a peasant girl, free to roll in the hay with her sweetheart.'

Bertha stared at her. Was that how I was got? As your duty to my father, to provide him with royal sons? But I was a girl, a disappointment. Yet still I have some value, a trading counter. Must I bear princes for Aethelbert, and princesses to be traded in their turn?

'That's settled then.' The men on both sides were beaming now. 'This calls for a banquet in your honour tonight, I think.'

The Frankish ship was in sight of Britain almost as soon as it left the harbour. The cliffs shone white through the haze, like a fairy fortress. It added to Bertha's sense of the unreality of what was happening to her. She stood on deck, feeling the breeze cool her face, staring ahead in silence. The wind was gentle, the grey-green waves running past them lightly.

Time passed, and still that shore came only slowly closer. It was some time before the princess realized that the ship's bows were turning eastward. It picked up speed with a following wind. As the Channel narrowed, it was creaming along a course almost equidistant between the Kentish and Frankish coasts.

She looked round for information, and saw Bishop Liudhard making his way along the deck towards her from a conference with the captain. He was not the man she would have chosen for her spiritual companion. Precise and formal in his manner, she would find it difficult to confide in him.

'Where are we going?' she demanded. 'The shore looked so near. I thought we should be there in a few hours.'

Her chaplain bowed his head. 'I beg you to be patient, your highness. The captain says his ship will carry you in comfort round to the River Stour and so to the very walls of Canterbury. It would be rough riding overland.'

It was strange to hear the bishop speaking to her with the same deference he gave her mother, as though she were already a married woman and a queen. To all intents and purposes she was; the contract was signed. Back in Paris, throughout her childhood, her parents' chaplain had laughed off her misdemeanours like those of a wayward child.

For a little while longer she could live in this protective cocoon, on a Frankish ship, surrounded by Frankish maids of honour, her soul watched over by her Frankish chaplain. It was true Aethelbert had sent two Kentish lords to escort her, the ambassadors Dirwine and Herman, and six soldiers, but she could not speak these noblemen's English language, and their knowledge of the Latin tongue was limited. She watched them chatting to each other, playing dice, scanning the shoreline. She had no desire to stir herself out of this trance to converse with them.

Hours stretched into another day. She sensed a new tenseness in the sailors negotiating the shoals and sandbanks around them. Then they were running north and the coast was lower, pale with sand dunes. Her homeland had fallen out of sight.

It was the third day, and Bertha had given up her first eager watching. She sat with her women, playing a game in which a ring was passed secretly from hand to hand and one of them must guess who held it. There was much laughter, some of it high and nervous. This too was unreality. Ordinarily, they would have had their embroidery laid on their knees, stitching away at works of skill and beauty, or spun flax as they chatted. But the rolling motion of the ship led to too many pricked fingers, misplaced stitches or tangled thread. A handful of salt spray might be whipped inboard to stain the work. And so it was a holiday, with tasks laid aside.

Bertha lifted her eyes and gasped. Over the side of the ship she saw a massive fort rushing past. Stone walls higher than the mast of the ship, projecting towers, a girdle of defences, masonry banded with red tiles. Between the fortress and the sea sprawled a township of common houses, wood and thatch.

The princess was on her feet. 'Is this Canterbury?'

Dirwine, the shorter of the Kentish lords, answered, 'No, lady, that's Richborough.' And then some English words she did not understand.

The captain of the ship translated for her. 'He says it's giants' work, my lady.'

Bishop Liudhard laughed, with an edge of unease. 'Heathen superstition. The barbarians who've conquered Britain know nothing of Rome's past glory. Ignorant folk who don't know how to raise one stone on another can only believe that it's done by magic.'

'Looks like their spell's broken, then,' said the captain. 'That castle's falling down.'

As she turned to look back at the fortress slipping away behind them, Bertha saw that was true. Not all the towers still stood to their full height. The girdle wall was crumbling in places. On the northern side, the whole structure had sagged, so that she could see through into the grass-grown space inside.

Would Canterbury be like this? The capital of the greatest king in Britain?

Richborough, it seemed, still stood as a massive gatepost to her husband's kingdom. The ship turned sharply west into a broad estuary. At its entrance, a tree-crowned landmass rose between the river mouth and the open sea.

'The Isle of Thanet, my lady,' the captain pointed. 'Sacred to Thunor.' He watched her face for recognition. 'Him of the Thunder Hammer. They say he's a jolly sort of god, if he's in a good humour. If you were a farmer, you'd want him on your side to give you rain. But he can hurl the lightning if you get on the wrong side of him.'

The bishop silently made the sign of the cross.

Bertha had the sense of threading a labyrinth, as the ship crept deeper and deeper into the land through narrowing creeks. The flat marshes were giving way to wooded slopes. She was gripping the rail now, close to the bows. Each time another fishing settlement edged into view, she thought it must be the outskirts of Canterbury. Only a glance over her shoulder at the two Kentish lords told her, from their relaxed stance, that it could not be. The crew had lowered the sail and were rowing now, against both breeze and current.

'Are we close?' The elderly Clotilda behind her spoke for them all. The women had put aside their games now.

When it came, Bertha did not need Dirwine's voice at her shoulder, 'Canterbury, your highness.'

These walls were stone, too, enclosing an area far wider than Richborough's. They showed the same uneven profile, the lost art of the stonemasons slipping away under the weight of centuries. Some towers still stood bravely erect, usable defences. Yet all the Frankish eyes were drawn to a ruin inside the walls. Towering above the perimeter rose the gap-toothed grin of a stone-built amphitheatre, such as Paris too had boasted. Its highest arches had fallen in. One side of the building had disappeared. Across the city, from still unseen habitations inside the walls, columns of smoke rose into the sky.

My capital, thought Bertha, with alarm and resolute pride.

A party was waiting on the quay ahead. Would Aethelbert be there in person to greet her? He should; she was King Charibert's daughter. The ship stole forward, ground against the crowded wooden wharf. The gangplank was thrown out. Dirwine held out his hand to escort her ashore.

She must concentrate on her feet for the next few moments. It would not do to trip and fall in front of all these people. Her women had readied her for this moment of meeting. Her long tunic was striped with cloth of gold and fine red wool. A cloak of sables fell from her shoulders, though the day was not cold. The white veil pinned to her hair felt odd. As an unmarried girl, she had not needed to cover her hair. The intricate braids beneath it made a heavy circle, like a crown already.

She was down, on Kentish soil, or at least the logs of the wharf. A man was standing close in front of her. She had tried not to let herself see him coming.

'Welcome to Kent, my lady.' The words were coarsely accented Latin, awkward, as if he had been coached to say them.

Bertha looked up then. The form of the greeting had given her no clue who he was. One glance convinced her. This was not a tall man by the standards of the Frankish court, yet he dominated the crowd of Kentish people behind him. Fair hair, clean and combed, fell to his shoulders. The shoulders themselves were padded out with bearskin. Within its bulk, she saw a warrior's figure, lean and straight-limbed. His teeth, she saw with relief at his smile, were good.

At last she made herself look up into his eyes. They were a vivid, penetrating blue, staring hard into hers. She was shockingly aware that this man might have less land, less wealth, less power than her father, but that he meant to be as great a king.

Instinctively, she went down in a deep curtsey. 'My lord.'

A hand grasped hers, strong, warm. Aethelbert raised her up. The gold of many necklaces swung before her eyes. He wore more jewellery than she did.

He relapsed into English immediately. He must know little of her language. The interpreter told her he was asking about her voyage. Stilted courtesies passed between them. She was acutely conscious of the power of his hand holding hers, the physical thrill of his strength. He was leading her the short distance to the city gate. The way the crowds fell back before him and the salutes of the guards were reassuringly familiar. So the crowds in Paris honoured her father. She was going to be a real queen, after all.

Inside the stone defences, the sight of Canterbury was both confusing and, in some ways, recognizable. Everywhere she looked she could see ruin, collapsing stonework, roofless buildings, pools of stagnant water. Yet timbered halls rose among them in a more accustomed magnificence. Their gables and doorways were carved with dragon heads, their thatch was thick and fresh, bright paint adorned the woodwork. Even a Frank might call such a cluster of halls a palace. She remembered her father's assurance: Aethelbert was the greatest king in Britain.

Suddenly, she was not contemptuous of these Kentish folk any more, but young and overawed. She must not show it. She was their queen now. Her future son would rule here.

She drew a deep breath and looked around her more steadily. She found Bishop Liudhard behind her, also studying the patchwork of the city. He was murmuring to himself. A prayer?

Catching her look, he closed the gap between them. 'One of these halls will be your husband's temple, your highness. But don't be afraid: you shall not enter it.'

Her father's cathedral church in Paris had been built partly in stone. It was disturbing to think that the gods of thunder and blood might live in a house here indistinguishable, outside at least, from her own hall. It brought them down to a domestic reality which she found more frightening than stories of sky-deities.

The grip of Aethelbert's hand on her own slackened and fell away. She was startled back into awareness of him. For a while, the pattern of the interpreter's voice had passed over her, telling her more information than her bewildered mind could hold. What must she do now? Where should she go?

The Kentish ladies were beckoning the way to her left. She studied their outlandish dress as she and Clotilda followed them with her own women: the chequered skirts and tight jackets, some barbarian fashion. The men were escorting Aethelbert a different way. This, then, in front of her, must be the queen's hall.

Lofty, dim, cool. She heard birds crooning from high in the rafters. Stray sunbeams fell across the space. There were humbler women, domestics probably, curtseying low to her. A cry went up in unison. They must be welcoming her.

She lifted her newly veiled head high and made her stiff face smile.

'I thank you.'

Bertha, Queen of Kent, stepped over the threshold to take possession of her alien realm.

Chapter Two

Bertha stood, pale with outrage, as the chief priest of the kingdom of Kent bound her wrists to Aethelbert's. Ordulf, servant of the royal god Woden, was a shocking figure, with tattooed face, blood-smeared hands, his cloak hung about with foxes' heads and the plumage of birds.

'I'm a Christian!' she protested. 'It was in the contract. I will not worship heathen gods.'

King Aethelbert turned to her. She caught surprise in those fierce blue eyes, and the verge of anger. Clearly he could not follow this much of her Frankish tongue, but he was not used to contradiction.

Herman, who had escorted her from Paris, summoned an interpreter. He was a slight man, with a crippled leg, who shook as he translated Bertha's defiance. There was a swift reply.

'His majesty says this is the custom of Kent. How else can man and woman be joined in marriage? He is respecting your religion, as he promised. As his royal bride, you ought to be making gifts of corn and beer to Frig, while he sacrifices blood to Woden. So Earth marries Sky. Instead, the king is graciously allowing you to pray to your own God in your own way for children. He, though, will honour our Kentish gods. You must respect that.'

Her skin flinched, as blood spattered their joined hands from a spray of twigs. She wanted to wipe it from her, but her hands were not free, and besides, she did not want to foul any other part of her.

Aethelbert turned, his anger dissolved, and kissed her strongly. Then, as their wrists were untied, he grabbed her hand and ran with her towards the king's hall. The crowd were clapping and yelling a rhythmic chant, from the nobles down to the youngest pot-boy. In front of the door was a circle of fire. In Aethelbert's grip, she had no choice but to leap with him over the nearest flames, across the centre, and out over the far side to the threshold of the hall. The king swept her up in his arms, tall though she was, and made a last bound into his palace. Cheers thundered as the court surged after them.

The chief priest was here again. He held out a red cockerel. The king took the knife and cut its throat. More blood sprayed her. The rafters shook with shouts.

A Kentish woman was holding out something to Bertha. Another shock. This must be a wise woman, a female priest. More tattoos, a cloak with cats' heads, this time. It was hard to distinguish the woman beneath this regalia. She was smaller, darker, than was common for Kentish women. Bertha looked in alarm at what she was offering.

It did not look immediately threatening. A basket of corn, ringed round with flowers. A flask of dark liquid, probably not blood. It reminded her a little of the bread and wine of the Christian Eucharist. The realization of what she was thinking shocked her anew. How could this be anything like the same?

What was she supposed to do with these things? Aethelbert had promised she would not have to offer sacrifice to his gods.

She looked round for her chaplain. Bishop Liudhard's blue cloak was nowhere to be seen. Had he turned his back in protest at these ceremonies? Or been shouldered out of the way by Aethelbert's priests?

The court stood waiting. She must do something to end the silence. Not knowing what significance it might have, she reached out her long fingers slowly and touched the corn.

More cheers shook the air. Now the woman was offering her the flagon too. Bertha shook her head. There was a rustle of unease.

She looked down into the woman's face. The hazel eyes were bright with malevolence. Bertha felt a thrill of fear.

Yet her actions seemed enough. Aethelbert was leading her to the high table. He was smiling broadly, as if satisfied. He seated her beside him in a tall carved chair. She felt a presence behind her place something on her head. The court was roaring again, stamping. She looked at Aethelbert. He too had been crowned. On his fair head he wore a circlet of gold, threaded with corn and flowers. She tried to picture how she must look herself, with the intricate braids of her own ginger hair surmounted now by this more colourful crown.

The feast began. A sea of sounds surged around her. Aethelbert offered her the choicest food, swan's breast and boar's cheek, roast venison and seethed cod. He had given up attempts to make conversation with her, even though the interpreter stood ready. Few others tried. Bertha found herself retreating into an untypical stillness, like a silent rock amid noisy waves. She missed her teasing sisters.

She was forming a resolve. I must learn this language, quickly. As long as I can't speak English, I shall be a nobody here, for all that I wear the crown of a queen. I can't talk to Aethelbert, I can't speak up for myself, I can't influence him. I shan't know what's going on at court if I can't share in the gossip.

She looked down the tables. Her retinue was there. Clotilda, looking disapproving, the younger ladies nervous, Bishop Liudhard was here now, upright and silent, his plump deacon Guntram attempting conversation, but snubbed. An island of Franks among the Kentish people. A wicked little smile curled the corners of her mouth. It would be so tempting to retire with them to her own hall, to lapse into the tongue of her homeland, to shut out this strangeness. How would these loyal Franks like it if she insisted that they converse in English with her?

After the feast, both the Frankish and the Kentish ladies prepared her for bed, in a room decked with more flowers and corn. Despite the difficulties of language, they were all laughing together as they left her. Even Clotilda allowed a difficult smile to her lips.

Bertha heard her bridegroom coming, and the shouts of the men escorting him. She would not need words for what came next.

It was strange to wake and find herself in bed with a man. The king seemed satisfied. Bertha examined her own feelings, a confusion of pain and achievement. She understood what should follow, but it was too soon yet to know.

Aethelbert left her. He had the brisk air of a man who had taken what he wanted and now had other important things to do. Already her women were filling the chamber, bringing her fresh clothes, exclaiming with satisfaction over the evidence of the bed sheets. Nothing in a queen's life was private.

A little Kentish girl carried in heated water for Bertha to be washed. As she set it down, Bertha's hand stayed her wrist. The girl was, she realized, not quite the child she had thought. Her small stature made her seem younger than she was.

'What's your name?' She could not even ask the simplest question in English. She had to point at the girl's chest.

Intelligence dawned in a shy smile. 'Edith.' The girl pointed to herself.

'Edith,' Bertha repeated the name. She reached up a hand and took an ear of corn from the wreath above her bed.

'What's this?' Pointing again.

A moment's puzzlement, then, 'Barley.'

'Bar-ley.'

The girl laughed. 'Good, my lady! Good!' Bertha could understand that much.

She laughed back. Edith's hazel eyes met her own blue ones merrily. Then she seemed to recollect with horror whom it was she was laughing with. Blood flushed her cheeks. She bent her brown head and hid her embarrassment in a deep curtsey. 'I'm sorry, my lady!' There was no need for an interpreter.

Bertha patted the girl's shoulder. 'It's all right, Edith. Thank you. You may go.'

14

The maid's frightened eyes asked questions. Bertha smiled and pointed to the door.

When she was dressed, she called Liudhard to her.

'The king asks that I pray for the success of our marriage to my own God. Where are we going to worship, Father?'

The bishop bowed. 'I don't know, your majesty. Perhaps you could ask the king to build you a royal chapel.'

'And until then?'

'A priest may read the divine office wherever he finds himself at the appointed hour. I have already made evening and morning prayers here with Guntram, though it was difficult to find a quiet place.'

'The queen cannot say her prayers in a corner of the yard.'

'No, my lady. But this hall is yours.'

'Look around you. It's full of Kentish heathen, as well as our own good Franks.'

'You are the queen. You may send them out.'

'Would that offend them?'

'It is the duty of the queen's household not to offend *her*.'

Power. She must get used to holding it, to wielding it. Yet warning voices sounded in her head. She was no fool. She had grown up at the court of Paris. Courts are webs of intrigue. Royal families can be divided against each other. Courtiers may fawn and smile, yet conspire behind their sovereign's back.

'I'm still a stranger here: it's too soon to make enemies.'

Liudhard bowed his respect. 'Your mother has counselled you prudently, I see. Very well. I shall say mass for you here, today. Ordinarily, only those baptized may witness the holy Eucharist, but, as you say, in strange places we must do the best we can. If the Kentish ladies wish to stay, I shall say nothing.' His thin lips spoke disapproval.

Bertha summoned her household. She knelt in front of her Frankish ladies. Liudhard chanted the familiar Latin words in a palace which had never heard them before. Bertha resisted the temptation to look round and see what the Kentish women were doing. Had they fled in fear of an alien god? Lingered out of curiosity? She thought she heard some English whispering from the doorway.

'The body of Christ broken for you.'

'Amen.'

The bread was on her tongue. This she could cling to. This had not changed. Everything else was new. It was hard not to be scared.

'Go in peace.'

She knew the bishop was scared too.

Chapter Three

It was too hot to be striding this fast through the streets of Rome in the hour before noon. They had left the trees of the Caelian Hill behind them. Buildings were closing around them, but their shadows were shrinking under the merciless stare of the sun. Augustine screwed up his eyes against the blaze of light from the Forum ahead and the glittering drum of the Colosseum.

He had thought when he joined Gregory's monastery on a hill over-looking the city that he would be entering a life of spiritual calm and prayer. It was more like being on the staff of a busy city governor.

He struggled to keep in sight of the tall figure in front of him. He could see Gregory's tonsured head, the bald scalp, the ring of black hair, and the broader shoulders of Peter, the deacon, following him. The crowd was surging against them now, threatening to separate Augustine from the others. These were sensible citizens, homeward bound for lunch and siesta. More sensible still were the aristocrats spending high summer on their country estates. But Gregory, noble though he was, would not leave the city, so nor could Augustine.

The sunlight struck him in all its brilliance. He was out in the market place of the Forum. Gregory and Peter were waiting for him. Augustine mopped his flushed face and drew up his cowl to shade his eyes. How could Gregory look so pale? And then he saw the sweat stand out on his abbot's brow, the muscles of his cheeks clench, and his conscience smote him. Gregory was not a well man. He never had been. It did not make any difference to the spirit which drove him. Perhaps it *was* what drove him.

Gregory smiled now for Augustine, with that radiant warmth which drew people into his circle of concern, and made them eager to follow him.

'Too hot for you? Only an hour, Brother, I promise you. Then we'll go home and eat and rest.'

'Why are we here?' Augustine wrinkled his nose as well as his eyes as he looked around at the confusion of neglected temples, new churches, open-air markets. Awnings were spread over food stalls, but they could not disguise the sweating cheeses and the stink of fish. Light scorched from the unshielded displays of glazed pottery, white and coloured cloth, sparkling brass and silver.

'To check that the city is still well provided.' Gregory was running a sharp, assessing eye along the food alleys.

'There were two ships docked this morning,' said Peter, 'with cargoes from the north, they say.'

'For how much longer?' The abbot lifted his dark gaze out over the city. 'The Lombards are advancing on Tuscany. If that falls, what can stop them reaching Rome?'

'And we no longer have an emperor here to receive them,' said Peter drily.

'No.' Gregory let the word fall, with its weight of sadness and resignation.

'It shouldn't fall to you, Father!' Augustine burst out. 'You're our abbot. How can you supervise the city's defences as well? It's too much to ask of you.'

Gregory's eyebrows rose in amusement, even though his smile was grim. 'The penalty of being born into a noble family, of having served time at the court of Constantinople, is that I have duties in this kingdom as well as in the eternal one. Though I wish with all my heart I had not. Sometimes I long to shut my ears and shut my heart to their cries, and spend my days in quiet prayer. But didn't our Lord warn us, to whom much is given, of them much will be expected?'

There was pain in his voice as well his face. Then he turned briskly, drawing himself up straighter, like the soldier he had once been. He strode away from them, and Peter and Augustine could only follow.

The smells and the jostling crowd among the food stalls did not deter Gregory. As he moved along them, he was examining their stock, greeting the stall-holders.

'Did they get a good catch last night, Lucius? You're not short of octopus, I see . . . Is the grandchild born yet, Maria? . . . What's the price of flour today, Thomas? Do you reckon it will last out till harvest-time?'

Some came back at him with grins and jokes, others with loud complaints. The abbot was a familiar figure. They trusted him enough to share their fears, as well as their triumphs. He listened intently, nodded, moved on with a word of encouragement.

Walking in his wake, Augustine tried to imitate his smile, to find a friendly word. It did not come naturally to him, as it did to Gregory. He saw the grins, the indignation, dying from their faces as their eyes moved on to him. His questions fell flat. He was nothing to them. He felt like an alien among the common people.

He felt a stranger, too, here at the hub of Rome's heathen past. Augustine had come to the monastery of St Andrew from a boyhood in southern Gaul. There had been statues from imperial Rome there, too, but nothing like this. He found it hard not to be overawed by the gigantic figures of gods and heroes who loomed over him from so many buildings in Rome. That temple of Saturn behind him, for instance. They were not real gods, of course. There was only one God. But they frowned down at him on all sides of this square. The men were large, muscular, some naked, the women scantily clothed. Many, perhaps the worst, had been smashed. But he could not help thinking that, since Roman emperors had been Christian for nearly 300 years, they should have removed all these images by now. He looked around him with sun-bleared eyes and realized why they could not. Palaces, council halls, courts, theatres, too many were supported on the heads of that pagan pantheon, or had them deeply carved into their façades. Rome could not lightly shed its past.

He came to with a start and looked round in panic. He had lost sight of Gregory and Peter in the pushing crowd. So many stalls, so many alleyways between them. Which way had they gone?

'Here, you fool.' Peter was gripping his elbow, tugging him sideways between rows of live geese. Augustine knew their reputation for being more menacing than guard dogs. He hurried past, keeping his arms folded, prudently out of reach of their craning necks and alarming beaks.

His steps slowed when he saw where Peter was leading him. The platform ringed round with ropes, the pens of huddled humanity. This corner of the square was the slave market. Even before his eyes focused on it his nostrils were assaulted by the stench. The dealers would have cleaned up their cargo as best they could, to make the goods more saleable. But there was still the rank smell of sweaty fear, of uncontrolled bladders, the lingering vomit of voyage.

He would have turned away, but Peter was hauling him closer.

Gregory stood, his hand grasping the rope which fenced the slaves in. His lips were moving. Augustine caught the murmur, '. . . Christ have mercy, Lord have mercy.' Then the abbot tensed. His head went up. He leaned half into the pen, peering through the nearest hunched figures at something on the far side. He began to work his way around the enclosure to the back of the auctioneer's platform. Peter raised his eyebrows to Augustine, shrugged his shoulders, and followed.

Augustine kept close to them. He was beginning to feel giddy in the sun and the pressing crowd. He needed his midday meal, sparse though it would be. He needed cool water, shade, quiet.

'*Who are they?*' The intensity of Gregory's question snapped Augustine awake.

He was staring at two boys, waiting their turn to be sold. They were like no one else in that motley collection of foreigners. There was the usual medley of olive, brown, black skins, black hair, oily and straight or frizzed into curls. But these two boys stood out with skin as fair as alabaster statues. Their hair was straight and blond, like combed flax. Their eyes, when the younger lifted his smudged eyelids to look up at the older one, were sky blue.

'Angles.' The slave-dealer tossed the word over his shoulder. 'From the Island of Britain.'

'No, friend,' – the breath caught in Gregory's voice – 'not Angles, but angels.'

The dealer turned the full force of his attention on the abbot. His eyes sharpened with the prospect of custom.

'You've a shrewd eye for a purchase, sir. It's not often any of these come on the market. Think of the stir they'd cause if you had them serving your guests on one of your feast days.'

'I . . . I wasn't buying.'

'No hurry, sir. We shan't sell these two yet. Come back late afternoon. We'll be keeping a pair as rare as this till siesta's over and the gentry are taking a stroll before supper. They'll go to a connoisseur . . . like yourself.'

The fair-haired boys evidently knew they were being talked about. The older one nudged the younger and whispered something. Were they brothers, Augustine wondered? How had they come to Rome? They looked too young to be prisoners of war. Had their parents sold them to relieve their poverty? Had they been kidnapped by pirates and spirited away, never to be seen by their families again? The boys' blue eyes were fixed on Gregory, as if in hope. Or was it fear?

'There are many English kings in Britain,' Gregory persisted. 'All as yet beyond the reach of grace. Which kingdom are these from?'

'One they call Deira. Up north, I believe.'

'In Latin *De ira* means "from wrath". Would that the mercy of God could deliver them from the wrath to come.'

'Wrath? I beg your pardon, sir? Gentle as lambs, these two. And they're safely shackled.'

The boys' wrists were bound with rope. A loose chain linked their ankles together.

'Tell me,' Gregory persisted, 'who is the king of this Deira?'

Augustine and Peter exchanged glances. It was like Gregory to be keenly interested in everyone he met, but there was an urgency in these questions they did not understand.

The slave-dealer scratched his head. 'I'm a trader, not a school-teacher.'

'Our king is Aelle.' It was the taller boy who spoke, in halting Latin.

All three monks started at the unexpected sound of his voice, high, nervous, but proud.

'Don't say "Aelle",' Gregory countered with his radiant smile. 'Say

19

rather, "Alleleuia", for Christ shall set you free.'

There was keen, protracted bargaining. The dealer protested that these English boys were a rare and valuable lot, the more so because there was a pair of them. If he waited until the afternoon and open bidding, he could expect to go away a rich man. No doubt the abbot had plans of his own for boys such as these. It would cost him dearly.

Gregory tried to keep the mounting anger out of his voice. At one time he turned away, as if the sale was lost. The dealer's voice called him back, newly obsequious. There was a lot more argument before the bargain was done. Augustine and Peter both gasped at the final sum. Gregory was a rich man who had inherited wealth from his noble family, but he had given most of it away to set up his monasteries. To pay such a sum for two slave boys seemed an act of reckless extravagance.

The price was more than a prudent man would carry in such a crowd.

'Bring them to the monastery of St Andrew this evening,' Gregory ordered. 'Your money will be waiting.'

The dealer, though no stranger to Rome, looked doubtful. 'Where?'

The muscles in Gregory's face tightened. 'Ask, if you must, for the Anici Palace on the Caelian Hill. Anyone will tell you where that is. The home of Gregory, formerly Prefect of Rome, who prefers now to be known as an abbot of God.'

'I'm sorry, sir! . . . I didn't recognize you.'

Gregory turned from him. He reached across the rope to put his arms round the boys' shoulders. 'Don't be afraid. I shall see you again. What are your names?'

'Edmer,' said the older one. 'And he's Saenoth.'

Augustine muttered to Peter. 'After all this, he'll give them their freedom.'

'He'll offer them a home first,' Peter answered. 'Where would they go in Rome, alone and destitute? If I know him, he'll tell them the Christ story, and then ask if they want to join us as monks.'

'English Christians?' Augustine asked. 'English *monks*? Do you think that could happen?'

'It *will* happen.' Gregory swung round on them. 'Did you think it was only for charity or their sweet faces I bought them, though either would have been reason enough? No. These boys are going to be our teachers. We must learn the English language. If we're to go to Britain and teach the angelic Angles the good news of the Gospel, we must tell them the story in words they can understand.'

'To Britain?' Augustine and Peter were shocked into unison.

'Why not? To the ends of the earth. Isn't that what the Lord said? After all, Britain was once part of the Roman Empire.'

'Us?' Augustine's voice wavered.

'I want you with me, Augustine. Come on, you're from Gaul. That's halfway there, isn't it?'

'Gaul is civilized, Father,' Augustine protested. 'And I left it for Rome, the holy city. Not the barbarian north!'

Chapter Four

'I'm going to ask the Holy Father for permission to lead an expedition to Britain.'

In his eagerness, Gregory was striding up and down the courtyard beside the pool almost as fast as he had swept them through the streets of Rome. His monks watched him with curiosity and no little alarm. For a man who said how much he longed for solitude and silence, for the ordered rhythm of murmured prayer and chanted psalms, the abbot was, Augustine thought, consumed by an exhausting energy. This inner space of the monastery of St Andrew, once the palace of Gregory's ancestors, should have been an oasis of peace. The evening sky was emptied of its fierce noonday colour. The colonnades offered cooler shade. The first star was reflected in the water, between the restful green of myrtle bushes.

I want to stay here, Augustine thought, with deep longing. I don't want to follow him to the limits of the known world, to that barbaric island of Britain, peopled by heathens as pale as ghosts.

'The Pope won't let you go,' Peter, the deacon, told Gregory with cheerful decision. 'The times are too dangerous. There'd be a riot if the people thought you were handing over the defences of the city to someone else.'

'Father.' A young monk spoke quietly from the shadows. 'The merchant is here.'

Gregory's hand moved in swift command to the other monks. 'Stay here.' He followed the messenger.

Peter rolled his eyes skyward. 'Seven monasteries, he's got, full of capable, intelligent men. Yet he has to go to the entrance hall himself and hand over the gold into the sticky hands of some thief of a slave-trader.'

'It's not the slave-trader he's thinking about,' Augustine said, 'it's the boys. Gregory's is the face they'll remember, not ours. Certainly not mine. When he smiled like that at them in the Forum, they trusted him. Everyone does.'

Gregory was back soon, with a blond English boy standing shyly on either side of him. The quiet chatter of the monks taking their social hour in the open courtyard fell silent as they stared. The abbot had stopped in the shadowed cloisters, respecting the boys' nervousness, the strangeness of it all. One hand rested reassuringly on a shoulder of each of them. In that deeper twilight they looked even more supernaturally pale.

'Father Augustine,' Gregory called.

Why did that summons send his heart pounding faster? As novice-master, he had already, on Gregory's orders, made provision for the boys' lodging. There was nothing unnatural in hearing his name called now they had arrived. But he felt the gaze of the other monks on him as he left the group and crossed the tiled floor to where the boys stood.

Gregory's words in the slave-market sounded, unbidden, in his mind. *'These boys are going to be our teachers.'*

There *was* something unnatural. Augustine was an ordained priest, a vowed monk, an ecclesiastical scholar trusted with the instruction of new recruits. Did Gregory mean him to sit at the feet of these strange barbarian children? Heathen slaves?

The abbot was smiling steadily at him, as though willing something from him.

'Here they are, Father. Do you remember their names?'

The first lesson. 'Edmer!' He felt relief at the recollection. 'And . . . Sid . . . Sith. . . .'

'Saenoth.' There was a gentle reproach.

'Saenoth.' Augustine made himself smile at the boys. 'Follow me.'

As Gregory took his hands away, both boys looked up at him in alarm. I'm not Gregory, Augustine thought. It's not me they trust.

The boys padded behind him to the postulants' dormitory. There were three Roman boys already there. They had begun their course of instruction and enquiry, which would, if successful, lead to their first vows. Just now, there was a scuffle and a swaying of beds which had just been jumped into. Augustine reproved them.

'Gravity is required of monks. Jude, Felix; report to me tomorrow morning after breakfast for a penance. Boys, we have two newcomers. Edmer and Saenoth, from the kingdom of Deira in Britain. Make them welcome.'

The Roman boys greeted them dutifully. One of them asked, 'Does your hair grow naturally like that? My father says the British warriors used to plaster their hair with lime to make it white.'

Edmer stared back at him. Saenoth sucked his thumb. Clearly their Latin did not extend this far.

'They're English,' Augustine explained. 'Strangers to Rome and everything Roman. They have much to learn. You must help them.'

'Yes, Father,' said the boys meekly. Then Jude, who had asked the question, buried himself under the blankets, as if to hide the fact that he was choking with mirth.

Augustine had spent too much time with boys not to know how cruel they could be to each other, especially to the more unusual among them. The black boy, Titus, from Ethiopia, for instance. But he could do nothing except warn the culprits. He would not be there when it happened. Gregory could give these English boys their freedom; he could not dictate what freedom would mean.

He motioned Edmer and Saenoth to the waiting beds and had to stop them getting into the same one. 'It's the Rule of Benedict,' he said. 'Each brother sleeps alone.'

Their tired faces looked back at him blankly. How could they understand him?

When they were settled in their chaste, narrow beds he spoke a blessing over them. As all too often, he was seized with self-doubt. Should he have done that? Could he ask for God's protection over unbaptized heathens? The assumptions of his ordered life were becoming confused.

It was a relief to hear the bell chiming for compline, which the younger boys were excused. He tucked his hands into his sleeves and made his escape. He put his hood up and bowed his head as he entered the church, focusing on the sacred things of God directly in front of him.

'Why me?' Augustine protested to Peter. 'You're his right-hand man. Why does Gregory keep calling on me to accompany him when he has business to do? I'm the novice-master. My work is here.'

Peter let his amused gaze travel over the monk from Gaul. 'Don't you realize, Brother? Gregory has high hopes of you. If . . . things change, you could be abbot one day. He wants you to know what he knows, see what he does, meet the people he must talk with.'

'The Holy Father?'

Peter nodded.

Again, the cold hand of fear, the sense of his own inadequacy. How could Gregory believe so much of him?

The afternoon sun was declining. They had followed their founder Benedict's rule and rested during the heat of the day. In the palace on the Lateran Hill, by St John's Cathedral, the Bishop of Rome would be rising refreshed too, to hold his audience.

Gregory could have had them carried there from St Andrew's, but that was not his way. He actually liked to walk the streets of Rome, chatting to soldiers, beggars, even women. He wanted his finger on the pulse of the city, which looked to his past experience of government to defend it, now that the empire in Constantinople was losing its grip and the Italian governor had retreated to Ravenna.

So he made himself vulnerable. His companions could not prevent people from surging up to him, full of their complaints, their fears, their demands that he do something about it.

'Father, do you know what they're charging for oil today?'

'Father, my wife's father died, but she's too scared to go out of the city for the funeral.'

'The emperor could be dead in Constantinople and we wouldn't hear about it, would we?'

Their smaller fears surfaced because the larger fear was too dark to be spoken. What would happen to them when the Lombards reached the walls of Rome? Gregory answered wearily, patiently, cheerfully. His firm resolve sent people away reassured.

The papal guard at the entrance to the Lateran Palace cut them off from the crowd. The sounds of the city ebbed as they walked through the gate and up the marble steps. There was no need to announce themselves. Everyone knew Gregory's face. They were bowed through to the audience hall.

The petitioners, great and humble, were ranged around the walls. Some were talking quietly, others nervously pleating the skirts of their tunics or fingering the scrolls they had brought. A hush fell. All eyes turned at the entrance of Pelagius, Bishop of Rome.

He was a small, plump man, his head thrust forward on its short neck, like a bird searching the ground in front of it for grubs. His eyes, when he looked out over the congregation, sparked with intelligence. He lifted his hand and pronounced a blessing. The audience began.

Augustine was unfamiliar with the protocol that governed the order of precedence, but he was not surprised when Gregory's was the second name to be called. Before leaving public office for the monastic life, Gregory had been Pelagius's ambassador to the court of the Emperor Tiberius in Constantinople.

Augustine looked to Peter for guidance. Following his lead, he stepped forward too. The two monks stood a little behind their abbot, a small escort symbolizing the standing of Gregory's seven monasteries.

Gregory and Pelagius were old friends. The Pope motioned the abbot to the chair beside him on the dais. Their heads bent in talk. Again Augustine caught the words, 'Angles . . . angels.' The Pope laughed. The name of Britain sounded many times and the debate grew serious.

At last Pelagius leaned forward and patted Gregory's hand. He rose from his gilded chair and Gregory went down on his knees before him. The other two monks did the same. Augustine's bowed head heard the words he had been fearing all along.

'In the name of the Father, and the Son, and the Holy Spirit, I, Pelagius, Bishop of Rome, grant you my blessing to take the Gospel of Christ to the English kingdoms in the Island of Britain. And may God go with you.'

Augustine stood, feeling himself swaying. It had come. It was reality.

He was aware that the Pope was beckoning Peter and him forward. He

25

knelt again and felt Pelagius's hand on his own head.

'God protect you, my son, and give you strength and wisdom for your mission.'

Two fair-haired boys had changed his life irrevocably.

The world was reeling as he followed Gregory out of the papal palace. No one had asked him. He should not have expected it. He was a monk under obedience. Yet he felt a dangerous surge of resentment, fixing his eyes on the back of Gregory's grey robe. A part of his mind was aware of a wry recognition. This was the same querulous complaining he heard from the Roman citizens, masking a deeper fear.

The pounding in his ears kept him for a while from the sound of the approaching mob. Only when Peter halted was he aware that something was wrong. Gregory was still marching ahead, a man with a mission.

Townspeople seemed to be coming from all directions, from the square around the Colosseum below them, from the narrower side streets. They were not armed, but their mood was angry. A thunderous shout went up when they saw Gregory. He, too, halted now, eyeing them warily, waiting.

'What's up?' growled Peter. 'The Lombards can't be here yet, can they? Without any warning?'

The crowd had converged in a circle round them, growling, threatening. Astonishingly, their anger seemed to be directed against Gregory. This time, they were not appealing to him to protect them from their enemies: he *was* the enemy.

Peter stepped up to his abbot's shoulder, shielding him. Quaking inside, Augustine did the same on the other side. He knew he was seeking protection, rather than giving it. He wanted the closeness of the other two monks. He needed to feel Gregory's strength.

A man was pushed forward, a butcher by the look of his bloodstained apron. He was red-faced, embarrassed but indignant. 'What do you mean, running away from us? They say you're leaving Rome. Is it true?'

The mob bayed with fear and fury.

Gregory held up his hand. His face was white. 'Has the news travelled so fast? Yes, I've come from the Holy Father. He's given me his blessing. I'm now Christ's apostle to the English in the Island of Britain.'

'What about us? What about Rome?'

'You can't leave us!'

'Who's going to see to our defences?'

'Think of the children!'

'The Lombards are coming!'

They were pushing, shouting, jostling the three monks. For once, Gregory's authority did not seem enough to calm the waves of rage. Augustine felt the cloth of his tunic tear as hands hauled at him. He was being dragged away from the others. He knew a naked immediate terror which blotted out the formless dread of an unknown future in Britain. He could die now.

Deep masculine orders cut through the frightened yells. The pressure was easing, the crowd falling apart. Soldiers of the city guard carved their way through to the monks with the flats of their swords. Even so, there was blood. The resentful citizens drew back, nursing cuts. The usually composed Gregory, Augustine saw, was shaking.

'Father Gregory!' The captain was visibly taken aback when he saw whom he had rescued. 'Are you all right, sir? What was all that about?' His soldiers had formed a ring, facing outwards. The crowd was backing away from their raised weapons.

Gregory told him.

'You're *what?* . . . Begging your pardon, Father!' Shock was plain on the officer's face. 'But you can't do that. You can't desert Rome. With the imperial troops holed up at Ravenna and the Lombards coming? And they *will* come.'

'I'm not the only man in Rome with administrative experience and wits. Someone else can organize the defences as well as I can.'

'There's no one else the people would trust. No one else *we'd* trust, the guards.'

'I'm a monk, not a general. My calling is to save souls, not cities.'

'You're a Roman, sir. And Rome is full of souls, looking to you for salvation.'

Gregory bowed his head, as if in exhaustion. His shoulders sagged. Augustine and Peter moved to support him.

'Let's get him home,' said Peter. 'He's a sick man. You ask too much of him.'

'And you'd let him go to the ends of the earth on some wild-goose hunt? Britain's so far away, it's not even *in* the empire now.'

A blessed gratitude washed over Augustine. They were not going to let Gregory go, not the citizens of Rome, not the army. He wouldn't have to do it. He wouldn't have to accompany his father in God halfway across the world into a kingdom of strangeness and terror, among the damnable heathen.

Rome was dangerous, too, but as long as Rome had Gregory, he would keep them safe.

Chapter Five

Bertha got up from her knees. She must steady herself before she turned to face the hall. She was the queen now. She must not show the English that she was afraid, unsure of herself. She must remember her mother's bearing.

She turned. At first the light from the open door confused her eyes. She saw only confused shadows in front of it. Then she made out the ranks of people in her hall. They were all of them on their feet because their queen had stood. It gave her a thrill of delight. Before she had lifted a hand or said a word, they had acknowledged her authority.

Immediately in front of her were her Frankish household, mostly women. Christians, of course, who had taken the sacrament from Liudhard as she had. Then the muscles of her neck tensed. Close to the door, across the hall, stood some ladies of the Kentish court, suppressing embarrassed giggles as she looked at them. A rapid assessment showed them to be the younger ones. It was those who had left, the ones too angered by her alien rites to stay and watch, of whom she must be careful.

She drew her eyes back to her Franks. A small, unfamiliar figure immediately behind them startled her. She was so slight and shy, Bertha had not noticed her at first, half-hidden by the tall Frankish ladies. This girl was not one of them. Bertha sought for a name, a context for that heart-shaped face, those mouse-brown braids.

'Edith!'

The girl's bowed head shot up. In the glow of the candles on the bishop's table, her hazel eyes went wide, scared.

'Come here.'

Edith's faltering steps betrayed her unwillingness. She fell on her knees before the queen.

'Why are you here, with us?' Bertha turned on Bishop Liudhard. 'Did she take the sacrament?'

The bishop nodded, defending himself. 'I couldn't ask her in English if she was baptized. She seemed to know what to do. She reached for the bread so eagerly, I felt it would be wrong to refuse her.'

'Are you a Christian?' she said to the girl.

The hazel eyes struggled to comprehend.

'Could she be?' Bertha questioned Liudhard. 'Might she be a slave captured from a Christian country? Oh, why can't I speak to her in English?'

The girl's hand reached up, towards the golden, ruby-studded cross Liudhard had placed on the table. Then she pointed to herself and said a word which was not her name, but which Bertha found she half-understood.

'Mutter? . . . *Mater?* . . . Mother!'

Edith nodded vigorously at the Latin word. '*Mater! Maria, mater Jesu.*'

'You know that? Mary, the mother of Jesus?'

The girl pointed again and again at herself. '*Mater. Mater.*' Then back to the cross.

'Fetch Herman, tell him to bring his interpreter.'

The English nobleman who had escorted her from Paris was fetched, with the Latin-speaking interpreter of the crooked spine. He questioned Edith in her own tongue and turned, bowing to the queen.

'She is a Kentish child, madam. A bondmaid, but not a slave. She's lived all her life in Canterbury.'

'How, then, does she know about Christianity?'

'Her father's English, one of the king's serfs. He honours our gods.' There was alarm in the man's pinched face. Was it in case he had angered his foreign queen? Or was it her God he was afraid of? 'But her mother's descended from the old British people of this land.'

Bertha frowned. 'I don't understand you. This island is Britain. The English folk live in it, in Kent and Essex and other kingdoms. Who are these British?'

The interpreter looked for help to Herman, who struggled with the differences of both thought and language.

'We English came in longships. We took this land from them, in my grandfather's time. The Britons ran away from our spears. But some stayed. This girl's people. Her mother's people.'

'And the Britons were Christian?'

Herman shrugged. 'This land belongs to Woden and Thunor now.'

Bertha's questioning eyes went to her chaplain.

'It's possible, madam. Long ago, Britain was part of the Roman Empire. There were priests here once, bishops even, churches, congregations. But all gone now, surely? In the west, where the British retreated, I've heard there is still a church, though the rumour is that some of their practices are scandalous. But here in Kent, so close to the empire, we should surely have heard if any of them were left.'

Bertha stared at the girl before her. 'If they were bondmen and women, a subject people—?'

29

'They would need to have priests. Educated men.'

Bertha pointed to Liudhard and back to Edith. 'Do you have one like this?'

The girl shook her head. She seemed overcome now, her words low.

'She says no. They have no priest. They only pray and sing together. Since she was a child, her mother has told her this story about the bread and wine. But none of them has ever seen it done, until today.'

'Then, she was not confirmed? No bishop has ever laid his hands on her?' Liudhard was scandalized. 'Then she has eaten the bread and drunk the wine to her own damnation!'

At the anger in his voice, Edith recoiled. Bertha went quickly to her and put her arms around the girl. 'She came in faith! You told me yourself, you could see how she hungered for it.'

'How do I know she's even baptized, though a layman or woman could do that *in extremis*?'

'Leave her alone for now. She's shaking.'

Bertha released Edith and smiled down from her greater height. 'Go now. *Vade in pacem.*'

'*In nomine Patri et Filii, et Spiritus Sancti,*' the girl echoed with shining eyes. She almost ran from the hall, leaving the Franks staring in astonishment after her.

Bertha walked towards the open door. Her heart felt warmed by this discovery. So Kent was not quite the spiritual wilderness she had believed it would be. She held herself tall, queenly. Her smile to the Kentish women by the door radiated a new confidence, a new hope. They drew back to make a passage for her.

The sunlight darkened. A man strode into the doorway, almost in front of her. It was Dirwine, her other escort from Paris. He started, as she did, and bowed. But it was a perfunctory courtesy. There was something more urgent he had come to tell her.

'My lady, the king commands your attendance.'

'Commands?' It was surprise, more than protest. Aethelbert was King of Kent, and she was his wife now. She knew a wife's duty.

Dirwine lifted his face, the fair moustache, the long combed hair. His blue eyes were concerned, avuncular. Her indifference to him had warmed into friendship on the four days' voyage. He, at least, like Herman, could speak a little of her language. Yet today, the subtleties of vocabulary again required Herman's interpreter.

'My lady, I could say the king *requests* your presence, but, since he is the king, it would make no difference.'

'I will come.'

They walked across the yard between the halls of the palace.

30

Everywhere there was morning busyness. Servants were coming and going, with pails and baskets, fodder and tools, leading animals, shouting orders, to maintain the court of the most powerful king in Britain.

'Do you know why he wants me?' Bertha had read from the haste of Dirwine's stride, the concern in his eyes, that something was wrong.

'It is . . . a matter to do with our customs. Franks and English. You, my lady, are used to different ways.' He appealed to the interpreter for his next words.

'He says it is probably a misunderstanding, madam.'

Bertha cast her mind back. She had been in Canterbury so short a time. Aethelbert had seemed in a good humour when he woke in her bed this morning. There could be only one thing since then to anger him. Her mouth set in an obstinate line.

She made full use of her Frankish height as she entered the king's hall. She held her head high and proud, under the married woman's veil. She was still King Charibert's daughter. Aethelbert might be a great king in Britain, but not to the Franks.

The light fell strongest on Aethelbert, seated in the king's carved chair. At first her sun-dazzled eyes made out only dim-coloured shadows at his side. She studied them rapidly; this was the confirmation she needed to have. Even while she swept a curtsey and questioned, 'My lord, you sent for me?' her eyes were focusing, distinguishing individuals.

There were more women than she might have expected in the king's hall at this hour of the morning. Her heart tripped, as knowledge leaped clearly of what she had feared. These were the older Kentish ladies, who had stalked from her own hall when Liudhard set his cross on the table. Mildgith, the most senior-ranking, was foremost among them. They were staring at her now, defiant, sure of their own righteousness.

Aethelbert held a staff up which a dragon crawled, twining its carved tail around the wood. He was thrusting it out, so that it stood between them. He looked angry and . . . scared?

There was someone else, at the king's left hand, singling her out from the indignant ladies gathered on his right. Twenty cats' masks swung and grinned at Bertha from the shaman's cloak. The woman's face was streaked with ashes. It made her look more withered and gaunt than she really was. This was the priestess of Frig who had offered her corn and wine on her wedding day. No doubt she had overseen those images woven in corn which hung over their marriage bed. How had she hallowed them? Bertha shivered, watching her.

The crash of the king's staff on the floor made her jump. She almost overbalanced. She heard the fury in his voice before the translation reached her.

'You offered a sacrifice in the queen's hall!' Aethelbert appealed for confirmation to the most senior of Canterbury's noblewomen. Mildgith nodded.

Bertha strove to steady her voice. 'You set your seal on our marriage contract, sir. It allows me freedom of worship. I should not have consented to marry you otherwise.'

When he understood, his left hand clenched convulsively on the bear's head carved on his chair arm. His right gripped the dragon staff, as though to ward off evil. Had she made a mistake, reminding him that she was not totally subservient to his wishes? The queen's chair still stood empty beside him. He had not invited her to seat herself.

'I never gave you permission to turn my palace into a foreign temple. The hall of English queens! My mother's hall.'

'Where, then, am I to pray, my lord?'

The question seemed to puzzle him, as though it was something he had not thought of. He thumped his staff. 'In the open air, I suppose, where your magic can escape to the sky without harming the rest of us. I don't want it trapped under my roof, to anger the gods of hearth and bed.'

'I prayed to God for my king and my country. For Kent. I asked a blessing on your palace, not a curse.'

The shaman leaned over the king's shoulder. Her hiss could have come from the cats' heads she wore.

'Werburh says your hall must be cleansed.'

'My lord. . . !' Behind Bertha, Bishop Liudhard's protest died away in a cough.

Bertha tried to control the trembling in her legs, which was part anger, part fear. She was beginning to see why Aethelbert was acknowledged as lord, even by other English kings. It took a huge physical effort to oppose him. 'My lord, you insult me and my Christ.'

'This is Kent, woman, ruled by an English king, protected by English gods. These ladies here fear you're putting us all in danger. If I say you will not make magic in the queen's hall, you will not!'

She must be wise. She must not anger these noblewomen needlessly. She had to spend the rest of her life here. Her children would be born in Kent, grow up as English princes and princesses. These hostile ladies, and the lords behind them, would help to raise her children. She needed their friendship.

'Then, my lord, I beg you, give me a chapel of my own where Bishop Liudhard can celebrate the Eucharist for us. We're not accustomed to worship on hilltops or in clearing in forests, as I believe you do.'

The interpreter had difficulty with this vocabulary. The bishop was obliged to explain further.

Aethelbert thundered back, 'We're not savages on this side of the Channel, madam! We have the royal temple here in Canterbury.'

'Then I may have my chapel, too?'

He glared at her. She kept her gaze steady. At last he said, stiff-lipped, 'It shall be built. Until then, you will not endanger my palace. Your priest must not sacrifice again in the queen's hall.'

'Then I must pray in the street?' She even made herself smile, though her heart was thudding. 'My chaplain offers the mass every day.'

Again, that grey-faced woman at his ear. King though he is, he's as afraid of her as I am, Bertha thought.

'Outside the walls. Not in Canterbury.'

Humiliation. The Queen of Kent, who may not pray in her own capital.

Oddly, the rage she should have felt was deflected by a sudden realization, a childish delight. She had understood Aethelbert's last words before she heard the translation.

'Very well, my lord. I shall wait to hear where you will allow me to build my chapel.'

Meekly. A balancing act as difficult as stepping stones across a rushing torrent. She must keep down the fury and insult she felt. She must step wisely, carefully.

Aethelbert relaxed. He leaned back smiling, the staff at his side now. He had asserted his mastery. The ranks of Kent's noblewomen in their striped skirts wavered, like a meadow when a gust of wind has passed over it.

The shaman crossed her arms and scowled at Bertha. Had she expected, even wanted, a furious confrontation between the king and the queen? Had she been sure she would inflict still greater humiliation on this Frankish Christian and her holy man?

Yet Werburh had won a victory. The little wise woman had banished the queen from her own hall. Meeting her fierce green-flecked eyes, it was hard not to fear her even more than King Aethelbert.

Rising to her feet, Bertha was not sure now whether she should have fought harder for God's dignity and her own.

Chapter Six

Bertha chose the Franks of her household to accompany her, with Dirwine and Herman as escorts, and the interpreter. She had a name for him now, Siric. A small man, whose crooked spine stooped him sideways.

She looked curiously around her at the streets of Canterbury. There was an unsettling ambiguity about this city. Nettles grew through cracked mosaic pavements. Ivy hung like ropes, ready to pull down the crumbling corner of a wall. Yet fresh paint blazed on other buildings. Dragons' and wolves' heads reared freshly carved. Thatch, only just beginning to fade from gold to brown, swept up to immensely high roof ridges. Aethelbert had not yet reached the prime of life. His power was still growing. Rome was the past here, England the future.

Was Canterbury so very different from Paris, after all? There, too, old stonework had crumbled; gods of antiquity had been smashed. The palaces raised by her father and his ancestors were in a Germanic style not too unlike Kent's.

They paused at the Water Gate.

'I hardly think the riverside will be suitable, your majesty.' Bishop Liudhard's expression of distaste was not without reason. The bustle of traders and watermen between the city and the River Stour certainly offered no quiet place for worship. Fishmongers called out their wares. Dogs ran everywhere, fighting over scraps. Alehouses beckoned. It was necessary to walk carefully on the slimy road.

'Where, then? Shall we walk inland and explore?' The optimism of youth was returning. Bertha felt like a small child who has been given a very large plaything. She wanted to try it out, to see what it was she now owned and what she could do with it. She was queen, not just of Canterbury, but of all this land around it. It was more than a site for a chapel she was eager to discover.

Away from the quay, the buildings continued. Some were cottages more wretched than those around the palace, others prosperous farmhouses, with orchards and gardens, before cornfields and open pasture began. Here and there, a remnant of stonework still spoke of the imperial past.

They were leaving the city walls now, and the land was rising. With the

34

strength of youth and long legs, Bertha set a brisk pace.

'I can send for horses, madam,' offered Herman, 'if you wish to wait here.'

She laughed. 'Canterbury is not such a large city, I think. We can walk round it.'

'My lady,' Clotilda scolded. 'Think of your dignity. A queen doesn't walk like a beggar.'

'King Aethelbert met me on foot at the wharf. He walked with me to the palace.'

Bertha saw the anger in the older woman's eyes, but her spirits rose at the tight-lipped expression of defeat which followed.

'As you wish, my lady.'

At home in Paris, Clotilda would have swept off to report the matter to Bertha's mother and overturn her decision. Here, she realized with delight, her will was sovereign, at least among her own household.

She chose a path up through a straggle of oak trees, between the open ground which had been cleared around the city for security and the forested slopes of the ridge. The young leaves were almost as golden as autumn. The sun and fresh air lifted her spirits further. She would not allow herself to be diminished by being banished from her own hall, driven outside the city walls. She would stake her claim here, on Kentish soil. She would build a chapel for herself, something never seen here before.

They had been walking for half an hour, studying the terrain and the roads radiating out from the city. There was a glint through the branches to their left, brighter in the dappled sunshine than the leaves. Bertha could just make out a base of stone. It stood higher than the track. The thickening foliage overhead screened out the rest.

'That masonry. Some Roman thing?' she turned to Liudhard.

'Another ruin from the empire, no doubt.'

'What's that?' she called to Dirwine.

'I don't know it, madam. There are no important buildings here.'

A still-childish curiosity that made her eager to know. At the risk of scandalizing Clotilda, she picked up her skirt and started to climb the bank.

Trees crowded around the building. In one corner, the roots of an elm had become so embedded in the stonework that it gave the impression of supporting it, rather than upheaving it. Above the first few courses of masonry, the style became more rustic, timber and plaster. Great cracks threatened to pull it apart, yet some had been filled with newer daub. The thatch was a patchwork. Most of it hung brown and tattered. Birds had scooped out nesting places. Others had pulled out its reeds, leaving untidy spikes. But here, too, some attempt at mending it had been made. Pale brown, faded yellow, brighter gold, showed how, over the years, holes had been mended.

Grass and wild flowers washed against its walls. Yet, Bertha saw, at the gable end they had been trampled down in front of a door, half-hidden behind a hawthorn bush. The merest trail of a footpath led to it.

'It's not a farm,' said Herman. 'No sign of animals. No barns or pens.'

Bertha held up her hand for silence. 'Listen!'

He was right. No pigs rootled for acorns under the oak trees. No sheep murmured from the hillside. There was only birdsong.

'What is it, then? It looks as if somebody cares for it, but there's no sign of life.'

Dirwine tried to answer in her Frankish Latin, though he spoke it less well than Herman. 'Some old thing. From Rome time, I think. English don't build with stone.'

'That roof was repaired not long ago.'

She was drawn to the door. The cracks in the walls warned her it might be rotting away, even gaping open. She rounded the hawthorn bush and found it was not. Stout oaken panels closed a rounded archway. There was a latch of iron.

Bertha put out a hand, clenching it as though she felt she should knock. Herman's shout over her shoulder startled her.

'Hey, there! Is anyone in?'

Bertha's fist was already unfolding, long fingers reaching down for the latch. The iron clattered. She waited for a lock to resist her push, but the door swung inward on silent hinges.

'It's been oiled,' said Herman, moving swiftly in front of her. His hand was ready on his sword.

They stepped down into dimness. The high windows should have let in sunshine, but the trees crowded too closely. A pale-green light washed the upper walls and left the floor shadowed.

It was a single room, only a little bigger than the chamber where the queen's women slept. A bare flagged floor. At the far end, two steps led up a dais, with a block of honey-coloured stone. It was the height of a table. On it stood a plain wooden cross.

Bertha and Liudhard caught their breath. They looked at each other in astonishment, wonder, almost fear. There were little cries of amazement from the women behind them.

'A Christian church?'

'I don't see how it can be anything else, your majesty.' Liudhard was mounting the steps. He moved his hand reverently over the bare stone of the altar. He knelt to examine the low relief of its carving.

Dirwine and Herman had halted inside the door. They looked more uneasy than if they had found armed men inside. Their hands were on their weapons, but their mouths muttered a different sort of protection. Warriors though they were, Bertha could see they were afraid to come closer.

The Frankish women crowded in after their lady, studying the place and exclaiming over their discoveries. Liudhard's young deacon, Guntram, was examining traces of faded paint on the walls.

'It's been swept and cleaned.' As mistress of the queen's household, Clotilda gave a nod of approval.

'Then could this be . . . the place where Edith's mother prays?'

'Without a priest?' Liudhard spoke sharply, getting to his feet. 'Without the sacraments? For so many years since Rome left? It's not possible.'

Bertha's head went up. 'If my father had sent me here without you, Bishop, if I had been a solitary Christian in a foreign land, I should still have needed a place to pray. I should have asked Aethelbert to allow me a chapel, even if no one ever came to feed me the bread and wine.'

'Madam, it's nearly two centuries since the Romans were here.'

'But if they had their own British priests, to begin with. . . ? When did the English conquer Kent?'

Dirwine counted the generations on his fingers. 'In the time of my great-great-grandfather.'

'Then it's possible. If they had real faith. We know from Edith that there are Christians here still.'

'British slaves or half-breed serfs.'

Bertha's women were still exploring the small space, whispering in excitement. Brunhild called, 'My lady, look here! See what Guntram's found.'

The queen crossed the twilit floor and looked up to the plastered wall below the windows. There were dark patches of damp and the surface was peeling. But here and there she glimpsed the ghosts of paintings. The remnants were faded, the wall crumbling between them.

'Can you see him, my lady?' the deacon pointed. 'A soldier in armour, with his sword raised?'

'Saint Michael, slaying the dragon of evil!' cried Liudhard, coming to join them. 'He must be the patron saint of this church. The archangel himself!'

'No,' said Bertha. 'Look closer. That's not a dragon he's about to split in two; it's his own cloak.'

'You're right, my lady! He's our very own saint from Gaul. Saint Martin!' cried Guntram.

The bishop peered up at the indistinct image. He sounded rather disappointed. 'Not a champion slaying evil, then, though that is a most noble symbol, but a soldier of the Roman Empire sharing his cloak with a beggar. An act of generous humility.'

'He was a soldier who turned his back on fighting, became a monk and lived in a cave,' Guntram enthused. 'Even when they made him Bishop of Tours, he insisted on riding a donkey.'

Just for a moment, Bertha, too, regretted the lost archangel. Wouldn't St Michael's warrior triumph have been more fitting for her as a queen? But she had discovered Martin of Tours instead.

A strange shiver ran through her. The Gaulish saint was here in Canterbury, his painted cloak still faintly glowing. He was reality.

She had found her chapel.

Bertha led them back downhill, making for the nearest gate in the city wall. There was no need now to complete the circuit of the capital. She had discovered what she needed, and more than she had dreamed: the Church of Saint Martin. She talked swiftly as she strode along the path.

'I'll ask Aethelbert to give me materials and workmen to restore it. They can cut away those trees, fill up the cracks, replace the rotting timbers, give it a fresh coat of plaster. And a new thick thatch over all of it.'

'It's a good job somebody's kept the rain out, my lady,' said Deacon Guntram, hurrying to keep up with her. 'It would have fallen down long ago, otherwise.'

Bertha talked eagerly with Bishop Liudhard as they threaded the half-ruined city streets. 'Do you think there's anyone in Canterbury skilled enough to repaint those wall pictures? Saint Martin himself, the Christ in Judgement above the altar, the three Marys receiving his body from the cross?'

'We can send a request to Paris, your majesty. Your dignity requires the finest craftsmanship. We must not have either you or Christ disgraced with second-rate work—'

He broke off. Bertha, too, halted. As they neared the range of halls which formed Aethelbert's palace, the sound of drumming had been growing louder. Now they saw that from the door of the queen's hall blue smoke was creeping.

'My lady, is your hall on fire?' Clotilda cried.

Bertha's long stride impelled her forward again, even faster.

'Where are the English ladies? Where are my servants? I pray to God they're safe.'

Herman overtook her. 'That's not a house-fire, madam.' He relapsed into English. 'If that's what the smoke meant, there'd be a crowd running about with buckets, and pulling the thatch off with rakes.' Lame Siric, the interpreter, was panting with the difficulty of keeping up with Herman's swift steps and words.

It was true. There was indeed a ring of onlookers. Yet they were keeping well back, as though they feared a worse danger than burning. There was an ominously empty space around Bertha's hall.

Something was clearly going on inside. Bertha felt the hand of fear grip her, as Herman and Dirwine cleared a way for her through the murmuring crowd. The English people fell back rather too quickly when they saw who she was. As she passed, she saw some of them make the sign against evil. She did not need to understand English to know that they were muttering charms to protect themselves from her. The skin of her face tightened as the blood left it.

'Am I evil?' she hissed to Liudhard. 'Is that what they think? That I will harm them?'

'Your majesty, I'm your holy man. They fear me too. And fear breeds hatred.'

She was walking alone now, across that empty space, with only the bishop beside her. Herman and Dirwine were falling back, as though unwillingness to face the supernatural risk was gaining ground over their duty to protect her. If a warhost with spears had been waiting, they would not have hesitated for a moment. Bertha would not let herself look round to see whether her Frankish women were still following her.

The smoke was bitter in her throat. Herman was right. This was not the too-familiar smell of burning wood and thatch, terrifying though that was. Someone had thrown on that fire things not commonly burned. She shivered, imagining poisonous herbs, roots, the carcasses of foul creatures.

It was not just drumming coming from inside the hall. There was a rising din of rattles, the screech of whistles, human voices chanting, shrieking. The noise was appalling. Bertha longed to clap her hands over her ears. She stopped.

'You must go on, your majesty,' Bishop Liudhard said in a firm voice. 'It's your hall. You are the queen.'

She gave him a look of appeal, and he made the sign of the cross over both of them. He was sweating.

More slowly now, less confident that being the daughter of a Frankish king weighed more than being the wife of English Aethelbert, Bertha made herself walk the last few steps to the half-open, smoke-filled doorway.

It was dark inside. There were no flames from the fire, only swirling smoke. The windows were clouded by it. She sensed a crowd of beings, dark-dressed, turning towards her. She must not let herself believe that they were not human.

'In the name of the Father, and the Son, and the Holy Spirit,' Liudhard muttered.

The chanting stopped. The rattles and whistles reached a crescendo, then fell abruptly silent. Only a low rapid drumming went on.

There was a hiss from the shadows, the stream of an incomprehensible curse.

'Lord have mercy, Christ have mercy, Lord have mercy.' Bertha's own charms of protection were a fierce whisper. She was almost face to face with the shaman now.

Fear made her voice shrill. 'Werburh! What are you doing in my hall? Get out!' She did not know if she had the authority to shout that. She did not know the extent of this woman's power. She was the stranger here, and Werburh its protector.

Yet this was her hall. If she let Werburh take it from her, she would have nowhere, no home that was truly her own – unless it was that half-ruined church up on the hill.

Before her terror could overcome her anger, she seized the shaman by her shoulders. Her greater height and strength forced the woman round to face the door.

Like the cats whose skins she wore, Werburh sprang back at her. Her nails raked Bertha's cheeks. A little higher and she would have caught her eyes. She was snarling, spitting in the queen's face.

Bertha's greater physical strength was ill-matched against the shaman's fury. She could order, she could impel. She could not fight Werburh like another cat.

Then there were masculine hands dragging the woman off her. Herman and Dirwine were pale and terrified, but they were recalled to their duty when they saw the blood on their queen's face.

Werburh writhed in their grip, shrieking curses. Bertha feared the men would let go. Dirwine looked ready to faint.

There was a different commotion in the doorway. The Frankish women had dared to come no further when they saw what was being done inside. Even Clotilda had left the field to the two English warriors. The ranks of Werburh's assistants still hissed from around the walls. King Aethelbert stalked into his wife's hall, creating his own wave of fear.

The drumming, the whispering, the cries of alarm hushed. Even Werburh stilled in the warriors' arms. Bertha stood facing her husband, with blood trickling down her cheeks.

The king surveyed the scene. His angry gaze came back to Bertha.

'I told you, madam, Werburh said this hall must be cleansed. She was doing what was necessary, with my permission.'

Bertha listened to the translation. She curtseyed, but rose again immediately. 'Your wise woman has done what she needed to do, and I have returned. This is my hall now. I have found another place where my bishop will celebrate the Eucharist, with your leave. I will observe your wishes, sir, in all other respects, but what the queen says in the queen's hall is law.' She looked at him levelly. She was as tall as he was.

Aethelbert stared back as Siric relayed this to him, as though seeing her clearly for the first time through that smoke-dimmed atmosphere, the

40

blood on her face, her straight gaze.

He started, and came the last few steps towards her. He reached out to touch her cheek, then examined the blood on his fingertips. He whirled round. 'Get her out!' he shouted to the men.

When he turned back to Bertha, there was a grin on his face. He raised his bloodstained hand to salute her.

'You are indeed a queen, madam. You have courage. More than most men here.' Bertha understood what he said to her.

Chapter Seven

'Father!' The young monk Titus tapped at Augustine's open door.

'Come.'

The prior of St Andrew's looked up. Beyond Titus's dark face and black tunic, he glimpsed another robe, creamy white.

'It's the Holy Father himself!' came the excited whisper.

Augustine leaped to his feet. Before he could speak, Gregory, Bishop of Rome, entered the room with that familiar eager stride. Augustine went down on his knees to kiss the ring of his former abbot.

'What are you doing here, Father? I would have come to you in the Lateran Palace. I didn't know. . . .'

Gregory held up the hand the prior had kissed. 'This was my home, Augustine, before I made it an abbey. I was born here. Can't I visit it, when I find an excuse?'

'Would you like some refreshment?' Already Augustine's mind was busy. If this energetic pope made an unannounced visit to St Andrew's, it could only mean that his 'excuse' meant important business to discuss. Augustine had known Gregory too long not to be alarmed. What would Gregory expect him to do now?

'A little wine and water, perhaps. Could we walk by the pool? I imagine it will be quiet at this hour.'

The monks were at their morning tasks.

Sunlight slanted brilliantly across half the rectangular pool and the cream, red and black tiles on the far side. The nearer colonnade offered welcome shade. It was like Gregory, Augustine reflected, to suggest they walk as they talked, not sit quietly on one of the stone benches. The new Bishop of Rome was still consumed by a restless energy.

Augustine's sense of foreboding grew. He had never been able to understand Gregory's high opinion of him. At each new responsibility, each promotion, he found himself astonished. But surely now the process was nearly complete? Now that the Church and city of Rome had unanimously proclaimed Gregory the new Pope, Augustine had become prior of St Andrew's. All that remained was to replace Gregory himself as abbot one day.

'How's your English coming on?' The question startled him. He was glad of a moment's reprieve as Titus brought them cool goblets beaded with condensation.

'I . . .' His answer trailed away in confusion.

'Those English boys I bought in the slave market to teach us their language.'

'Saenoth died. The swamp fever last year.'

'I know that. God rest his soul. But Edmer?'

'But . . . that mission was cancelled. The city wouldn't let you go.'

'You haven't been learning English from him?'

'Edmer has taken his first vows. He has work to do. So have I. Now that I'm now longer novice master—'

'Yes, Father Augustine, you have work to do.' Gregory stopped pacing the poolside. He stood looking at the prior with a gaze which compelled Augustine's eyes to his. 'I can't go to Britain. Now that I'm Bishop of Rome, that door is finally closed to me. But for you the way is open.'

'Me, Father?' He felt the indignation of a housewife whose helpless broom vainly tries to sweep back the flood invading her home. He knew what Gregory meant, but he must not let himself understand.

'Yes, you. Augustine, prior of St Andrew's. What better man to do what I cannot. There are seven English kingdoms in Britain, they tell me, and all of them heathen, under the sway of savage gods. If you could deliver just one of them into the light of the loving Lord, I should die content. It's been my dream since the day I saw those two boys.'

'But . . . I'm not a travelling missionary. I'm no great preacher. I know nothing of the English.'

'Take Edmer with you. He was heaven-sent.'

The wine chilled Augustine's stomach. He found he was clutching his goblet so hard he feared the stem would break. The truth, now it was spoken out loud, shouted in his head. No crowd of Roman citizenry would block his own way. No one would protest that Rome could not survive without him. Where Gregory had been forced to stay, they would willingly let Augustine go. Nothing could prevent him taking the road to Britain, if Gregory said so.

The whole abbey community met in their church of St Andrew for Pope Gregory to give the travellers his blessing. He kissed Augustine warmly on both cheeks and delivered into his keeping a silver processional cross.

'Father Augustine, I create you abbot of this travelling band of monks. Raise this in Britain, for Christ and for me.'

As his hands rested on the heads of each of the forty monks, he asked their name. 'The blessing of almighty God be over you, Domitian . . . Honorius . . . Laurence . . .' He reached the end of the line of bowed, tonsured heads before the altar rail, the two youngest monks. 'Titus . . . Maurice. Go in the power and love of the Lord, to do his work.'

'Amen.'

The monks rose. Some kept their heads bent, as if overcome by the immensity of what they were undertaking. Others lifted faces to the far west window, seeing visions of all they would do. The light shone brightest in the dark eyes of young Titus.

Gregory had hardly lowered his hands before he turned swiftly to Augustine. His joy had sharpened to concern. 'Where's Edmer?'

'He . . . I. . . .'

'When you chose your companions, you knew beyond doubt that Edmer must go with you, as your interpreter, your teacher. Why isn't he here?'

'I called him to my study and explained our mission to him. I said that we would take him back to his homeland. That he could help us enormously, help the kingdom of God to grow. Change Britain.'

'He must have been overjoyed, surely? To go home at last, to the island from which he was so cruelly snatched into slavery.'

'No.'

'No?'

'He begged me to allow him to stay in Rome. He said he was afraid to go back. That he had suffered savagery, the killing of his parents, kidnapping. That he was now a Roman Christian. That if we challenge the English gods, our very lives will be in danger. Britain is a land of darkness and thunder, of bloodthirsty deities, of cruel rites.'

'That's why you're going! To rescue the English from darkness. Edmer has taken his first vows: he's a monk under obedience. You're his prior.'

'I fear . . . Edmer may no longer be a monk.'

'What do you mean? Why not?'

'When the novices woke for matins this morning, Edmer was not in his bed. He didn't appear in chapel. No one has seen him since. We fear . . . he has run away.'

'I bought his freedom. He chose to stay with us and become a monk. You offered him a passage home, and he refused?'

'It seems he would rather be a fugitive in Rome without a family than go back to Britain.'

Gregory's long face fell further. Then he shook himself and straightened his shoulders. 'God protect him, poor boy, wherever he is. No matter. You can find interpreters among the Franks before you take ship across the Channel. Besides, you won't be going to Edmer's kingdom of Deira. He's right, there. It seems they're a wild people north of the Humber. I doubt if they'd even let you land. But we have a key to another door. The Franks have dealings with the kingdom of Kent, in the south-east. One of their princesses has married its king. I've written to her and to her earthly lord. For her sake, King Aethelbert may let you in.'

'It's not certain? They might not even let us land? Might they attack our ship? I thought—'

'Peace, brother, peace! We think Kent may be halfway civilized. The Lord will watch over you. Remember the boys in the slave-market, our two Angles? Augustine, I'm sending you to the Land of Angels!'

His laughter did little to reassure Augustine.

Pope Gregory insisted on walking to the city gate with Augustine and his missionaries and their mules. The two of them walked down the hill together at the head of the expedition, through curious crowds. The monks led their pack animals. They could hardly ride while the Pope walked on foot. The white papal robe shone in the sunshine beside the abbot's black. Augustine noted with approval that every one of his forty monks wore the same sober dignified robes. Benedict, their founder, had said only that his followers should wear cheap cloth of whatever kind and colour was to be had locally. This could lead to a motley flock of white, brown, black wool. With the thrill of his new status as abbot, Augustine knew that he would impose uniformity. Even so, it was unsatisfactory that even some black sheep's wool tended towards a rusty brown.

The stone-arched gate in Rome's walls was still imposing. They passed through its hoof-echoing shadows into the glare and disorder of the outer city. Here, the pedlars' stalls and the shacks of the poor crowded up to the foot of the walls.

Here, too, the rest of their caravan was waiting: merchants, eager to exploit the current lull in hostilities with Lombardy; the armed escort they had hired to protect them; pilgrims who had made a once-in-a-lifetime journey to the holy city and must now go home. Like the monks, they sought the protection of travelling companions.

Heads were turning to greet them. They were almost committed.

'Are you sure it's safe now going overland?' Augustine turned to Gregory with a last plea. 'What if the truce breaks while we're in Lombardy?'

'You worry too much, Augustine. The Lombards saw their troops were over-committed. They have their work cut out holding all they've conquered so far. Trading with Rome is worth more to them than besieging it at the moment.'

He clapped his hand on the new abbot's shoulder. Augustine winced. For a monk, Pope Gregory II was not entirely circumspect in the custody of his hands. The warm way he embraced people was more appropriate to a soldier or a politician than a chaste churchman.

The caravan was forming into an orderly procession. Armed men took up positions at the front, others as outriders. Gregory's arms went round

Augustine for the last time. He spoke a final blessing over them all.

The abbot mounted his mule, a little awkwardly. He had separated Gregory's silver cross from its staff and packed it away in his saddle-bag. He felt the pressure of its uncompromising shape against his leg. One of the merchants' horses neighed. The column was moving.

Augustine knew a sudden desperate longing to be wherever Edmer was, an anonymous runaway, hiding from his destiny somewhere in the back streets of Rome.

Chapter Eight

As the day wore on, the hot blue sky thickened to grey. Though the sun was dimming, the heat grew more oppressive. The monks sweated in their black wool tunics. Gregory had advised them that their winter garments would be better for the inhospitable north.

It was becoming harder to see ahead. A loud rumble of thunder made Augustine's mule shy. From the clatter and shouts behind him he knew that more of the animals had been frightened. The merchants in front of him were eyeing the clouds and turning to unstrap their cloaks from their saddles. Augustine did the same.

The very first drops were large and heavy. The monks pulled up their cowls to shield themselves, but quickly the rain turned to hail. Stinging pellets drove in their faces. Several of the mules halted and refused to go on. There were cries of distress from some of the more lightly dressed pilgrims in the rear.

The captain of their escort reined in his horse and consulted with the leading merchants. Servants went running to obey orders. The ground was already streaming with melted ice, dancing with hailstones, before tents were pitched for the more wealthy travellers.

The monks had brought no such provision, trusting to the hospitality of other abbeys or wayside inns. They huddled in the scant shelter of some olive trees, though even there the force of the hail broke through the branches.

The storm raged on and on. Sometimes the lightning and thunder moved away and the deluge lessened. But each time they emerged to see if it was fit to go on, the downpour returned. It was hard to tell if it was only the thunderclouds which were darkening the air now or the approach of night.

At last the captain of the hired guards approached the monks, his eyes screwed up in his wet face. 'We're stopping here for the night. There's a river between us and the next village and it'll be a raging torrent after this storm.'

'Where will we sleep?'

The merchants were snugly inside their tents.

'Wherever you please. The sun will dry you off tomorrow,' the captain grinned.

'The bushes look thicker over there, Father,' Titus offered. 'The ground might be a bit drier underneath them.'

'We must light a fire,' the elderly Domitian protested. 'What's to keep the wild animals off? You boys, fetch some sticks.'

Titus and Maurice looked at Domitian in silent astonishment. Every stick, every pinecone was drenched. Augustine felt cold, inside and out.

'Wild animals?' Laurence, their infirmarian, faltered. 'What sort?'

'How do I know? Wolves? Bears? I'm a stranger here, the same as you, Father,' Domitian snapped back.

'Brothers!' With an effort, Augustine moved out of frozen immobility to restore discipline. 'If you can't speak in love, keep silent.'

They were unwillingly chastened. Conscious of the uncertainty of his authority, he led them in the singing of vespers. Before their chants were ended, the rain had eased to a gentle shower. The clouds began to break apart to show occasional stars.

Titus was right. The ground under the myrtle bushes was gritty and damp, broken by boulders, but it was not as waterlogged as the sandy soil around the olive trees. The monks crawled in amongst them and curled up in their wet cloaks.

Augustine slept badly. From the scared whispering around him, he knew that he was not the only one who was disturbed by the howls. They echoed first from a distant hilltop, then closer. When they fell silent and he tried to sleep again, each movement seemed to bring him into contact with something wetter, colder, harder.

The first grey light of dawn was stealing into the sky when he heard the sound he had been dreading all night, the rustle of leaves stealthily approaching him. He froze.

'Father?' A shock of relief this time. Honorius's voice. A large, steady monk of middle age. His inclusion in the party had given Augustine some little reassurance.

He tried to sit up. A shower-bath of droplets cascaded from the leaves above. His heart was still thudding. He sensed that whatever Honorius had come to say at this hour, it would be something he did not want to hear.

'Yes, my son.'

Honorius's fleshy face appeared between the twigs. 'We . . . the brothers have been talking, Father.'

'The tongue is small member, but dangerous. Benedict's Rule lays down that the night hours are silent.'

'I know, Father. But they fear this expedition is far too rash and dangerous.'

'Pope Gregory himself commissioned us. Do you want to turn back because you got wet in a thunderstorm?'

'It's not the rain, Father. The Holy Father knows all about imperial Rome; he's never been to barbarian Britain.'

Augustine was becoming aware of a larger audience. Other monks were creeping into earshot, their black tunics deepening the shadows. He stood up, to assert his uncertain authority.

'Gregory, Bishop of Rome, is a great and wise leader. He was the previous Pope's ambassador to Constantinople.'

Domitian snorted. 'Constantinople's the capital of the empire; Britain's an island off the edge of the world.'

'We're monks under obedience. If Pope Gregory tells us to go, we must go.'

'Couldn't you go back and persuade him, Father, before it's too late? Make him see it's a hopeless idea. You're a friend of his. You could beg him to release us from this mission.'

'We can't turn back! It's going to be such a great adventure!' A young voice, hardly more than a boy's, came out of the shadows. Titus had only taken his full vows a year ago. 'In the postulants' dormitory, the English boy Edmer used to tell us stories about Britain. About the English warrior kings leading their spear-hosts. Their longboats with a hundred oars. Their sailing ships. I've never been on a ship.'

'And where's your precious Brother Edmer now?' Domitian broke in. 'He was supposed to be our interpreter. He ran away. Rather than go back to his own country, he broke his vows! Doesn't that tell us enough about the risk?'

'He has a point, Father,' urged Honorius. 'Edmer knew what was in store for us, and he was afraid to go back there.'

'Stop this, all of you,' Augustine ordered. 'It must be time for the morning office. We should rather be praying to God to give us courage.'

He must stop his ears to their pleas. They were too much like the treacherous voices in his own heart.

'Yes, Father.'

Meekly they backed out of the bushes into the growing light. Sunrise was brilliant on the wet hillside.

They were passing from the golden hills of Umbria into Tuscany, moving north along the coast on the Aurelian Way.

'Are you sure this is safe, Father?' Honorius nudged his mule closer to Augustine's. 'We're getting into Lombard territory. Do we know the Holy Father's right about the truce? What if it breaks when we're right in the middle of them?'

'Be easy, Brother. You know our Pope is a statesman as well as Bishop of Rome. If anyone knows what's happening beyond Roman rule, he does. We must trust his wisdom.'

'Yes, Father. I'm sorry. But I've never been this far north of Rome before.'

'God protects us.' Augustine tried to put the confidence of leadership into his voice.

They had turned away from the sea towards a low pass through the hills. The town on the slope ahead of them grew slowly larger. All afternoon it had danced in the heat-haze. Now it loomed clear-edged against the evening sky.

'Will they have inns enough for all of us?'

Augustine looked around. They were a large convoy. The merchants were at the forefront, close to the leading guards. Poorer pilgrims straggled in the rear. Between them, the party from St Andrew's made an almost military impression, uniformly dressed in black, moving at a sober, steady pace, four by four.

He would be relieved to spend the night within town walls. He told himself that he and his monks were not an obvious prey to brigands, with their plain dress and carrying the most meagre personal possessions. Yet he knew that this simplicity disguised a dangerous truth. Did these Lombards know what any peasant in Roman lands did? That monks vowed to poverty worshipped their God with golden chalices, silver patens, jewel-studded Gospel books and Psalteries? They were going to dazzle the faithless English with the glory of God. But the road to Britain was dangerous itself. He felt the precious processional cross Gregory had given him must surely blaze through his leather saddle-bag.

They were approaching the town gate. Hoofs clattered on the paved ascent. There was only a brief halt before they were passed through into a square, with narrow streets beyond. The sun was dropping below the walls.

'See if you can find us an inn for the night, Brother,' Augustine ordered Honorius. 'Take Laurence with you. We'll wait for you here in the square.'

He was not enjoying this journey. He did not like this feeling that he had total responsibility for these men. The challenge ahead was so big, their future clouded with so many uncertainties. Every day of travel brought new difficulties.

It was a long wait. The brothers were beginning to look uneasy. Around them, people were crossing the square, homeward bound. Voices came and went, liquid Italian speech contrasting with the harsher Germanic tones of the Lombards. If the monks had been a group of laymen, they would have passed the time grumbling or joking to each other about the delay. But these were men under obedience, trained to silence. They waited in the deepening twilight without speaking, but Augustine sensed the unquiet in them.

A group of young local men passed, staring at them. 'Romans!' One spat accurately, to hoots of laughter.

Domitian looked scandalized. 'Aren't they Christians here? Do they spit at monks!'

'They call themselves Christians, but they foul the name. The Lombards deny that Christ is of the same substance as God the Father or his equal in the Trinity.'

The old monk crossed himself in outrage. 'But everything rests on that! The threefold name of God the Father, Son and Holy Spirit.'

'We're travelling through a wicked world. Savage wolves and bears are not the only danger.'

Augustine broke off. Honorius and Laurence were coming back at last, though from a street directly opposite the one down which they had disappeared. Their steps were weary, their faces dejected. Augustine braced himself to hear bad news.

'I'm sorry, Father,' Honorius apologized. 'We weren't well received. We probably don't look as if we'd spend enough money, when there are so many guests here with fatter purses, and the Lombards billeted on them, too. There's nowhere that will take anything like forty of us.'

'If we split up? Six or so of us an inn?' He saw the doubtful looks that passed between his monks. They seemed to draw closer to each other for reassurance.

Honorius shrugged. 'We could try. The watch won't let us sleep in the street, will they?'

Augustine looked with longing at the large church at the other end of the square, half stone, half timber. 'In a Christian country, the church of Christ should shelter us.'

Even as he spoke, he heard the clang of the heavy door shutting for the night. The curfew bell would ring soon.

There was nothing for it. He took the youngest monks and the oldest monks with him and left the others with his blessing for the night.

The first two inns rejected them, with a curse or a burst of laughter. Their reception at the third was surly, but they and their animals were admitted.

'You're late. There's only two more bed spaces to be had. The rest of you will just have to roll yourselves in your cloaks in the stable yard with the mules. It's a warm enough night.'

The innkeeper took money from them for six men's lodging all the same, and more for a bit of bread and cheese. When they had eaten, there was an awkward hesitation. Then Augustine left Titus and Maurice with two others under the stable eaves and took Domitian back indoors with him. It was, he told himself, more fitting that an abbot should have a bed.

He regretted it. Better to have lain separately under the stars, than squashed up in one huge bed with six snoring strangers. After the chaste solitude of his cell, their physical closeness was a torture to him.

It was a relief to meet the others next morning at the city gate, where the convoy was reassembling. The day was fine, the breeze still cool in the early morning. But the muttering had begun, as though the ties of their vows made in Rome were loosening as the distance between the monks and the holy city increased.

'If we're as unwelcome as this in Tuscany, what's it going to be like outside the Empire?'

'At least most people understand our language here. We won't even be able to talk to the English.'

'Those heathens will kill us before we've time to tell them we've come to offer them eternal peace.'

They were all looking at Augustine. Their faces were expectant, frightened, questioning.

'The Lord of hosts will protect us. The Spirit will guide us.' Augustine's voice made it sound like a rebuke to them. Inside him, it felt like a prayer, rather than an affirmation.

'Amen!' Titus's lone shout of enthusiasm echoed back from the walls. The young black monk looked round at his companions and hung his head in embarrassment.

The others' response was slower, a reluctant 'Amen.' Augustine saw them cross themselves in uneasy obedience. He felt he was holding them under his will, but only just.

The caravan moved out of the gate into the brilliant nakedness of another morning.

It came at noon. They had crested a rise where the sea coast glittered below them. Now the road turned inland, avoiding the highest cliffs. The way plunged down, between walls of rock. The sound of the horses and mules sounded louder in the confined space.

There was a heart-stopping yell, shattering the air, taken up from across the gorge by many more. The pass was a wild confusion of shouts and echoes, impossible to tell how many. Down from the skyline, out from behind boulders, came leaping terrifying figures armed with swords and knives. The monks' donkeys brayed. Their riders were trapped in close formation between walls of rock. Pilgrims screamed.

Gregory's cross was digging into Augustine's thigh. Should he draw it out? It was the nearest thing to a weapon he had, save for the short table knife in his girdle.

But he thought of the silver and the jewels. How long before the bandits realized what the monks carried?

Some of the leading merchants were galloping away, trying to break through the line of armed men blocking the lower end of the gorge. The mercenary guards had their swords out and were laying about them. Blood spattered the boulders. A speared horse screamed.

It was all over before Augustine could summon a coherent prayer to his lips. Robbers lay dead or dying by the roadside. Others were fleeing over the hill. One of the guards was tying a fast-flowing wound in his comrade's arm. Laurence was dismounting, hurrying to help with his physician's skill.

Augustine was shaking uncontrollably. No one had got near him. He was untouched. He saw Honorius looking with amazement at the knife in his hand. There was blood on it. They were all pale and shocked.

'Gregory was right to send us with an armed caravan,' he said at last.

'Gregory was a fool to send us at all.'

Augustine's ears were still ringing with the shouts and screams. He could not have heard Domitian correctly. His puzzled eyes took in the rest of his party. Almost all were staring back at him, their eyes both scared and defiant. The old monk had said aloud what they felt.

'Father Domitian, you will do heavy penance for that this evening,' his shocked abbot told him.

They fell short of their objective that night. They stopped instead at a surly village, whose solitary inn was inadequate to house and feed all of them. The purses of the merchants secured what hospitality there was. Honorius and Laurence managed to purchase three tents. The rest of the monks would again sleep rolled in their cloaks. They looked with silent dismay at the few loaves and olives the villagers had sold them.

Yet again, Augustine gathered them under an olive tree for their evening prayers. He knew with sick foreboding what would follow. Gregory would have laughed their fears aside, thrown a warm arm round their shoulders, made them feel that even the wildest dream was possible. He was not Gregory.

Even in the night-time, when they should have maintained the Great Silence, he heard them muttering outside his tent.

As the dawn broke, they were waiting for him. This time, they had appointed Laurence as their spokesman.

The soft-spoken physician smiled apologetically. 'I'm sorry, Father. We must be a great disappointment to you. But you see how it is. Three days on the road, and already we've encountered storm, hostility, robbers. God clearly doesn't mean us to take this road. If it's this bad in a land which at least calls itself Christian, what will it be like among savages who hate the very name of Christ? We don't speak their language; we don't understand their ways. How can we possibly do any good there? We must heed the warnings Heaven is giving us and turn back.'

Augustine swallowed. He knew what he should say. He knew what

Gregory would say. The words would not come.

'Is this the view of you all?'

'It is.'

'No! Not me.' A breathless squeak of protest from the back of the group. Titus's dark eyes were round with dismay. 'I'll go with you, Father, to the end of the world!'

'You'll be lucky to get to the end of Italy,' growled Domitian.

'And you, Honorius?'

The large monk still looked shaken. He took out his knife and stared down at it. 'Yesterday, I stabbed a man. I may have killed him. It wasn't for that I turned my back on the sinful world and became a monk. Let's go home, Father, before it's too late.'

Augustine felt a wave of relief sweep over him. Perhaps this mission was not, after all, inevitable. He could never have abandoned it of his own volition. But was there not sense in what they were telling him? Not just pessimists like Domitian, but reliable men like Honorius and Laurence. Faced with the overwhelming pressure of these companions, his brothers whose lives he held in his hand, was it not his duty as their abbot to plead for their safety? The safety, as Honorius had pointed out, of their souls as well as their bodies?

Even as he clutched at this plank, fear struck him from another direction. How could he possibly go back to Gregory and ask to be reprieved? Gregory, who had longed with all his heart to lead this expedition himself? Gregory, who had such unrealistically high hopes of Augustine? Who seemed, for all his worldy and spiritual wisdom, not to be able to see his abbot's doubts and inadequacies?

'Let me pray about it.'

'The merchants are starting to saddle up,' said Honorius. 'We're already three days away from Rome.'

Chapter Nine

The church of St Martin was being resurrected. Aethelbert lent labourers to slash the grass and tall weeds from around its walls. Trees were cut down and the walls shored up where their roots had trespassed. New thatch shone golden. The walls were plastered outside and cleaned inside. The faded paintings glowed gently by candlelight.

Bertha went often to see the work. She rode now directly up the hill from the palace. Sometimes she stood outside in the clearing above the road, watching the footpath, the woods, for movement. No one came, except the workmen Aethelbert had placed at her disposal. She studied them instead. Many of the lowest slaves were Britons. Had any of them ever come here to pray? Their faces betrayed nothing.

She always brought Edith with her. She had promoted the half-British girl to be her personal maid. On the queen's orders, Edith conversed shyly with her mistress in English. Bertha was making progress. She began to hear how some words of her own Frankish language, ones which had no place in the formalities of Church Latin, were not unlike their counterparts in Edith's tongue.

'Your mother?' she said in English. 'Does she still come here?'

Edith hung her head. 'No. They can't, my lady. Not while the workmen are here.'

'Tell her, when it's done, we shall have a . . .' – she had to resort to the Latin word – 'mass. We must make this work holy to God. She must come. She and her people.'

Edith's eyes shot up to hers, startled. 'My mother? Pray with you?'

'If she's a Christian. Liudhard may have to baptize her again, and certainly confirm her.' She could see from Edith's puzzled face she was using too many ecclesiastical terms for which neither of them had English words. She was startled to realize that there probably *were* no English words for these things. 'But in Christ there's no queen or serf, no man or woman, no Frank or English. He says all are one under God the Father.'

These everyday words Edith did understand, but not the reality they described. Her round hazel eyes stared up at Bertha's, as though she must have misunderstood.

'Tell them,' Bertha said, 'next week, on Sunday morning.'

Guntram, Liudhard's deacon, led the way with a golden cross. The bishop followed and then the queen. Behind her came all the aristocratic ladies of her Frankish household. The Englishmen Herman and Dirwine escorted her, with their spearmen, but they stopped outside the church. They had sometimes entered it uneasily while the restoration was going forward, but now that Liudhard was going to reconsecrate it, now that her god might suddenly appear, they were more afraid than before.

'Please excuse us, my lady. We'll stay in the open, if you don't mind.'

It was strange to see fear in the eyes of these warriors. She understood that they felt the walls and the roof of her church as a trap, within which the magic of her god would be concentrated too powerfully for them to escape. Woden was their Sky Father, Thunor their Thunder God. They would stay under the protection of the open heavens.

At the door she cast a last look round, past the procession following her. She felt a pang of disappointment. No Britons had crept out of the trees, or followed the royal party respectfully up the path. There were only herself and her fellow foreigners. A small panic seized her. Where was Edith? She, at least, should have had more courage than the heathen warriors and followed her mistress into the church. She had often come here with Bertha. There was no sign of the small brown-haired girl.

The queen swept up the short aisle to take her seat on the royal chair facing the altar. Her retinue stood behind her. Looking around at it all, Bertha felt there should be more gold, more jewels, more blazing lamps. At least there were candles in plenty, like luminous honey. She had bestowed on this church what she could. Aethelbert had provided for the outer fabric. She could hardly expect him to beautify the temple of a different god. That would come.

Liudhard was chanting the words of consecration, scattering holy water on the altar. Guntram, the deacon, was swinging the censer, releasing clouds of pungent smoke.

Bertha risked a glance over her shoulder. Again that pang of loss. Only the Frankish ladies were ranked behind her. Just then, she caught sight of a movement. Edith's small head was peering round the doorpost. The girl would not come inside, but she was lurking on the threshold. Bertha beckoned. It was as much a command as an invitation. Blushing, beneath the fall of her hair, Edith crept just inside the door and bowed her head.

The service moved into the familiar liturgy of the mass. When Bertha closed her eyes and heard the chants, she could imagine herself back in Paris, worshipping in the cathedral with all her father's court, not in a patched-up church in the woods, surrounded by heathen foreigners.

Yet today this alien world was moving forward. Not only would the bread and wine be transformed into the body and blood of Christ on Kentish soil, she herself had a gift of flesh and blood to present to Kent. The happiness grew inside her. This would make her the queen Kent wanted, the wife Aethelbert needed, the mother of his child. The timing could not have been more favourable. 'This,' she would tell Aethelbert, 'is the miracle of my God. Because you built this church for Him, He has rewarded you with a son.'

If it is a son: if I and the child live.

The Eucharist ended. The Amen should have pealed out from the throats of a cathedral choir. Neither Liudhard nor Guntram had particularly musical voices. The murmurs of a dozen or so in the congregation did not shake the rafters.

Liudhard bowed to her. She rose and followed the clergymen towards the door. As she passed Clotilda and the rest of her ladies Bertha started. Now she could see that in the shadowed back corner of the church beyond Edith, three women in dun-coloured dresses were crouched so low, their heads bowed to her, that she could see nothing of their faces. They might have been hedgehogs curled into defensive brown balls.

Her heart raced. So it was true.

'Edith!' she called.

The girl came slowly, fearfully, head hanging, as though it might be dangerous to walk across this space newly made sacred. Besides, there was the severe bishop in his gold and white vestments, a powerful holy man standing between her and the queen.

'Who are these?' Bertha demanded.

'My mother,' the girl whispered, 'my grandmother, a friend.'

The British women were uncurling their servile posture. A glimpse of pale faces showed behind stringy hair. One had a baby strapped to her chest. How had she kept it silent all this time?

'Don't be afraid,' she called to them. 'You are welcome.'

The women said nothing. They looked more frightened.

'Are you really Christians?'

They nodded.

'Just the three of you? No more?'

At last one of them spoke. It was Edith's mother. 'The rest of us are working, my lady.'

'On a Sunday?'

'They're slaves, my lady. They can't choose.'

Was that a note of contempt in her voice? The woman's eyes were veiled by downcast lids.

Bertha turned her head to Liudhard. Would there be some time when he could say evening prayers for people like these? Or could they come in the very early morning? She realized she knew so little of the lives of slaves, what freedom of movement they had. Edith's mother was not a slave. She was married to an English serf. But what of the rest?

She needed time to think.

'Clotilda.' She turned instead to her chief lady-in-waiting. 'Take the pearl from my ear.'

'Madam!'

'Do it.'

Clotilda's hands expertly unhooked the jewel and placed it in the queen's hand. Her tight lips spoke disapproval. Bertha offered it to Edith's mother. 'For all of you.'

The woman started back. She looked more scared than overjoyed, though the worth of the gift must have exceeded a labourer's wages for a year.

'She's afraid they'll accuse her of stealing it. What did you expect, madam?' Clotilda scolded. 'It's not a fitting gift for the likes of her.'

'Then what else? Can you arrange for food? A length of woollen?'

'That would be more appropriate to her station, madam. And more use.'

Bertha felt herself rebuked by both sides. She had wanted, today of all days, to make an overwhelmingly generous gesture, to celebrate her double triumph. Her exuberance had been reduced to what was prudent, practical.

But still she hugged the secret she must tell to Aethelbert.

It was a boy. Bertha lay back in bed, exhausted by pain, but feeling like a warrior whose wounds are the price of triumph. She watched the king lift his baby son in his arms. A grin of joy flashed through his moustache.

'The future king of Kent. Now my kingdom's secure.'

There was a flurry of arrival behind him. To her alarm, Bertha saw Ordulf, the Chief Priest of Woden, in her chamber. This was the first time men were admitted. Hours ago, when the pains had gripped her, she had been terrified to find the shaman Werburh bending over her. The wise woman of Frig had dominated the birthstool, chanting spells, waving the sacred things of her religion, offering some dark drink. Bertha had ordered her out of the room. Nevertheless, the Englishwoman had crouched in the doorway, knees splayed, rocking from side to side, intoning monotonous charms, until Bertha could no longer hear or see her for the agony racking her own body, threatening to split her apart.

Now she knew with unspoken dread that she would not be able to order out the king's chief priest in Aethelbert's presence. His authority would always be greater than hers.

Tattoos marked Ordulf's face. They made shadows where the lamplight should have illuminated it. He was peering at the baby, unwrapping its swaddling bands, probing the tiny exposed body. Bertha was horrified. What was he doing? What could he do?

The English midwives stood by impassively. They did not move to protest, even when their wrappings fell away from the baby's body. They must have expected this. They understood it, as she did not.

Now the priest was passing the little naked boy to and fro through smoke seeping from a pot held by a lesser priest. Bertha was confused. Why was the incense in St Martin's holy, rising like a prayer to Heaven, and this was not? She felt it as heavier, earthbound, oppressive.

'There, your majesty.' The chief priest transferred the baby back into Aethelbert's arms. 'He'll be safe for nine days. His name is . . .' Ordulf leaned forward and whispered in the king's ear. 'Tell no one. Names are dangerous. Never speak his name aloud until the ceremony.'

'Trust me. I'll keep him safe.'

Suddenly it was over. The chamber was clearing. People and smoke were both receding into the antechamber, out into her hall. Only Aethelbert and few of her women were left, with the midwives.

Aethelbert beamed and gave the baby back to her. 'You've done well, madam. You shall have gold, horses, land, for this.'

'My lord.' Her voice came thin and tired. 'Knowledge of this child came to me the day Bishop Liudhard hallowed the church you rebuilt for me. I thank you for that with all my heart. Now the God of that church has blessed us with a son. We should show Him our gratitude. May I baptize this child in the name of God who gave him to us?'

Aethelbert's face could change from sunshine to storm instantly. She thought he was going to strike her. She cowered back against the pillows, protecting the baby.

'Trust my firstborn son to foreign magic? Ead—' An expression of terror came over his face as he caught back his son's secret name he had nearly spoken aloud. 'This boy will be king of Kent. An English king for an English people. He carries the blood of Woden the Sky Father in his veins. Only Woden and Thunor shall have him.'

Through her tired mind drifted the thought of her own Sky Father. Hadn't He descended from Heaven to Mount Sinai, to give Moses the Ten Commandments? He had spoken from the clouds at Jesus's baptism. How could she explain the difference?

It was useless to argue. She would have to let her baby, descendant of Frankish Christian kings, be carried into a pagan temple, undergo barbaric rites, probably be smeared with the blood of sacrifices to heathen gods. She had no power to prevent it.

In less than a week she felt well and strong. But the midwives were adamant. She must stay in her chamber until the nine days were over. Even if she had not been a Christian, they would not have let her go to the temple for this ceremony. She was their brood mare; she had done her work. This was for the men.

'Eadbald,' said the king, dropping the swaddled baby into her arms afterwards. He looked like a man well pleased with his day's work. 'His name is Eadbald.'

Bertha held the little boy in her arms. She had been right. There was a smear of blood on his forehead. He felt like a stranger.

When the king had gone, she exercised her newly restored right to leave her chamber. She called Bishop Liudhard to her.

With only her most trusted Frankish women within hearing, she asked, 'Couldn't we baptize him now? Give him the protection of the Trinity against the powers of the dark? Aethelbert need not know, but I shall.'

The bishop stuttered, 'Your majesty . . . the king ordered . . . You asked him if Prince Eadbald could be baptized as a Christian, and he refused you. We are bound to obey our lawful rulers. Much as it grieves me, madam, I dare not deceive him. And, forgive me for speaking plainly, nor should you.'

Bertha found her strength suddenly leave her. She looked round for her chair and sank into it, faint and exhausted. Would it end with her, then? This brief foray of Frankish Christians into heathen English territory? Could she pass nothing on to the next generation, not even to her own child?

Edith came hurrying to her with a cup of wine. As ever, she was shy, nervous, but solicitous. She had hardly needed Clotilda's summons when she saw the queen's distress.

Bertha took the cup from those small hands and tried to smile. Had Edith's British mother felt like this too, seeing her own daughter follow her English husband into the temple of Woden and Thunor? Yet she had managed to plant in Edith a hunger for something else.

Would this be subversion?

Chapter Ten

Augustine turned south. He chose Honorius and Maurice, one of the younger monks, to accompany him, leaving Laurence in charge of the remaining party.

Augustine spoke little on the road. It should have been a relief to be going back to Rome. It was not. If they had been apprehensive about journeying in a large convoy through what had recently been enemy territory, the three felt even more exposed now. They had had to join a much smaller group, without well-armed guards.

An air of apprehension hung over the three. The nearer he got to Rome, the more nervous Augustine felt about meeting Gregory. He glanced sideways at the solid figure of Honorius, jogging on a mule which seemed too small for him. He wished he could unburden himself to Honorius and seek reassurance. But it would not be fitting. He was the abbot. He must preserve his authority, his dignity. It would certainly not do to let young Maurice see that he had any doubts about the rightness of his actions.

The other two monks themselves seemed reluctant to talk about it. For the usually steady Honorius to speak plainly would be to admit to the others his troubled conscience. Maurice's delicate, intelligent face showed only the reticence due from a newly vowed monk towards his superiors.

For all their private worries, the sight of the Eternal City, raised on its hills against the blue spring sky, reached out to welcome them like a mother's arms. Augustine had truly believed he would never see this again. Even shamed by failure, he longed to creep back into the embrace of those familiar streets, to beg her forgiveness. When he pleaded his case, he would surely be absolved. He could go back to the familiar order of St Andrew's. Shut the doors on the threat of violence and barbarity. Everything would be as before.

It was late in the afternoon when they and their mules passed under the gateway into its sun-baked streets.

'We'll spend the night at St Andrew's,' Augustine told the others. 'It's too late to expect the Holy Father to receive us today.'

'How do you think he's going to react, Father?' asked Honorius. 'He'd set his heart on this mission, hadn't he?'

It was out at last.

'Pope Gregory is a monk under discipline, as we are. We're trained not to allow our personal wishes to affect our judgement. Wise counsel must prevail.'

'I know what *my* personal wish would be.' Maurice managed a nervous laugh. 'Not to end up with an English battle-axe in my skull . . . I'm sorry, Father!' With the release of his tongue, he had been bordering on hilarity. 'I just mean, I'm not as bold as Titus.'

The recollection of the young black monk's eagerness to go on was like a slap to the face.

'The Rule of Benedict includes the avoidance of laughter.'

'Yes, Father. I'm sorry, Father.'

The gate of St Andrew's was as it had always been. The situation inside was not. There was a new prior of St Andrew's, a big, broad-shouldered man with a jowly face. Augustine felt smaller in his presence. Mellitus greeted the returned travellers with a surprised lift of his eyebrows. To Augustine, the movement conveyed more than a hint of scorn.

'We didn't expect to see you again, Father. Has some calamity struck your mission? Why are there only three of you?'

'The rest are well, though only by the mercy of God. My business is with the Holy Father.'

There was a coolness between them. It struck home to Augustine for the first time that he would not be able to sleep this night in the prior's chamber which had once been his. That belonged to this large, confident monk now. Rome had already replaced him, as a footstep on a beach is quickly smothered by the tide.

'We have beds enough for you,' Mellitus said. 'With so many monks gone, there are many vacant cells in the dormitory. Unless you would prefer the guest house?'

He should have been welcoming them with open arms, as returning brothers. Instead he spoke as if they were almost strangers.

That night, and at the early morning services, the monks of St Andrew's kept their heads studiously bowed, but Augustine felt their curious stares over the meal table. Only days ago, he would have called these men 'his' monks. Now they were Mellitus's, as the prior in charge of the abbey's discipline. They ate in silence, while a brother read to them. The direction of their eyes told him how little they were attending to the homily.

Later that morning it was time to set out for the Lateran Palace, where the Pope would be holding his audience.

'Will you be coming back to us afterwards, Father?' Mellitus asked.

For another night? For a lifetime? Augustine hesitated. 'That's for Pope Gregory to decide. We await his orders.'

Mellitus gazed down at his former prior from his greater height. His eyes seemed to say, 'You had his orders.'

The walk to the Lateran Palace brought back difficult memories. He and Peter had accompanied their abbot along these streets. Gregory had gone to beg another pope to allow him to go to Britain. Now Augustine was following his footsteps to beg Gregory to excuse him from going.

If the Bishop of Rome was astonished to see those three in his audience chamber, he hid it well. Even from a distance, his posture, the inclination of his head, showed the energy and attention he gave to each dignitary or supplicant who came before him. It was some time into the session before Augustine heard his own name called. He felt a treacherous dizziness as he crossed the floor and knelt to kiss the Pope's ring. When he looked up, Gregory's dark eyes were brilliant with concern.

'What's this, Augustine? When I embraced you at the city gate, I thought I'd parted bodily from you for ever, even though you carried my heart with you to Britain. I knew there might be dangers, yet I hear all forty of you are still alive. So what are you doing back in Rome?'

How could he know so much? Had Mellitus sent him a message? Had the two of them been communicating over his head?

It was hard to convey the message of his monks. Augustine struggled for the words to make abandoning their mission sound like a counsel of wisdom and not a confession of weakness. Here in the ancient and familiar solidity of the city, the terrors of a small group of men on a journey into the unknown were difficult to recreate convincingly.

'But you weren't *there*!' he wanted to cry out. 'You don't know how it *felt*! We nearly died. And we were still in Italy.'

The Pope's expression spoke bewilderment, rather than anger. 'But God preserved you. You were their abbot, Augustine. I promised to make you their bishop, too, as soon as you've gained a foothold in Kent. I've given you authority. They've all sworn to obey you.'

Pain scorched Augustine's soul that Honorius and even young Maurice should be hearing this rebuke. He was well known as Gregory's favoured protégé, his friend, and now his substitute. He had been singled out to do what the Bishop of Rome longed to, and could not. He had lowered himself, not only in Gregory's eyes, but in those of his own monks.

He set his mouth in what might have looked like an obstinate line. It was necessary to prevent the trembling of his lips, which he knew would accompany any further attempt to justify himself.

Gregory gazed at him for a long while. Then a smile dazzled his dark face. 'Courage, Brother! Look, let's meet in my private garden as soon as I've finished this audience. I promise not to send you away comfortless. Peter will show you the way.'

With a swift blessing, he turned his face away from them and lifted his hand. The name of the next supplicant was called.

The late spring sunshine was gentle enough for them to leave the shadowed colonnades and walk in the open along paths among beds of green
herbs. The terrifying thunderstorms of northern Italy had merely refreshed
the gardens of Rome.

Peter, the deacon, left them alone. The other two monks followed
Augustine in nervous silence. He knew that if he had not been there, they
would have broken their monastic discipline to exchange anxious
enquiries about what the Pope could do for them, what he might still be
expecting from them. Had Augustine's plea failed? The abbot wished he
could have eased his own pain by sharing his doubts with them. But
Gregory had recalled him to his duty. He must maintain what was left of
his dignity. He must keep his lips steady, his steps measured. If Gregory
sent him back to Lombardy, how could he now reassert his authority in the
wake of his foolish weakness?

At last there was the slap of sandals along the tiles of the cloister.
Gregory and Peter came into view, blinking in the sudden sunshine.
Gregory had laid aside the fine linen and damask of the robes he wore
when he sat on the papal throne. He dutifully upheld the honour of the
Church and the lordship of Christ, whose representative he was, to the
dignitaries who courted him, but his own taste was for monastic simplicity. He was dressed now not much differently from Augustine, except that
his long plain tunic was white, where Augustine's was black.

His stride was no less eager than of old. His skirt swept the aromatic
leaves bordering the path. Augustine flinched. He found Gregory's
warmth almost as hard to bear as his anger or disappointment. Now the
Pope's arms were round him in a strong embrace. Augustine would have
reproved any of his own monks who had shown his love so physically. Yet
the strength of those arms made the frightened little boy inside him want
to weep.

Gregory stood back, his hands still on Augustine's shoulders. He studied his friend's face. One hand lifted, and a long finger stroked away a tear
that had brimmed from the abbot's eye.

'There, Brother. Courage. It's not so bad. Peter and I have a plan. Peter
will write to your monks and I'll sign it myself to put fresh heart into them.
I'll tell them that in future they must do everything you say without question. The tougher the task, the greater their eternal reward. And I'll give
you a letter to a friend of mine on your route, the Archbishop of Arles.
You're from south Gaul yourself, aren't you? He'll be proud to know that
one of his countrymen is passing through on a mission from me. He'll help
you. He'll know conditions further north better than I do, and give you
more introductions and advice. For my sake, as well as Christ's, I need you

to make this journey.'

His eyes searched Augustine's. It was more than the authority of the Bishop of Rome over his missionary abbot. Augustine was as helpless before the appeal in those dark eyes as he would have been had the Pope ordered him to obey on pain of hell-fire.

'I will go, Father.' He heard his own voice make what sounded astonishingly like a brave affirmation, as though he had never turned tail and run from his mission. The squaring of his shoulders gave no impression that he had just given in to the mutiny of monks who should have obeyed him without question.

Gregory's eyes brightened with that amazing smile, which threatened to undo Augustine's new-found resolve in a flood of tears. He had not deserved it, any more than he deserved the love of Christ. But Gregory always gave himself to people, freely, generously. He made you feel you were a better a human than you were, because he believed in you.

Oddly, Augustine found he was starting to believe in himself. It was not a feeling he was accustomed to. Peter had gone indoors to prepare the letters. With a smile of apology, Gregory followed him.

When, a while later, Augustine held the scrolls with the papal seal in his hand, an uncertain imagining of places ahead began to feel more like physical reality. It was becoming possible to think past the danger and squalid discomfort of travel, the scarcely veiled hostility of the Lombards, the fear of their unknown route and the terror of Britain. The creamy parchment in his hand spoke to him of the golden stones of Arles, of cultured Latin ways, still safely within the Roman Empire and the Roman Church.

'If your mission is successful,' Gregory told him, 'I shall need you to be more than a bishop to the English. Write to me often. When the time is ripe, when you've converted the king, I'll send you the stole of an archbishop, with all Britain as your province. You can travel back to Arles for the archbishop to consecrate you there.'

So it would still be possible to go back. Not all the way to Rome, but at least to southern Gaul, to the warm sunshine of that Mediterranean land, to the ways of civilized Christians, to the Latin-speaking people he understood. His life might not be lost for ever on an island of cloud and rain, with heathen savages.

He turned his own smile, newly bright and determined, on Honorius and Maurice.

'Come, my sons. We've wasted enough time. The brothers in Tuscany will be wondering what's happened to us.'

65

Chapter Eleven

With every step of the mules' hoofs away from Rome it got harder. The glow of Gregory's presence faded.

'Nothing's changed, has it, Father?' said Honorius. 'Bandits, wolves in the mountains, floods on the rivers. The Lombards could declare war on us again.'

'And then there's Britain,' said Maurice. 'I wish I was brave, like Titus.'

'Peter and Paul went to their deaths for the Gospel,' Augustine countered. 'Whatever happens, Gregory assures us of a crown of glory.'

I must go on saying that to them, he told himself. I must repeat out loud Gregory's reassurance until, little by little, I come to believe myself that no matter how great the danger, it's going to be worth it for Christ's kingdom.

Honorius was right. The fear was no less alarming than before. Yet something had changed. The gates of Rome were closed to him now; he could not go back. He would rather face the axe-wielding savages in Britain than disappoint Gregory a second time.

Three days later, the waiting monks surged towards them, eyes questing, naked faces begging him to release them from their worst forebodings. Domitian's mouth was carved into lines of pessimism. Laurence's questions expressed concern, as much for the rest of the party as for himself. Only Titus's gleaming eyes showed a different fear, that he might lose his boy's desire.

Augustine held up the letters, as if the flimsy rolls of parchment were weapons that could strike down any enemy, or thunderbolts he could hurl to confound the elements. He felt astonishingly bold. Perhaps there really was power in them.

The monks looked at the scrolls suspiciously, apparently unimpressed.

He read Gregory's letter to them, 'My very dear sons . . .' Words of encouragement, of admonition, the promise of great reward in Heaven flowed. With an effort, he kept his voice steady as he read, 'We have appointed Augustine your abbot. Whatever he directs you to do will always be for the good of your souls. Obey him humbly.'

The words of the Pope died away. Doubt and discipline struggled for mastery in the faces of the listening monks.

'We still have mountains to cross to get to Arles, Father.'

'And then the sea between Gaul and Britain.'

'Did he give you letters of introduction to their savage gods?' Domitian's lip curled. 'It won't be Pope Gregory's head that's separated from his neck, will it?'

Augustine tried to turn his angry frown into a smile of encouragement. He knew no smile of his could ever dazzle men as Gregory's did. He was conscious of the stiffness of his face, the uncertainty with which his lips arranged themselves. He feared his eyes must look troubled, betraying his bold words. But he had made his decision: if he could not inspire these men to follow him, he must command them.

His voice came harsher than he meant it to, but at least it had authority. 'There must be no more questioning this mission. The Pope has sent us to Britain, and to Britain we shall go. If it is the Lord's will, nothing can prevent us. From now on, if I find any brother stirring up dissent, I shall chastize him severely with my own hand.'

The smile had slipped. He knew this was not how Gregory would have spoken to them. The words of the letter sounded too late in his head, '*My very dear sons.*' Gregory would have rallied them laughingly, made jokes of their fears, led them forward with energy and a high heart. Because Gregory was fearless himself, he would have made them brave.

I can only be what I am. I'm not Gregory. I never asked to do this. But I've promised him I'll lead them to Britain, and I will.

The crossing of the Maritime Alps was behind them. Provence spread its sunlit welcome. The warmth of their greeting in Arles was enough to make the deepest doubters relax a little. The archbishop was a small, plump man with a face creased like a dried plum. When he had read the Pope's letter, he embraced Augustine almost as eagerly as Gregory had.

'My boy, my boy! I'm so proud of you. Forgive me. I should call you Father, shouldn't I? But it seems only yesterday you were a young lad setting out for Rome, and look at you now! The Pope's own ambassador to a foreign country. And soon to be a bishop, too, if the English will receive you. Gregory's letter tells me you could become even more.' He winked at Augustine. 'I shall have to look to my laurels. You'll be after my job next!' The folds of his face shook with merriment.

The largeness of Gregory's promise began to dawn on Augustine for the first time. If the English did not kill or expel him, he would certainly become their bishop. But it need not stop there. He could become an archbishop himself. Never mind that his province would be some poor benighted land beyond the limits of the Empire. In the eyes of the Church, he would be equal to the Archbishop of Arles. He, Augustine, a prince of the Church. The prospect overwhelmed him.

Gregory's optimism proved right, in one respect, at least. The arch-bishop gave him an introduction to the King of Paris.

'The Franks are some sort of cousins to the English, I believe. Only they're Christians, after a fashion. Still heathens under the skin, I fancy, but there, we must accept them in charity as brothers, mustn't we? I believe King Clotaire has some sort of pull over his neighbours across the water.'

'Clotaire? I thought their king was Charibert. Didn't his daughter marry the king of Kent?'

The archbishop's laughter bubbled over. 'Charibert? Goodness, he died years ago! No, this Clotaire's a bigger king than Charibert ever was. Cheer up. I'll put in a good word for you.'

Augustine struggled against the shock of disappointment. His cheeks felt bloodless. His hope in Queen Bertha, Charibert's daughter, was retreating into unreality. He would not meet her father in Paris. He could not rely on his influence.

As the monks left Arles, Augustine had a keen sense that the line from Rome was lengthening out, growing thinner, weaker with every mile. Yet it still held. There was still a destination where his name would be made known at court, still a letter in the pouch on his belt.

They journeyed on by boat up the Rhône. There came a point where they must leave the river to fall green and tumbling from the Alps and take to mule-back again. They crossed the watershed into the valleys that ran down to the Seine.

Paris lay before them on its island. Roman grandeur was crumbling here, as everywhere else. A sprawl of wooden Frankish houses had colo-nized the banks of the river, leaving the island to its king. Even so, Clotaire's court was more often elsewhere. Augustine had to deliver his letter of introduction to the Frankish king in Soissons, further north.

King Clotaire was a more barbaric figure than the Roman monks had met since they left Lombardy. He lounged in his carved chair, picking at meat caught between his teeth, while a clerk read the archbishop's letter to him. To the dark-tonsured Italians and Gauls, his red hair and his great height gave him the air of a giant from a supernatural race. He laughed and leaned forward to Augustine. His Latin was guttural and hard to follow.

'So, you want to go to Kent? Yes, my cousin Bertha's queen there. But she has her own bishop already. I don't know what she'd do with forty monks.'

'With respect, the Pope has not sent us to the queen alone, sire. Our mission is to the whole English nation.'

'Is it indeed? We'll have to see what Aethelbert thinks of that! He's done pretty well for himself under his old gods.'

'But, sire!' With an effort, Augustine controlled the shocked protest in his voice. 'You're a Christian, as we are. Surely you must long to see the English gathered into Christ's fold, as much as the Bishop of Rome does. A king's faith is the key to his kingdom.'

'Ye-es. It's true, Paris and Soissons-Tournai are Christian lands, because I am. What the common people get up to behind my back is their affair. My family's certainly been successful under the banner of the cross. That's what counts, monk. Victory in battles. You'll have to convince Aethelbert your Lord is a more reliable champion than Woden and Thunor.'

'Victory may not always lie on the battlefield. From the beginning, there have been Christian martyrs, sire. Our Lord himself was crucified. We may have to suffer for our faith.'

'The Franks are not afraid to die in battle. Nor are the English. But we respect the gods who give us victory.'

'Then . . . will you not help us?'

Clotaire shrugged extravagantly and played with his luxuriant red moustache. 'I'll get my clerk to write a letter to my cousin. I'm sure her bishop, at least, will be glad of your ecclesiastical company. As for Aethelbert . . . there was a time when he was a puppet to the Franks, but he's grown a greater king since then. I'll commend you to him, but if he's as superstitious as they say, I can't guarantee the warmth of your welcome.'

His queen stood listening behind his chair. She leaned over and laid a hand on his arm. 'Can they read at the court of Canterbury, my dear?'

'Bertha's bishop can. He'll tell her husband what I write.'

'You think Aethelbert will listen to a Christian priest?'

Augustine strained to follow their conversation. Their heavily accented Latin was laced with Germanic words. Nothing he heard gave him confidence. Only a narrow strip of water lay between the Franks and the English. It might have been a raging ocean.

They came to the sea. It was like no water Augustine had known before. Gone was the vivid blue of the Mediterranean, the purple waves of the Adriatic, the jade green over the sandy shores of Provence. This was grey, cold even to look at, the breakers heaving on to the shingled shore like growling guard-dogs.

Laurence hunched in his cloak. 'Is that land on the horizon, or just a bank of cloud?'

'You've clearer eyes than I have,' Domitian told him. 'Beyond this harbour, it's all grey fog to me.'

'Not all!' Titus cried. 'Didn't you see when the sun shone out just now, a flash of white, like a seagull's wing? The cliffs of Britain, for sure.'

Augustine's hand slid into his satchel. It closed round another letter, with its wax seal. This time it bore the imprint of Clotaire, King of Paris, cousin to Queen Bertha of Kent. The Roman part of his mind was tempted to despise the moustachioed Franks. Clotaire's kingdom was barely converted to Christianity yet. The monks had ridden past hilltops still crowned with sacred groves. These people spoke a barbaric form of Latin. Their leaders gloried in war and conquest, not in scholarship and charity.

Yet it was comforting to know that King Clotaire might be an ally. He was a halfway staging post between the Roman magnificence of Arles' archbishopric and the English court of Aethelbert. What would a heathen king care for a letter from the Pope himself? The king of the neighbouring Franks had greater political weight. And, after all, Clotaire's cousin Bertha was a Christian.

Coming from a community of chaste men, in an imperial city which gave little power to women, Augustine felt shamed that he should have to rely on the Queen of Kent for protection. All his hope was centred on Aethelbert's wife. If that failed, he had no other key to enter Britain.

He looked regretfully at the line of pack asses which had brought them to the very edge of the Continent. The monks had cursed and grumbled at the jarring ride over the roads of Italy and Gaul. They had accepted with relief the smoother passage of river boats. Now the asses looked like old friends they would never see again.

'Take your saddle-bags,' he ordered. 'Each brother is responsible for his own load.'

They had little of their own. They wore their heaviest clothes, though this was what passed for midsummer among the Franks. But if Gregory's impossible dream in the slave market, of Britain as a land of angels, ever came true, a new monastery would rise in Kent, with these forty monks. They would need communion silver, books, tools, a bell. The saddle-bags were heavy.

Augustine lifted from his own pack its most precious burden. He unwrapped the folds of blanket. The silver cross gleamed in the uncertain light. There was a staff of ebony over which the silver socket fitted. He heard the voices of his monks fall still. When he looked up, their heads were turned to him. He smiled, wanting to put the reassurance into his face he knew Gregory would have radiated. He raised the cross, symbol of faith, of hope, of love. He was willing courage into them, as well as into himself.

'Time to board, my sons. Brother Titus.'

At a sign from his abbot, the young man sprang forward.

'Carry this before us.' And to the rest, 'Follow it in faith, and do not dishonour the cross, whatever happens to us.' He traced the sign of the threefold blessing. 'In the name of the Father, and the Son, and the Holy Spirit.'

70

'Amen!' He heard the fervour in their voices. They wanted to believe in him.

He had obeyed Gregory. He had got them to the sea, to this last crossing. They would follow him now, though it cost them their lives.

Titus led them proudly up the gangplank, with the silver cross held high. Augustine followed and turned to watch his monks come aboard. He caught sight of the scared young face of Maurice, his eyes darting around the details of the ship. The lad crossed himself. Probably he had never been to sea before. Next, the stolid gloom of Honorius's face, obedient, loyal, now that he knew he had no choice. Behind them, Domitian, frowning as his short-sighted eyes strained to see where he was going, still sourly pessimistic. Only Titus's face was alive with hope and excitement. He moved eagerly to the bows and stood there, planting Gregory's processional cross boldly as a figurehead.

Hawsers were loosed from the quay, splashed into the dirty water of the dock, and were hauled aboard. The sail was spreading. The sturdy trading vessel began to lunge and kick out into the open sea.

Chapter Twelve

'A Kentish sail, and flying the royal flag.'

A frisson ran through the forty monks on the Frankish ship. The grey-green coast of Aethelbert's kingdom had been slipping by on their port side for hours now. To starboard, was the gleam of sandbanks and the rolling white of surf, climbing and slipping back with the tide as the shoals rose clear and vanished again. Dangerous waters. Even a landsman like Augustine could see how skilled a pilot must be to negotiate them.

Now the captain's stance had altered from practised watchfulness to a sharp immediate concern. A smaller ship was bearing down on them, with a fast precision of oar-strokes. A bank of shields was plainly visible, the bristle of spears. This was no trading vessel. As the Englishmen's challenge rang across the water, Augustine felt as helpless as if he were deaf. The only word that sounded out clear to him was the king's name, Aethelbert.

Clotaire had provided them with a Frankish interpreter. Ebroin was used to trading in the English language. He had become voluble now. He was gesturing at the Roman monks, explaining their purpose to the newcomers. Scholars in theology and Hebrew listened like baffled children as the torrent of English words flowed between ship and ship.

The ready smile of the Frank was stiffening. The captain of the Kentish ship barked sentences that were shorter, curter. Augustine grabbed Ebroin's arm.

'What's wrong? Did you tell him we come in peace? We only want to present our courtesies to the king and to speak with Queen Bertha. As Christian monks—'

'Holy men. They don't like that. You're bringing strange magic to their land.'

'Magic? We're all good Christians!'

'From the Kentish point of view, sir, you're sorcerers, servants of a foreign god. That makes you more dangerous than a shipload of warriors.'

'Blasphemy! To equate us with sorcerers!'

'Simple prudence, sir, in their eyes. The coast warden's ordered us to follow his ship into the Wantsum Channel, and moor where the River Stour flows out from Canterbury. He needs to report this to the king before he knows whether he can let you land.'

'That's ridiculous. We carry no weapons. What harm can we do to Kentish folk?'

'You carry your god's totem on a pole, sir. They saw it.'

Augustine's eyes went to the bow. All his waking hours, Titus had held the cross gripped in cold hands, as though it, and not the helmsman, led the ship northward over the waves. The young monk was watching the English longship. His face had lost the shining eagerness with which he had embarked, but it was still taut with subdued excitement. Kent was close. The humps of its fields and wooded ridges were clearly visible. Smoke from clusters of thatch spoke of living people, English men and women. Titus at last saw his life's work almost within his grasp.

And Augustine? A treacherous question surfaced in his memory. Was this like the monks' mutiny on the road through Lombardy? Was he going to seize again on the hope that his mission might, after all, not be possible? Could he turn round with honour this time, go back to Gregory and say, 'I really tried'?

Almost to his own surprise, he found it was no longer what he wanted. A steely resolve was hardening in him. He had come this far, through fear, through difficulty, through danger. He would not be beaten back at the last mile. He would get to Canterbury. He would raise the cross of Christ on English soil. He would be Kent's bishop.

Their ship was moving again, oars out now and swinging against the current, closer into the land. The Kentish vessel executed a swiftly disciplined turn and led the way.

Now the details of the shore were becoming clearer: individual oak trees, under which cows grazed, women and children bare-legged in the mud, looking for shellfish, a country estate with a fine hall, set back from the huddled village above the beach.

A silver dart between wooded banks widened into a broad spearhead, a sword of light, a street of water. As they turned into this channel, there was land on their right now, where this morning there had been only sandbanks. No mud flats, these. There was a sizeable line of hills, banked with trees. In one high place the woods had been cleared, leaving a single mighty tree against the sky. Augustine knew enough of the practices of heathens to shudder.

'Is that their World Tree?' said Domitian at his elbow, peering up at it short-sightedly.

'I think so.'

'A heathen abomination!'

'But we have our own tree, don't we?' put in Maurice.

'There's no comparison,' spat Domitian. 'One blood, and one only, was shed on Christ's tree. You can be sure that human blood, even children's, waters those roots up there.'

The eyes of the monks turned up to the skyline, in thoughtful silence.

'You've got it right, sirs,' said the interpreter Ebroin. 'That's Thanet. Thunor's island, they call it. Sacred to their god of war and thunder. The one with the hammer. A real joker when he's in a good humour. Popular with farmers, because of the rain. But he can wade through blood if you get the wrong side of him, so they believe.'

The Romans watched, stifling more questions, as the anchor dropped in the channel. A smaller boat was taking the coastguards' captain to the opposite shore. It was dwindling now into the mouth of a river that must lead deep into the heart of the mainland.

'Kent,' murmured Augustine, 'and all the kingdoms of Britain beyond it.'

'We're here at last,' said Honorius. 'You brought us safely, Father.'

'By the grace of Holy God.'

'But are they going to let us land?' growled Domitian.

Augustine was silent for a while, staring westward at the shore. It was strange to see it almost still, save for the dipping of their ship as it rode the swell, no longer slipping past them, habitations seen only to vanish astern. He was here. This was reality. He felt a shiver of eagerness, almost like Titus's.

'Once,' he said thoughtfully, 'all this was Rome's. There were bishops from Britain who came to the great councils of the Church, in Arles, in Sofia, in Rimini. It's going to happen again. Britain is lost to the Roman Empire, but we can reclaim it for the Kingdom of Christ.'

'Are there none left, Father? No Christians at all?'

'Outside of the queen's court and her chaplain, none I know of, where the English have conquered. The old Britons were driven into the far west. I believe they still keep up some sort of Christian practice. But Rome has had no oversight for many years. Gregory tells me there are rumours of irregularities, of priests and monks more like pagan druids than sober Christian clerics. Perhaps one day, when Kent is converted, we'll be able to venture further west and bring them, too, back into the fold of the Church.'

His sense of reality was fading. For the moment, anything seemed possible.

The day wore on and the shadows lengthened slowly into evening. For a long time the wide channel held the light, though the tide had slipped down, revealing banks of gleaming mud. The Frankish merchants chafed at the unexpected delay. Augustine led his monks in the last office of vespers, and their obedient voices chanted the familiar words. The evening hymns of reassurance floated away across these foreign waters as they surrounded themselves with prayers of protection for the night.

*

It was mid-morning again before the smaller boat returned. This time there was a stranger with the coast warden. They were scarcely within hailing distance before Augustine could see that this man was more richly dressed. The pale northern sunlight sparkled on a heavier array of jewellery. It was more than his cloak fastenings; there were chains around his neck, bracelets on his bared arms. Closer too, they could see the red glow of fox fur round his deep-blue cloak. His beard was fair and neatly trimmed, though the brisk wind was tangling his long hair.

He stared intently at the newcomers as the rowing boat passed the coastguards' longship with its vigilant sea-warriors and closed with the Frankish ship in mid-channel.

The two captains shouted questions and information to each other, while the interpreter listened.

'That nobleman comes from the king's court,' Ebroin the Frank translated for Augustine. 'His name's Herman, one of their noble thanes. It looks as if King Aethelbert is taking you very seriously.'

'Give him greetings from Pope Gregory to his lord and tell him we ask permission to land.'

The courtesies and the request were called in English over the water. It was frustrating to have to wait to understand Herman's reply. The frown on Ebroin's face forewarned the abbot.

'Yes, the king will let you land. But not on the mainland of Kent. He needs to be satisfied that you mean no danger to his country. He says forty holy men is an army of magicians. His queen brought only two. He has to put you under the guardianship of a god strong enough to protect Kent and its people from evil.'

'Evil? You call Christ's Gospel evil?'

The interpreter held up his hands in mock submission. 'Not me, sir! I'm a good Frankish Christian. But with Kentish folk, it's Woden and Thunor and that crew they look to for protection. They think the Holy Trinity are enemies to them. If they anger their own gods, they fear they'll suffer for it.'

The thane Herman had delivered the king's message himself. It was the coastguard captain who was now rapping out orders. Ebroin listened intently.

'They're taking us to Thanet. They reckon Thunor's power is mightiest on his sacred island. They'll land you there. Then my merchant friends can get clearance to cross the Wantsum Channel and make landfall in Kent to sell their goods at last. They've lost money by this hold-up.'

'And you? You'll stay with us?' Augustine had a swift, painful longing for Edmer, the English boy they had rescued from the slave market, and lost again. He was suddenly alarmed that this slender cord which connected them to the foreigners might be untied and slip away with the merchants.

The Frank grinned. 'You're paying me well enough. We shook hands on a fair bargain.'

The ship's bows turned away from the mainland. Suddenly Herman's voice rang out again from the smaller craft. 'The queen asks for your prayers.'

It was a moment before Augustine realized the significance of what he had heard. These words were Frankish Latin. It was too late now to take advantage of the knowledge that the English nobleman spoke it. He could only cry, 'Tell her I pray for her daily,' and make the sign of the cross. The thane gave no further acknowledgment.

It was not a long row to the wooded island, but it called uncomfortably to Augustine's mind tales of voyagers on the rim of the world who had been ferried to an island of the dead.

Thanet loomed large. He could still see its southern end and the bright sea beyond. To the north, the low ridge of forest stretched on out of sight, seeming to merge tantalizingly with the mainland as distance narrowed the channel to a shining thread. He looked over his shoulder at the retreating shore of Aethelbert's kingdom. It was perhaps two miles away. So close, but would he ever cross that water to set foot on it?

Titus at the prow began to chant a psalm, lifting the cross high. He had stood as their figurehead for so long it was difficult to think of him stepping down on to firm soil. He had been their inspiration. He would never again be quite the naïve youngster he had once seemed in all their eyes.

Beyond Titus's dark tonsured head, the edge of Thanet swung vividly close. Augustine could make out the distinction between mud and shingle, see separate branches on the lowest trees. For a moment longer, he forced himself to concentrate on these small harmless details of nature. But he could not then deny the more threatening evidence of his senses.

A throng of men and women was coming down the beach to meet them. Again Herman's voice startled Augustine, calling from the small boat which still accompanied the Romans. This time the words were English, and shouted at these guardians of the island.

The monks could see them all too clearly now. The exotic fur and feathers of their robes, the tattooed faces. Augustine did not need to be told these were servants of the territorial god, priests and acolytes of Thunor. He murmured a prayer and tried to stiffen himself against a visible tremor of fear. Gregory had made him shepherd of his flock.

'In the name of the Father, the Son and the Holy Spirit,' he called, to strengthen himself as well as his monks.

'Amen!' they chorused fervently.

'Alleluia!' cried Titus

There was the lightest jolt, as the nose of the ship grounded against the shelving shore. At once the anchor splashed down. Titus was shouldered out of the way by the crew as the gangplank was run out.

'After you, sir.' The interpreter waved Augustine forward. 'Welcome to Thanet.'

Chapter Thirteen

Queen Bertha sped across the orchard, setting apple blossom tumbling as she passed. No longer would Clotilda's voice pant in her wake, chiding her to behave more seemly. Clotilda was dead two years since. Now it was an English noblewoman, Mildgith, who headed her household. Mildgith could not understand her mistress's excitement, but her legs were nimbler than Clotilda's had been.

At the far end of the orchard, Bertha saw what she had been looking for. The tall, intent figure of Bishop Liudhard seated on a bench under the damson tree, bent over a book.

'Bishop!'

'Your majesty?' He rose, punctilious as ever. She saw how he kept his finger in the book, marking his page. He would do whatever she commanded him: he would still rather be left alone to read.

'There is a ship in the Wantsum Channel, from France!'

'Indeed, your majesty? Perhaps there will be a letter from one of your sisters.'

He could no more understand the impetuosity of her stride, the flash of her eyes, than Mildgith could.

'There are monks aboard. Some forty of them. From Rome! They've brought an introduction from my cousin King Clotaire and a letter from the Pope.'

At that, his head did go up and a gleam came to his grey eyes.

'For me?'

'For my lord Aethelbert. His majesty commands that you come and translate it for him.'

She saw the winged eyebrows rise. Liudhard was plainly wondering, as Mildgith was, why the queen must run across the orchard herself with this message.

'Forty monks, you say? From Rome? Here?'

Bertha had expected a flame of excitement leaping to meet her own. What she saw instead was alarm. Guntram came hurrying up to join his bishop, bowing to the queen. Liudhard's eyes went swiftly to him. In a court of lean English warriors, the Frankish deacon had grown untypically

plump. She sensed Liudhard's arithmetic. These two were the sole repre-
sentatives of the Christian clergy on Kentish soil. For fourteen years they
had ministered to Bertha's spiritual needs, and those of her dwindling
Frankish retinue. To Bertha's sorrow, King Aethelbert had allowed none of
his growing brood of children to be baptized.

What would forty Roman monks do here? The bishop's private little
empire within the English court had been invaded.

There was a jabbering of English tongues all around Augustine, harsh as a
flock of rooks disturbed in a harvest field. His eyes went from face to darkened face, trying to read the expressions in those unfamiliar lineaments.
Long, bony features, blue eyes glinting with a chilling anger, violent as
their northern seas. Augustine had reproved his own monks often enough
for unbecoming laughter, but he would have welcomed now a broad
Italian smile, an expansive gesture of hospitality. With surprised joy, as if
conjured up by his need, he felt again the strength of Gregory's arms
embracing him. It was a token, he told himself, of Christ's presence.

He and his monks were not wanted here. A fierce argument had broken
out between the leaders of Thanet and the king's representative. The thane
Herman crossed his arms, the furrow deepening between his brows. While
the priests of Thunor poured out a torrent of abuse and denial, he
answered them with single terse orders. Alone, he held his ground. The
storm of words fell to an angry swell, from which hisses burst like spray
from broken wave-tops. The atmosphere was still thunderous.

One of the priests was pointing at the silver cross Titus held, demanding something. Herman turned to Augustine. All this time, the Romans had
stood speechless, unconsulted, like so much contraband cargo seized and
deposited on the beach. Now the thane said in his careful, heavily accented
Latin, 'He says you cover that.'

The monks looked at their abbot in alarm. Titus gripped the staff
tighter, as though nothing could tear it from him. There was a fearful
blank in Augustine's mind. What should he do? Here, on English soil, he
had no rights. He could only beg for entry. He must plead Christ's cause
like a would-be bridegroom bringing his suit to the court of a foreign
princess.

But there was Christ's honour to uphold. The cross was on the sacred
territory of the Thunder God. Would he concede defeat at the outset if he
hid it for a while? Or would it be merely prudent?

Christ had alternated between declaring himself openly in Jerusalem
and retreating secretly into the wilderness, hadn't he?

It was not just the monks. The heathens, too, were staring at him. He
must say something. This was his moment of decision. He felt by the stiffening of his spine, the rigidity of his jaw, that what he did now would set

79

the pattern for the years to come.

'This cross is why we have come. It offers eternal life to your king and his people. It means riches in Heaven. It is not a thing to be hidden, as if it were shameful.'

This was more than Herman's Latin could cope with. Ebroin translated into English. The thane's face brightened.

'In the name of my king, I thank you.'

There was a moment of farce as he reached out to take the cross from Titus. He clearly thought Augustine had meant that the silver object itself was the gift.

'No, no!' Augustine cried in despair. 'This is a symbol. The gift is the Gospel, the words of hope, the blood shed, the promise of Heaven. I have other material gifts for King Aethelbert and his queen.'

To his astonishment, Herman appeared to understand the thoughts, if not the Latin words. He nodded. 'Yes, yes. The bread and wine, these too are signs, I think. There was a man, yes? Your Christ. A man-god. These things are signs of him, as the stone hammer is a sign of Thunor. But you must put your cross in a place of safety, where it can do no damage.'

Augustine smiled thinly. 'We have not come to damage Kent, but to heal it.'

Herman rapped out an order. There were more furious protests from the heathen priests, but the point was made. Titus held tightly to his cross.

Augustine signed to Honorius, who drew from his heavy satchel gifts Gregory had given them for the king and queen. A precious Gospel book, its cover tooled with filigree gold and set with lapis lazuli. A silver cup of Byzantine workmanship. Herman's eyes widened, and he lifted a corner of their wrappings. He seized them with an eagerness which made Augustine hope they would please his royal master too.

A procession was forming. The Roman phalanx was tightly hemmed in by a seething mass of Thunor's people. The mask of a stoat snarled at Augustine over a priest's shoulder. There was the rank breath of meat-eaters. Waving wands, clashing bells and beating drums to ward off evil, they began to march up the beach. Some of the leading priests grasped the animal masks, which swung on their robes, and pulled them down over their faces.

'I feel,' Honorius muttered beside Augustine, 'like Jonah in the belly of the whale.'

It was indeed as if the monks had been swallowed into the stomach of some monstrous beast. The animal cries and the thunderous drumming made it difficult not to be afraid.

Titus was clutching the cross close to himself now, like a mother protecting her baby. He was no longer the brave enthusiastic missionary, carrying his symbol high.

The way led through a township. It was hard to see much of it for the press of Thunor's servants all around them. English folk, Augustine realized, were taller than most Romans. He had glimpses of women staring, of open-mouthed children. Everywhere he looked, curiosity was matched with hostility.

'We don't seem to be very welcome here, Father,' whispered Maurice.

'This is their sacred island. You wouldn't expect their priests to open their arms to a greater god than their own.'

'Will it be like this at the court?'

'I think not. The queen is there already, and she has her chaplain. Somewhere in Kent Christian people are kneeling before the King of kings.'

He clung on to that thought. They were not the first. Queen Bertha had brought her faith to Kent and had not renounced it. She needed help. He must, he would give it.

'If they ever let us get near Canterbury,' muttered Domitian. His aged voice spoke what Augustine had not dared to let himself think.

'That's more like it!' Titus had raised himself on tiptoe to see further ahead.

The steeply soaring roof of a great hall broke on their vision. Dragons sprang from its gables. Red and green and blue paint shouted vibrant colours. There was a flash of gold from the ornamented door.

'Surely a king's palace!' Augustine's heart lifted. They were not to be prisoners, after all, but honoured guests.

The pace of the march did not falter. They were swept past the lofty hall. Ahead of them the woods loomed darker. There was a sudden turn, a smaller path. The leading priests halted and barked at the monks a sound that had no more meaning than if it had come from dogs.

'They request that you will go in there,' Ebroin translated. The Latin words were more courteous, Augustine was sure, than the original curt command.

A building, big enough for a barn, but without the paint of the palace they had passed, stood on a knoll among the trees. There were carvings here too, weathered by time and dark as the planks of its walls. Doubtless the local guardians of this place. Augustine found himself reluctant to look at them too closely.

Thunor's people stood aside. He had no choice but to lead his monks into the dark unknown of its interior.

The floor was almost bare, drifted with golden dust and bits of straw. A few bales were scattered around the walls. Sparrows searching for grain scrambled into the air and beat their frightened way past him back into the daylight.

As Titus carried the silver cross in under the lintel, Augustine could almost feel the sag of relief in the heathen shamans. They clearly believed it had dangerous power. Did he believe in its power as strongly as they did? When it was gone from their sight, the chief priest of Thunor cried a last incantation. The drums fell silent, the chanting stopped.

In the hush that followed, Augustine felt his own relief wash over him. They had arrived. A dirty barn, not a king's palace. An island brooded over by a bloodthirsty god, not a court fit to receive ambassadors. Yet this was a building on English soil, a destination. The Isle of Thanet was a place set apart, yet it was within the kingdom of Kent. They had brought the cross Gregory had given them to the country Gregory had dreamed of. He need not be ashamed.

'What are you going to do?'

Bertha laid a tentative hand on her husband's shoulder. Aethelbert's moods were hard to gauge. It was difficult to control her own excitement. For fourteen years she had kept her faith alive with only Bishop Liudhard, Deacon Guntram, her Frankish household and a handful of the poorest Britons for comfort. Death had reduced their number. There were more Englishwomen than Franks attending her now. But not one of these Kentish ladies had joined her Church. Why should they? Bishop Liudhard never preached the Gospel outside the little church of St Martin's, safely remote from the king's palace.

There was just one joy. Bertha's eyes went fondly to the slight young woman behind her. Edith, her half-English maid, had fallen, shy and trembling, to her knees and begged to be baptized, like her British mother. She had served Bertha devotedly all this time.

Now, there were forty Roman monks on Thanet. Pope Gregory's gifts lay on the table in front of Aethelbert. His eyes widened, sparkling, not only at the precious materials but at the quality of the workmanship. Warrior though he was, he had an eye for beauty. The sumptuous, jewel-studded filigree of the Gospel's cover entranced him. The greater treasures within that cover were a mystery to him.

King Clotaire's letter remained in Aethelbert's lap. The king handled it obsessively with battle-scarred fingers. He traced the embossing of the wax seal. That, at least, he could understand. For the rest, it was just black marks on creamy parchment. He ran the curled sheet through his hands as though the meaning of those marks might be transmitted by physical contact. Bertha's bishop had read it to him, of course. He was not so naïve as to think the written word was magic. Kent and the Frankish kingdoms were in constant touch. Ever since the arrival of his queen, there had been letters.

Yet he felt their threat, and it made him angry. It was not just the writing itself, but the language in which they must be written. Latin, the language of the Franks and all the nations south of them, to Rome and further. It spoke of a brotherhood, a family to which he did not belong. The Christian priest had not only had to read it for him, but lame Siric had had to translate it. Even now, the Frankish Liudhard spoke only broken English. He had not shared his queen's passion to learn the language of their adopted homeland.

Aethelbert put up his hand and clasped Bertha's, in a rare gesture of affection. 'What am I going to do about these holy men? I must protect my country.'

'You do that well, my lord. Half Britain's rulers acknowledge you as king over them. Why should these unarmed Romans threaten you?'

'For the same reason I've kept you and your magic man well outside my capital. The blood of the All-Father Woden runs in my veins. That's what fits me to be king. That and my sword-arm. When I hack my way to victory, I do it in the power of Woden and Thunor. What do you suppose would happen to me and to Kent if I turned traitor?'

'My family in France changed their old gods for the true one. The kingdoms of Paris and Soissons, Burgundy and Orléans are greater than ever before.'

Aethelbert's grey-blue eyes sharpened suddenly as they fixed on hers. His other fist clenched the letter and his gaze went back to it.

'A man would have to dare much to make war on his own gods.'

Bertha's mouth went dry. 'You are such a daring man, my lord. The bravest.'

Chapter Fourteen

A mist of rain drifted across the doorway, cutting off Thanet from sight of the mainland. The barn was damp.

'They might as well have set us adrift in the Northern Ocean,' complained Domitian. 'Why does nobody come? What's the king doing?'

'What do you suppose we have to do, Father, to convince him it's safe to let us set foot on the mainland?' Honorius asked.

'We're not likely to convince him of anything, if no one comes to talk to us, are we?' Domitian countered.

'Listen,' said Titus. 'They're starting again.'

This was the sound which troubled them even more than the silence and the waiting. The beat of drums, deep, large drums, which rolled like thunder. Occasionally a horn would shriek, swift and sky-splitting as a bolt of lightning. The chants which rose were, at this distance, less threatening. They were not too unlike the incantations sounding from any Christian abbey as the seven offices of divine worship marked out the passage of the day. The monks could only guess how different were the rites which they accompanied. Imagination coloured them red with blood, black with smoke, white with fear.

Augustine began his own counter-chant. *'The Lord bless us and keep us. The Lord make his face to shine upon us. The Lord lift up the light of his countenance upon us, and give us peace.'*

'Amen!' they chorused fervently.

Yet anxiety, and not peace, was the mood which hung over them as the days of their quarantine lengthened.

There were footsteps squelching on the wet path. The sound of a number of people. The monks were all suddenly alert. Until now, only a few servants, truculent or fearful, had brought them food. The tonsured heads of the Romans went up, their eyes questioned each other, torn between alarm and hope.

Augustine turned to face the door, drawing himself up tall. Honorius and Domitian positioned themselves immediately behind him. All forty monks were now on their feet, prepared. Their black robes darkened the shadows still further. Only Ebroin the interpreter stood out in his blue tunic and grey cloak. The lighter colours seemed almost frivolous.

They watched the approaching party block out the view of the wet woods and the misted channel. Some of these English had hoods drawn up against the drizzle. Their leader was bareheaded.

Augustine felt a start of relief as he recognized him. This was not a priest of Thunor in his savage regalia; it was Herman, the nobleman from Aethelbert's court. Moisture beaded his beard and darkened his blond hair. The men behind him were mostly plain soldiers or better-dressed laymen like himself. Only two wore the hammer and animal skins of Thunor's holy men.

Ebroin stepped up to Augustine's shoulder, ready to interpret.

'Greetings, Lord Herman,' said the abbot. He was pleased he had succeeded in steadying his voice. 'The peace of God on you and on your king and his household.'

'Greetings to you, Father,' said Herman, not waiting for the translation. 'The king hopes you are well.'

'Well, my lord, but somewhat damp, and eager to speak with the king himself. Did he receive the gifts from our Pope?'

Herman looked to Ebroin for help. Across the barrier of words, civilities passed.

'The king thanks you. The richness of your lord's gifts honours him. He hopes he may do you some small service in return.'

'The only service we seek is to speak with the king and his queen face to face, and to be permitted some place to stay near his court.'

'On one count, then, you may be pleased with what I come to tell you. On the other, perhaps not.'

Augustine stared at him questioningly. 'You speak in riddles, sir.'

'The English are famous for riddling.' Ebroin conveyed this additional information with a grin.

'Are we to go to Canterbury, then?'

'No.' The word fell like a blow. All of them understood the English monosyllable. They listened in frustration to what followed, before the sense was disentangled into Latin.

'The king will meet you. You are honoured. He's coming himself to Thanet.'

'To see us?'

'The chief priests of Kent have warned him that so great a body of magicians as you Romans poses a threat to his kingdom. He won't let you out of the power of Thunor until he's satisfied you bring no harm to Kent.'

'We bring salvation.'

The thane held up his hand. 'I'm a plain warrior. I don't pretend to be a judge of these things. But I've served as head of the queen's bodyguard for fourteen years and seen no harm come to us from her Christian priest.

Kent's mightier now than it was before the king married her. But our priests say differently. Thunor brings the rain we need to grow the harvest and keep the grass green for our cattle. Anger him, they say, and there'll be drought and famine. If you upset him and All-Father Woden, Kent could start losing wars. The king's afr—' With a wink, Ebroin indicated that Herman had been on the brink of saying 'afraid', and added for himself, '. . . But that's not a word you use about a king, is it?'

Herman corrected himself. 'The king's duty is to defend his country, from human enemies and the anger of the gods.'

'Superstition!' muttered Augustine. 'No, don't translate that.' More loudly he asked, 'You say the king's coming here?'

'Tomorrow.'

'To that palace we passed on the way from the ship? I may speak with him there?'

Herman shook his head with a slow smile. 'No, Father. The priests of Thunor have warned him that would not be prudent. They fear to have so much magic — the power of your God — concentrated within four walls, under one roof. Thunor himself needs to see what you're up to and hurl a thunderbolt from the sky if he needs to stop you. King Aethelbert will only grant you an audience in the open air.'

A tremor of surprise ran through the monks. Their eyes questioned each other. Were they really so powerful, then? Did even the chief priests of the heathen fear them? Titus's eyes flew to the cross he had carried so faithfully. He had set it up in this barn, wedged between bales of straw. Its silver glinted faintly in the gloom.

Augustine bowed. 'I will meet King Aethelbert wherever he chooses. Will I be free to speak to him, to tell him why we've come?'

Herman inclined his head courteously. 'You may have your say, Father. On the impression you make before the king will depend whether he lets you cross the Wantsum Channel to his court, or whether he sends you back to Frankland. I should warn you, my lord is a shrewd judge of men.'

The Romans kept a vigil through that night. Relays of monks knelt on the damp floor, praying through the darkness. Domitian and Honorius persuaded Augustine that he must get some sleep.

'We're all depending on you tomorrow, Father. Let us do the praying for you, while you rest.'

It was hard to sleep. His monks had tried to create a more retired space for him, but the bales of straw were few. He felt an unbearable ache for the privacy of the prior's cell at St Andrew's. Even though he was accustomed to spend the most significant part of his day worshipping with his monks in the church, and to rise from sleep to join them for the night office, the constant presence of so much humanity close around him was an affliction.

His restless body longed for the warm Roman nights. How could he ever have complained of summer heat?

All these were secondary complaints. He knew his mind was dwelling on them to prevent him from facing the greater challenge. What should he say to King Aethelbert tomorrow? On him, and him alone, rested the responsibility which would see them admitted to the greatest court in Britain, or sent back to Rome like dogs stoned out of a village with their tails between their legs.

'No!' The tortured word broke aloud from him in his dark corner of the barn. 'God forgive me, to think that it should be my own words I speak! Surely the Holy Spirit will take possession of my tongue and teach me what to say?'

He must have slept. The morning dawned fine. The steadying routine of the early service of prime called all of them to consciousness. There were even smiles. They were glad this moment had come. Triumph or disaster hung on it, but this day marked their journey's end. When the sun set, they would know whether they were to remain in Britain or turn back. Their mutiny on the road from Rome seemed like some far-off sin of boyhood. They were grown men now, hardened travellers, men with a mission. After the smiles at one another, most faces set with a firm resolve. Even Domitian tried to hide his scepticism.

It was mid-morning when the summons came. Augustine had hoped Herman would return to lead them to the king. Instead, two files of Thunor's priests, men and women, made a long corridor from the barn to the road. They would keep these foreign holy men well guarded on their sacred soil.

Augustine turned to Titus. 'Lift up the cross. If they're afraid of its power, let them see we trust in it.'

The young monk raised it reverently. Domitian went down on one painful knee to it, and all the monks made the same homage. The cross passed before them to the open doorway, where the morning light shone on its outspread arms. A snarl burst from the waiting ranks of Thunor's servants.

'Maurice,' said Augustine to the other young monk, 'it's time.'

Maurice flushed. He lacked Titus's boldness. But he had carried his own burden right across Europe for this. It was larger than the cross, and heavier. In embarrassed silence, under the eyes of his older companions, he let fall the canvas wrappings which had protected it from damage all these weeks. They revealed a rectangular board, painted on one side. There was a murmur of reverence as he fitted his staff into position behind it, and lifted it high for them to see. The large dark eyes of Christ looked down on them; their Saviour lifted his fingers to bless them. Suddenly they felt that the words of their prayers were not empty. Their Lord was with them here.

Shyly, Maurice took his place behind Titus, turning the face of Christ to greet the world.

'God be with you, Father,' said Honorius. Breaking the custom of their order, his hand gripped his abbot's shoulder.

'Into your hands, O Lord, we commit ourselves this day.'

The cross dipped under the lintel, and straightened into the glory of the morning. The wooden banner followed. As the monks followed two by two out into the open air the Wantsum Channel flashed in front of them. The rain had washed the air, making the mainland of Kent clear and close, every detail drawn with aching clarity. Across that narrow water lay their goal. The next hours would determine whether they attained it.

Julius their cantor raised his fine tenor voice. He pealed out the opening lines of the litany. *'Blessed be the Lord our God.'*

And the monks gave back their answer, *'For he has visited and redeemed his people.'*

Gregory had taught them the music for their chants. The measured, disciplined, antiphonal rhythms of their voices rose in a recreation of their services in Rome. All their vows, all their obedience, all their personal battles with doubt and fear and weariness, all their constancy, had been for this. Today, they were singing the Lord's song in a new land. Today, Augustine would preach the Gospel of Christ to the greatest ruler in Britain, Aethelbert, King of Kent.

Chapter Fifteen

It was strange to be sitting on her throne beside this great heathen king in the open air, on an island sacred to his thunder-god. What would her sisters in Paris say if they could see her now in this barbaric setting? Bertha looked around her uneasily at the circular clearing in the woods, packed with the devotees of Thunor in their savage regalia. Even the familiar English faces of her court, Mildgith, Herman, Dirwine, looked fearful.

This was the first time Bertha had set foot on Thanet in all the years of her marriage. Aethelbert came here to worship his gods, to sacrifice for his people. She could never be persuaded to join him. There had been angry scenes, but she insisted on the nuptial contract which upheld her freedom of religion. It was not only the priests of Thunor who chafed at that. Behind her, Bertha could hear Werburh, priestess of the goddess Frig, making incantations in a scarcely concealed undertone. She had never forgotten the horror she had felt when she found Werburh conducting a ritual of purification in her hall, nor the malevolence in her eyes when Bertha had halted it. She knew Werburh cast spells against her. She tried not to be afraid, especially when she was pregnant. Yet the spells seemed to have done her no harm. She had borne six healthy children.

All the same, there was an irrational tremor of fear as she turned to Eadbald standing beside her. Yes, she was right. He was growing into a princely boy, tall, fair and well-muscled. Aethelbert's thanes were schooling him to follow in his warrior father's footsteps. The puppy-fat of boyhood was giving way to a determined jut of his chin, like his father's. She was foolish to think he could be harmed by such spells. Still, it pained her heart that her sons and daughters had never been baptized. What if Eadbald fell in his first battle? What if he died a heathen?

These alien surroundings of Thanet were troubling her. If she did not let herself look too far, the scene was familiar enough. She and Aethelbert on their carved chairs of state, the court around them, ranged according to their status. The nobles of Canterbury had come richly dressed and hung with the gold chains they liked to flaunt. Around them were ranks of spearmen, guarding the royal family. From what? It was no surprise attack of sea-raiders Bertha feared on this island; it was the native presence that lived here, in its dark surrounding woods, in the World Tree towering on the hill, in every rain cloud that passed over it.

She did not have to look far to see how different this was from an audience at Canterbury. Behind the spearmen, there were no palace walls hung with embroidered curtains and gorgeous parade weapons. This circle of grass had been levelled out of ancient forest. Dense curtains of leaves surrounded it on three sides. The twisted boughs of oak and elm and holly had been carved into fantastic shapes by no human craftsman. Instead of a raftered roof blackened with smoke, the blue heavens arched above them, with puffs of fair-weather clouds today. How close were her husband's sky-gods, Woden and Thunor?

At least, she told herself, I was not required to enter a heathen temple or sit on my throne under Thunor's great tree on the hilltop. If Aethelbert's priests fear the power of the cross in an enclosed space, I too have been spared the sanctuaries of their dreadful gods.

She stared down the empty avenue through the trees, along which the monks must approach. She had felt compelled to come here. When she heard that Pope Gregory had sent, not one, but forty monks from the very heart of the Church in Rome bringing the good news of Christ to Kent, her heart had leaped with joy. For fourteen years she had clung to her lonely, obstinate faith here. Bishop Liudhard served her loyally, but he had never gained permission to do what this Augustine was about to: to preach Christ's Gospel before Aethelbert. Had he ever really wanted to? Should they both have pressed her husband harder?

Too late now for regrets. Her pulse was quickening. Surely that was the distant chanting of the Romans she could hear in the distance?

As if in confirmation, there was a burst of whistling and the tattoo of drums. Thunor's servants were hurling defiance back.

Bertha looked sideways and saw Aethelbert grip the arms of his chair and draw himself up taller. She realized with astonishment that he was afraid. Aethelbert of Kent, overlord of Britain, whom all the other kings acknowledged as their superior. Did he really fear unarmed monks?

Aethelbert glanced up at the sky above him, as if for protection. The day was fine, the small clouds harmlessly white against the blue canopy. There was no evidence of the thunder-god.

Now Bertha could see movement down the pathway cut through the woods. The glint of sunlight on something silver, a larger standard carried behind it, and the moving column of black-robed monks steadily marching nearer. An undisciplined crowd of the people of Thanet surged alongside them, trying to drown out their chanting. In snatches, she could begin to make out words of their Latin litany.

'. . . *that we should be saved from our enemies.*'
'*And from the hand of all who hate us.*'

Brave words. Bertha's heart thrilled. She had an overwhelming desire to weep. Fourteen years in Kent. Only the small thin hymns of her own household, growing less each year. She had forgotten the full-throated sound of many male voices chanting confidently the praise of her God. She was suddenly back in the cathedral of Paris, a small princess attending church with her family, Why had she fidgeted and yawned and wriggled her toes with impatience then? The sound of this choir was the most glorious music this side of Heaven. There were tears running down her cheeks.

She heard the hiss behind her. Werburh had insisted on coming too, though Thunor was not the god she chiefly served. She was the high priest of Frig, goddess of fertility. Bertha knew that if she turned her head she would see the English wise woman weaving her hands, muttering curses half aloud. There would be hatred in her eyes, born of the same fear as Aethelbert's that the Christians were bringing a magic more powerful than hers.

Bertha kept her eyes resolutely fixed on the monks.

The silver cross came first. The young monk who carried it scarcely watched where he was walking. His round face and the thick black circle of his tonsure were turned up, so that he gazed at the sacred emblem he carried. Even so, his face seemed darkly shadowed. A start of astonishment made her crane forward to see better. The monk's face was black. So were the hands that held the cross. His expression was radiant with excitement.

The lad behind him looked more nervous. His thinner face and narrow shoulders were almost overshadowed by the wooden board he bore on a staff. A nobler head than his was emerging now into the full sunshine of the clearing. A halo of gold threw into vivid relief the painted features of Christ, her Lord. His face was a beardless oval, his eyes full and dark. Two fingers of one hand were raised in blessing. She could see the nail mark in his palm. A moment more and she felt those serious lips would smile at her. She was on the edge of her throne, wanting to dash forward and throw herself at his feet.

She steadied herself. It was the third man she must concentrate on. He carried nothing but a book and his pilgrim's staff. Augustine was a smaller man than she had expected, used as she was to long-legged Franks and Anglo-Saxons. Beside her, she sensed Aethelbert relax a little. He was accustomed to meet his opponents with a sword on the battlefield. This little southerner could never be a match for him. They both watched Augustine approach their thrones. Bertha could see sweat on the Roman's face, though the spring day was not warm.

Behind him, his monks advanced, two by two, still chanting insistently.
'*You will go before the Lord to prepare his ways.*'
'*To give knowledge of salvation to his people.*'
'*To give light to those who sit in darkness.*'

'*And in the shadow of death.*'

She felt proud of them, as if she were one of their number. They were surrounded by the hostile servants of Thunor. In contrast to the sober black-gowned monks, the English priests had decked themselves with animal pelts and masks, with feather capes, with symbols of their gods painted on their skin. She knew the cacophany of rattles and whistles were meant to scare away the magic of the Christians. The Roman cantor held the rhythm of the litany in his pealing tenor.

The procession stopped before the king. The two young monks lowered their standards and planted the poles on either side of Augustine. They turned to watch their abbot.

Aethelbert barked an order. The servants of Thunor fell back, reluctantly silent.

Abbot Augustine halted before the thrones. He bowed deeply to the king, though he did not bend his knee. Then he bowed to Bertha. His hand traced the sign of the cross for her. She felt the blessing warm her, as if his fingers had touched her.

The king raised his hand.

'You may speak,' Herman told Augustine in Latin.

'Your majesty, I bring you the peace of God and the blessing of the Bishop of Rome.'

A Frank in secular clothing stepped forward from among the monks to translate.

Aethelbert barely acknowledged the greeting. 'Tell your pope, I thank him for his gifts. Now, let's get down to business. Why have you come here? What do you want from me?'

Bargaining, Bertha thought, the buying and selling of advantages. Conquest or trade, the bargain of loyalty between a lord and his followers, these are the transactions Aethelbert understands.

'I come to offer you the kingdom of Heaven.'

'I have a kingdom already. And power over half of Britain.'

'And when you die? Whose kingdom will you enjoy for eternity?'

Bertha had no need to wait for the translation. She had time to watch the play of emotion over her husband's face. The English were a stoic people. They sang of ships carrying their dead out into the grey sea, disappearing into the mist. It was said that heroes who fell in battle were snatched up by Woden's daughters and carried to the Sky Father's feasting hall above. But for those who died in bed, for the old, for the commoners, for women, only the cold shadows of the North Sea awaited them. As the years began to grey Aethelbert's beard, did this fear haunt him? Was that why he threw himself into battles of which he had little need, to die the hero's death which would carry him up to Woden's feast?

Augustine began to tell of a heavenly kingdom, of a royal court more glorious than any known on earth, of a King of kings before whom all the monarchs of the world gladly cast down their crowns. Emperor after emperor of Rome and Constantinople, the victors of mighty battles which had changed the history of Europe and Asia and Africa, all had died with this hope in their hearts, that the glory they had known in their lives was nothing compared to the glory to come.

'And what is the price of this kingdom?'

'The price is paid already, your majesty, and not by you. The King's own son, Jesus, who is called the Christ, laid down his life and shed his blood for you. We may all enter freely into His Father's kingdom. We have only to repent of our sins and claim His blood as our ransom.'

'I don't have to make sacrifices to your God? I don't have to give him gold? Where's the trick?'

'No trick, your majesty. It was a gift of love. The greatest gift there could ever be. God made the sacrifice Himself. There need be no other. The Father gave us His Son, a gift more precious than any gold. He asks only that you love Him, as He loved you, that you serve his people.'

'Love? Serve? You're talking to a king, sir!'

'God the King loves you. Christ the Prince serves you.'

And Augustine began to tell him the Gospel story.

Bertha watched her husband curiously. What would he make of a carpenter's child born in a stable? Of an itinerant preacher with less of a home than a fox or a bird? Of a shameful gallows death?

But she underrated Aethelbert. His fierce English warrior blood rose to the challenge of the hero who defied His enemies. Who rode into Jerusalem where they plotted His death. Who faced His torturers with a proud silence. Who mounted the cross like a battle steed which would carry Him to glory.

'He was a brave man, your Christ.'

'He calls for brave men to follow Him, your majesty.'

'And you say that those who do this ride through death into glory?'

'There is no glory on earth to compare with the glory of the kingdom of Heaven.'

'And I must lay down my wrongdoings at His feet? These are the trophies He wants?'

'You will be washed clean of them.'

Aethelbert gazed at him without speaking. His eyes travelled round the listening ranks of his court, the priests of Thunor, Woden and Frig, at the contorted features of Werburh, plainly willing him to resist. His eyes came at last to Bertha's face. She held her breath. Was there anything she could say which might make or mar this moment? Let her eyes speak for her.

'You speak nobly, monk. But I carry the weight of a great kingdom on my shoulders. What I choose, my followers will choose. My priests tell me that, if I call down the anger of the gods, the people of Kent will die of war or famine. Enemies will snatch back lands I've conquered. You ask me to take a great risk.'

'Those gods are nothing, your majesty. Painted idols. There is only one God.'

There was an outcry at that. Before the spearmen could stop them, the priests of Thunor sprang on the monks. They began thrashing them with sticks, tearing at their robes. In an instant, the king rose in anger and thundered a command. Belatedly, the spearmen levelled their weapons at the priests, though they had to control their shaking arms. The mob subsided, let go of the monks, fell resentfully silent.

Aethelbert turned to the shaken Augustine. 'I thought you had brought your god to do battle with my gods. You say there is only one power?'

'None but the Trinity of Father, Son and Spirit.'

'Then how have I won so many battles in the name of Woden and Thunor?'

'My God has watched over you, sire, to bring you to this day. He is the Lord of history.'

Aethelbert smiled. 'You have an answer for everything, haven't you, monk?'

Augustine coloured. 'I speak only as the Spirit gives me the words.'

Again a silence, while the king's fingers played on the arm of his chair.

'Very well. You may come to Canterbury. I will give you a place to lodge and food for your men. If any of my people wish to follow you, I won't prevent them. You may visit the court and speak with the queen. She'll be glad of your company.' He grinned through his beard at Bertha. 'She's had only that lanky Frank for the past fourteen years. He never explained things to me as you did. I don't think he understands about heroes.'

'And you . . . your majesty?' The abbot's voice trembled with daring and hope. You've heard the Gospel. Will you accept baptism from me?'

'Hah!' snorted Aethelbert, snatching back the advantage. 'Don't presume too much, monk! Be thankful I let you this far inside my defences.'

Chapter Sixteen

If only Gregory could see me now.

Augustine did not speak the words aloud, but an astonished pride made it hard to breathe. He stood by the mast of the royal ship powering its way up the River Stour. Farms and hamlets flashed by as the oarsmen swung to their task. This was Kent, the gateway to Britain. This was Aethelbert, Britain's overlord. And he, Augustine, had won the royal warrant to set up a Christian mission in English Canterbury.

If only he could go back to Rome in person. If he could wait in that cloistered garden of the Lateran Palace next to St John's and hear the Pope's feet approaching again. This time, he would go down on his knees and announce, not failure, but triumph. This would wipe out the shameful past. This would restore him in Gregory's eyes to all his friend once believed he could be.

'As soon as we arrive in Canterbury,' he said to Honorius, 'I must write a letter to Rome. Aethelbert must have messengers between his court and the Franks. There will surely be frequent communications between the kings.'

'It'll be a while before it gets from there to Rome.'

The reminder of the journey that letter must take before it reached Gregory's hands was like a cold wave breaking over the bow of the boat. So great a distance, so many months of separation from all Augustine had counted as security.

'Have you been to Paris?' The queen's voice interrupted them. He had to look up at this tall woman. Thick plaits, a gingery red, hung over her shoulders beneath her white veil and golden coronet. There was a dusting of freckles on her nose between the blue eyes. This was a middle-aged woman, with a growing family, but there was still something of the awkward eagerness of the adolescent about her. Queen Bertha asked him questions as though she really wanted to know the answers, not just as the courtesies of polite conversation.

'Yes, your majesty. We went to Paris hoping to meet King Clotaire there, but he was further north in Soissons.'

'So you didn't stay there?'

'No, your majesty, not more than one night.'

'Did you go to the cathedral on the island in the Seine? The royal palace?'

'We made our morning prayers in the cathedral, before we took to the road again.'

Her face lit up in an amazing smile. She had, he noted, good teeth, square and regular, though with small gaps between them. 'Isn't it fine? Do you think one day, Father, we might have a cathedral like that in Canterbury?'

'With God all things are possible, your majesty. But we must walk before we can run. If I can found an abbey there, that will be a good beginning.'

'I wish you'd visited the palace in Paris. There might have been some of my family still there.'

He saw from her wistful expression that she still felt an exile in Kent, as he would now be.

'Do none of your sisters or brothers visit you?'

She made a face. 'The Franks are much too grand to come to little Britain. But Rome? Is that grander than Paris?'

Words fled from Augustine. How could he convey to her the vast and ancient splendour of the former capital of that huge empire? The acres of marble, cracked by time and defaced by Christian converts, true, but flowering with more recent churches just as beautiful and costly as any pagan temple. The stone-paved roads leading from every part of the horizon. The libraries of scholarship. The tombs of the saints, great Peter and Paul themselves.

'Rome is like Paris multiplied a hundred times, your majesty. But some things you would find familiar. We too have a Colosseum, and ours is crumbling, like yours. There, Christians were martyred by wild beasts, in the time when the pagans ruled. Now, thank God, its cursed stones are falling apart.'

'Oh!' Queen Bertha had clearly not considered that the amphitheatre she remembered might be a source of shame, not pride. 'In Canterbury too, we have a little one like that. Look, there it is.'

She turned to face upriver. The breeze of their passage blew in their faces. Augustine saw a jagged outline beginning to emerge above the swell of fields and orchards.

'Now God be praised! That's Canterbury?'

'My husband's capital. Though we have palaces in many other places, of course.'

The jetty swung into view. The motley crowd awaiting them was edged by a line of steel. An escort stood ready to greet the king, doubling the bodyguard who had travelled with him.

Suddenly the arrival of Augustine and his monks became a matter of secondary importance. King Aethelbert's presence commanded total attention. Through phalanxes of spearmen and cheering crowds, who flocked from their work for a sight of the royal couple, the king and queen processed. They entered the city through a turreted gateway in its crumbling wall. When the hubbub had subsided, the monks were left standing awkwardly on the landing stage.

'What do we do now?' Honorius asked, dropping the weight of his satchel to the boards.

Augustine looked round for Ebroin and found him talking earnestly with Herman. He must appear to take control of the situation.

'Titus, Maurice. Raise the cross and the banner again.'

The young monks, more self-consciously this time without a royal audience, set their standards upright on the dark planks of the jetty. As the king and queen disappeared, some at the back of the crowd looked round curiously at the mass of black-clad strangers.

Ebroin came towards them, with Herman following.

'Sirs, the king has assigned you a hostel close to the palace. You'll be supplied with food. You're free to go where you will and to speak to his people.'

'Speak with them? But for that, my friend, we need an interpreter. Will you stay with us?'

The Frank shrugged. 'A day or two, perhaps. But I've a family of my own across the water. It's not my intention to settle in Kent. You must find Latin speakers here, or learn the English language for yourselves.'

There were some moments of silence.

Laurence said, 'I wish we'd learned more from Edmer and Saenoth, when we had still those boys with us in Rome.'

'Father,' Maurice spoke shyly from his post holding the banner of Christ. 'I picked up a few words. Well, I could hardly help it, sharing the novices' dormitory with them, and the two of them chattering away to each other in English. Until Saenoth died.'

Augustine swung round with hope. 'You could translate for us?'

'Oh, no!' Maurice flushed. 'Not enough for that. But I think I could learn their language.'

'We shall all have to,' snorted Domitian. 'No sense in coming to spread the Gospel if we can't even talk to these savages.'

'Not savages, Brother,' Augustine reproved the older monk. 'Think of them as strayed lambs.'

'Hm! I doubt that King Aethelbert would thank you for calling him that. He looks to me like a man who'd far rather play the wolf.'

'A wolf who is giving us a roof over our heads and food for our table. Be thankful.'

'Oh, I am, Father, I certainly am.'

He must hold on to that sense of pride and victory, with which he had sailed up the River Stour. The honour was not for himself. He was the representative of the Church of Christ.

'Justus, it's time. Put your best voice into it. The kingdom of God has arrived on English soil.'

Maurice and Titus lifted their standards. Augustine felt the historic importance of this moment as both awesome and delicious. As Justus's fine voice raised the litany, he began to lead his monks across the wharf. They were passing staring Englishmen and women, many of whom, he could not help noticing, were making signs against evil. Behind him the monks thundered their responses to Justus's chant.

'We pray thee, 0 Lord, in all thy mercy,'
'That thy wrath and anger may be turned away from this city,'
'And from thy holy house, for we are sinners.'
'Alleluia!'

The outer walls of Canterbury were immediately in front of them, rearing over shacks and warehouses which crowded the riverside. Yet it was a shock of disappointment to see how uneven and broken down they were, and to glimpse the ruins within their sagging boundary. Augustine kept chanting with the rest, but his eye was roving swiftly, assessing the dilapidation of such a great king's capital.

The road was making for that gaping gateway where the royal couple had disappeared. All Augustine could see ahead was the gap-toothed remains of a once-noble amphitheatre. On either side of the street, thatched English hovels crouched between roofless walls of Roman masonry.

A few more verses up the main street and Herman turned sharply to the right. Suddenly the truth of Aethelbert's Canterbury swung gorgeously into view. The palace of the king of Kent rose before them in all its splendour. Huge halls, with towering roofs, row upon row of stables and storehouses. Smoke climbed from kitchens large enough to feed an army. Gold, brilliant paint, a riot of intricate carvings. This, Augustine had to admit, was the equal of anything he had seen among the Franks. The English could not build in stone, as the Romans did, but what they raised in wood and thatch was awe-inspiring. He would do well not to underrate this king.

Herman stopped short of the palisade which surrounded the royal halls. They were outside a lesser hall, which looked small only by comparison with the king's palace.

'Here's where we often lodge guests who've brought a big retinue with them. You'll be comfortable enough here, till you can have a place of your own.'

Inside, the wide living space had partitions jutting from the walls, providing separate stalls for sleeping. It would, Augustine realized with respect, sleep a hundred. Herman led him across it to a door in the far wall.

'Some private chambers, for the nobles leading a delegation, and any ladies who might accompany them.'

So he would sleep alone at last, enjoying the privacy and privilege of an abbot. The overcrowded squalor of travel was behind him. He had not realized how enormous a relief that would be. There was even a proper bed.

'Thank you!' He had to suppress the urge to seize Herman's hands and squeeze them with joy. 'And thank your king for his generosity from the bottom of our hearts.'

Herman looked at him with a shrewd smile. 'My duties as captain of the queen's bodyguard have brought me close to her for many years. To begin with, I have to admit, I was afraid of her god, and kept well away from their rites. But I've watched the comfort she gets from them. I think you'll find some doors will open readily for you, now that the king's given his permission.' With a nod, he strode away.

When Augustine stepped back into the hall, he found the monks in a circle waiting for him. Titus and Maurice were still bearing the cross and the painting. Their abbot moved through the silence to join them and fell to his knees.

'*We praise thee, O God.*'

'*We acknowledge thee to be the Lord,*' they chorused back to him.

He had delivered them safely to Britain.

Chapter Seventeen

Bertha sat on the bench outside the queen's hall, spinning flax in the sun. She found it a restful occupation, busying her hands with the physical, while letting her mind roam free. There was a pride, too, in glancing down occasionally and seeing the pale fine thread lengthening from the distaff. She rarely snapped or knotted it.

Around her, her women were soothingly at work, too. Even noblewomen must not sit idle. Their small children played on the grass, crawling after insects or tottering on chubby legs.

'I think, your majesty,' a male voice said at her elbow, 'it might be more dignified to receive the Romans in your hall.'

Bertha squinted up into the sun. The long melancholy lines of Bishop Liudhard's face frowned down at her. He was such a stiff man. He would never rebuke her openly. He was too conscious of her royal status. But she sensed, beneath his grave politeness, that she was still in his eyes the freckled princess who had leaped and laughed with her brothers and sisters in the wild games of her girlhood.

She hesitated, then sighed. Perhaps her chaplain was right. There had been no opportunity for more than brief conversation with the Roman abbot on the journey from Thanet. Today she must give him a longer audience. He came direct from the Pope. She should do him proper honour.

She had been so delighted when she first heard of this mission from Rome, and when Aethelbert gave the monks permission to land in Kent. In a single day, it had more than trebled the number of Christians in this kingdom. Yet there was something alarming in the thought of forty of them in the hostel so close to her palace. Kent was surely about to change. For her, most of all, life would be different from now on. It was difficult to imagine what this would mean.

'Very well.' She rose and smiled at Liudhard. Edith, her maid, moved swiftly to take the distaff and spindle from her.

Obediently, the ladies of her household, Kentish and Frankish, laid up their own work and accompanied her indoors. The Queen of Kent moved into the shadows of the hall and crossed to where her chair stood facing the door. She seated herself and waited. Her ladies ranged themselves around her. Liudhard stood just back from her chair, a little to one side, where she could turn and speak to him. Mildgith stood on the other side. Bertha sensed the Englishwoman's unease.

The door stood open on the sunlit space between her own hall and Aethelbert's larger one. She could still hear the children's voices, just out of sight.

Two fair-haired page boys, stationed either side of the door, sprang to proud attention. One of them, Tyrri, called self-importantly, 'Father Augustine from Rome, to see the queen.'

The sunlit doorway darkened as the abbot entered, with a burly middle-aged monk and a wrinkled older one behind him. The Fathers Honorius and Domitian, she remembered. Augustine had, she felt, chosen his most senior monks to reinforce his status. The abbot was the smallest of the three. As on Thanet, their plain black garb struck Bertha as almost shocking, used as she was to the swagger of Anglo-Saxons in their heavy gold neck-chains, the flash of garnets and bright enamel, the costly dyes of the cloth the nobles flaunted, which no serf could afford. These monks, she knew, would be from aristocratic families, yet they chose this dramatic denial of all they could have had. Suddenly she felt the splendour of her queenly dress, which Aethelbert regarded as essential for his wife, to be the subject for challenge rather than admiration.

She smiled uncertainly. She had so looked forward to their coming. Now they were making her nervous.

'Welcome to my hall, Fathers.'

She saw the smile of relief which illuminated Augustine's shaved face. Her sense of alienation deepened as she gazed at him. The blackness of his cropped tonsure, the yellower skin, the rounded features, his short stature, made him seem as though he came from another continent than the English warriors she lived amongst.

Yet to Augustine, she evidently represented a blessed familiarity.

'God be with you, your majesty. I cannot say what a delight it is to find someone here who speaks Latin.'

A jolt of surprise. Yes, she had spoken to him in the language of her girlhood. It was easy to slip from one tongue to the other. She did it all the time. She had simply not thought about it. By now, English was as natural to her as the married woman's veil which Edith pinned to her hair every morning. It had become part of who she now was.

'You will learn English,' she said, smiling widely. 'As I did. I'm sure that monks who study the ancient scriptures in Greek will find no difficulty with the language of Kent.'

Augustine bowed. 'Let's hope you're right, your majesty. We have a great work in front of us.'

Bertha's eyes wandered above his head to look through the open door-

101

way and beyond. 'All Kent. Do you think you can really make these people Christians?'

If Augustine had doubts, he was suppressing them. 'Once, the whole of Europe was in the grip of pagan superstition. It is not now.'

'And yet . . .' She levelled her gaze at him. 'That was the work of kings as much as missionaries. I'm a daughter of the king of Paris. The Franks were not converted household by household. When my great-grandfather Clovis changed, they all changed.'

He bowed again. 'In that, you show considerable wisdom, your majesty. If we could win the soul of the king of Kent . . .' The eyes of all three men were raised to her, full of hope.

Bertha spread her hands in a gesture of powerlessness. 'He's the key. I know that. I'd hoped, when I came as a Christian princess to a heathen land, I might have some influence over him. But you've seen Aethelbert. He hasn't become the greatest king in Britain, for nothing. He's a man who sees very clearly what he wants and he means to hold on to it. He believes the gods of his people – Woden and Thunor and Lady Frig – give him victory. He's afraid to change.'

She had said, with her toothy girl's smile, what Herman had not dared to. There was a rustle of unease among the Kentish women.

'Yet your chaplain has preached the Gospel of Christ to the king?' The abbot's gaze went past her, to where Liudhard stood stiffly behind her.

Bertha sensed the unspoken condemnation. She turned with a hasty smile for her chaplain. 'Bishop Liudhard, I beg your pardon! I should have introduced you long before this to these gentlemen.' To the newcomers she explained, 'I brought my own bishop with me from Paris. This is Liudhard, of the Frankish Church.'

The clerics bowed to each other silently.

'He has freedom to act as chaplain to my household. He leads the services in our little church. But Liudhard is not, like you, a missionary. Many times I've asked the king to hear him preach, but he has never consented. He won't let him speak in the palace, before his royal priests.'

'Does he say why not?'

'Aethelbert speaks only English. Bishop Liudhard preaches in the Latin tongue. The king grows impatient with translation.'

'But, your majesty, you've been here . . . how long?'

'Fourteen years,' said Liudhard flatly.

'And still you don't speak enough English to tell the king the good news of salvation?'

Behind Bertha, the Frank's voice rose. 'English is a barbaric language, for a barbarous people. Latin is the tongue of the empire, of the Holy Roman Church, of civilization. Our scriptures are in Latin, our sacred liturgies. I would coarsen the Gospel to reduce its cadences to the spits and snarls of English.'

'And yet,' – Domitian lifted his white eyebrows – 'your own Latin, Father, is – how shall I put it? – not quite the same as we speak it in Rome. You've already dropped in some Frankish words I don't understand.'

The bishop drew himself up even taller, facing the southerners. He was stiff with rage. 'I'd looked forward to your coming. Here, at last, I thought, I would find brothers. Men I could speak to as intelligent beings in a civilized tongue. I did not expect to be insulted in my queen's presence.'

A little smile of mischief played around Bertha's mouth as she looked from one churchman to the others. They were startlingly different. Liudhard lacked the jewellery of a nobleman, save for the large pearl-studded cross on his breast and the ruby of his episcopal ring, but his clothes were as colourful as any of Aethelbert's court, a long blue gown, with slashed sleeves, over a tunic of dark red. He was not a monk. He wore his reddish hair cropped, but not tonsured.

Liudhard shot a question back at Domitian. 'And you, Father? Do you claim to speak English?'

The Roman bridled. 'We've only just arrived!'

Honorius moved in to smooth things over. 'I regret to say I don't speak English either. We had a chance to learn while we were still in Rome. There were two English boys Pope Gregory saved from the slave market. We let that chance slip. But now we're here . . . Your majesty, can you help us to find teachers and interpreters?'

For a moment, Bertha was startled. Then, 'I think I can.' In delight, she clapped her hands. 'Tyrri, Gosfraeg!'

The boys attending the door were jolted into attention. They ran forward and knelt before her.

'My little friends, you can still speak Latin, I think?'

'Of course we can!'

She looked over their fair heads at the monks. 'Two of my ladies married English nobles. These are their sons. They normally talk English, like all the other children here, as, of course, my own children do. But as infants, they stayed with their mothers, playing around my hall. They learned our Frankish Latin as babies.

'Gosfraeg, Tyrri, you will go with these Fathers and be their teachers.' Her smile was wide and merry now. 'See that they learn good English, and quickly.'

She turned to the Romans more gravely. 'Take these boys with you as interpreters. They are young, I know, but quick. The folk of Canterbury already know them as my pages. When these boys speak for you, the people will know that you come to them with my authority. And now . . .' – she slapped the arms of her chair eagerly – 'tell me about Rome!'

103

'Do you really think anyone's going to listen to children? You're demeaning yourself and the Church, Father.' Domitian glared at the two eleven-year-olds.

Augustine tried to suppress his own misgivings. 'Doesn't the scripture say, "Out of the mouths of babes and sucklings". . . ?'

Tyrri and Gosfraeg led the monks towards the quay on the River Stour, with a swagger of self-importance. To Augustine's eyes, they might have been brothers, though they had told him they were not related. All English boys looked alike to him, leggy, blond, pink-cheeked, with faces as long as horses', once they lost their infant chubbiness.

'Here.' He halted the party where Canterbury's city wall had collapsed into a mound of stones. 'Titus, climb up with me. Domitian, too.'

The abbot clambered to the top of the mound, lifting the skirt of his black robe clear. His sandalled feet slid awkwardly on the tumbled masonry, grazing his ankles. Titus mounted more nimbly, even though he was carrying the cross. Domitian laboured after them, muttering under his breath. The ten remaining monks accompanying them arranged themselves in a semicircle below. After some whispered words with Gosfraeg, Tyrri scrambled up to join Augustine.

Gosfraeg, the smaller of the two boys, put his hands to his mouth like a trumpet. His high-pitched voice shrilled out, evidently announcing what was going to happen. He strutted through the crowd of traders and market-folk. The news he called out was already making them turn their heads. Augustine caught no more of its meaning than his own name.

'What's he saying?' he asked Tyrri.

The taller boy grinned. 'He's calling them to roll up and hear the great Father Augustine. You've come all the way from Rome, over the mountains and across the sea. You're going to tell them of wonders they've never heard before. Anyone who loves a good story must come and listen to you.'

A stab of alarm went through Augustine. A story? Was that what these people were expecting?

'The boy makes it sound like a public entertainment, not a call to repentance, to save their immortal souls,' Domitian growled.

Tyrri flashed his smile at the elderly monk. 'We're English, sir, and we love a good story. It's a pity your abbot hasn't brought a harp. That's how it should be done: the poet striking a chord, after the mead has gone round in the feasting hall. All of us falling silent, with our mouths open to listen. Tales of monsters and heroes, of treasure and dragons. That's what we love.'

With growing nervousness, the abbot watched the promise of a story begin to work its magic on the crowd. Shoppers stopped their haggling, with their baskets only half full. Stall-holders, seeing their customers going, accepted the inevitable and positioned themselves to see the Romans better. There were, he noticed, a disconcerting number of women in the crowd. In Rome, you saw fewer women of the respectable sort in the markets. All these faces, he realized, were turned to him.

He checked to either side. The young Nubian Titus made a pleasingly dramatic figure, black-robed, black-faced, steadying the silver cross. Domitian, on the other side, lent the gravity of his years. But the monks stationed below him were glancing nervously from the gathering crowd back to their abbot.

Gosfraeg was coming back, looking pleased with himself. He bowed extravagantly to Augustine. 'Here you are, Father. You can begin now.'

Before Augustine could speak, Tyrri shouted from his perch on a massive stone beside him. Again, Augustine heard his own name echo across the river. Even the men on the wharf paused in their work and began to shuffle nearer.

'What shall I tell them?' he sent up a murmured prayer. 'Inspire me, Lord!'

'In the beginning,' he called, his voice surprisingly loud and confident, 'God made the world, and he saw that it was good.' He paused for Tyrri to translate. 'And in that world he made the first garden, and set in it a man and a woman. . . .'

It was like talking to children. He would not have needed to tell his congregation in Rome the story of Adam and Eve. They would have heard it from childhood. But the English knew nothing. He must tell them the great history of sin and salvation from the beginning.

A few sentences later, his curious audience came suddenly to life. He heard their eager gasps, was aware that they were pressing closer to where he stood. He smelt their close-packed bodies, saw their gap-toothed mouths agape.

Augustine shot a questioning glance at Tyrri. The boy finished what he was saying and grinned back. 'It's the serpent,' he mouthed. 'They love dragons.'

Augustine pictured the carved dragons jutting from the beams of the king's palace, with open jaws and scarlet tongues. Was this how Tyrri was describing the Serpent of Eden? How much else in this story of Palestine would grow distorted on English soil?

The story spun on: the people's broken relationship with God, the prophets rejected, the incredible gift of God's own Son.

There was a disturbance growing at the edge of the crowd. Those at the front, until now rapt in the enjoyment of this tale, were turning round to look. Augustine's monks had abandoned their attention on their abbot and were on tiptoe to see, over the heads of the taller English, what was happening.

Augustine's words began to falter.

Suddenly a missile flew from the crowd. Tyrri dodged it. Behind him, Titus rocked backwards on the uneven rubble and went down. The cross clattered on the stones. A roar went up from the back of the crowd.

In a moment, the monks below were clambering to help their fallen brother and drag him to safety. Augustine sprang away from another hurtling stone and called out to Tyrri, 'What are they shouting?'

The boy ducked and came up swiftly. 'They're saying there's only one All-Father, Woden. He's the one who hung on the tree for nine days. She says you're teaching the people lies.'

'She?'

He was aware of Domitian, pulling him away from the dangerously exposed summit of the mound. Clods of earth, stones, rotting vegetables, rained down around them. Something sharp struck Augustine's shoulder.

Tyrri and the two monks tumbled down the mound, on the side away from the crowd. All the brothers had retreated there. From somewhere out of sight a childish voice yelled.

Tyrri grimaced. 'That's Gosfraeg. He's trying to tell them you're here on the king's authority, with Queen Bertha's blessing.'

The crowd came storming towards the pile of masonry behind which they cowered. The tumult was almost upon them when it fell abruptly silent. A man's harsh voice rapped out an order. There was the clash of weapons.

'Soldiers?'

A growl from the mob, like the undertow grinding down a bank of shingle, rose and fell. A sharp voice, shrilled back defiance.

Tyrri looked suddenly pale. 'That's her. She's cursing him.' His humour and confidence had deserted him, leaving him a small scared boy.

'Who?' Augustine stood up. He must not be found crouching in fear. Even martyrdom might be better than further disgrace. He saw the blood on Titus's face as his friends bent over the wounded monk.

'Werburh!' answered Tyrri, getting reluctantly to his feet as well. 'Lady Frig's chief priest.'

Augustine nerved himself to walk back into view. There was a hiss from the crowd, quickly subdued by the soldiers. A thane with shield and spear was confronting the mutinous mob. His feet were planted apart, his brows frowning under his leather cap, as he stared them down. Augustine recognized Dirwine, one of the English noblemen who served the queen. A ring of his soldiers was, somewhat nervously, surrounding an angry woman.

Werburh was small for an Englishwoman. Her grey hair was not covered with the conventional veil, but hung in elf locks around her face,

106

inadequately confined by two sparse braids. Her features were contorted; there was spittle on her twisting lips. Augustine shuddered at the strange markings darkening her skin. Instead of the skirt and neat jacket of the other Kentish noblewomen, she seemed to be wrapped around in an assortment of shawls and scarves. They were strangely fringed. The tiny corpses of mice, of bats, of shrivelled toads, adorned them. Her shaman's staff had dropped to the ground, but her fingers were ceaselessly weaving ominous patterns that could not be anything but curses.

Augustine had grown up in a Roman-style community in southern Gaul. He had moved to the ordered serenity of Gregory's Christian abbey in Rome. What he saw before him was utterly alien to him. Yet he recognized its power instantly. It was as if the knowledge had been sleeping within him all this time, and was stirring now, like the serpent coiled around the apple tree in the Garden of Eden. He acknowledged and feared it.

'Father, are you hurt?' Dirwine could speak a little Latin.

'No, not much. But one of my monks is.' He gestured at the mound behind which Titus still lay. 'Domitian!' he cried suddenly. 'The cross!'

It lay where Titus had dropped it, on top of the heap of rubble. It looked no more than a beam fallen from some collapsed building. With an exclamation of dismay, Domitian scrambled up to retrieve it, moving now with the speed of a much younger man.

'I must thank you from the bottom of my heart,' said Augustine to Dirwine. 'You came just in time.'

'We were watching you. It was the queen's orders.' The English warrior seemed calm, but Augustine saw the inner turmoil in his eyes. Dirwine would have been brought up in awe of shamans like this. If this officer was afraid, how long could he hold his men obedient?

The abbot looked back at the ring of frightened soldiers guarding this one defiant woman. There was more than one power at work in this kingdom. He might have the king's permission to teach here, but there were others who would fight him to keep Aethelbert's heart, and with methods he dared not even guess at.

Chapter Eighteen

Bertha approached the church of St Martin on its hill with more than her usual ceremony. This Sunday morning would be different. It had been strange, both wonderful and shocking, to hear the voices of forty monks in their hostel just beyond the palace walls, singing the divine office seven times a day. Aethelbert, she noticed, had not forbidden the Romans to worship their foreign god so near his hall, as he had forbidden her in the first days of their marriage. The balance was shifting. These Romans brought with them the echoes of Empire. Aethelbert coveted that power.

Now, this first Lord's Day, she had invited the monks to join her at St Martin's. It was no fine cathedral, such as Paris could have offered, but it was a consecrated Christian church. Bertha had ordered her servants to carry more benches to the almost-empty building. Until now, there had been only her chair facing the altar and Liudhard's episcopal seat in the sanctuary. Now there would be seats for a choir of monks, on opposite sides of the chancel. At last the thin voices of the elderly bishop and his deacon would be engulfed in the full-throated praise of a male-voice choir. She had not seen the monks climbing the hill ahead of her, but they would surely be there, waiting for their royal patron.

The stone and thatched church came into view. She tried not to regret how small it was. There was silence within. She pictured the hush of disciplined, black-gowned men, awaiting her entrance.

Attendants swung the door fully open. Candle flames blurred her vision. She stepped inside.

The church was almost empty. Bishop Liudhard was standing just inside the door, with Guntram, as always, at his shoulder, ready to greet the queen and conduct her to her seat. In a back corner there was the usual little huddle of drab-clad women from the British village. There was no one in the new choir stalls.

Bertha stopped in a moment of anger. 'They haven't come?' she demanded of Liudhard.

Her bishop bowed. She sensed a smile of revenge, which made her angrier still. 'No, your majesty.'

She and her Frankish retinue followed him the length of the nave. Bertha seated herself. Liudhard mounted the chancel steps to begin the mass.

They heard the singing from a distance. Unable to help themselves, the Franks turned to look at the door, though there could be nothing to see yet.

The chanted litany grew louder. Even in her indignation, Bertha knew it as a thrilling sound. So many years, so few Christians, and now this. The door flew open and the paean of praise burst upon them. The small congregation craned round to look. Bertha remained resolutely seated.

The double file of black-robed men swept past her. At the chancel steps they parted, filling the benches of the choir, as she had planned they should. But she had not planned how overwhelmed she would feel by their presence. They packed the small chancel, as though they must burst its walls.

Behind his monks came Augustine. For this mass, he wore the white and gold vestments of a priest.

I am the queen, Bertha told herself, clenching her hands. I will not rise to him like everyone else. I will not let him assert dominance over me.

Augustine paused as he drew level with her chair. She thought he would bow to her, as Bishop Liudhard always did. There was indeed an inclination of his head, yet at the same time his hand drew the sign of the cross over her. She should be grateful for his blessing, but she was not. She knew it was a gesture of superiority.

She felt a rush of sympathy for Liudhard, whose tall, spare figure stood paralysed before the altar, unable to begin the service. For fourteen years this had been his church. Whose was it now? Augustine mounted the steps and paused in front of the altar rails, looking from one side to the other. For a moment, she feared he would take Liudhard's episcopal chair. Did he think I should have set a chair for him too?

With a genuflection to the altar cross beyond the Frankish bishop, the Roman abbot took his place at the end of the bench next to Honorius. He turned his head to Liudhard, as though giving him permission to begin.

It was a strange service, beautiful and heart-wrenching to hear such singing at last. They reached the breaking of bread. The queen knelt, like everyone else. The bishop bowed stiffly to Augustine and motioned the Roman forward to join him at the altar, as co-celebrant. Liudhard blessed the bread and wine with the words of the body and blood of Christ and fed the abbot and himself. Then he took the paten of consecrated bread. He handed Augustine the chalice, the lesser role. Bertha saw the Roman's involuntary recoil. A flash of satisfaction warmed her, as Augustine recovered his composure and reached out to take it. This round, then, to the Franks. It was now the bishop's turn to assert his superiority, relegating the abbot to his assistant.

Liuhard raised the silver paten in invitation to the congregation. The queen rose from her knees and moved forward to the rail, leading her people. Liudhard placed the bread on her tongue. A few heartbeats later, Augustine was in front of her with the chalice. It was disturbing to kneel so close to him, to feel him standing over her, to brush his sleeve as she took the cup.

This is a man with authority, she thought, in surprise. In my hall, I had thought him somewhat nervous, challenging Liudhard to disguise his own uncertainty. But when he preached before Aethelbert on Thanet, and now, wearing the priestly mantle of Christ, he has no doubts. He is sure of the authority given him by Rome. For today, Liudhard, as bishop, has precedence over him, but Augustine will not accept that for long.

She got to her feet and walked back to her seat. Her head, which should have been bowed in prayer, looked back at the newcomer. Perhaps he is braver than I gave him credit for. Perhaps he is a small man, called by Christ to do a great thing. Only his sureness of purpose gives him the courage to come here, among barbarians, as he thinks we are. Augustine, the man, would turn and run from us. Augustine, the abbot, would give his life for us.

As indeed, he almost had.

'How's Titus?'

'He still has headaches. Father Laurence is giving him a herbal infusion the queen sent over.' They paced the road back from the palace to the hostel. Honorius glanced at his abbot. 'Strange, really, don't you think, Father? He was felled by a mob incited by some English witch, yet we have to rely on their wise women to heal him.'

'One day we shall have an abbey with a herb garden of our own.' Augustine raised his eyes to where, through a gap in the city wall, the meadowland of Kent spread around Canterbury. Cows moved slowly, tearing at the grass. Swallows darted after insects. 'There's stone in plenty here. Other Romans used it for building before us.'

'The English don't have a use for it, that's certain.'

Vegetation smothered the heaps of broken masonry, where the wall had collapsed. Sometimes it was only the coping stones, leaving a ragged, sagging edge. In other places the whole wall had bowed outwards and shot its stones across the meadow as it fell.

Honorius picked up a piece of clay tile, which must once have roofed some house on the wall. He stroked it with his thumb, as if it spoke to him of a more familiar city. 'When do you think your letter will get to Rome, Father?'

His sideways glance at his abbot betrayed the eagerness behind his studiously casual tone. They were all of them keyed up with a mood of excitement, anticipation, even elation. Far from dismaying them, Werburh's attack and Titus's wound seemed to have changed the way the monks thought about themselves. They were real missionaries now, martyrs almost. The Church in Rome must hear of them.

'Weeks, months maybe, if it gets there at all.' Augustine was more sober. He was alarmed that even steady, sensible Honorius seemed dangerously inflamed. He saw more clearly than they did that it was not a good start. If they needed royal protection even in Canterbury, how would they be greeted further afield?

Honorius looked over his shoulder. 'Father, the king!'

Augustine turned. A group of noblemen, escorted by soldiers, was coming swiftly along the road which led from the palace out to these meadows. Aethelbert strode in front. There could be no mistaking him. The morning sun glinted on his gold coronet. The fur-trimmed sleeves of his gown swung, like the corpses of foxes hung on a branch as a warning. His boots were the finest red leather, though yellowed now with dust. Everything Aethelbert of Kent did or wore was calculated to show the world he was king.

Augustine had a fleeting, painful vision of Pope Gregory, guardian of Rome, in his plain white tunic.

The two monks drew back respectfully to the side of the road. But when he came level with them, Aethelbert stopped and stared at them. The challenge in his blue eyes was so direct it might almost have been a glare.

'Where's your leader? That Augustine fellow?'

They caught the name, and half understood the question. Honorius gestured at his abbot. 'This is Father Augustine, your majesty.'

The king looked Augustine up and down with incredulity. The plain black tunic, the simple cross of ebony edged with silver. He threw back his head with a laugh which sounded like a bark of contempt. 'You?'

Augustine winced. The flash of teeth in the king's beard was too like a wolf. He doesn't remember my face from Thanet, though I preached to him for an hour. He looks for outward symbols of authority.

It was a chance meeting. Aethelbert was surely not on his way to the hostel in person, when he could summon the abbot to his palace. Yet the king had evidently something he wished to convey. He was conferring with Herman.

The thane stepped forward. 'The king says you can't stay in his hostel. He will have delegations from other English kingdoms soon. He must have room for his guests.'

111

Augustine's heart fell. Were they to be cast out so soon? Had those promises of protection and maintenance meant nothing?

He bowed. 'As your majesty wishes.'

His letter to Gregory, telling of their successful landing, would not even have arrived yet.

A grin spread slowly over Herman's face as Aethelbert's hand fell like a blow on Augustine's shoulder. Is he not my friend, either, Augustine wondered bitterly, though I thought he seemed on the edge of changing his faith?

'The king says,' Herman explained, 'you have a face like a sick crow. But he is going to show you a nest that will make you feel better. Come.'

The royal party moved on, deeper into the city, with its motley of Roman ruins, half smothered in foliage, and busy new English homes and market stalls. Augustine and Honorius looked at each other in bewilderment as they followed along its dung-spattered streets.

They came to a crossroads. In front of them, the encroaching greenery was denser, the smoke of thatched roofs thinning.

'It's yours.' The king made an abrupt gesture, from the road to their left to a more distant thoroughfare. A rattle of sharp decisive sentences followed. Augustine struggled vainly to follow. Hope was stifling his breath.

Herman translated. 'The king says his wife has told him there is the ruin of one of her old churches under here. You may have it back. And the land beside it for your monks. He will supply builders.'

The site for an abbey, even if a small one? Augustine started to stammer incredulous thanks. Another burst of words from Aethelbert spoke royal anger, rather than kindness.

'The king says he gave you his authority to enter Kent and speak to his people. He will not have anyone question that, even a priestess of his gods. He is the king. He is overlord of all the kings of Britain. His word is law. You will be protected.'

So, this gift is not for the King of kings, not for repentance and salvation, not for humility and gratitude. For Aethelbert's wounded pride, for his determination to be absolute ruler, I get land for a first abbey, a mission church.

'Thank you! Thank you, your majesty!' The guttural English words tumbled off his loosened tongue.

Aethelbert's eyes widened. 'You speak English? So soon?'

Augustine had to shake his head. 'A little. Only a little, your majesty.'

Again that warrior's blow on the small man's shoulder. The ringing laugh. The king was pleased. Augustine vowed to himself to double his lessons with the boys. He must make his way in Kent on Aethelbert's terms, in Aethelbert's language, on Aethelbert's land, with Aethelbert's protection. He needed that power.

Another snort of savage laughter.

Herman translated. 'But don't think this means the king is about to embrace your Christ.'

Chapter Nineteen

Augustine walked through the round-arched door of St Martin's with a sense of elation. He went down on his knee to the cross, feeling an overwhelming rush of thanksgiving. Then he rose and looked slowly about him. Today, this church was his: the narrow nave, the walls striped red and yellow with brickwork and stone, in the Roman style, the rustling thatch the Anglo-Saxons had roofed it with. Six of his monks knelt in the choir, murmuring prayers. The rest would arrive soon for the midday office of sext. Liudhard would not come today, and not only because he was not a monk. At the next mass, it would be Augustine's hands which raised the bread and wine, Augustine's priestly words which consecrated them. He would be the one to pass the chalice to someone else, Honorius probably, to assist him. He, Abbot Augustine, was in control.

The king and queen had gone from Canterbury. Dirwine had explained to Augustine, the two of them stumbling between English and Latin.

'A king as great as Aethelbert can't stay in one place all year round, not even in his capital. A court like ours would eat its way through the harvest in no time. Besides, he needs to keep his finger on what's going on in Dover, Rochester, even over the river in London. And he gets them to feed him for a few weeks, while he's about it. Fair's fair. He's made Kent strong. They're grateful. They'd be fools to mess with him.'

'And the queen?'

'She goes with him, of course.'

And where Queen Bertha went, her chaplain must follow, leaving Augustine undisputed leader of Canterbury's church.

The monks were filling the choir, their black-clad figures welcome to him as shadows on a hot Italian road. Gravity, simplicity, obedience. Augustine noted with approval their startling contrast to the swagger and show of the Kentish court. With the royal family away, he could breathe a more congenial atmosphere of restraint.

And yet . . . he eyed Bertha's empty chair as he intoned the appointed psalm . . . this English swagger and show was not a sham. It spoke of real power. He needed that. He could go nowhere, do nothing, without Aethelbert's support.

Somewhere across this kingdom, was Aethelbert entering a different temple, bowing before a different god, sanctioning by his presence the rituals of a different priesthood?

There was silence around him. His monks were waiting. Conscience-stricken, he realized that they had reached the end of the service. He turned to face the door and raised his hand in blessing. 'The grace of our Lord Jesus Christ. . . .'

Past the rows of monks by their benches in the choir stretched the empty nave. No Britons at this hour, this day of the week. The local people would be at work. This was a service for monks, part of the chain of ceaseless prayer which bound them to the throne of God. Even the queen would not have attended, had she been in Canterbury. An abbey would shoulder the work of prayer for the laity.

He led the silent procession down the nave to the low doorway. Sunlight greeted him. There was a basket on the step. Augustine checked. A clutch of eggs, sheltered from the sun in a nest of cool dock leaves. He looked up quickly. The trees had been cleared back from the entrance. The edge of the woods was a little way off. There was no one in sight.

'Father,' Honorius approached him, 'I've been thinking . . . What's that?'

Augustine lifted the basket. 'A present, I think.'

'Better than a stone to the head. Father Laurence is beginning to worry about Titus.'

'Out of their poverty, someone is giving us presents, though we're guests of the king and well fed.'

'Perhaps because we *are* guests of the king.'

Augustine looked around again, more keenly. 'Is someone there?' he called in halting English.

A rustle among the leaves. The other monks stopped on the homeward path and stared. Augustine looked back at them, seeing them with the eyes of a frightened native. A solid, uniformed phalanx, like an invading army. An army of shadows, perhaps, in their unrelieved black.

He gestured them to stay and walked forward to the edge of the trees, still carrying the eggs. 'Did you bring these? Thank you.'

The rustle was startlingly close. A woman in greyish drab rose from behind a holly bush almost in front of him. Her hair hung raggedly about her face, the cropped hair of a bondwoman. Tied across her chest was a baby, curiously silent. Its pale face peeped from the coarse weave of the shawl which bound it to her.

'What do you want, daughter?' For the first time, Augustine found himself using this foreign language with no interpreter to hand. This was not the translated formalities between the king and himself. This was not a lesson, which Tyrri and Gosfraeg made almost a game. This was not the exchanges with the thanes Dirwine and Herman, chopping English and Latin sentences to achieve understanding. This was the reality of direct encounter with a stranger who needed him. He read that in her face.

She held up the baby to him. 'Will you sign her with the holy water?'

Baptize the child? Augustine's blood checked. He still found it difficult to distinguish one English face from another, but he was almost sure this was not one of those women, mostly members of Edith's family, who frequented the church.

'Are you a Christian?'

She shook her head.

Augustine set down the basket of eggs and held out his arms awkwardly. The woman lifted the sling over her head and placed the bundled baby in his arms. She said something more, which he failed to understand.

He stood looking down at the infant, the hollow, almost white cheeks, the blue-veined eyelids, the brush of golden down beneath her grubby cap. He felt an overwhelming surge of emotion. He did not have the English words to ask her why she, a heathen woman, should bring her baby to a Christian monk and ask for baptism. Why the basket of eggs? In return for what favour, already given or required?

Was this his first true convert? Had she heard him preach, in those boys' cheerful translation, as if the kingdom of Heaven was a game for children?

'Come with me.'

He led her back to the church, still carrying the baby. The woman picked up the basket and followed him.

The monks should have been filing down the road, back to work, but they stood gaping. It was the young monk Maurice who held out his arms to take the baby, 'Father, let me.' He took the baby and cradled her in the crook of his elbow, smiling down at her.

'Father Peter, fetch some water for the font.'

The woman looked scared as she stepped into the church. She looked around her swiftly. Some of the fear went out of her face. There were no threatening idols. The candles had been extinguished. Only the cross stood on the altar.

Augustine permitted just a handful of monks to re-enter the church. The woman was frightened enough already by the ring of foreigners. He began the baptismal service, intoning a Latin he knew this woman could not understand. At his bidding, young Maurice and old Domitian stood sponsors for the child.

'What is her name?' That, at least, he could manage in English.

The woman was silent, looking at him with wide, frightened eyes. To name something is to have power over it, Augustine remembered. Will she trust me?

'Ellen,' she whispered.

A shock. He had expected a mouthful of English syllables he would have trouble repeating.

'Helena? The sainted mother of the Emperor Constantine?'

She did not understand, of course, but nor did he. Sometimes he felt like an explorer in a land no civilized human had trod before. At other times he stumbled across strands of imperial memory which showed this Britain and his Rome had been linked centuries ago.

He sprinkled the child with water in the threefold name and placed her back in her mother's arms. He felt a pang of regret that there was no white robe for this first tiny, newly baptized Christian. This was a far cry from the longed-for baptism of King Aethelbert, yet surely it was significant?

There were so many things he needed to ask this woman. Who are you? What is your name? Where do you live? How will you see that this child is brought up in the Christian faith? With Maurice's help, he managed some of this, but not all.

'The baby's sick,' Maurice explained. 'You're a wise man. She thinks you and your holy water can save her.'

Augustine laid his hand on the infant's head and closed his eyes. If only he could. If the strength of the Saviour, who healed lepers and made the blind see, could flow through his hands, here, now. He murmured prayers, and stopped, exhausted.

A little smile was playing round the baby's mouth. Two blue eyes opened, then the almost transparent lids fell over them again.

Augustine smiled at her mother, willing reassurance into his eyes. 'Go in peace, daughter. Look after her well.'

The woman left, the baby cradled against her breast again. The eggs still lay at Augustine's feet, nestled in dock leaves.

'Father, I was trying to tell you before we were interrupted—'

'Interrupted? Honorius, that was our first convert.'

'Not quite a convert. The mother hasn't asked for baptism herself. What can she know about Christianity? It's probably only superstition. She thinks our holy water may give hope for her child.'

'Hope indeed. A child was won for Christ who would have known only darkness.'

Honorius bowed his head. 'I'm justly rebuked, Father. Paul tells us hope is one of the three great virtues. Still, this small success reinforces what I wanted to say. May I go on?'

'Speak plainly, Father. I count you one of my most sensible counsellors.'

'Well, then. Pope Gregory sent you out as abbot, in charge of us forty monks. But didn't he say that if you gained entry to Kent and established a mission to the English, you should become a bishop?'

Augustine felt the word grip his heart, almost like terror. A joy was waiting he could scarcely acknowledge. 'Yes,' he said faintly.

'Even an archbishop, with authority throughout Britain?'

Augustine said nothing. He was picturing Bishop Liudhard, all these years in Kent, ministering only to Queen Bertha and her Frankish retinue and the handful of servile Britons who remembered the old tradition. In all that time, what had Liudhard done to save the English from eternal damnation? Yet at the Lord's Table that Sunday, it was the bishop who had been the senior celebrant, Augustine, the abbot, his junior. Besides, the Frankish manner in which he celebrated the mass had been reprehensibly more flamboyant than the sober practice of Rome.

The knowledge swept over him. By obeying Gregory's wish, he could change all this.

'My letter telling him of our safe arrival, won't have reached Rome yet. It will be months before we get his answer.'

'With respect, Father, you don't need our beloved Gregory's reply. The Pope made his will clear before we left. We're here. We now have a plot for an abbey. We're preaching the Gospel to the people. A heathen woman has come forward bringing her baby for baptism. It's happening. What more authority do you need?'

Augustine stopped walking and stared down at the city in front of him, the broken-down wall and crumbling amphitheatre, the royal palace with its soaring roofs and thrusting dragons. In the north-east corner, trees had been felled. The old stonework of the Romans was being revealed. Here, a fine church would rise on the ruins of an older one. But first, they needed roofs over the monks' heads. Perhaps all this was only due to the power struggle between the king and the priestess of Frig, but it was becoming reality now, wood and stone. Would Canterbury be his episcopal see, this church his cathedral?

He could hardly speak for the fluttering of emotion in his throat.

'You think this is God's will?'

'I do. You must go back to Arles for your consecration, Father. Yes, I know the Franks have bishops as well as Liudhard, who could do it. But it's what blessed Gregory advised you. You've said yourself, the Frankish rites don't entirely conform to Rome's. We don't want any questions raised about your episcopal authority. Southern Gaul is firmly in the tradition of the Roman Church. Archbishop Virgilius is your man.'

'Go back to Arles? So far?' It seemed a colossal task, to undertake that journey again, so soon. Augustine found travelling daunting, oppressive. Yet a wave of delicious nostalgia was creeping over him. To feel the sun of the south again. To talk freely with Latin-speaking people. The thought of how the archbishop's face would light up at his news. In Arles he would be welcomed, recognized, praised.

'You have the courage to make the journey, Father, for all our sakes.'

Augustine's hand was halfway to Honorius's shoulder in a gesture of goodwill not unlike Aethelbert's. He arrested the impulse and folded his hands chastely in his sleeves. Saint Benedict, their founder, had not approved of such physical warmth. An ache of homesickness betrayed Augustine. Gregory, saintly though he undoubtedly was, cared little for such regulations. His hands were warm, his smile was ready, his arms were strong. If only, Augustine thought, he could be here with us in this cold country.

He began to walk again, faster. Soon they were in through the city gate. Already houses were rising where Aethelbert's men had cleared the trees. Posts were being interwoven with coppiced wands. Soon they would be ready for plastering. These were no more than temporary shelters for the monks. One day, they must build more lastingly in stone. Could they do that? Augustine wondered. Would he have to send to Gaul for skilled masons? The English had none. He must ask Archbishop Virgilius in Arles.

Arles. A vision of sunshine on its cathedral. Could he, Augustine, one day become an archbishop like Virgilius? Could he raise such a cathedral here?

They paused to watch the younger monks, who were already hard at work again, labouring alongside the English craftsmen. Then Honorius and Augustine followed the older ones back to the royal hostel they must soon leave.

Father Laurence met them in the dim-lit hall. His plump face always looked as if it had been freshly oiled. Today its usually reassuring placidity was scored with concern.

'Father, I'm glad you're back. I'm worried. Would you come and have a look at Titus?'

Augustine quickened his step. There could be no separate infirmary here. Titus lay in one of the stalls partitioned off around the walls. He had made a simple bed for himself, as had all the other monks. A mattress stuffed with straw, his cloak to cover him.

The young man lay tossing under this cover. Against the darker cloth, his clenching hands looked more pink than black. More shocking was the colour of the wound in his forehead, where the jagged stone, thrown at Werburh's incitement, had struck him. Laurence had tried to draw the edges together, but the split still gaped. The raw red flesh had crusted over and drops of yellow pus congealed.

'I've tried to keep away the fever, but we're not winning. The potion the queen sent is helping, but not enough.'

'What else do you need? We've no herb garden of our own, but if you know anything that would help I'll ask the queen if . . .' He paused. Bertha was many miles away now, at the port of Dover.

'Father . . . I hardly need to tell you, but healing's not a matter of medicine alone. Herbs must go hand in hand with prayer; body with spirit. Who knows where the queen's herbs come from, or what chants were sung over them?'

'You're saying some English witch has been at work?'

'They call them cunning women here, I believe. How do we know? It was that priestess of Frig, Werburh, who incited the crowd to throw this stone. What if she and her cronies brewed this potion?'

'The queen would surely not allow that!'

'A great queen can't see everything which is done in her name.'

'You suspect poison? Didn't you say the medicine was helping a little?' Honorius asked.

Laurence shrugged. 'Not enough.'

'Then what can we do for our brother, if we can't trust their medicine?'

Titus cried out suddenly. His large dark eyes opened terrifyingly wide. Their huge dark irises were edged with bloodshot yellow. Laurence laid a steadying hand on his chest. 'There, son. Lie easy. Father Augustine's here. He'll help you.'

Laurence turned his eyes back to his abbot's. A knot of fear twisted in Augustine's stomach. The word 'abbot' meant 'father'. They were all depending on him.

There came unbidden into his mind the vision of a pale-faced baby, frighteningly tiny and light in his arms. Under his touch, her sleepy blue eyes had opened, her delicate mouth had curved in the ghost of a smile. He felt a rush of awe. All he had done was pray.

All? Had he not invoked the power of almighty God, the name of Father, Son and Spirit? He had laid himself open as a channel of that power. Could he do it again?

He fought to keep his hand steady as he stooped to touch the young monk's wounded head. The festering cut was rough and sticky, the skin of his brow hot and damp. He forced himself not to recoil from the contact. Father Laurence was right to be concerned.

Augustine went down on his knees at the bedside. Honorius and Laurence did the same. What should he do? He could say the words of benediction, but surely something more was needed?

'Lord,' he prayed aloud, 'if it is Your will, make me a channel of Your grace. Not my desire but Yours be done. Look with pity on this Your servant, wounded in Your service. Cast out the evil of your enemies which has entered into him. In place of pain, bring peace. In place of fear, bring calm. In place of wounding, bring wholeness.'

The other two monks lent their fervent 'Amen' to his threefold blessing.

Augustine took his hand away, half-afraid to look at Titus. He rose to his feet.

Laurence rose too. 'What shall I do with the rest of the potion, Father?'

'Throw it out.'

'The queen's gift, Father?' Honorius fears were different from Laurence's.

They were both staring at him. Could he really accuse his Christian patron of poisoning? Augustine recovered his diplomacy.

'Bring it to me.'

Augustine took the leather flask from Laurence warily. It felt still half full.

'As you reminded us, Brother, healing is not just a matter of the flesh, of water and leaves.' He traced the sign of the cross over the flask. 'It is God, not we, who gives the water of life, that whoever drinks of it will never thirst again. It is God, not we, who provides the plants of the field to supply our daily needs. It is God, not we, who breathes the breath of fire to change water and herbs, as the Spirit transforms Christians. May this medicine be blessed to our use, in the name of Him who makes all things holy.'

He kept his eyes fixed on the flask in his hand. Had he compromised his faith? Had he colluded with evil?

'Father,' said Laurence softly, 'I think Titus is sleeping now.'

Augustine turned slowly. The eyelids had fallen shut in the young monk's dark face. His breathing was easier and the twisting fingers had relaxed. Augustine felt a terrible desire to reach out and touch the lad's head. Would he still feel fever? Would the movement betray doubt? Doubt in himself, doubt in the power of God?

'Blessed be the name of God,' he said firmly, and walked away.

'Oh, dear,' sighed Gregory. He paced the cloisters of the papal garden, turning over the pages of the letter. His amused smile had yet a little sadness in its down-turned corners.

'Is the news from Britain not good?' prompted the deacon Peter.

'Good, and not good. On the Kentish side, it's as well as could be expected at this early stage. Better, perhaps. They've landed. King Aethelbert's come to hear Augustine preach. A fine sermon, by all accounts, though he gives God the glory. The king's allowed the monks access to his capital, guaranteed them lodging and food, and given them permission to evangelize. Short of instant conversion, it's as much as I dared to hope.'

'But. . . ?'

The Pope laughed. 'You're right. The "but" is Augustine. I love him dearly, but I don't think I'd realized how anxious a man he is. Not till he came back to Rome after only a few days on the road, with his tail between his legs.'

'You would never have turned back, would you, Father, whatever the danger? But you put new heart into Augustine, to finish the journey, and he did.'

'No credit to me if I'm made differently, Brother. It's God who created me fearless, and him fearful. So it took more courage for him to do what he has done, and land in Britain.'

'And is he not pleased with his own success?'

'He says his soul is filled with darkness when he looks at the evil around him. The heathen priesthood, their bloody rites, the sacred groves and terrible temples. He longs to fell and burn the lot of them.'

'Isn't that why you sent him, Father? To convert the English?'

'To make them fall in love with Christ, yes. But these English are children, Peter, not devils. How can they love Him they've never known? We must all worship something, and if we don't know any better, it will be wood and stone, thunder and corn. Our hearts are made for God. We seek Him everywhere.'

The tiled path brought them to the fountain at the centre of the garden. Gregory held his fingers under the cool stream and shook them. His wet hand caressed the marble. The bowl of the fountain was carved with dancing fauns and nymphs, playing with lyres or reaching up to pluck the dangling grapes.

Peter watched him. 'You love this too, don't you, old heathen Rome?'

Gregory flushed, and drew his hand away quickly. Then he relaxed into rueful laughter. 'You understand me too well. Look at it, Peter, this little, perfect piece of our past. Feel the joy of their dancing, hear the music, taste the God-given juice of those grapes. Oh, I know. The blessed Benedict enjoined something stricter for us. I'm still a monk under obedience, as well as Pope. But what of the common people? Would you have me tear down the glory of ancient Rome, and leave them with . . . what? Isn't it better to do as we are doing? Purifying old temples and transforming them into Christian churches? The lewd and idolatrous statuary must go, of course, but only to be replaced by something finer. What will Augustine gain, if he ever has the power to burn temples across the land? A people in mourning, rebellious, hating him. And what can he give them instead, he and his forty monks?'

'You'd have them worship Christ, in the temples of their northern gods? You'd take that risk?'

'With both hands. Think, man. If they love their gods as we love ours, they'll have built them the finest palaces that art and wealth can raise. Isn't that what we want for God the Father? For our dear Saviour? For the Holy Spirit and all the saints? Let him cleanse and consecrate them, and give them back to God. And make a lot of common people happy to come and worship where they've always done.'

Peter grinned affectionately. 'That's how you've always worked, Father, isn't it? As Pope and governor of this city, you're powerful enough to order people to do whatever you decide, but you don't. You'd rather persuade them than bully them. You always find a way to make it easy for them to do what you want, so they hardly notice how big the changes you've talked them into. Look at Augustine. He never thought he could lead a band of men across Europe and land in a heathen country, whose language none of them speaks. But you coaxed him into it, and he's there.'

'Yes, he's there.' Gregory looked down at the letter and sighed again. 'But did I pick the right man for the job?'

Chapter Twenty

White water flew from the oars, tumultuous as a flock of seagulls. The rowers bent and heaved, sending the longships shooting across the waves. A fitful sun made the wet shields sparkle along the ships' sides.

King Aethelbert sat enthroned on the cliff-top, cheering his navy as the longships raced each other. They were a formidable sight. With its prow dragon- or wolf-headed, raven-beaked or boar-tusked, the ship itself was a weapon of war, not just a transport for armed warriors. The king thumped the carved arm of his chair with satisfaction.

'That'll make those Sussex pirates quake in their shoes! Just let them try stealing along the coast and poaching from Kentish villages again. They'll find their ships smashed and their crews slaughtered before the tide turns.'

The longships powered past the stationary boats which marked the finishing line. One ringing cheer from fifty throats split the sky. Far below the watching court, the other crews slumped over their oars, drained, defeated. Aethelbert tossed a handful of gold to his steward. 'Give the winners something to wet their throats with.'

He sat back, well pleased with this regatta. More ships were moving into position for a training battle. The race crews braced their weary muscles to row for the shore. Down came the threatening figureheads, the red-tongued dragon, the snarling wolf, the glittering-eyed raven, the malignant boar. Their strong war magic must not threaten the home port.

In the lull, Bertha summoned her nerve. It was always dangerous to question Aethelbert, King of Kent.

'Will you hear that man again? Augustine the Roman?'

'Hear him? Haven't I given him a plot of land for his monks and permission to rebuild a church in the city?'

'Your majesty is famous for his generosity.'

'Remember that when next harvest comes. You'd better pray to that god of yours it's a bumper one. Mother Werburh's breathing every curse she can think of against me.' He laughed savagely. 'She says Frig will blast my crops.'

He's afraid, Bertha thought. He doesn't want to be in the thrall of his old gods, but he is. He's defied Werburh to prove himself master. He can't

124

undo that now, but he's afraid of the consequences.

'I shall pray with all my heart for Kent and its king, as I've always done. Bishop Liudhard will too. And now we've forty monks who dedicate their lives to prayer. They'll be making intercession for you as their benefactor, not just daily, but every three hours.'

'Pah! Werburh spits curses with every breath she draws.'

'She prays to a sheaf of corn, to a wooden doll. Augustine prays to Almighty God. And . . . God answers him. You know that young black monk, Titus, was struck on the head? They're saying Father Augustine laid his hands on him and the lad recovered at once.'

He turned his look on her with sharpened interest. 'You were never so bold before, madam, to say the gods of Kent are nothing, and your god everything.'

She felt herself colour. Should she bow her head, backtrack, apologize?

'I've perhaps been a coward, my lord, fearing to anger you. The bravest king in Britain deserves better of his queen. I shall honour you more by speaking honestly.'

Aethelbert looked astonished. Then he laughed, more genuinely this time, making his golden moustache quiver. 'I liked you that first day, when you faced down Werburh and threw her out of your hall. You showed yourself a true daughter of kings then.'

'If I have been less brave since then, I beg your pardon. I've tried to go quietly about my faith, with dignity and prudence. Perhaps I should have spoken up more boldly sooner. Abbot Augustine will not stay quiet, as Liudhard has.'

The horns blew. Aethelbert's attention was suddenly on the sea below him. The battle formations were in place. Six ships on either side. Not rowers only this time, but warriors standing, armed with spears. The shield wall along the gunwales was now in earnest.

Another single horn, and the ships drove towards each other. The watchers heard the terrifying yells with which men stave off their own terror. Spouting water made wings on either side of the ships. They flew together.

The crack and grinding of wood against wood made Aethelbert wince and curse. These were real ships being put at risk. The shouts, and sometimes screams, of their crews were real too. Men would be dead at the end of this exercise.

Bertha was glad of the foam that hid the details from her. There were rules, umpires, she knew, for these things. It would not be a fight to the death, yet some would die.

She let her eye shift beyond the struggle to the smudge of grey along the horizon. She knew it was not a cloudbank. The land of the Franks had once been her homeland. It seemed impossibly far away now, in time as well as distance.

The sea fell quiet. The ships drifted apart. Aethelbert was on his feet, applauding. She did the same. All the spearmen turned their faces up to the cliff-top. Both sides punched the air, yelling allegiance.

'Who won?' she asked.

'The men of Deal. They're always the best boatmen. A naval battle's as much about sailors as about spearmen.'

'When I'm grown up, Father, can I have a ship of my own?'

Both parents turned in surprise. Eadbald, their eldest son, had been cheering the sport with a group of his friends. Now he was at his father's elbow, shining-eyed.

Aethelbert ruffled his blond hair. The lad already stood as high as his tall father's shoulder. Another year or two, and he would make a splendid warrior prince.

'What figurehead will you put on the prow of your ship to terrify the enemy?'

'A horse! Woden's grey stallion, with eight legs.' He turned his blue eyes to his mother with a challenging stare. 'I'm descended from Woden. All of us are. Ordulf says so, and he's Woden's chief priest.'

'True enough, true enough,' said Aethelbert fondly. 'Every English king can trace his line back to Woden, Lord of wisdom and battlecraft.'

'*She* doesn't. Mother says *her* god is the lord of battle-hosts.'

Bertha's eyes flew to her husband's. 'My lord, I've never tried to turn your son against Kent's traditions. It was a grief to me that you wouldn't let Liudhard baptize him, but I've respected your orders.'

Eadbald grinned, not entirely pleasantly. 'Tyrri and Gosfraeg tell me what your holy men say, though. They have to take those foreigners' words and turn them into English. They're beginning to half believe it, too.'

Aethelbert's eyes narrowed. 'Are they, indeed?'

'Ordulf says Woden will be angry. He says if we don't go on making the sacrifices and hailing Woden as All-Father, Kent won't go on winning battles. Doesn't that mean that you won't be—?'

'Silence!' thundered the king. The boy cowered back, knowing too late he had been about to utter the unsayable. 'I'll flay Ordulf's painted skin from his flesh. I'm Aethelbert, lord over all Britain's kings. I fought my way to that through British and English armies. Do you think that weasel-faced soothsayer can tell me what to do and whether or not I'm fit to win battles? Look at these!'

The victorious crews were trooping up on to the cliff-top to receive praise and prizes from their king. At his angry shout they stopped in alarm. Questions shot from one face to another.

'Look at them,' Aethelbert snapped at his son. 'They're terrified of me.

That's kingship for you. And so should anyone who conspires behind my back be terrified, including you. . . . Come along, come along,' he called to the men irritably. 'Don't stand there bleating like a herd of sheep. Do you want your prizes or don't you?'

Men hardened to battles, gales, shipwrecks shuffled forward with placating smiles, bending their heads before him. It was hard to meet King Aethelbert's eyes. He did not touch their calloused hands. It was his steward who handed out the king's favours: a piece of valuable metal, a knife, an arm ring. Aethelbert needed wars to fill his treasure chests, to give gifts to the men who fought those wars for him. The oarsmen muttered their thanks and escaped. Only when they were out of sight down the cliff path did their voices rise in exultant boasting. Aethelbert allowed himself a smile in the direction they had gone.

'So.' The king fixed his gaze again on his son. 'Does that mean that if I were to turn Christian, you'd refuse to follow me?'

It was Eadbald's turn to bow his head before his father. But his voice was obstinate. 'You won't change your gods, Father. Ordulf says you won't. He says you're Kentish to the bone. You couldn't turn your back on Kent's gods.'

'Does he indeed? Couldn't? Can a great king not do exactly what he pleases? And you? What about your mother's blood in you? She comes from a line of powerful kings too, you know, and they're Christians.'

'I'm my father's son! The King of Kent's greater than any Frank.'

There was a silence. Bertha knew that was not true. She knew that Aethelbert knew this too. On this side of the Channel his power ran unchallenged. The view from Frankland was different. The Frankish kings of her family had power, even over Aethelbert. Her marriage to him was evidence of it. Aethelbert wanted a larger share in that power.

'The King of Kent will do what's good for Kent.'

She saw the mutinous flash in Eadbald's eyes, before he dropped them again.

'Yes, Father.'

Neither mother nor son dared to ask Aethelbert what he meant by the good of Kent.

'Give me the letter to sign.'

Maurice passed the carefully penned script to his abbot. The youngster had, Augustine noted, a good hand. The pressure of the strokes was perhaps a little too light and tentative. Firm black words would speak more authority. But the letter seemed free from smudges and corrections. This would witness to Virgilius in Arles of a community in England which was well ordered, observing high standards.

He read through the phrases of his own dictation. Had he judged the tone right? There needed to be a degree of deference at this stage. He was, as yet, only an abbot. The Archbishop of Arles was a father in God to him. Augustine was seeking a great gift. And yet . . . once that gift was given, he, Augustine, would be almost Virgilius's equal. Bishop of Canterbury, and one day, if his hopes were fulfilled, Archbishop of Britain.

The thought was dizzying.

'You write a fair hand.' He smiled encouragement at his young scribe. 'Hand me the pen.'

Maurice was holding it ready. The goose-quill nib shone with black ink. There were no lumps in the liquid, to cause a shameful blot. The young man had ground his mixture meticulously. Augustine signed the letter in his own firm, neat hand. It was done. He had committed himself to this journey. By the time Virgilius read these words, Augustine and his small escort would already have crossed the Channel.

He stood for a moment, looking down at the document which would change his life. He could have wished, on second thoughts, that his signature was larger, more obviously confident. His writing, though firm, was small, tightly controlled. Perhaps it was better like that than an untidy sprawl. Discipline was a virtue in a monk.

'Seal it for me.' He pushed it back decisively to Maurice and handed him his ring. 'It must be nearly suppertime.'

When the bell summoned him, the abbot walked into the hall, where his monks stood by their benches, waiting for him. He sensed immediately some change in the atmosphere. Usually their heads would be bowed within their cowls, eyes cast down until he had spoken the blessing which released them to eat. Yet today he had not reached his place at the high table before he was aware of suppressed excitement. He lifted his eyes from the chair on which he was advancing. The faces within the hoods were all turned to him. They were staring. There was even a subdued whispering, breaking the discipline of silence. He frowned and quickened his step to stand in the abbot's place.

'Silence, Brothers! Let us give thanks for this food.' But the power of their eyes drew his to theirs, when his own head should have been bowed. They were still gazing at him, as though there were a quality about him they had never seen before. Was there something improper about his dress? Some soiling of his face? Surely Maurice would have warned him?

It was not mockery he met in their faces. Something more like awe. He hurried the words of the grace and sat down. Better to concentrate on the food put before him. It was the custom of his monks to serve one another, anticipating each other's needs, so that no brother needed to ask for anything or go hungry. Yet the senior monks around him were offering dishes to him with an air that had less of fraternity about it than reverence. He took what they gave him with thanks. He dared not ask, 'Why are you looking at me like this?'

It was Honorius who nudged him as the meal proceeded. Under cover of the reading which accompanied the meal, of the martyrdom of St Stephen, he murmured, 'Father, haven't you noticed? Our numbers are complete again.'

It took Augustine some moments to make sense of this. He glanced down the table to where Honorius was nodding. The monks had put back their cowls from their heads to eat. The face near the end of the table where the youngest monks sat was hard to miss. That earth-brown skin, its faintly golden hues accentuated by the contrast with black wool. It could only be the Nubian.

'Titus!' The name was startled from his lips. It was Augustine's turn to stare. Only this morning this monk had been unconscious with fever. Now he was dipping his spoon in his broth with relish, breaking off bread with strong hands.

'Yes,' Honorius grinned. It's a miracle, isn't it?'

The word rippled down the lines of seated monks. '*Miracle!*' *Miracle!*' '*Miracle!*' It reached the far end, where Titus suddenly looked up, his large dark eyes drawn to Augustine's. The voice of the monk reading rang suddenly loud in the silence which followed. All eyes were back on the abbot.

'God is good,' said Augustine. 'Give thanks to him.'

'Amen,' they chorused.

He must not look at Titus again. He must not let himself wonder how this had happened. He was a vessel, nothing more. God's grace alone could do this. It was becoming harder to swallow. He wished it were not the custom to forbid idle conversation at mealtimes. The buzz of talk around him might have shielded him from the intensity of their attention.

After the meal, the rules were relaxed for an hour. Yet this evening the monks did not lapse into casual conversation. As Augustine moved through them, down the hall towards Titus, he was aware of the company drawing back from him. It was no longer simple courtesy, to allow their abbot passage; this was more like awe. He reached the space around Titus. Everyone else stood back.

'You're well, my son?'

'Yes, God be praised, Father.'

'Yet this morning you were very ill. Father Laurence was beginning to fear for you.'

'So they tell me. Father Laurence says the change began the moment you left us. I feel like a new man now. Thanks be to Almighty God, and you, Father.'

'All your brothers prayed that you would be healed.'

The big lad's face was suffused with embarrassment. 'Father Laurence said you laid your hands on me.'

'As your abbot should, in need.'

'And I got better.' In a sudden, startling movement, Titus went down on his knees. He seized the hem of Augustine's tunic and kissed it. All around them, other monks were kneeling.

'Get up, my son!' There was anger in Augustine's voice. He steadied himself. 'There is One, and One only, you should praise for this.'

'Yes, Father.' Meek, obedient, standing now with his head bowed.

Augustine's look of command brought the rest to their feet. It made little difference. He understood now what all forty of his monks were seeing in him. Had this begun with that English baby at St Martin's? What had they heard? How had the story grown in travelling? And now Titus, brought back from the brink of death. The coincidence of these happening in a single day.

Or . . . the thought shook him to the core . . . was this a real gift of healing? Could it have been given to him, for just this hour, this place, this kingdom? He felt the thrill run through him, of fear and excitement.

The sun blazed down on the procession. It did not penetrate the heavy crimson and gold canopy under which Augustine was being carried, but the heat inside was stifling. Augustine felt his small frame wilting under the weight of the vestments he wore. White and gold, encrusted with precious embroidery. Sweat trickled down his face. One last weight had not yet been placed upon him. On his head he wore a simple white cap. When he came out of the cathedral he would bear the towering mitre of a bishop.

Light dazzled from the square. From under the canopy he could see only the legs and lower bodies of the cheering crowd, and the occasional bright-faced, curious stare of a little child, twisting sideways to peer up at him.

Why were they cheering? Did they know who he was? Where he came from? Why should these Gauls, Italians, Spaniards, North Africans care about far-off misty Britain? Probably they did not. They were just enjoying a good procession.

They were passing the blue obelisk in the square now. It could not be far to the Cathedral of Arles. Almost at once the bearers set him down. A deacon stepped forward to hand him down from the chair. He must enter the cathedral humbly, on foot. He would leave it, wearing his mitre, carried aloft by a host of fellow bishops.

The sun smote him. The interior of the cathedral looked impenetrably dark through the doorway, its myriad lamps and candles merely spangling it like the night sky. As soon as he stepped inside he felt the coolness of stone.

Though he entered on foot, he felt carried up the aisle on wings of song. Virgilius was waiting for him, smiling welcome. Around him, a fan of other bishops, from Aix, Marseille, Avignon, Toulon and all the region round the Camargue. Names known to Rome even before Christian times, when Britons huddled in their wooden huts and the English had not yet crossed the North Sea from Germany.

The sanctuary ahead of him was not shadowed like the nave, but ablaze with golden light. All the bishops wore gold. For a wistful moment Augustine wished King Aethelbert could be here to see this. He was a sovereign who knew the value of outward show to impress the reality of his power on people. Would he not be awed by this ecclesiastical magnificence? Would he not understand that the service of the King of kings ranked above any earthly ruler's?

He was kneeling now, and the words were flowing over him. Questions were put; his tongue was ready with the responses. He was pronounced worthy. Virgilius's hands were descending on his head. All the bishops were crowding round, eager to add the authority of their own hands to the archbishop's. Augustine braced his neck as the mitre was lowered on to his head. It was done. They were raising him up, embracing him, congratulating him. He was part of their brotherhood.

Virgilius took his hand and turned him to face the congregation. 'I present to you Augustine, Bishop of Canterbury in Britain.'

The applause seemed to send the multitude of hanging silver lamps swinging.

The bishops took him up on their shoulders and carried him out into the blaze of the square.

Dinner was lavish that evening in the archbishop's palace. Normally, Virgilius, like Augustine, ate frugally. Tonight, there were many guests, princes of the church and of the state. Virgilius had provided the best that southern Gaul could offer.

It was a feast for the eyes, as well as the stomach. The rich flesh of swan and venison could be had at any English court. What brought the saliva to Augustine's throat were the mountains of shellfish, the white and red flesh of the abundance of Mediterranean fish, the forgotten familiarity of fresh figs and sun-sweet grapes. He had not realized until now how much he had missed these things in the north. It was the gleaming black olives, such as any peasant could eat, which spoke to him most poignantly of home.

'We used to have Britons in Arles,' Virgilius was saying, 'when the great councils of the Church met there. They sent their bishops.'

Augustine looked up and blinked. Even judiciously watered, the red wine of Provence was making it difficult to focus sharply. He felt drunk with more than wine tonight. 'British bishops?' That was long ago. They haven't even priests left, since the English invaded.

Virgilius's eyes narrowed. He tapped his fingers together, trying to retrieve a memory. 'There was something in the records about that. Didn't most of them flee to the west when the English came? For a while a few still came to the councils, though they were sometimes so poor that the other delegates had to make a collection to pay their travel expenses. I fancy there are some left in their mountain fastnesses. You should make contact with them. You're the Pope's representative in Britain.'

Augustine started. 'I've hardly begun my mission in Kent yet. The king's still a heathen.'

'I know, I know. I meant in the fullness of time. You'll succeed in Kent. Look at the king's generosity towards you. You've impressed him. Then, when Kent is secured, you must look west.'

'The Britons have no dealings with the English. Those that stayed in the east are already slaves. The rest of their kingdoms are waiting to be conquered.'

'They are souls waiting to be saved.'

'You said they were Christian.'

The Archbishop of Arles spread his hands. 'In a way, yes. The common people are doubtless heathens still, as they are all too often under the surface, even in Gaul. But their British Christian leaders give us cause for concern too. We began to feel, before we lost contact with them, they were – how shall I put it? – going native.'

'I don't know what you mean, Father.'

Virgilius sighed. 'I'm not sure that I do, either. These contacts were not within living memory. But there was apparently some fear that the British were not entirely conversant with Roman thinking, reluctant to adopt the latest decrees of the Church. They clung rather obstinately to their own ways of baptism and ordination. They may even have been influenced by the rites of their pagan druids.'

Augustine shuddered and made the sign of the cross.

'Yes, Brother.' Augustine blushed at this acknowledgement of their equality. Virgilius smiled. 'They need you too, to bring them back to the pure, unadulterated practice of the Church. You must enlighten their provincial ignorance.'

'When time and opportunity allow me. Even if Pope Gregory makes me an archbishop, I should need the king's consent to venture into their territory.'

'Yes, yes. You have a mighty task on your hands. To evangelize the English. I know. Be assured, I pray for your success night and day. And when Pope Gregory receives my report of our meeting, he'll redouble his own prayers. He's very fond of you, Augustine, as I am.'

A warmth crept round Augustine's heart. He would not need to boast of his own exploits to Gregory. Virgilius would do it for him. Domitian, who had accompanied him, had made sure the Gauls knew the stories of Augustine's healings. Augustine had not reproved him. Perhaps, on second thoughts, Gregory would want to hear the story in Augustine's own words, when he wrote of his consecration.

'Thank you, Father. I need all the prayers I can get. Aethelbert of Kent's a strong-minded man. He will not easily be influenced.'

'Perhaps not, but such kings, once won, make powerful patrons.' He smiled with direct frankness at the new Bishop of Canterbury. 'You are playing for high stakes, Brother, and you too can be an obstinate man. I think you will not give up until you've won.'

Chapter Twenty-one

Augustine heard the distant sound of Gosfraeg's voice as the boy came running into the building site in Canterbury.

Some of the ruined houses from Roman times had already been made habitable again. The queen had provided workmen to help. They knew nothing about masonry, of course. The new walls must be wood and wattle, their poverty disguised with a coat of plaster and a good thick thatch. Monks laboured alongside the English craftsmen, slapping daub under their instructions, shouldering bundles of reeds. The work was going fast. Some monks had already moved out of the hostel.

Across the street, Augustine was conferring with stonemasons he had brought back from Gaul for a grander project.

The foreman shook his head. 'It's too far gone, sir. There might have been a fine church here once, but what you've got left is worth no more than a goat pen. And, begging your pardon, Father, I wouldn't be surprised if that's what it's been used for, judging from the dirt on my shoes.'

Augustine felt the light brighten in his eyes. 'You mean, it would be better to level the site and start again? I wouldn't be confined by the plans of the Britons?'

'You can have anything you like here, Father, if the king says you can, and you can pay. I could build you as fine a church as you'll see between here and Arles. You'll need an architect, mind. I need to work to a plan.'

'Father!' Gosfraeg's cry burst through the building site. Augustine shook his head with a wry smile. Those two English boys made nothing of monkish discipline over noise and haste.

He saw heads turn towards the youngster. Men accustomed to spend their time in prayer and study were glad of an excuse to pause their aching arms and backs.

There was a man behind Gosfraeg. A common man, by the look of him, in a coarse brown tunic, with cross-gartered hose, and an unkempt beard. He limped as he walked. From his haggard air of weariness it was hard to tell if the lameness was habitual, or due to the soreness of a long journey on foot. The boy was looking around him.

'He's over there,' called Titus, 'at the new church.'

'Father! Father Augustine!' Gosfraeg's shrill voice penetrated more easily on this quieter site. Augustine and the foreman broke off their conference. Behind them, workmen were heaving at fallen stones, marshalling them into piles, away from the trampled earth which had once been the tiled floor of a church.

Augustine's eye took in the boy and the weary man limping after him. Whatever the pain, the stranger was still trying to hurry, his breath coming hard. The abbot stepped down from the ruins into the street. He reached out to steady the man, but the peasant fell on his knees before Augustine could grasp him. Urgent hands clutched at the abbot's knees. He suppressed the instinct to recoil, to preserve his physical integrity.

'My son,' he said, his English more confident now, 'what's the matter?'

'My daughter!' the man gasped. 'She couldn't get her breath. It was cruel to watch her. And then, all of sudden, she gave a sort of strangled cry and fell still as a stone. She hasn't breathed since.'

'You mean she's dead?'

The man shuddered. 'I don't know, sir. She looks so sweet and peaceful. I can't believe she's gone where the shades walk. Not after all the little ones died of swamp fever. She's our only one left, my eldest, my sweetheart.'

Augustine felt the chill inside him. 'Why do you come to me? Can I raise the dead?'

The man lifted his head. There was a look almost of craftiness in his appeal.

'They're saying you heal the sick. And your holy men go around telling of a man who was hanged on a tree and came to life after three days. My daughter stopped breathing this morning, about dawn. Her spirit must still be near the body. If you come before the three days are up . . . please, Father! She's all I've got left.'

'How far have you come?' Augustine glanced at the sky. It was nearing noon. The man must have been walking fast for hours.

'A long weary way on foot. But if your worship has horses, we could be back there by late afternoon.'

The clatter of stones behind Augustine had stopped. The workmen were listening. Gosfraeg stood wide-eyed, alight with excitement. There was a terrifying air of expectancy, as though they believed he could really do this.

'Christ who rose from the dead was no ordinary man: He was the Son of God.'

'But didn't He raise the dead himself, Father?' the Gaulish foreman urged. 'Lazarus? And there was a girl too, wasn't there? Like this poor soul's daughter.'

'I'm not the Lord Jesus, just his humble servant.'

'It wouldn't be the first time you'd healed someone,' Gosfraeg said eagerly. 'Remember Titus? You've got to try. You can do it, Father. I know you can.'

I know no such thing, Augustine's heart was telling him. What if I fail? What if news of my failure gets back to Canterbury, to the priests Werburh and Ordulf, and all the heathens who hate me?

What if I succeed? Rather, what if Christ succeeds through me? All Kent will hear of it. The king will know.

'Call Father Laurence,' he ordered Gosfraeg. 'And Titus.' To the man, 'What's your name?'

'Wulfric, sir.'

'Wulfric, I'll come and see your daughter, and tell you whether anything can be done. It may be that's she's not truly dead, but sleeping. Let's pray I come in time.'

Should he go himself to the palace and beg Queen Bertha for horses? Send a messenger? Set out on foot?

Speed was important. 'Maurice!' he called.

His young secretary emerged from the group of workmen, where he had been making lists of the building materials available from the site of the tumbled church.

'Write this request to the queen on your tablet. . . .'

Wulfric's way led them to the coast. Autumn had stripped the fields and pigs rooted amongst the stubble. Mist dimmed the air. It had the cold and clammy feel of the sea not far away. Augustine and Laurence were riding horses borrowed from the royal stable. Gosfraeg had brought his own frisky pony, but Augustine detected him looking enviously at the abbot's black mount. The peasant and Titus bestrode mules. The young Nubian's legs almost trailed on the ground. For his own part, Augustine was not a confident horseman. He would have preferred to be nearer the ground. Yet a bishop must maintain the dignity of the Church.

The tedium of the journey almost numbed his senses. It was not the habit of Augustine and his monks to chatter as they travelled. Even Gosfraeg had gone quiet. Wulfric seemed cowed by grief and by the company of these foreigners who were rumoured to work powerful magic.

They were jolted out of their separate reveries. A grey building loomed out of the dun mist. There was a sound of women's voices keening.

'Here, sirs.' Wulfric pulled at his mule's reins, with the awkwardness of one not accustomed to ride. He almost fell from his mount, and immediately let go of it. Gosfraeg prudently grabbed up the trailing leathers.

'Please,' urged the peasant, 'if your worships would go in. I know it's not much of a place for the likes of you.' The apology was merely the habit of deference. He could hardly wait to shepherd them into his hovel.

The man was indeed lame, Augustine noted as he dismounted. The left foot twisted inwards, so that he must walk on the side of his foot, rather than treading firmly on the sole. It must have been a painful journey to Canterbury on foot and in haste.

The monks made to follow Wulfric into the hut. Augustine passed Gosfraeg his horse's reins.

'But you'll need me to interpret for you, Father!'

'Perhaps not. I'll call if I need you.'

He saw the excitement and self-importance fade in the boy's eyes. Was that a flash of resentment? Gosfraeg was, after all, a nobleman's son, not a stable-lad.

Inside, the swirling mist was replaced by a drier smoke that caught the back of his throat. Augustine coughed. The poor girl might well have had trouble with her breathing, living here.

The laments were hushed instantly.

At first he could see little. Then the smoke moved and a woman came forward. Her back was bowed by work as well as by the low roof. She too fell on her knees to him. His hand rested on her kerchiefed head. He murmured a blessing. He was still a little uncertain whether it was right to do this for a heathen.

He groped his way after them to the wall furthest from the door. There was no light in the hut except for the doorway, now blocked by Laurence and Titus, and an occasional spurt of flame from the central hearth. Gradually his eyes made sense of the shadows.

The girl lay stretched out on a low mattress. She was no more than a humped shape in the gloom. He stumbled against other figures kneeling beside her, which he had failed to see. Mourning women shuffled sideways to make more room for him. Now he could make out her pale hands clasped on her chest, the ashen face. Bending closer, he saw that she was older than he had expected, perhaps fourteen.

Augustine motioned to Laurence. He too bent over the girl. He lifted her closed lids and bent his ear to her mouth, felt the side of her neck where the pulse should beat. He straightened up and looked seriously at his abbot.

'The body's not stiff yet, but she's cold.'

What does that mean? Augustine's heart was racing. Is she dead, or isn't she? He was acutely aware of the infirmarian gazing at him with warm-eyed confidence. Even more, he was conscious of the living bulk of Titus behind him. He was certain the lad was remembering Augustine's healing touch on his own body. Their faith was impelling him to act. He could not hold out against them.

He turned to the girl. What should he do or say? Would it be presumptuous to use the same words as Christ had when he had stood at the bedside of a dead girl? He could think of nothing else.

His hand clasped one of the girl's, lying limp on her chest. He was shocked how cold it felt.

'Little girl, get up.'

Did he only imagine that hand growing warmer in his grasp? The hut was intensely still. They heard the merest sigh from her lips as her head fell sideways.

The shock to Augustine was more terror than joy. The mother swooped between him and the girl, frantic with relief. But Laurence held her back.

'Gently, daughter, gently. Wait for her spirit to come fully back to us.'

The girl's eyes opened vacantly and fell shut again. Her pallid face was darkening. Colour must be creeping into her cheeks, though it was hard to make out the red in the shadows. It was the abbot who now stood pale and paralysed.

Laurence took control. Care of the sick was what he understood. 'How long is it since she last ate? Do you have food? A spoonful or so of broth to begin with. . . .'

Titus was hugging the girl's father, who had tears pouring down his haggard cheeks.

Words seemed to be dredged up from a painful depth in Augustine's chest. 'Thanks be to God,' he said at last.

The monks 'Amen' thundered around him, caught up by the disconsolate voice of Gosfraeg outside.

Augustine found himself out in the yard, without really knowing how he had got there. The air was lighter. A little breeze was shifting the sea-fret, allowing the late afternoon sunbeams to glisten on the drops beading every twig and blade of grass. The dun sky had softened to a pale blue.

Gosfraeg's cry seemed to come from a long way off. 'Did you do it, Father? Have you really brought her back to life?'

Titus was at his elbow with a beaker of warm broth. 'Father Laurence says you should drink some too. The strength you put into the girl has been taken from you.'

'I did nothing. Give God the glory.'

'Yes, Father.'

Titus was too young to argue with his abbot and bishop, but Augustine sensed the obstinacy of the young. Nothing he said would change Titus's mind. Augustine was a miracle worker. He could raise the dead.

Had he? The thought was terrifying.

Slowly the sounds of the normal world returned to him. Gosfraeg had tethered the three horses and the two mules to trees. Their mouths tore at the wayside weeds. Further off, the freshening breeze was sending water lapping against wood. He turned to look. Beyond the hut a broad river had come into view, curving towards the sea. Little boats lay on the mudbanks. He had nearly reached the coast of Kent. This seaway could take him back to Gaul.

Gosfraeg was still gazing wide-eyed at him. It was he who had come running to Augustine, shouting his certainty that the abbot could help Wulfric. Yet now he looked shocked into silent awe. Worse, a crowd was beginning to gather. Augustine dimly remembered shouts, women running from the house to tell their neighbours. But the clamour had died. Peasants were edging closer, murmuring, as if afraid of him. It was like fire creeping through the beams under the thatch, which will suddenly roar out into the open.

Laurence appeared from the hut and took in the situation. 'Father, give them your blessing, then I think we should go. You've done enough for one day. It's a long ride back.'

For once, Augustine was glad to accept the orders of his infirmarian. He felt bone weary. He raised his hand over the advancing crowd in blessing. They fell to their knees.

'Look smart,' said Laurence, 'before they start bringing us any more of their sick.'

Augustine let Titus hoist him into the saddle. They were none too soon. The girl's parents were running out of the house. Wulfric reached to clutch the abbot's leg, but Gosfraeg on his pony was there between them, manoeuvring him out of the way. The boy had found his voice. He was forging ahead, clearing a path for them through the crowd. Speed was necessary. The peasants too were finding their voices, getting to their feet, shouting things Augustine barely understood. He need not listen. He had fulfilled his summons. All he wanted now was to get home.

Home. A quiet cloister in a monastery in Rome, where the slap of sandalled feet on warm tiles was all that broke the silence.

Home. A crowded hostel in a country of barbarians.

They took the road inland.

'I suppose we just follow our noses,' said Laurence, 'back to Canterbury?'

They had left their guide Wulfric behind with his recovered daughter.

Almost immediately the brief, belated sunshine vanished. The air was thickening again, darker this time. Even if monastic discipline had allowed it, no one wanted to talk much. They jogged along the rough track, with Gosfraeg leading the spare mule which had carried Wulfric. Each of them was absorbed in his own thoughts.

As they left the coastal farmland the way began to climb. Trees closed in around them. The light was failing rapidly.

Titus peered around him in bewilderment. 'Why's it getting dark so soon? It can't be time for vespers yet, can it?'

With an effort, Augustine broke his silence. 'Haven't you noticed? The days here are different from those in Rome. In midsummer it seemed the birds would never stop singing and the light still lingered in the sky when we retired to bed. But here, with each day that winter approaches, the days get shorter. Britain must be a dark place in midwinter.'

'We'd better quicken our pace, then.' Laurence's heels inexpertly kicked his horse into a trot. Only Gosfraeg on his pony was an experienced rider.

Each crossroads presented a decision. There was no setting sun to guide them. Sometimes they passed a village. The bustle of the day's work was already over, people gathering indoors for supper. Gosfraeg approached a doorway and asked for directions. He returned to say that their way led over the next hill, and another.

'Do you think we should stop at the next village, Father?' Laurence asked. 'Ask for beds for the night?'

'We'll see. Maybe they'll be able to tell us how much further it is. It can't be so very far now.'

He felt an unreasonable fear of spending the night outside Canterbury. Since they had left Thanet, he had walked or ridden around the country-side, telling the story of Christ's coming in many villages. But always he had retired at night to the security of his monastic community. He could not rid himself of the dread of the surrounding darkness, this heathen land, these barbarous people. He would have said he did not believe in the dark gods who ruled from Thanet, yet he felt their presence at every turn.

They were leaving the trees now, approaching another crossroads at the top of the ridge. The woods had been cleared back from the road. A wind blew in from the sea, cold, damp. It shivered the mist, but did not clear it.

'On a fine evening, we'd probably get a sight of Canterbury from here.' Titus dragged his cloak closer.

Below them was brown dusk. Even the edge of the wood was shrouded from their view.

'Do we still go forward?' Augustine asked Gosfraeg. It was odd how he had become so dependent on this boy, who only two hours before had been staring at him in awe.

'That's what they told me at the last village.' Gosfraeg moved his mount forward, down the path ahead, then reined in abruptly. He swung out of the saddle and bent over the track.

'What's wrong?'

'I'm . . . not sure.' Augustine caught the defensive rise in his voice.

'Let me look.'

He handed the reins of his horse to Titus and bent beside Gosfraeg. Something glimmered on the darker mud. If he had been riding in front, he might have dismissed it as a scatter of white pebbles. The boy's sharper eyes had seen more truly.

These were not white stones. A line had been drawn across the road. Those bone-white skulls had once been living creatures. Gosfraeg was whispering over them. 'Rat? Mouse? Weasel? Badger?!' His last gasp was almost a shriek.

Even now, Augustine had assumed that the larger mass at the edge of the road must be a rock. As Gosfraeg recoiled, the abbot moved with a swiftness he half regretted to see what was shocking the boy.

It was a human skull. There was no mistaking the cavernous eye sockets, those grinning teeth. Small, but a human. A child's.

'God rest its soul.' Laurence's voice spoke over their shoulders. 'There's wickedness here. What's that line between them?'

Gosfraeg reached out his hand to feel the darker thread linking the skulls, then drew it back. He mumbled something. His usually high, clear voice had become as indistinct as the fog which surrounded them.

'I thought it would be hair, but . . . it's sticky and it smells. I think it's guts.' He shuddered visibly.

'Why?' said Augustine. 'Who put this here? What's it supposed to mean?'

'Do you suppose it's for us?' Titus asked what they were all thinking.

'It's a magic bar across the road.' Gosfraeg had risen to his feet and was backing away. 'We daren't go this way.'

'But this is the road to Canterbury.'

The English boy shook his head violently. 'We mustn't cross *that*.'

Augustine took him by the shoulders. 'Are you afraid this is some work of the Devil against us?'

'Not a devil, sir. It's a message from our gods. Thunor, Woden, Frig.'

'Idols!' snapped Augustine, made angry by his own fear. 'You're receiving instruction in the catechism for your baptism. You don't believe in those gods any more.'

Gosfraeg hung his head. He could not stop trembling.

'Should I just kick them out of the way?' Laurence offered. Yet he stood still. It was hard for the monks not to share Gosfraeg's dread. Augustine himself did not want to touch these signs.

'We may be sure they didn't get here by magic,' he said. 'Someone put them here. Probably recently, after other travellers had stopped for the night. Who?'

'Someone who knew we'd be travelling this way.'

'No English heathen would dare to cross it,' Titus said, 'but why should they think it would stop Christians?' He took a step forward.

'No!' yelled Gosfraeg, and bolted off down a path to the left.

They heard his scream. At once they were with him, leaving the horses untethered. The boy was sobbing and pointing to the ground.

Another line of skulls linked by a dark cord. Titus moved swiftly back to try the road on the right. Before his cloaked form became lost in the mist, they saw him stop.

They retreated to the crossroads. They were all of them breathing fast, trying to control terror. Laurence met Augustine's eyes.

'What if we go back the way we came?'

He walked away, down the road towards the coast. Agonizing moments passed. Augustine missed the point when the indistinct form of the older monk turned. Laurence was standing in front of him again. Even in the dusk his face loomed pale.

'There too?'

Laurence nodded.

'Then. . . .'

'They're all around us.'

They felt the need to be physically close to each other. Augustine led a low, urgent murmur of prayer. In the silence that followed they waited, nerves stretched to breaking point. The slightest shift of their horses' feet caused them to gasp.

'Should we press on?' Laurence whispered.

As if in answer, there came the crash of a drum. Augustine leaped with shock. There was drumming all around them now, quieter, a low, insistent roll. It was no less menacing for that. It had started from some little distance, yet it was creeping closer up the hill.

'If we'd travelled on foot, I'd have had my staff,' Laurence muttered.

'Could the horses ride them down?' Gosfraeg's voice sounded frighteningly loud. Yet the quiver in his breath told of his supernatural horror that animal muscle and flashing hoofs would be powerless here.

When the ring of voices shrieked out, it was startlingly closer than the drums. Women's voices as well as men's. No words were distinguishable to the Romans. Probably, Augustine thought, not even to Gosfraeg. The intensity of this rhythmic chant surely rose out of the darkness of antiquity, born in the blood rather than taught in the mind. He felt with dismay his own blood caught up in the drumbeat, responding. He raised his voice in a sudden shout.

'Get behind me, Satan! Christ is the Light!'

There was a check in the chant. Then a woman shrieked and the noise redoubled. They were closing in fast now, shapes beginning to emerge out of the mist, gigantic shadows. The horses were pawing and snorting in fear.

'Let me deal with them, Father!'

It would be fatally easy to obey his young monk's order, to accept the protection of the body thrusting in front of him, to retreat between Titus's raised fists and the bulwark of the horses behind. Aethelbert's bodyguard would do the same in battle, giving the last drop of their blood to defend their lord.

Yet the way of the cross was often the road to martyrdom. Was this the last news Gregory would hear of him? Augustine made himself stand alongside the Nubian.

They were coming at a run now. Not weaponed soldiers, but robed figures with hair streaming, wielding staves or reaching clawing hands. Titus threw up his arms to grasp a stick descending on him. Augustine wrestled against hands that tore at his tunic, at his face, even at the cross around his neck. Was Werburh one of these hissing, spitting, roaring demons? Or the chief priest of Woden, Ordulf?

He heard a scream. He hardly knew if it was human or a terrified animal. Certainly there was a stamping of hoofs, the sounds of panic. The lunge of a horse's hind quarters threw him and his assailant sideways, but did not separate them. He parried the tearing nails. The woman snarling in his face rolled up her eyes. Blood gurgled from her contorted mouth. She crumpled at his feet. Had he done this? Or the horse?

There was a chaos of shrieks and curses, a shifting of the shadows. The circle was widening, weakening, scattering. Now there was groaning, low on the ground in many directions. Augustine stumbled on a shadow blacker and bulkier than the woman. He was close enough to see what it was. Denial tore through him. It could not be Titus.

He knelt, trembling. 'My son, my son!'

There was no answer. The miracle that had cleared this ambush like autumn leaves before a gale meant nothing. He put his hands on the young Nubian, hands that had healed the lad from fever, hands that this very day had raised a girl from the dead.

'In the name of the Father, the Son and the Holy Spirit, wake up, Titus!'

The monk did not stir. Augustine was dimly aware that the nature of the commotion around him was changing. Gosfraeg was calling to the horses and mules, trying to collect and calm them. Laurence was busy among the fallen shadows. He was calling out Augustine's name and Titus's. Augustine knelt on, nursing Titus in his arms. Neither of them moved or spoke.

The infirmarian stumbled upon them. 'Father? Thank God!' Then he saw what Augustine was holding. 'God have mercy! Is he bad?'

He was down on his knees. Augustine relinquished his burden to him. Tears were cold on his cheeks.

'Father,' said Laurence urgently, 'can't you do something? What you did before?' Augustine shook a head that felt impossibly heavy on his neck. 'I tried. I put my hands on him, I prayed, but nothing happened.'

'The Lord moves in a mysterious way. God rest his soul.'

With the burden taken out of his arms, Augustine's mind moved wider.

'What happened? Why did they run away? Why didn't they stay and kill us all?'

Laurence nodded his head towards the clink of jewellery that told of Gosfraeg's approach. The boy looked taller, coming out of the mist, almost a young man. He was holding a sword, a little awkwardly. Augustine looked at it in surprise. His mind had hardly registered the fact that Gosfraeg was wearing it when they rode out of Canterbury. An English nobleman, even one so young, would not set out on a journey unarmed. Why then should he feel astonishment that Gosfraeg had used it? It was not an ornament, like his gold chains. There was enough light left to show the blood on the blade.

Gosfraeg's voice was unsteady. 'I knew all those hours on the practice ground had to come in useful one day. I just didn't think it would be . . . wise women and priests.'

He had been terrified of these enemies. Now he was terrified of what he had done to them.

Augustine rose and placed his hands on the boy's trembling shoulders. 'Blessed be the queen who gave you to us for a friend. And blessed are you, Gosfraeg, for what you've done. When we saw those signs, I feared you were slipping away from us, back to your old gods.'

The boy hung his head, then looked up defiantly. He answered Augustine in English, though he was fluent in Latin. 'I'm Kentish. I do what's right for Kent. I saw what you did today. Ordulf and Werburh have never done anything like that. I was going to tell the queen, so she could tell the king. But then . . . when they attacked you, I had to decide right away. So I did. You're my lord. I had to defend you.'

He looked down at his sword as if in surprise. He was still shaking. He broke free from Augustine's grip and began to wipe the blade furiously on the grass.

'I'm not your lord,' Augustine said. 'Christ is. Never forget that.'

'We'd better get home.' Gosfraeg's head was still lowered. 'It can't be far now.'

'Do you think they'll come back?' Laurence asked.

No one answered.

'Should I do what I can for the wounded before we go?'

It took all three of them to lift Titus's body on to his mule. They led it on down the hill into the thicker dusk. The first glimmer of candlelight came out of the gloom.

Chapter Twenty-two

'It's an outrage!' Bertha strode from her own hall into the king's without ceremony. Her voice rang across the shadowed space. 'Brother Titus is dead. Your priests killed him.'

The king rose. The men around him fell back and turned to stare at her. The clamour of their voices was hushed.

Aethelbert's anger matched her own. 'Do you teach me my job, madam?'

Bertha sank in a belatedly curtsey, still defiant. 'I am jealous of your honour, my lord. You gave the monks safe conduct. I will not have Kent shamed.'

'And did you think I would stand by and see my orders disobeyed?'

As her eyes grew accustomed to the dim morning light she saw that Gosfraeg was there before her, his slight boy's figure dwarfed by the warriors and counsellors surrounding Aethelbert. The face that he turned to her was alight with the story of treachery and heroism he had been delivering.

'So Gosfraeg has told you everything? What are you doing about it, my lord?'

She was answered by a commotion behind her. Two of Aethelbert's bodyguard were entering the hall, with a small, snarling figure between them.

Bold though she had been a moment before, Bertha flinched back from the shaman Werburh as she was led past to the king's chair. The battle-scarred spear-wielders on either side of her were far less intimidating than this little woman in her cats' pelts. The men's faces were set in a determination not to betray their own fear of their prisoner. She spat the ferocity of her anger at them all.

'My lady.' Aethelbert motioned his queen to join him on the dais.

More dignified now, Bertha crossed the hall. She was aware that she was being followed by Mildgith and her ladies. There were more Englishwomen in her retinue than Franks now. More heathens than Christians. If she herself was afraid of Werburh and her power, how much more must women like Mildgith fear her?

145

Was Aethelbert as afraid?

Bertha sat in her chair beside her husband and watched him warring with his fears. The priestess of Frig stood below him, proud and scornful. She had dressed in her full regalia.

The king turned unexpectedly to the courtiers around him. 'Ordulf. Stand beside her.'

Surprised and alarmed, the chief priest of Woden stepped from the ranks of counsellors and took his place facing Aethelbert. He wore secular dress, a loose, fur-trimmed gown over his long tunic. Only the dark patterns on his face marked him out as a shaman.

Aethelbert addressed him first. 'Did the priests of Woden have anything to do with this treachery?'

The representative of the father of the gods bowed, then drew himself up straighter. 'My lord, I've made no secret of my advice. I have counselled you against these foreigners. I have reminded you respectfully that you are descended from Woden. I have warned you that your famous success in battle could desert you, if the gods remove their smile from you. But Woden is lord of the battlefields. He does not attack in the dark, like some alley-cat. He uses warriors, not women.'

The king stared at him in silence for a long while.

'So you say, but doesn't Woden go about hooded and disguised as Grim? And you?' turning to Werburh with a ferocity to match her own. 'The boy says there were as many women as men in that ambush. Do you deny this shameful murder was your work?'

'No!' Scornful and proud.

'I gave those monks safe-conduct and liberty to preach,' Aethelbert thundered. 'You've dishonoured me. You dishonour Kent.'

The woman spat. 'Foreign devils! Traitors to Kent.'

'I could have you executed for this.'

'My dying words would put a curse on you.'

Bertha heard her husband's intake of breath. She has infuriated you, but you will not execute her, Bertha thought, with a sudden shudder. You still fear her. You dread the wrath of her fertile goddess too much. What if Mother Frig shuts up her womb? What if Kent becomes barren? Yes, you're ambitious to be like the Franks and the Romans. You're wavering on the point of change, but you're not sure yet. Not while this woman is weaving her magic in front of you, cursing you.

She studied the woman priest's face, made vicious by outrage. It was very like a cat's. That pointed chin, the wide brow, those greenish eyes rounded with charcoal. She was snarling now, too, like an angry cat, a small, tense, spitting creature.

Small. It struck Bertha with sudden force that she had never realized until now how far Werburh was from the ideal of English womanhood.

Ladies of the Kentish court were praised for standing tall and proud, though none were as tall as Bertha. Werburh was a cat among deerhounds. Poets sang of maidens with tresses fair as corn stalks. Werburh's hair was mousy brown, its rebellious strands not bound into plaits, but flicking into wild curls. Beautiful eyes to the English should be blue as cornflowers. Werburh's were flecked with flashes of green.

Was she wholly English? What had it meant to grow up small and brown among these leggy blondes? Was it this difference which made the English fear her so? Was this what had separated her out as a holy woman?

Aethelbert feared her. Bertha listened to him rasping out the sentence of banishment from his court for Titus's death. She felt a burden lifted from her spirit after all these years. And yet. . . ? What was the power-play still between the angry king and this little woman hissing curses back at him? Was Aethelbert the sovereign, and she his courtier, to be appointed or dismissed as he willed? Or was it Werburh's ritual authority which legit-imized this man's reign? What would the king believe himself to be without her?

Sitting so close, she sensed the thrill in her husband. He was venturing out into new and dangerous ground. She felt both his terror and the intox-ication of risk. This must be how he led his warriors into battle. This was the madness which made him great. Aethelbert might yet become a Christian, not for faith in God, or love of Christ, but just for the lure of danger and the lust for a kingdom not yet won.

It was done. The words of banishment were spoken. The little woman had to withdraw, still spitting malevolence. As she reached the door, she turned her back on the court. From behind, in the twitching fur cloak of her regalia, she looked more animal than human. Then she was gone, like vermin chased from a barn.

To what? Could Werburh still be chief priest of Frig, without the king's authority? Might Aethelbert appoint another woman in her place? Bertha did not believe so. He had taken too bold a step down the road towards Rome.

The faces of the Kentish courtiers were pale. Herman and Dirwine looked dismayed, though they often seemed more than half Frankish by now, living so closely with the queen's court. Our childhoods never wholly leave us, she thought. I was brought up a Christian; these men have other memories. Werburh's claws will never fully let go of them.

She rose with the king.

'Thank you, my lord.'

'Don't think I did it for you, madam. I don't need a woman to give me lessons in honour.' But the grin he gave her spoke of a shared victory, in the face of great and continuing danger.

She walked from the hall across the yard. In the distance she could see the small bent figure of Werburh going away. People drew back a wide distance as she approached them, disappeared into doorways or round corners. No doubt she was still scattering curses.

The priestess was passing the orchard now. A figure separated itself from the trunk of a tree. He did not shrink back or run away. Bertha watched the tall, slim young man walk towards the path. Werburh turned her head, stopped, as if he had called to her. The blood left Bertha's face. She watched her eldest son, Eadbald, walk up to the banished priestess, and place something in her hand. The woman raised her arm, as if in blessing. Then she went on her way to the gate. The prince stayed watching her.

Bertha stood motionless.

'Is something the matter, madam?' Mildgith asked. 'Are you well?'

'It's nothing.' Bertha shook her head, as if to shake off the dark thoughts. Had no one else seen? What did it mean? Should she tell Aethelbert?

A shiver of fear for her son ran through her. The king of Kent was not a man to be challenged, least of all by the boy who would succeed him.

'Follow me.' There was still a dark blaze of anger in the king's face.

Augustine motioned silently to Honorius and Domitian to accompany him.

The king strode ahead through Canterbury. The barely controlled energy of his muscled body challenged everyone in his path to move hastily aside, before they bowed and touched their foreheads. He ignored them all. The monks were swept along in his wake, between an escort of spearmen.

He led them west, out through a gate in the sagging city wall. They left the highway and turned aside through a cluster of hawthorn trees. Level meadows stretched away from the tumbled stonework of Canterbury to the foot of the hill up which St Martin's lay. The king strode though a herd of cows and stopped in this open pasture. He grasped a spear from a startled soldier and planted it upright, just missing a warmly steaming cow pat.

'Here!' He plucked up the spear again and jabbed it at a distant oak tree. 'From there,' tracing a circle in the air, 'to there, and there, and there.' With a grim laugh, he brought the haft of the spear back and stuck in the hole it had left.

'I give you a bigger kingdom than before. Let that mangy cat tell me I dare not! She'll see! I know what your monks' houses are like in Rome and Gaul. Bertha tells me about them. Houses for your men, a school, a place for the sick, a hall for your guests. She says your little place in the city will not be enough. Very well! Make this grander than anything in Frankland. Ask me for whatever you want.'

And the king was not yet a Christian.

'Your majesty! Heaven will bless you.'

'Your heaven had better, since I'm told my own gods will curse me.'

It was hard to meet the fury, the resolution, in his eyes.

Was it for this Titus had died?

As work began on a bigger abbey, the new cathedral in Canterbury was finished.

King Aethelbert was coming to the consecration. Augustine was both flattered and alarmed. He had tried to explain, hesitantly, that it was normal for the unbaptized to gather outside, looking into the holiest area from the rear, hearing the praise of the congregation to which they were not yet admitted.

The words had died before Aethelbert's fierce blue stare. This was not a king you said 'no' to.

And so, this disturbing prospect. The monks were by now well accustomed to the queen's presence. Augustine was no longer overawed to find royalty in his congregation. Queen Bertha was, after all, a woman, and not a sovereign monarch. He was bishop now. He could hold himself confidently the equal of her chaplain Liudhard, perhaps his superior.

King Aethelbert was something else. The king carried everywhere that aura of power, of danger.

Augustine's anxious mind flew around the rebuilt church he had been so proud of until now. This was no little St Martin's, tucked away in the woods on the hillside outside the city. This was his cathedral of Christ Church, his episcopal seat. The walls were of stone, at least for the lower courses. The roof soared skywards. The queen had contributed her wealth to equip its sanctuary with silver lamps, a gem-studded cross on the altar, the exotic smell of incense.

Would King Aethelbert be impressed?

The cheering of the crowd outside the church announced the royal party. Domitian led them forward. Augustine stood his ground as they came towards him, resplendent in their gold necklaces and coronets, the rich stuff of their gowns. He was not sure if a bishop should bow to a king, but he did. There was probably not a knee in Kent which could resist the pressure to bend before the advance of the overlord of Britain. Aethelbert was a tall man, though only a little more so than his Frankish queen. The face under his crown had stayed lean in middle age. The monk's own disciplined body recognized how Aethelbert's was hardened by the different punishment of constant training for battle, scarred by the battles themselves. This king never wearied of war. His kingdom was still growing. Only last month, Bertha had told him, Aethelbert had advanced to the Welsh border at the River Wye. The face that drew closer was craggier about the cheekbones, the eyes deeper set and flashing. As the king walked up the nave, he seemed like a tethered beast, chafing to spring. Never mind that his anger was on the Christian monks' behalf, his rage against his own people for the death of Titus.

The courtesies were done. The king and queen were seated. The royal children were ranged around them, from the tall, frowning Prince Eadbald down to the chubby little Princess Eanswythe staring about her with round eyes.

The king nodded. The faces of everyone in that packed church were focused on Bishop Augustine.

It was time. He had travelled this impossible distance from Rome, come through a disorientating first year. He stood here in his newly raised cathedral of Christ the Saviour, in the heart of royal Canterbury. Today, he would dedicate it proudly to God Almighty, in the presence of Kent's heathen king.

He led his monks in procession around the church, all of them walking behind Gregory's cross. There would not be one of them who did not feel a pang of grief that this cross must be carried today by Maurice. He had a vivid memory of Titus, holding it up like a figurehead on the prow of their ship, leading that solemn procession across Thanet to their first encounter with King Aethelbert under the oaks. Would the king remember that too?

Augustine spattered the holy oil over the twelve crosses cut on its walls. He anointed the doorposts, for the safekeeping of all who entered. He ascended to the altar, where the relics of the saints Gregory had sent him were enshrined. Five crosses were engraved on the bare altar. He signed them with oil.

He signalled to Tyrri. The English boy, recently baptized, was clad in a white surplice. With a painful thrill, Augustine recalled that morning in the slave market of Rome, when Gregory had seen two captive English boys, and said of them, 'Not Angles, but angels.' He must describe all this to Gregory in his next letter.

Tyrri was well schooled in court formalities. It had not been difficult to teach him this liturgy. His usual exuberance was overlaid with a proper gravity. He handed the bishop the smoking censer. Augustine burned incense over the five crosses. He handed the censer back to the boy, who grinned at last and swung it now exuberantly, sending clouds of pungent smoke over everyone.

The bishop clothed his new altar for the first time, in white and gold. Other priests set upon it the bread and wine, which would be consecrated for the first mass afterwards, when the unbaptized had departed. The monks were chanting the divine plainsong Gregory had taught them. The music, the ritual, the smoke, the feel of the chalice in his hands, these were as much intoxication to Augustine as the snort of warhorses and the clash of weapons were to King Aethelbert. He was in his element.

It was accomplished. Canterbury's new cathedral was made holy for the worship of the one true God.

Now he must preach his sermon. The exultation was fading. Knots of anxiety tightened his stomach, his throat, his breathing. His hand holding the script on the desk in front of him was shaking. Lord God, let me not fail.

He forced his eyes to look up, beyond the rim of the desk, to the full congregation. There were far more heathens than Christians here, obedient to their king. The choir was a reassuringly solid mass of monks, many wearing priestly vestments today over their habitual black. The Franks stood on one side of the nave, behind their queen. The rest were warriors, ladies, counsellors, children of the Kentish court. Christian or heathen, they counted for nothing. There was only one man who mattered: the king of Kent, seated in his chair directly in front of the sanctuary, with the royal family ranged behind him.

Aethelbert folded his arms. He was staring at Augustine with an almost belligerent intensity. Augustine summoned up the courage to meet that stare. As their eyes connected, the thought leaped out at him, like an unleashed wolfhound. He wants me to convince him.

Even so, his voice trembled on the first words. 'In the name of the Father, and the Son, and the Holy Spirit . . . This day, Christ has made holy His own church in Canterbury. No words of mine could do this. No oil sprinkled. No incense burned. No offering made. Christ, Son of God, is His own High Priest. I, Bishop of Canterbury by the grace of God, am His meanest servant. All around this city are other temples, where those who call themselves priests offer sacrifices to placate their gods. When bread is broken and wine is poured in this church, it is our God Himself who gives His own body and blood as the sacrifice. Given for me, who am not worthy to undo the buckle of Christ's sandal. Shed for all of you here, from the greatest king to the smallest child. You are of such infinite value that God died for you. . . .'

'As a great king lays down his life on the battlefield for his people.'

The shock stopped Augustine in mid-sentence. He had never been interrupted in a sermon in any church. True, when he and his monks walked the villages around, or when he climbed on a pile of rubble in Canterbury to harangue the crowds, there were hecklers. But here, in the ordered sanctity of his newly consecrated cathedral?

Aethelbert, the warrior king, was responding to Christ the Hero.

Augustine swallowed his astonishment. He must make good this moment. Whatever the words he had so carefully penned yesterday, on the desk before him, he must speak now, directly, to this man, this ruler. Aethelbert of Kent understood, as no one else in this congregation could, what it meant for a king to die for his people.

Afterwards, Augustine could not recall what he said, though his words had resounded around the new rafters. All he could remember was Aethelbert's burning blue eyes, fixed on his, as though the two of them had been the only men in this packed building. The Roman had not even wondered how to translate his thoughts into English. The phrases had flowed, strong, sure, true. He heard his last words ring out, and the sound die away in the hush that followed. Had he uttered some challenge? He could not remember.

The king sat as still as the carved back of his chair. His eyes had dropped. He seemed to be staring intently at his feet. Very slightly, the queen turned her head to watch him.

A shudder ran through the seated man, like a wild beast when its cage door is opened. Suddenly, he was on his feet, shouting. 'Bring me my sword!'

By courtesy and custom he had come unarmed into this house of prayer. Yet the sword that had made him so great a king was never far away from him. Gosfraeg, the page, came running and threw himself on his knees, offering up the weapon. Aethelbert took it, looking at it almost in surprise, as though it was, after all, strange to him. Then he walked forward, with that slow firm step that made everyone fall back before him, though there was already a respectful space between the king and the rest of the congregation. Augustine nerved himself to walk from the desk to meet the English lord on the central step of the chancel.

King Aethelbert, overlord of Britain, knelt before him, causing a huge collective gasp from the congregation. He held the sword steady across his lifted hands. Even now, Augustine had enough sense to move a little to one side, so that the king could offer his sword, not to him, but to the cross on the altar.

'I pledge my loyalty to the King who died for all kings.'

It was hard for the bishop not to stutter. 'God welcomes you into the Kingdom of heaven, my son.'

Chapter Twenty-three

Aethelbert checked at the door of his great hall, as though even now he doubted his own decision. He looked up, narrowing his eyes at the bright sky.

Is he remembering Thanet? Bertha thought. Is there a part of his pagan self which still fears to leave the open air of his sky gods? He could have ordered our chairs to be set outside, and the court gathered round us on the grass. In many places across Kent we do this, where the local palace is not big enough to hold so many.

Yes, I'm sure he does remember the oak tree of Thanet, and for that very reason he's defying the advice of the chief priest of Thunor. He will not display his fear, precisely because he *is* afraid. He's making a dangerous gamble, with his life, his tribe, his country. And because he's Aethelbert the King, he's going to meet that danger eagerly, like a lover rushing to his bride.

The doorway was tall, but the king seemed to stoop as he entered, as though the dimness inside was not a high-raftered hall, but a low cave. After the sunshine it seemed dark, though the windows were unshuttered.

'Lights! Bring more torches!' shouted the king.

Servants thrust brands into the smouldering daytime fire. Flames sprang to life in iron cressets around the walls, though not so close as to endanger wood and thatch. Will we ever live in a stone palace, like Romans? Bertha wondered, thinking of far-off Paris and Augustine's new church.

Aethelbert's hand was warm and vital around hers as he led her up the steps of the dais. The torches had sparked smaller flames in the weapons on the walls, the rims and bosses of the shields, the blades of spears and axes. Yes, this is part of why we must meet Augustine indoors. This is royalty. When the time comes, Aethelbert will kneel humbly, stripped of this finery, and accept the plain white gown of baptism. But first he will show the Roman bishop how much he is giving up, how great a sacrifice of wealth and honour and power this English king is laying at Christ's feet. Even his humility is a source of pride to him.

I shouldn't be thinking like this. This is the thing I've longed for since I was betrothed to him as a girl. The greatest of the English kings is becoming a Christian. I shouldn't criticize him: I should rejoice and honour him.

Aethelbert is a child, who loves to vaunt himself above other boys. He is a sovereign, playing a devious power game. He is a soul in need of salvation, coming to God.

There were real children around Bertha, the family she had borne her husband. From little Eanswythe, round-eyed and solemn, whose fair, braided head scarcely topped the arm of her mother's chair, to the eldest Eadbald, tall and restless behind his father.

She half turned to watch her son. He was frowning, his lips twitching impatiently, where the first hairs were beginning to show. This was hard for him. Bertha was uneasy. Thurwald, high priest of Thunor, had come from Thanet on the king's orders. She had seen Eadbald talking with him several times. All the priests of the old gods had fallen under Aethelbert's suspicion, since the murder of the monk. As yet, only Werburh had been banished. Eadbald was playing a dangerous game.

She sighed. It would make little difference what Eadbald wanted. There would be no choice for Aethelbert's sons and daughters. Just as he had forbidden their Christian baptism as babies, so he would command them to make their vows to Christ now. He was not a man to ask his children for their opinions. She could only pray that Eadbald would accept that. The inevitable consequences of refusal made her shiver.

She heard the chanting of monks approaching. It gave a lift to her heart, as though she had been captured by pirates and heard at last the sound of rescue. All these years she had kept her lonely faith with a handful of retainers. These had dwindled through death or marriage. Now, in a single year, her world had changed. What had been scorned in Kent was triumphant. Her faith was vindicated.

Even as Augustine and his monks entered the hall, with the cross before them, she shot a sideways glance at her chaplain Liudhard. He was biting his lip, as though more angered than overjoyed. A new thought came to her. Had they failed Kent, she and Liudhard? Had they been content with too little? Had they lacked Augustine's courage to convert her husband?

'Your majesty.' The little Roman bishop bowed in answer to the king's gesture of permission to speak. 'We have come, at your gracious invitation, to instruct you and your household in the sacraments of the Christian faith before your baptism. A year ago, I told you the story of Christ the King, who came to us in a humble stable. Yesterday you knelt before his cross and offered him your soul and your sword. The armies of angels rejoiced. Today, I must tell you what else Christianity will demand of you. If you and your court accept the challenge I lay before you, the Church will welcome you to baptism with open arms.'

'Begin, begin! I'm a soldier. I understand discipline. What are the rules of honour your king demands of his warriors?'

Augustine looked up, startled. He was, Bertha thought, a very unwar-like man. Yet he had fired Aethelbert's imagination with a vision of Christ the Hero, riding the cross like Woden's stallion. He must go through with it.

'In baptism,' he began, his voice faltering, 'we die to sin. We go down under the water, as if to the grave. It takes courage. You must believe that arms will lift you up into new life, as the Father raised Christ from the tomb. You will rise washed from your past.'

'Good, good! When a man pledges his loyalty to me, I care nothing for his past, as long as he serves me loyally from then on, to the death.'

The bishop led them through the Last Supper, with an anxious glance at the unconverted court, who should not be listening to this.

'Yes! Yes!' Aethelbert beat his hand on his chair, grinning like a small boy who has suddenly discovered he can aim a spear. 'That's just how a king behaves on the eve of battle. He feasts his warriors with mead. They raise their cups to the lord they will die for.'

'Yet,' said Augustine quietly, 'in this case, it was the Lord who died for his followers.'

Aethelbert glared at the bishop. Bertha feared they had lost him.

Then the king muttered into his beard, 'Just as I shall die one day, on the battlefield, for my people.'

The shock stopped her breath for a moment. All the court knew that any hint of the king's mortality must never be spoken. Was this the turn of the tide which had washed him to the shores of Paradise? Aethelbert, at last, was facing the certainty of his own death. He must know, though he still dared not speak this fearful alternative, that it might not be in the glory of battle, but sick in bed, or thrown from his horse in the hunt. There might, after all, be no battle maidens of Woden to sweep down from the sky and carry the fallen warrior up to the gods' feasting hall. Only the longship going out into the grey fog and an eternity of uncertainty. No wonder the jewelled city of Christ's Heaven dazzled him with a new hope.

In Augustine's story of Christ's anguish in the Garden of Gethsemane the king read the warrior's vigil. He had known, Bertha realized, as she and the monks did not, that sweat of fear.

Aethelbert watched Augustine's face intently as he listened to the wounds of the Crucifixion. She saw him wince, and sensed his own scars were hurting.

When he heard of the women preparing the precious body for burial, his hand went out to hers. Bertha, who alone knew his vulnerability in the secrecy of the bedchamber, was less astonished than the rest of the court at this admission of weakness. Her husband was pleading with her: when the time comes, do this for me.

At the joy of Resurrection morning, he leaned back in his chair, smiling

155

satisfaction at last. The King was secure on his throne for eternity.

'I must teach you now the rites of the sacrament in which we take for ourselves his body and blood.' Augustine looked round the crowded hall. 'But this is not for the uninitiated. It is our rule that those who have not been baptized must leave the church before the celebration of the Eucharist. So too, I may teach its mystery only to those who are candidates for baptism. The rest must leave.'

His eyes came back to the king, who alone could dismiss them.

Aethelbert barked the answer Bertha knew that he would. 'I'm the King of Kent. What I say, Kent does.'

Bishop Augustine proved a braver man than she might have expected. 'With respect, your majesty, no one can compel another soul to salvation. I would gladly baptize your whole nation in a single day, but I may not. Each must choose for himself, and for no one else, unless it be a little child too young to answer.' He smiled at Eanswythe, and her solemn face slowly relaxed in an answering grin.

But he was on dangerous ground. The king shifted angrily in his chair. 'May not? May not?' Then the crafty flame of power lit his eyes. He swung on Ordulf, chief priest of Woden. 'Well, priest? Woden's the god of wisdom. What do you say to that?'

The priest bit his lip. He bowed. His hanging hair hid his face. When he straightened up, he said carefully, 'Your majesty, whatever wisdom God sends, it rests in the king. You have guided your people well these many years. I've served you faithfully as a son of Woden. If you wish, I will serve you as a child of Christ.'

There is no conviction there, Bertha thought. Ordulf is no Werburh. He's a courtier, more than a shaman. If Aethelbert shifts, Ordulf will shift too. He will keep his place in the king's circle.

Aethelbert nodded. His grin spoke satisfaction.

He rounded suddenly on Thurwald, chief priest of Thunor. Thurwald had managed to absent himself from the consecration of Christ Church. It had not gone unnoticed.

'Well, priest of Thunor? You've heard of a god who died to open heaven to us. The very sky split when he died on the cross. What does your thunder lord say to that, eh? Are you ready to turn your back on Thunor and follow your king to glory with Christ?'

For all Augustine's scandalized caution, Bertha knew there were few in that English court who would have courage to defy the king. Each one of them had to make their decision here, in front of him.

Thurwald began to tremble so violently that the thunder axe round his neck rattled against the shells and pebbles of his many necklaces. 'M-my lord . . . I too have served you faithfully. I've made the sacrifices to the god for you. It's my prayers and spells have kept this land safe. I . . . cannot . . .

I . . .' Bertha feared he would be sick on the spot.

Aethelbert half rose, pressing his hands on the arms of his chair so that the wood creaked under the pressure. 'I, the king, can, and you . . . *cannot?*'

'Forgive me, your majesty! The great Lord Thunor . . . the thunder . . . the rain—'

'Go! Get out of here! And never cross my threshold again! You are no priest of mine!'

Thurwald shuddered back across the floor in his blue- and white-feathered cape, like a gust of rain driven before a storm wind. He was out of the door and fleeing. The faces of those who remained were stricken, fearful.

More quietly, but yet more venomously Aethelbert turned back to Ordulf, chief priest of Woden. 'And you? I ask you again. Do you prefer your Sky Father to mine?'

Ordulf had dignity. He did not bow his head and mutter his submission. He looked at his king, eye to eye. 'Your majesty, the poets sing you descended from Woden, Sky Father of English kings. Woden, we know, sacrificed himself to gain wisdom. He hung nine days on a tree. This new priest tells us of a Christ who hung on a tree and died and lives again. He goes among us disguised as the Spirit, as Woden went about cloaked and hooded as Grim. When I heard his story, I felt it was one I had known all my life, but with this difference: I've served Woden since I was a boy, and I've always feared him. The gods may favour us one day and turn on us the next. We live in terror of their moods. Until now, I'd never heard of a god who loves me, whatever I do. For that, I'd risk much.'

Bertha started in her chair. I've underrated him, she thought. He's more than a self-serving courtier. This is real faith.

The king stared at his chief priest, then a slow, broad smile split his face. 'Well said, Ordulf, well said! . . . And the rest of you? Raise your hand if you're willing. If not, there's the door behind you. You can follow Thurwald if you dare.'

All round the hall a thicket of hands went up, as Bertha knew they would. There were very few brave enough to creep behind their ranks and flee through that door, out under the clouds of Thunor and Woden and a chill future without the king's favour. Aethelbert noted each one.

When they were gone he shrugged, swinging back to Augustine. 'So. I and my children and my court are ready for you, Bishop. You can tell us your secrets now.'

There was a little shuffle behind the royal couple. Eadbald, their eldest son, stepped out in front of their chairs. He was sweating. The torchlight sparkled on the beads of moisture and on the silky gold of his first moustache.

'Father.' He gulped for air. 'I don't want this. Ordulf's right—'

'Ordulf will take his oath as a Christian!' thundered Aethelbert. 'You heard him.'

'He ... he said we ... we're descended from Woden. And we are. We're Kent, and we've always been the best because of Woden. How can I change? I w-won't.'

'You *won't*? You're my *son*!' The king was on his feet in a towering fury.

Bertha leaped down the steps to put her arms around Eadbald.

'I know ... I'm sorry!' It was all the boy could do not to burst into tears.

'I'll whip the hide off you for this!'

'Your majesty—' Augustine came hurrying forward, in distress.

Aethelbert shouted at him, 'You said I must give them a choice. I have, haven't I? You saw them go. But my own son? My heir?'

'Your majesty, God knows I pray the next king of Kent may be a Christian too. But we cannot compel him.'

'He's only a boy. You said a child can't answer for himself.'

'But he has!' cried Bertha, heartbroken. 'I wanted to have him baptized as a baby. I would have saved his soul. But he's not a child now. It's too late.'

Slowly she took her protecting arm away and looked at her firstborn son. The tears were starting to creep from her eyes. 'They've turned you against us, haven't they? Thurwald and Werburh. They've led your soul to damnation. And I must let you go. Love may not compel you.'

With an effort, Eadbald straightened himself to face his father. He could scarcely speak through stiff, pale lips. 'I'm sorry, sir. I'm still your son, whatever you say about me. I'll fight for you and for Kent as you've trained me to do all these years ... I'm not sure what we'll do, if there's no priest of Woden any more to make the sacrifices.' He turned reproach-fully to Ordulf. 'But there's still Thunor and the priests of Thanet. He isn't the god of kings, like Woden. But he's a god of war, and he's all you've left us. And may our ancestors forgive you if we lose the next battle.'

It was a brave speech, and it struck home. Aethelbert stared after his son as the boy backed towards the door. He was gone, like the others. For once, Aethelbert was deprived of words.

But not for long. He rounded on Augustine. 'What are you standing there with your mouth open for, man? Proceed! Do you think I'm going to change my mind for a beardless boy?'

Chapter Twenty-four

Aethelbert might not compel his inferiors to baptism, but he would make them watch his own. He exerted his authority over Eadbald, his defiant son, and others of his kin.

He had summoned his nephew Sabert, under-king of neighbouring Essex. Sabert and his own sons must be made vividly aware of the risk they ran by not following Aethelbert through the waters of baptism. It did not please the King of Kent that Sabert boasted the busy port of London for his capital, but he was still a client king to his uncle.

There was another who came with them. When the Essex court arrived at Canterbury, Bertha ran across the yard to greet Sabert's mother with the genuine joy of long friendship. Queen Ricula rode into Canterbury mounted like her menfolk. She had her brother Aethelbert's square jaw, the piercing determination of his eye. She could still ride a horse almost as well as her warrior son and grandsons.

There were three of those boys, Sexred, Saeward and Sigbert, flamboyantly tossing long hair, making their many gold neck chains jingle, trying to look like the grown men they almost were. These East Saxon boys jumped down in the yard to greet their Kentish cousins. Bertha's eyes flew sideways to watch as her son Eadbald strode to meet them. The princes of Essex turned their faces up to him in hero-worship. They were all growing up to be proud young men. Soon, like Eadbald, these Essex princes would be at that age when high blood is looking for a reason to defy the older generation. Bertha looked uneasily from them to her husband. Aethelbert bore that certainty of kingship which still brought a tremor to her knees. She feared the power struggle that was beginning between her husband and her adolescent son. Eadbald surely could not win it? She feared now for his life, as she already feared for his soul.

'Are you too proud now to give your sister-in-law a kiss?' Ricula was grinning down at her from the saddle.

The Queen of Kent gasped at her discourtesy. 'I'm so sorry! My mind was miles away. Be most welcome, Lady!'

It was more than formal courtesy. The older woman swung down from her mount, scarcely needing the assistance of the waiting Dirwine. The two queens embraced warmly.

'What's all this about, then? Is Aethelbert really giving up our English gods for the Lord of Rome and Constantinople? I'm sorry, my dear. Of course, you're one of these Christians, and I've never held it against you. When we're together, you seem like one of us.'

Too much? thought Bertha. Should I have shouted my difference louder? Should it have needed Augustine and his monks to come and make this change?

'Still,' – Ricula removed her riding gloves – 'we've missed you at the ceremonies. The queen should play her part to please the gods. I've always wondered that Aethelbert let you get away with that. But' – she flashed her brother's wolfish grin at Bertha – 'he admired you from the very beginning for standing up to him. There are few who dare to do that.'

'There's another now. Eadbald. All the children are being baptized tomorrow, after Aethelbert. Except our eldest. He refuses to abandon Woden and the rest of his gods.'

The other queen's eyebrows rose 'Does he, indeed? So he's inherited his father's courage . . . and his mother's. Though I doubt that Aethelbert will be as tolerant with his son as he's been with you.'

'I'm afraid for him,' Bertha said candidly.

'With reason.'

Bertha led her sister-in-law into the queen's hall. The East Saxon women followed, eyeing their Kentish counterparts. Civilities were being exchanged, fashions noted, who was missing through death or marriage, who was pregnant. Proximity to Frankland had made the Kentish ladies somewhat superior, though ships docked in London bearing cargoes from lands further still.

'Listen, my dear.' Ricula sat down and leaned confidentially towards Bertha. The ladies attending them drew back tactfully. Only Edith stayed curled at Bertha's feet, an almost invisible maidservant, ready to attend her mistress at any moment. 'We both know what's going on, why Sabert and I and the boys have been summoned to Canterbury. Aethelbert was always like this. Don't forget, this is where I grew up with him.'

She stared down the length of the hall through the open doorway. Aethelbert and her son Sabert were still in the yard, in conference over their horses.

'Aethelbert was the greatest daredevil you ever saw. But it was never enough for him that he should be brave himself. He always had to be taunting the others to follow him, whether they wanted to or not: his own brothers and foster-brothers, other boys of the court too scared to say no to him, and yet too scared to do what he could do safely.

'My husband Sledda was one. As a boy, he was fostered at our Kentish court.' She nodded to the yard. 'Do you see that great oak tree? One day,

Aethelbert climbed it and leaped from there across to the gable of the king's hall. We thought for sure he'd break his neck. But he didn't. It's only the ones who're scared they'll fall who do. All the rest of us were standing under the tree, gawping up at him.

'He jeered down at Sledda, "A prince of Essex will never be the equal of the prince of Kent." So, of course, Sledda had to try, though he was shaking with terror. He made himself climb, branch after branch, until he was higher than Aethelbert. Then he crawled out along the bough. It was shaking so hard the leaves were raining down on us. The rest of us had gone dead quiet watching him. I wondered if I should run and get someone to stop it. The servants in the yard had put down their buckets and what-not to stare, but they hadn't the wit to shout for someone with authority.

'Sledda needed to stand up on the branch before he could jump. That was the worst bit. The bough was swaying about like a mast in a gale. Aethelbert had gone across like a squirrel, so quick and nimble you hardly saw how he did it. Sledda took his time. We saw him gather himself into a kind of knot and then fling himself out over the empty air. My heart turned over. When he made it on to the roof, we all let out a great cheer. But we were too soon. He slipped on the thatch. He grabbed for the carving on the gable end, but missed. And down he went, slipping and sliding, over and over, till he tumbled over the eaves and went crashing to the ground.'

'Was he killed?' But Bertha knew as soon as the gasp was out that he couldn't have been. Sledda had become king. His widow and son and grandsons were here.

'Lucky for him it was only a broken leg. He limped ever after.

'But Aethelbert swung down, hand over hand by the gable boards, and dropped on his feet as light as a cat. There wasn't a mark on him. He looked down at Sledda, groaning on the ground, with everyone fussing over him. Then he dusted his hands on his breeches and said, "Too bad you missed your hold", and sauntered off.

'I made up my mind that day. I told my father it was time he made a marriage alliance between Kent and Essex, and I was the princess to do it.'

'I know what you're telling me,' Bertha said slowly. 'To throw over the gods of your ancestors is a daring thing. In heathen eyes, it could have terrible risks. And risk is what Aethelbert loves above everything else. He's summoned Sledda's son here to taunt him with being too scared to follow him into Christ's kingdom.'

The grin flashed, without humour this time. 'He's never changed.'

'But Christ *should* change him. In baptism, he should be dying to his old life, rising as a new and better person.' Bertha looked round in alarm, but only her maid Edith sat studiously sewing at her feet. The ladies of Kent

161

and Essex were exchanging gossip and renewing friendships. She lowered her voice. 'Well, you're his sister. There are things I can say to you and no one else.'

'Aethelbert may not change because he's baptized a Christian, but Kent will. And in your favour. You'll be looking to the Continent now, even more than you already do, to Frankland and Gaul and Rome. The rest of us will be barbarians, who can't speak Latin. Oh, don't look so startled! I may be Dowager Queen of Essex, but I was born Kentish, too, remember. I was the one who told Aethelbert he'd do well to send overseas for a Frankish queen.'

'We women are gaming pieces on the board. If you married Sledda for love, you were lucky. But Aethelbert hasn't been such a bad husband to me.'

'He admires you. You stood up to his priests. He liked that. I'm surprised it's taken him this long to do the same. There are few men he'd let stand out against him, let alone a woman.'

'Perhaps it was *because* I'm a woman.' The blush was high in Bertha's cheeks. 'He didn't know how to fight me.'

'And so, we've all got to listen to this new priest of yours, before the baptism?'

'Aethelbert has commanded Bishop Augustine to preach to Sabert and all the East Saxon court. He wants to give you the chance of joining him in baptism tomorrow.'

'He's throwing down a challenge to Sledda's son.'

'Yes.'

'I wonder how poor Sabert will limp away from this one.'

It was Ricula herself who capitulated. Next morning, the Dowager Queen of Essex joined her brother, King of Kent. In the cathedral of Christ the Saviour, Augustine watched them come as in a dream. In turn, the tall Angles were divested, one by one, of the trappings of royalty: the golden coronet, the robe encrusted with more gold, neck chains heavy with jewels, precious rings, their fine woven tunics, down to a simple white tunic over naked flesh, like any commoner.

Aethelbert was first, of course. He would be the leader of his people in this, as in everything.

Bishop Augustine had touched no wine. He came fasting to administer this sacrament, like the baptismal candidates themselves. He felt that the slightest error or weakness on his part might invalidate this ceremony, bring his dream crashing in ruins on the very day of his triumph.

This was his triumph. This is what was intoxicating him. Here in Canterbury, this day, he, Augustine, was making Gregory's vision come true. The King of Kent was kneeling before him to ask for baptism. All

Kent would surely follow, and the other English kingdoms after it.

The warrior king was on his knees. The short white tunic barely hid his muscled body. He was as disturbing in his energetic physicality as when he wore the crown. Augustine looked down and saw how the pale hair was threaded with wiry grey. This was a ruler at the peak of his power. This conversion came at a God-given moment. The bishop bit his lip. He should be putting these power games out of his mind. This was a soul won for Christ. That was all that mattered.

It was not. Here before him was the king. The eternal salvation of thousands more hung on this. Christ Church was filled with the smoke of incense, making hazy the packed congregation when Augustine lifted his eyes. Blue clouds billowed under the rafters, until they became the massed faces of angels looking down. This was a pivotal moment in history. One man, one kingdom, a whole island.

He began the questions challenging Aethelbert to affirm his faith. Even as he spoke the familiar words he felt a warmth steal over his shoulders. This baptism, surely, would bring him the fulfilment of Gregory's promise: not Bishop of Kent now, but Archbishop of Britain. Gregory would send him the lambswool stole, embroidered with crosses by the nuns of St Agnes in Rome, the traditional symbol given to every archbishop.

'I will, so help me God.'

Aethelbert's grating voice recalled Augustine to the present. The king had sworn his oath to his new Lord. He would never dishonour himself by breaking it now. These Englishmen ranked loyalty to their lord above everything else.

It was time for the sponsors to pledge their support for him. They should have been kings, for a royal baptism. That had not been possible. There were, Augustine acknowledged, Christian kings in the west. Britons. No, that would never have done. Since the English invaded, the British had been cut off in their mountain refuges. They had drifted away from Rome. It was said their baptismal rite was suspect. So he had to make do with a Frankish prince, cousin to Bertha, and Bishop Liudhard, as baptismal sponsors for his royal convert.

These two were leading Aethelbert to the lead tank now. Augustine found himself standing thigh deep in the water. He did not remember how he had got there. The water the deacons had warmed for the first highborn candidates had cooled somewhat during the liturgy. The bishop felt the growing chill around his legs, but as if it was happening to another person.

Aethelbert stood before him now. He was alarmingly tall. Augustine saw with relief that Laurence was standing on his other side to help lift the king.

'I baptize you in the name of the Father ... and the Son ... and the Holy Spirit.'

He encircled the king's waist with his smaller arm and leaned swiftly forward. Aethelbert, no longer the King of Kent but a poor sinner, went under the water, dead to the works of Satan. It needed two men's strength to lift him upright again. He had not gasped or flinched. He went as bravely to this death as to an enemy's spears. But now a battle-cry burst from him. 'Alleluia!'

It was not in the liturgy.

Aethelbert shook the water from his eyes and grinned at them.

The two sponsors were quickly there with the large towel and the longer white baptismal robe. They replaced the golden crown on his dripping hair. He looked like an archangel: he smelt like a wet dog.

It was done. As short and simple as any other Christian baptism.

It changed everything.

Queen Ricula was next. Her sister-in-law, Bertha of Kent, was her royal sponsor, as was fitting. The wet white shift moulded itself against her still slender body, before the towels enfolded her. The brief immersion had hardly penetrated her tightly plaited hair. She, too, emerged clad in her baptismal gown.

The bishop and Bertha led her, smiling, out to the acclaim of the congregation. At the front of the nave, her son Sabert was seated, as was the right of a king, though her grandsons stood. He was chewing his beard. It will not be long, Augustine thought, staring hungrily at the King of Essex. You will give in to Aethelbert. Everyone does. You are only a client king. He is your overlord.

The dream was growing, as his monks chanted their psalm of joy, '*Oh be joyful in the Lord, all you lands!*'

Kent was secure. Then Essex, across the Thames. He must have a suitable bishop ready for the great port of London when the time came. Laurence? But he had planned him to be his own successor at Canterbury. Domitian was getting old. The hard journey across Europe had aged him further. Honorius?

And beyond? What if all the seven great kingdoms of the English fell under the spell of the cross? What if Woden and Thunor and Frig were no more?

His imagination widened as the psalm pealed out, '*We are his people and the sheep of his pasture.*' North and west, to the distant fastnesses where the Britons lingered still. Gregory had wanted him to be archbishop of the whole island. English and British under one primate. He would be a shepherd, too, to these wild ignorant tribes. They were truly lost sheep from the Christian fold. He would seek them out and bring them back to the flock of Rome, rejoicing.

Ricula was seated now in the chair beside her son. Not everyone was joining in the applause for her baptism. Three boys, arrogant, princely, behind Sabert's chair. Ricula's grandsons, with those impossible English names which all began with the same letter for one family. A frown brought tension back to Augustine's forehead. It was not hard to see from the asides behind the boys' hands, their barely suppressed laughter, that yet had anger in it, that they resented their grandmother's conversion.

King Sabert, he was almost sure of. He was a fish already hooked, who must be patiently drawn in. His mother would be a formidable ally. But the young princes? He glanced in alarm at Aethelbert's eldest son, too. The king had commanded Eadbald to be there. He had come. But no one could command his soul.

Suddenly the fragility of this great day hit Augustine. A kingdom could change overnight, with the conversion of its ruler. It could change back again, just as swiftly, when that king died.

Chapter Twenty-five

Peter, the Deacon, panted behind Gregory up the hill to St Andrew's monastery. He was getting overweight. He had not always got so out of breath. Gregory, by contrast, grew more cadaverous every day. Yet the pain of his illness did nothing to slow him down. Rather the opposite. It seemed as if he knew he could not have many years to live, and meant to waste no moment of them.

As the gap between them widened, Peter had more opportunity to see the ripple of recognition that ran through the passers-by. It was first surprise, then joy. Here was their Pope, their 'Papa', still walking among them. Yes, there were half-a-dozen of the Papal Guard, some little show of ceremony and security. But Gregory himself was the people's security. As long as he went among them, as long as they could cry out to him, they felt safe.

He turned his smile on them, out of the pallor of his face, and raised his hand to bless them. All up the road, people went down on their knees.

He knows, thought Peter. He knows what he needs to do to connect with people. It's worth the pain to him to be their Papa, Father to all the Romans.

Yet when he reached the gates of St Andrew's, Gregory put his hand on the bar and leaned his weight against it, his eyes closed. His face was grey, under the sweat. Peter pushed past the guards. He had the flask ready. He guided Gregory's shaking hand to his lips.

The porter was already swinging the gate open. Gregory was inside, in the house where he was born, in the monastery he had given to the Church, in the retreat where he wished, Peter knew, to die.

Gregory faced Mellitus across the abbot's parlour. The burly monk, with a red-veined nose that spread across his fleshy face, had been promoted from prior to the highest office since Augustine left. Gregory ran his fingers through what was left of his tonsured hair. The other hand held Augustine's latest letter.

'What am I to do with him? He tells me of victory, the king converted, miracles done. He's apparently even raised the dead. Julius, their cantor, brought the letter from Kent himself, and he confirms it. And yet, poor Augustine! He's such an *anxious* man. Look what he asks me. Can an expectant woman be baptized? Should he excommunicate converts if he finds they've married their stepmothers? How long after a sexual dream must a priest wait before he can celebrate mass?'

'These are serious questions, surely, Father? Our souls are daily endangered by our impure bodies.'

Gregory turned. There was another monk in the corner of the room. Paulinus was another who was tall for a Roman. He shared Gregory's energy too, though it took a different form. Where the Pope's face lit with laughter between his more habitual gravity, like an April sky, this younger monk's was always intense. The forward stoop of his shoulders, the hooked nose, the burning black eyes, made him look like some predatory bird, watching for carrion.

Gregory looked between the smiling, blunt-featured abbot and this cadaverous monk. He sighed and laughed. 'Of course. Adam sinned, and we all suffer. But God is merciful. When the first man and woman were driven from Paradise and lost immortality, God gave us instead childbirth. Yes, it's painful. You could say it was a punishment, but it's also God's gift, so that humanity will never die out. How can that gift make a woman unclean? Would you deny her baptism, even if it were in the very hour of her delivery, if you knew that without it she would die unredeemed?'

'You have a generous heart, Father.' From Paulinus's lips, that might almost have been a reproof.

'I learned my generosity from God, who gave His all for me, a sinner.'

Paulinus bowed silently. Abbot Mellitus shot him a look of reproof, and turned back to his papal visitor.

'I trust you're still going to tell Augustine that the English must break utterly with their heathen customs?'

'Of course. We can't have a Christian sleeping with his father's wife. But it would be unjust to excommunicate people for something done in the time before they know it was wrong. Augustine must guide them on the upward path, step by step, like little children.'

Gregory stood, gazing out of the window with a faraway expression. His hands held Augustine's latest letter against his breast. This is his little piece of England, Peter thought. Where he would have gone himself, if the Romans hadn't stopped him. His heart is there, though his feet will never be able to walk that land.

'Why are you telling me all this, Father?' Mellitus's matter-of-fact voice cut the silence. 'Augustine was prior here once, but he's Bishop of Kent now. What have his missionary problems to do with me? . . . Or is this why you've called for Father Paulinus to be here? Are you going to send him to the English too?'

Gregory's eyes swung slowly back to the abbot, as though he found it difficult to focus on this room in Rome. 'Why? I . . . Yes, of course, forgive me, I'm forgetting myself.' He looked around the sparsely furnished room, a little vaguely.

Mellitus hurried round from behind the desk where he had been standing. 'Please, holy Father, sit down.'

Peter helped Gregory to a seat and made him drink the watered wine Mellitus offered. Paulinus watched them, immobile.

'You're shrewd, as always, Mellitus. I have a reason for coming here.' Gregory leaned forward, his intensity matching Paulinus's now. 'I've long had a vision for Britain, and Augustine has begun it. Virgilius of Arles consecrated him a bishop. Now the King of Kent's converted, it's time to make good my promise of the archbishop's stole. Augustine, first Archbishop of the English. He'll like that.'

The abbot compressed his lips, as though stifling a comment.

'But, Father Mellitus,' Gregory went on, 'the field is now wide open. Aethelbert is lord of more than Kent. Augustine tells me all the other English kings acknowledge him their overlord. Surely Aethelbert's archbishop can gain access far beyond Kent? Canterbury needs reinforcements.' He twisted in his seat, spreading his hands to demonstrate his vision to them. 'We'll need more bishops, at other capitals and trading centres. A second archbishop, before long, for the north.

'The greatest port in Britain is London, in the neighbouring kingdom of Essex. Augustine has already baptized its queen, and he says Aethelbert will not be satisfied until the king is converted.. That's where our next bishop must be. I thought you, Mellitus, might be the man for the job.'

Peter saw the abbot's shock.

'I? Go to Britain?'

'That's what Augustine said,' Gregory laughed. 'But he went. In the end.'

'You want me to be Bishop of London . . . under Augustine as archbishop?'

Gregory's eyes were shrewd. 'You were chosen abbot of St Andrew's, where Augustine was prior. Does that mean you're too proud to serve under him?'

What could Mellitus do but bow his head in obedient humility.

'Of course,' Gregory added, 'you're the younger man. It is possible the see of London might one day have pre-eminence over Canterbury.' The silence that followed was full of understanding.

Gregory turned his gaze to Paulinus. 'And yes, you're right that I need Paulinus too. There is much to be done. The whole of north Britain is unexplored country for us. Those boys I found in the slave market were from Deira, with its capital at the old Roman city of York. We must find a way to reclaim it for Christ, too.'

Augustine hurried to the quayside. His skirt flapped at his ankles and the mud of the river road spattered from his sandalled feet in his haste. He was annoyed that he had been caught unawares by a freshening of the wind. A coastguard had galloped overland from the coast to say that the ship bearing passengers from Rome had turned into the River Stour. Augustine had calculated there would be several hours yet to prepare a dignified welcome.

The market crowds gave way before the hurrying monks. They were friendly enough now, since the king's baptism, yet they looked surprised at his haste. What is happening to my dignity? thought Augustine. Is this how the Archbishop of Britain should behave? Could I not have waited for them within the abbey with more decorum?

He forced a smile for a snot-smeared little girl and her still shorter brother, holding up their wondering faces to be blessed. The word had long run through Canterbury that this foreign priest could work miracles. His hand and lips moved instinctively. He still found it difficult to grasp the enormity of what had happened to him. To be plucked from his ordered life as prior of St Andrew's, where he had been not only disciplined himself, but disciplining others, and set down in this chaotic, unmapped situation. There were no rules, unless he made them. A whole kingdom, all his monks, even the young English converts he was beginning to train for the lowest orders of the clergy, all looked to him for answers. There was an infant English Church, and he was its father. He felt totally inadequate for the responsibility.

The sail coming up the river smote his heart a succession of shocks. First, relief that he would reach the wharf in time. Second, joy that into the strangeness of this foreign country, this alien language, were coming men from the heart of Rome, from his friend and spiritual father Gregory, from the dear abbey of St Andrew's itself. He could talk with them — gravely, of course, without excessive chatter — of events in Rome, of recent deliberations at the heart of the Church, of ecclesiastical scholarship. They would doubtless bring another letter from Gregory, his first since the great news of King Aethelbert's conversion. Gregory must surely be delighted about that.

Third, and unexpected by him, because he had so looked forward to this moment, he felt alarm.

Who were these men whom Gregory was sending to supply his need? One he knew certainly. Mellitus, abbot of St Andrew's. Mellitus, who had received Augustine when he came back to Rome with his tail between his legs, to say his monks were too afraid to go on to Britain.

Augustine came out on the wharf and the cool wet wind should have cooled his cheeks. But he felt his face hot with shame, remembering. Whatever his successes since, he would never forget Mellitus's eyes when he admitted his former prior back into St Andrew's. Surprise, scorn, condemnation. The new prior had been courteous, of course, and Augustine had saved the details of his story for the Pope, but Mellitus had known enough, and judged.

He watched the heavy Frankish ship bearing down on the quay, as once he and his monks had sailed up to Canterbury from Thanet. The sail was collapsing on the deck. A dark cloud was sweeping down on Augustine. Was this Gregory's judgement? That Augustine was not fit to hold the office he did, and better men must be sent from Rome to replace him?

'Father!' Honorius was at his elbow, steering him out of harm's way as mooring ropes flew through the air, crewmen sprang ashore, the big trading vessel was brought sweetly up to the wharf and made fast.

The gangplank was down. He had not scanned the ranks of passengers staring down from the deck. He would meet them soon enough. It would not, in any case, be seemly to wave, like some girl reunited with her sweetheart.

People were streaming ashore. And now there was no need to hunt through the throng of strangers for those he sought. They stood out at once, dramatic in their monastic black among the motley of browns and greens and yellows, as he and his party must stand out on the quay for them. Benedict, Augustine recalled, had decreed that his monks should wear only the natural colours of the local wool, but unrelieved black had become their custom.

They moved towards each other. He recognized Mellitus at once, though it seemed a lifetime since he had left the sunlight and the shadows of St Andrew's for a second, and final, time. That broad head, with the tonsure shaved close against it. The ample gown across a chest that was more brawny than plump. Mellitus looked more like a prize wrestler than a scholar, as though his features had been squashed by a fist.

'Welcome to Kent, my brothers.' With an effort, Augustine took the initiative. He even embraced Mellitus with a chaste kiss to each cheek. Then his hands retreated swiftly into his sleeves.

He looked beyond the abbot. That tall, lean, slightly stooping figure, with the intense face. Surely he had seen those burning black eyes before? The name edged back to him out of his past. 'Paulinus.'

The younger monk gave a half-smile, which lit his face with a sudden vividness, and vanished. 'Father Augustine.'

Still young, and yet evidently high in Gregory's favour. Out of older, more experienced monks in St Andrew's, Paulinus had been plucked to strengthen the English Church. It was a strange combination. The abbot

170

of St Andrew's himself, as though no one else could be good enough to meet this great need, and one much junior. Augustine knew from one look at those fierce dark eyes that Paulinus would not remain in obscurity long.

'And Rufinianus.' This monk, at least, Augustine felt no compulsion to remember. Older than Paulinus, but less impressive, with a pleasant olive-hued face and a deferential air. He was clearly relieved to be on solid ground again, and was looking around him at the English crowds with eager curiosity. He returned Augustine's greeting with a gratifying expression of admiration.

'And Father Justus.'

Augustine started. So strong was the bonding effect of the Benedictines' black habits that it had not occurred to him to include any other passenger. Now Mellitus was drawing forward a middle-aged man in a russet cloak. Not a monk, evidently. His dark brown hair was not tonsured, though neatly clipped. Yet 'Father'?

'A secular priest?' He could not help the surprise in his voice rising almost to censure.

'I'm afraid so, your grace,' smiled Father Justus. 'Does that upset you? I know you're all monks here, up to now.'

'Not at all, not at all. Be welcome.' Augustine offered the kiss of peace, belatedly. Thoughts were flying through his head. The unfinished abbey of Saints Peter and Paul in the meadow was not yet ready. They had been busy enough at their first crowded house within the walls, preparing makeshift quarters for yet more workers. It had not crossed Augustine's mind that these might include more than monks. Would a secular priest be content to live inside the abbey? Would he conform to their discipline of prayer and silence? Or would he require lodgings outside, among the English community of Canterbury, and a stipend to support this? Might he even, the thought made the archbishop shudder, have on his staff lesser secular clergy who might wish to marry?

They were turning for the city now, his own monks coming forward to escort the new arrivals, lifting the most precious personal baggage on to handcarts, arranging with the ship's master for the unloading and collection of the rest. What would they have brought with them? What books? What communion vessels? What relics of the saints?

'I have letters for you,' said Abbot Mellitus, tapping a bulge in his tunic. 'From the Pope himself.' His smile widened. 'I gather you've been asking him a lot of questions.'

Augustine felt the mockery. 'We're in a situation here no churchmen have faced before. There's never been a Church for the English. Everything is new to them. They're not like the Franks or Germans or Carthaginians. The first Archbishop of the English must seek counsel to

171

shape this Church to the converts' needs and our own missionary situation. You'll find out.'

'I bow to your judgement, Father,' said Mellitus gravely.

Chapter Twenty-six

It was an awkward meal. The king had summoned the newcomers from Rome to his palace. As he paced outdoors in front of the hall, waiting to greet them, Aethelbert's face was turned up to the restless sky. Bertha sensed the widening of his ambition. Her powerful Frankish family were no longer enough for him. Augustine had brought him the breath of a warmer wind from the south, old echoes of empire. Aethelbert boasted that his Germanic forebears had never been conquered by that Roman Empire. Now he dreamed himself the equal of its emperors.

She smiled, more in tenderness than mockery. Poor Aethelbert. He could have no idea what that empire meant. How could he imagine the glories of Rome, of Lyons, of Arles, with only the crumbling stones of Canterbury for evidence? How could he compare a horde of English spearmen to the disciplined might of the Roman legions?

No doubt he saw this new wave of Romans coming as ecclesiastical servants to do his bidding, to enlarge his influence. He, Aethelbert, carrying the banner of the King of kings, alone among the English rulers, until he had bullied all the lesser kings into submission to the Cross, and to himself.

And yet . . . Her heart twisted at the sight of that bearded face, the energy of this man striding to and fro in front of her. The flash of his blue-grey eyes still thrilled her. Here was a warrior like few other men, and she had grown up among powerful kings. After all, the empire of the legions was long past. The imperial court had retreated to faraway Constantinople. Rome itself was defended now only by Pope Gregory. Hadn't Europe become a forest in which the stags of many nations were locking their antlers in battle? Old Rome had given them a vision of ultimate power, and then abandoned them. Why should it not be an English king who won pre-eminence over the new nations? She felt a shiver of excitement.

They were here. Father Mellitus, that big bluff man who seemed to overshadow the smaller Augustine. The younger Paulinus, tall and unsmiling. Even standing behind his superiors he had an intensity which dominated the group. She felt a tingle of recognition. For all the contrast between his unrelieved black, his grave silence, and Aethelbert's gaudy finery and loud-voiced hectoring, these two tall men were not unlike. Neither had a presence you could ever ignore. Father Rufinianus she noticed only as a pleasant, unassuming supporter.

Justus was the one who caught the king's attention. Aethelbert looked the Roman up and down, taking in his blue gown, trimmed with a discreet border of richer braid.

'Are you a priest?'

He was taken unawares by Justus's incomprehension. So diligent had Augustine's monks been in learning the English language that Aethelbert had forgotten the experience of meeting men who spoke only Latin. Bertha moved swiftly to translate, and registered too late that her husband was subtly humiliated by this. She beckoned Tyrri forward. The boy was studying enthusiastically in Augustine's school. The king could take pride in the cleverness of an English boy. He need not be reminded of the more cosmopolitan culture of his Frankish wife.

'I am indeed a priest, your majesty.' Justus bowed. 'But not a monk.' Seeing the puzzled frown which greeted the translation, he explained. 'You're familiar with Father Augustine and the monks of his monastery, but not all the priests of the Christian Church are monks, by a long way. Monks take vows to live under a rule of obedience, in community, away from the temptations of wealth and women. A little like your own army, I imagine, when you lead them to war. But with monks, the discipline is for life. I'm a secular priest. I live among my people. I'm the father of a varied family. Men, women, children. Not of the flesh, you understand; I'm unmarried. Think of me as a shepherd who wraps himself in his cloak and curls up in the sheepfold with his flock at night.'

He smiled, urbane, courteous, as though already at home in this Anglo-Saxon feasting hall.

Aethelbert eyed the other newcomers suspiciously, aware that here too, his lack of Latin, more than theirs of English, would wrongfoot him. Language was a barrier to him, but not to his wife.

Deliberately, he steered Augustine, Laurence and Honorius, to Bertha's side of the table, Mellitus and his three companions to his own. Here, her fluency could no longer disguise these strangers' ignorance of English. The contest became equal again.

The monks picked sparingly at the hunks of meat, laying them aside when they had eaten enough to satisfy courtesy. The priest Justus, though, ate with appetite and enjoyment. Mellitus complimented the Kentish king on the quality of his wine. His voice betrayed genuine surprise that the English were quaffing more than home-brewed beer. Aethelbert grinned. His status was rising in their eyes.

Bertha was aware that her husband's glance was going frequently to the heavy satchel Mellitus had brought with him. She, too, was excited by the knowledge that it must contain gifts from Rome, from the Pope himself. There would doubtless be letters as well, all the way from the centre of the Church to this island on the edge of Christendom. But first, etiquette demanded that she feed their guests and talk pleasantries until the meal was over.

The time had come. Aethelbert's eyes widened as the bag was opened. Byzantine jewellery, like nothing the English king had ever worn. Plaques of silver, set with lapis lazuli, hung row upon row, like a breastplate. A set of twelve gold spoons, each with the figure of an apostle. A lovely flagon of twisted green glass, which must have cost Mellitus heart-stopping moments to bring safe from Rome. Bertha leaned forward with an instinctive gasp as the last gift was unwrapped. Within the linen was the hilt of an ancient sword with a broken blade.

Mellitus explained. 'This is the weapon with which Saint Peter struck off the ear of a soldier who was arresting Jesus, whom the Lord immediately healed.'

Aethelbert touched it, frowning. 'Why does the Pope send me this? A broken sword may be well enough for a Jewish fisherman, but an English king must defend his land and his people.'

'It is a symbol, your majesty,' Mellitus said smoothly. 'The greatest kings on earth submit their weapons to the Lord of Hosts.'

'And take them up again to defend his honour?'

'As you say, your majesty.'

There were indeed letters. With a wave of his hand, Aethelbert summoned Bertha's chaplain, Liudhard, then waved him aside and chose instead Honorius, who spoke fluent English. The king leaned back in his chair, apparently at ease, as though his dignity, not his illiteracy, required someone else should read this letter aloud.

Pope Gregory spoke of his joy in the king's conversion, of the good he was already bringing to his kingdom, and of the hopes that Aethelbert would use his influence to spread the Gospel of Christ further still. He should stamp out the worship of idols.

'Do you hear that?' Aethelbert rounded on Augustine with glee. 'What say we make a raid on Thanet? Cut down that oak tree. Set fire to their temple. Let the god of thunder and lightning go up in flames. See how Thurwald likes that!'

He was half drunk by now. Bertha could see he was driven by fear as much as zeal. All his life, that sacred island had thrown its shadow of terror and awe over him and his people. It was there he had quarantined Augustine and his monks, as sorcerers carrying foreign magic. It was there she had accompanied him to hear the Romans, setting foot for the very first time on its bloodstained soil. She and Aethelbert had sat under that

175

oak, hearing the chant of the litany coming nearer and nearer. She had watched the silver cross emerge from the trees, then the banner with the face of Christ. Poor Titus! She had a fond vision of that proud boy, with his shining black face, carrying the silver cross.

Hearing Aethelbert's shout, she knew what was making his voice rise. Did he really have the courage to destroy the sanctuary of his family's gods? Precisely because he dreaded this act, his honour was goading him to do it. What agony might he suffer afterwards, when Thanet lay in ashes?

She ached to lay her hand over his in reassurance. Would he accept it? She began to move unobtrusively towards the fist grasping the carved armrest beside her.

Mellitus's hand moved too, to a fold in his tunic. He brought out a slimmer letter.

'Permit me, your majesty. The holy Father did indeed give me that letter for you, with another for Archbishop Augustine.' He bowed to the abbot of Canterbury, and crimson flooded Augustine's face. Gregory had fulfilled his promise. Mellitus had brought him the archiepiscopal stole.

Mellitus turned back to the king. 'But when we were already in Gaul, a messenger came galloping after us. The Pope, who cares for all of us like a father, was concerned that he had had no news of our progress. He feared for our safety. But also, he had a fresh message for me, to add to your letter. After much prayer, the holy Father is convinced that it would be a mistake to destroy utterly the temples of your people. Where are the churches yet, to replace them? Where are your people meant to worship Christ?

'He recommends instead that you take out the idols and burn them in public. That will be enough. The buildings, if they are sound, can remain. We priests will cleanse them thoroughly and rededicate them to the one true God. The people will come more readily to worship in a place they already know. And if they've been used to sacrificing beasts to their gods at certain seasons, Pope Gregory bids us find a saint's day thereabouts. Then your people can still hold a feast, and give praise to our God instead of their heathen rituals. He wants to open his arms wide to draw in as many of your subjects as possible, not to drive a wedge through your kingdom.'

Aethelbert stiffened into silence, chewing the edge of his moustache. Bertha knew the turmoil he was feeling. To drag those sacred idols out of the temple and burn them was dreadful enough, but something of the past would remain. It would be like stepping into a fast-flowing river, yet keeping hold of a tree. Aethelbert's warrior spirit raged at the thought that he might seem to be clinging on from cowardice.

Mellitus laid the second letter before him on the grease-spattered table.

Aethelbert stared down at the writing, as though he could indeed read it.

'You churchmen are soft,' he said. 'That's not how a real king wins victory. You need to destroy the enemy's stronghold, so he can't take it back from you.' He shot a venomous look at his eldest son. 'Well, have your way, then. Let the temples stand.'

At last, Bertha allowed her hand to fall over his. The lightest squeeze complimented him on his statesmanship.

Augustine's hand unfolded the wrappings and the slightest gasp escaped his lips. Here was his dream made reality. A simple stole, no splendour of purple or gold. Soft white lamb's wool, embroidered with crosses by the nuns of St Agnes in Rome. The stole sent to every archbishop by his pope. Gregory's gift to Augustine. His hand reached out, and hesitated.

'Go on, Father,' Laurence's quiet voice urged him. 'It's yours, and richly earned.'

His fingertips touched the softness. Still he hardly dared to pick it up, in case this dream should dissolve in the daylight.

'Let me, Father.'

Laurence might be prior now, but his hands retained their infirmarian's sensitive touch. He lifted the stole and placed it gently around Augustine's neck. The understated white wool now made its own drama against the monastic black robe.

'Archbishop to the English,' he smiled at his leader. 'Congratulations, Father.'

Augustine could not speak. He had fulfilled his mission. Gregory was proud of him.

He was still feeling the remembered touch of the wool against his neck as he paced the new abbey estate outside the city walls. He had no great love of the English countryside. The lushness of the grass, the sprawling copses, the brambles and weeds which seemed to spring fully-grown overnight, all threatened his sense of simplicity and discipline. Yet a possibly unworthy warmth was beginning to grow that all this was now his. Not personally, of course, a monk renounces personal property, but as Archbishop of Canterbury, head of the English Church. The construction activity in this meadow, given him by the king, was the visible measure of his achievement in Kent.

Workmen and monks were busy here now, as once they had worked to build the monks' first community house within the city. Here, there was room to expand the monastery. The reinforcements from Rome had made demands on the already limited space. They were attracting more English recruits to the school. Augustine examined the foundation holes for the new classroom with satisfaction. One day, when these boys were competently literate and schooled in Latin, when they had passed through the ranks of acolyte and minor clergy, he would be able to ordain the first English priests.

If he lived that long. There was a nagging pain in his belly which troubled him.

'It's very impressive. You must be proud of it. But it doesn't feel quite so much our place, any more, does it, Father?'

Laurence was at his elbow, interrupting Augustine's agreeable train of thought. He had been promoted from infirmarian to prior, and shadowed Augustine more often now as his second-in-command than Honorius.

'It was never our place. It's God's.'

'I'm rebuked, Father. . . . But all the same, we'd got into our own way of doing things. Now these brothers come fresh from Rome, I feel as though they're inspecting us, putting us right. In love, of course.'

'Pope Gregory has sent me invaluable advice. There were many things troubling me about our new English Church. He recommends that I take the best of all I've seen, in Rome, in Gaul, among the Franks, and bind them into a sheaf suitable for the English.'

'And he sent you the archbishop's stole. That's all the confirmation you need, Father. It was well deserved.'

A spasm crossed Augustine's face. Could Laurence see the hurt?

'His letter was not all congratulation. He rebukes me for taking pride in healing miracles.'

'Father!' the former infirmarian protested. 'Those were cases far beyond my own skill. When Titus was struck by a stone. Oh, I know, you couldn't save him afterwards in the ambush. But there was that girl given up for dead. Surely these are signs which turned the hearts of the Kentish people to the Gospel?'

'The Holy Father is right. I should not have boasted about it.'

He had wanted so much to rise in Gregory's estimation.

'But Pope Gregory has great confidence in you. He's sent the Abbot of St Andrew's himself to serve under you. All the same, I confess I wasn't sorry when you packed Father Mellitus off to Essex with King Sabert.'

'Did I do right? His English is still so poor.'

'He has interpreters, as we did at first. You must admit, Father, Canterbury feels more our own place again without him.'

'We're only sojourners on this earth. . . . You don't suppose . . . that the Holy Father sees Mellitus as my successor?'

'As abbot here? Or as archbishop?'

Augustine stopped his measured pace and turned to face Laurence. The other monk's face was lined now, making him look older than his years. Long nights watching at sickbeds had taken their toll, added to the regular calls to prayer in the darkness which every monk submitted to. The new role of prior, overseeing the discipline of the abbey, carried its own burden, but Laurence must find its more predictable timetable a relief.

'When this new monastery is complete, we shall need a new abbot. But that's not a job for either of us. The English Church is growing far bigger than Canterbury. An archbishop must take care of a wider family, monastic and secular, ordained and lay, from royal households in their palaces to the humblest slaves tending pigs. One day, it will stretch across kingdoms we haven't even set foot in yet. It's my wish that, when I'm dead, you should follow me, not as abbot, but as the head of this Church.'

He saw the shock in Laurence's eyes, the moment of doubt when he thought he must have misunderstood, and then the joy.

'Me, Father?'

'You are, in every way worthy. Mellitus can't even speak English yet. You know these people. I think you love them.'

Colour and confusion in Laurence's face. 'Yes, particularly the young ones. That half-British maid of the queen's, Edith. And young Tyrri and Gosfraeg. I see the future in their faces. But is it . . . can you. . . ?'

'Is the Archbishopric of Britain in my gift? Well, no. Only the Pope can send the stole from Rome. But Gregory trusts me. When I tell him my decision, I think he will respect my judgement.'

A boy came running from the city gate across the meadow towards them, jumping the foundation holes in his way.

'What news, Gosfraeg, that gets you so much out of breath?'

'The king wants to see you, Father.'

'When?'

'Now.'

'Do you know why?'

Gosfraeg grinned. 'He didn't say. But there were horsemen from Essex in the yard.'

Laurence raised his eyebrows at his archbishop in an unspoken question.

'Yes, Laurence, escort me. Do you have your wax tablet with you? Take notes, if necessary.'

Archbishop and prior quickened their steps towards the palace. Gosfraeg skipped alongside.

'Do you know what I think, Father? If there's a message from Essex, and the king's sent for you, I reckon Father Mellitus has persuaded King Sabert to turn Christian.'

Augustine and Laurence's eyes met, but not with unmixed joy. Augsustine read the sympathy in his prior's face. They were both reappraising the score of success between the Archbishop of Canterbury and the former Abbot of St Andrew's.

*

There was a new church on the hill just north of the Thames. No stone walls here, yet it was a fine English hall to honour the King of kings, planked and thatched. The port of London was Sabert's, in his kingdom of Essex, yet it was not he who had provided this church for his own baptism. His uncle and over-king, Aethelbert of Kent, had stamped this visible mark on his nephew's city.

Power, Augustine thought, walking in procession up the hill from the river crossing. When I preached to Sabert in Canterbury, I wanted him to respond from his heart to my offer of the good news of Jesus Christ. No doubt Mellitus did too. But for the overlord of Britain, this is one more occasion to assert his dominance over a vassal king.

Yet, at the top of the hill, the archbishop stood in the wind outside the new St Paul's and his spirit lifted with the wind which tugged at his mitre. They were winning. Across the rolling woods beyond London reared another hill, with another temple. Great Harrow, sacred to Woden and Thunor and the rest of that heathen crew.

'A pity we couldn't have set a torch to that,' muttered a voice behind him. Augustine swung round. It was Justus, the secular priest sent from Rome with Mellitus.

'It's beyond Sabert's borders, and Gregory forbade it,' the archbishop reproved him. 'He'd rather we cleansed and changed such places.'

'Playing with fire. We'd be better off using real flames on it. Leave one bit of dirty bedding in a house, and the fleas will be all over you again next morning.'

Augustine looked about him at the procession marshalling itself to enter the church. Here was the King of Essex. To the joy of his mother, he was coming to join her in Christ's family. But Augustine saw, too, the story of Kent's conversion repeated. Aethelbert had not been able to compel his own son Eadbald to baptism. Augustine himself had forbidden coercion. So King Sabert's three arrogant sons, Sexred, Saeward and Sigbert, stood fiddling with their jewellery and tossing their hair, ostentatiously distancing themselves from their father's decision. He could compel them to witness his baptism, but not to share it.

Beyond them was a knot of Roman churchmen, waiting for their archbishop. Augustine should have viewed their presence with joy. Instead, he felt threatened.

It was time. The archbishop led the royal procession into the long, lofty nave. The twittering of sparrows on the new-cut rafters was overwhelmed by the full-throated chant of men's voices as the cross was carried up the steps to the altar. Kings and queens, princes and princesses, nobles and courtiers, took their places. Augustine turned to face the splendid congregation which filled the nave. Now a second procession entered.

This is the next generation, Augustine thought, as Mellitus was led forward by his companions, Paulinus and Rufinianus. Did Laurence speak the truth when he said the Pope sent him from Rome to serve under me? Or has Gregory at last seen me for what I am, weak, inadequate, irresolute, and sent this man as my successor?

He watched the blunt-featured, brawny missionary approach. Mellitus would not have run back from that first journey. He would never have yielded to the fearful complaints of his monks and returned to ask Gregory to release them. Mellitus would have thundered at them to obey the Pope's command, their Lord's command, though death was their reward. Mellitus would not send letters to Rome full of anxious enquiries about whether he was doing the right thing. He will make up his mind what is good for the English, and tell them his rules.

The bigger monk approached, grave now, dark-haired, dark-eyed, through the ranks of fair Saxons. The richness of his gold-embroidered cope blazed in the light of hundreds of candles. As yet he wore no mitre. Why do I feel, thought Augustine, that he is a greater man than I am? That he is Gregory's favourite and confidant now, not I? That when he is bishop here, London, not Canterbury, will become the ecclesiastical capital of Britain?

Fool, you're still archbishop, not Mellitus. Gregory does see the power of Canterbury passing to London, but not in your lifetime. He's promised. And there'll be another archbishopric in York, for the north, God willing, to balance London's power. You're safe. You're Archbishop of all Britain, for now.

Yet he felt a smaller man than Mellitus, when the former abbot of St Andrew's knelt at his feet. Augustine spoke the words of consecration. There were no other bishops, as there should have been, to crowd around and lay their hands, with his, on Mellitus's tonsured head. The elderly Liudhard lay sick in Canterbury. Augustine's authority alone made Mellitus Bishop of London. When his hands had set the mitre on the Roman's head, he alone raised the new bishop to his feet, planted the fraternal kisses on his stubbly cheek.

There were other shadows too, beyond the gold of Mellitus's cope. Tall, saturnine Paulinus, watchful as a hawk. Rufinianus plumper, less threatening. Justus, always a jolt to his senses in the vestments of a secular priest, with his untonsured hair. They would need more bishops yet as the number of converts grew. Which of these would he pick?

For a moment, he had almost forgotten the royal baptism which was still to follow. Mellitus had not. It was his preaching, not Augustine's which had at last brought King Sabert to this decision. This was his day of double glory. A bishopric, the first in the kingdom of Essex, and the King of Essex coming to him for baptism.

The ceremony passed in a haze of incense, candle smoke, vows demanded and made, the splashing of water. There was the shedding of royal robes and the donning of baptismal white. And still the princes of Essex smirked and fidgeted, while their father changed the course of his kingdom. Scores of East Saxons followed their king, like loyal warriors into battle. The three princes did not.

Afterwards, outside, the wide English horizons swung again across Augustine's view. Essex, Kent across the river, Middlesex to the west. How many more, rolling away to the unseen hills over the horizon? Sussex, Wessex, Mercia. All with their heathen kings. All hanging, like fruit waiting to drop. That was how Gregory saw it from Rome.

And still the temple on Harrow reared towards the sky, where the thunderclouds were beginning to gather.

'It could come back,' growled Justus. 'Another generation could overthrow everything we're doing.'

'We must change the people's hearts,' said Augustine. 'Loyalty to their earthly king is not enough. Kings change.' He looked round hastily, lest Aethelbert should have overheard.

'That's what the British did,' said Laurence, unexpectedly, on his other side. 'A hundred years and more, some of their people kept the faith without a priest. Women, mostly, mother to child, according to Edith. That's how the Word survived until we came.'

'British priests?' Justus almost spat. 'They cut and ran when the English longships appeared. Off to their mountains in the west. And will they come out to preach salvation to the English? They will not.'

'The British suffered,' Laurence said gently. 'By all accounts they were slaughtered by the thousand. The English didn't spare priests or nuns. The rest were driven westward, or enslaved. You'd hardly expect them to extend the hand of love to their enemies.'

'If a man hits you on one cheek, turn the other to him. Isn't that what the Lord said?'

There was silence. Then, Laurence murmured, 'Yes, but it's hard to do.'

'Father,' Justus insisted, 'how long are you going to put up with that disgraceful crew of Welshmen? The British bishops, or so they style themselves. You're archbishop of the whole island, aren't you? So Pope Gregory says. Isn't it time you brought them to heel? Made them face up to their responsibilities? Put them right on their barbaric ways, like the wrong date for Easter and their outlandish baptismal rite?'

'I?' Augustine was startled.

'Who else? We've only got one archbishop.'

Again, that sense of threat. Why did this new wave of Romans seem so much more confident, more sure of their power?

The procession was forming again, back to King Sabert's palace for a feast. Augustine was grateful to let himself be swept up in it. Mellitus, resplendent in his new mitre, was talking animatedly to the East Saxon king. His English, Augustine noted with some alarm, had improved rapidly. Queen Ricula and Queen Bertha were laughing with King Aethelbert. Archbishop though he was, Augustine felt small and redundant. He looked again to where the clouds were darkening in the west. The horizon that had offered such promise was lowering, closing in on him.

Aethelbert turned suddenly to him, with that savage grin which he found so alarming. 'Well, Archbishop? That's Essex captured. Where shall we move next?'

Chapter Twenty-seven

'You're coming on a progress with us. It's time I showed my face in the west. Make sure those bucks in Sussex and Wessex understand who's king of the forest.' That glare and grin combined, which could send a shudder down the spine of another Saxon king. Aethelbert of Kent leaned forward to his archbishop, as he might to examine a newly bought horse. 'I particularly wish to leave my mark on the Hwicce on the banks of the Severn. Too far from Kent for comfort. They need to know who's boss. You could be useful to me there.'

'I?' Augustine flinched from the intensity of Aethelbert's eyes. They demanded so much of those who came under their scrutiny.

'Why not? My wife never stirs from Canterbury without that beanpole of a Frankish chaplain, and those two are staying at home this time. I'm a Christian king. I need to take my priest with me, don't I? And mine comes all the way from Rome.'

Augustine thought, that's all I am to him. Not his spiritual director, but a status symbol. He wants to flaunt me before his Saxon underlings. I'm Roman, symbol of metropolitan culture, of empire, of world dominion. His wants to show his fellow Englishmen they're still barbarians.

'Your majesty, I have many able Roman priests I could assign to your household for this honour. Father Justus, for example. I'm Archbishop of all Kent and Essex. I have a growing church to administer.'

'And you're content to stop there? Two kingdoms? Are your ambitions so small? Little priest, I'm offering you the chance to preach the Gospel to kings from Kent to the borders of the Welsh.'

Augustine's mouth fell open. Could that be true? Did Aethelbert have the authority to demand that the King of Sussex, the King of Wessex, the King of the Hwicce listen to him? Apparently he had.

To the borders of the Welsh? There swam into his mind a vision of blue mountains, inhabited by a race like Edith's mother's people. The Christian British, separated from Rome by two centuries of loss and ignorance.

'I see you take my meaning. Power, Augustine. I have power and I mean to use it, and increase it. You shouldn't turn white when I offer you a share in the spoils.'

'No, your majesty. I'm sorry. I should have understood the meaning of your invitation sooner.'

His heart was racing. If only this was St Andrew's in Rome, and Gregory just a few streets away in the Lateran Palace. He could have sped to his friend and hero, and told him the joyful news. I'm to preach to half the English kings. I may even, God willing, find a way to reach the recalcitrant Britons and bring them back into the fold of the Mother Church. I'm fulfilling your dreams!

Deep into the west they rode, into a land Augustine thought of as wrapped in superstitious mystery. The king's party, with a cohort of picked spearmen at their back, passed over the bare chalk hills. The tracks sank deeper into the softly yielding earth, banks rose taller on either side, trees grew more lushly, cloaked with emerald moss on their northern sides. At last the ridgeway ran out and they dipped down towards the vast wet plain of a mighty river.

'The Severn.' Aethelbert reined in his horse to survey it. There was the glint of challenge in his eyes. 'For now, it serves as a boundary between us and the Britons. But it won't be for ever.'

Augustine looked down on the glistening mudflats with relief. The end of this long journey was in sight. It had been a painful ride.

Beyond the broad estuary, grey mountains rose indistinctly into rain-clouds. Even in this poor visibility, Augustine could see the difference. No such wilderness had reared above the rolling English hills they had crossed. These Germanic conquerors had tamed the lands of Kent and Sussex and Wessex. Even the contours seemed to bow to the rule of Aethelbert and of the kings who honoured him as overlord. No one had yet tamed those Welsh mountains, where the Britons had fled.

'Strange.' Honorius was the most senior of the small retinue of monks Augustine had brought with him. He voiced his archbishop's own thought. 'We're standing in a land of heathens here, and they say the British across that river are Christians. Yet somehow I feel more at home among Saxons than I would over there. If the Britons are as wild as their mountains, who knows how they've mangled the Christian faith by now. There are rumours of strange rites among them, aren't there?'

'I'm told their monks know nothing of St Peter's tonsure.'

'The British have monks?'

'They use that name, though whether their practices conform to the Benedictine Rule is another matter. We shave our scalps as a reminder of Christ's cross of thorns. Apparently they shave their heads in front and let the hair hang down long behind. I've heard . . .' – he gave a fastidious shudder – 'this was the fashion of their old pagan priests.'

'The ones they call druids?'

185

'I fear so. Who knows how else they've become corrupt. They keep a different calendar of festivals from ours. Their calculation of Easter may make it fall on another Sunday than ours.'

'Well, then, Father, we're here to set them right.'

'If we ever meet them.'

They followed Aethelbert down the slope to the flood plain and the last Saxon stronghold before the Severn, the palace of the King of the Hwicce.

Augustine preached to the court at Aust, as he had in other palaces across the south. None of the lesser kings they visited had made a commitment to Christ, braving Aethelbert's wrath. Here, King Tondbert listened courteously. In the presence of his overlord he had little choice. He even gave the archbishop a silver cup in praise of his sermon. Augustine accepted it courteously for the use of Church. But behind the royal smile there was little to encourage him. The king's visitors must understand he could not make such a grave decision lightly. The foreign priest had spoken winningly, but a king must first gain the consent of his nobles and sages in council. King Aethelbert and Archbishop Augustine could be sure he would try his best to persuade them. His smile was wide, but without warmth. This Christianity was obviously the coming thing. If such a great lord as King Aethelbert believed, who was Tondbert to argue for their old gods?

'I feel as though I'm beating my staff on one of his mud-banks,' said Augustine to Honorius afterwards in frustration. 'I think I've made a deep impression. Then, before my eyes, the mud oozes back and it's as if I'd never been there. I fear if I stayed here long, I might be sucked down too.'

But next morning, Tondbert had news for them. 'King Aethelbert tells me you want to speak with the British holy men over the Severn. The writ of my spears runs on both banks of this river. I can send a boat across with a messenger to their local chief. He'll know where to find them.'

'Well enough for these priests, my friend, but I have business further up the Severn.' Aethelbert was a man to grasp whatever opportunity he saw to strengthen his power.

'I'm not kicking my heels on your mudflats, while you round up these Welshmen from their hills like stray sheep. The Mercians on your northern border sit a bit too lightly to my authority for my liking. I think I'll surprise them, with the sight of my face and the edge of my spears.'

'Do you require me to accompany you, your majesty? What if the Britons arrive while I'm away?' Augustine was dismayed. Never before had the King of Kent demanded his services as a military chaplain.

'No, little monk,' grinned Aethelbert. 'Stay here and wait for your Welsh cousins. But don't think I'm ever going to own them as brothers, just because they call themselves Christians. I mean to finish the job I've started. With your God on my side, the Island of Britain is going to be English from the east coast to the west. I'll take Honorius off your hands to pray for my victory over any Mercian warbands.'

The older Roman paled, but he could not refuse. Augustine was left with only the younger monks to attend him.

The reply came four days later. Bishops and abbots from the British kingdom of Gwent, across the river, would meet this ambassador from Rome to hear what he had to say to them. The place was set at a great oak beside the River Severn.

Chapter Twenty-eight

Augustine and his party of monks, with their escort of English spearmen, approached the oak tree on the banks of the Severn. As so often, Maurice was carrying Gregory's silver cross before them. The monks were chanting. It woke disturbing echoes of that procession on Thanet, when they had emerged from the woods to find King Aethelbert and Queen Bertha seated under Thunor's Oak.

A wave of optimism surged through Augustine, banishing temporarily the chill of doubt. He had preached Christ to the heathen king then, and won him. First, he had gained a foothold in Canterbury, then the conversion of a kingdom. God would surely aid him here, too.

There was a knot of people already waiting. The British party were here before the Romans. As he drew closer, Augustine was dismayed to find that this was, indeed, to be another conference in the open air, with only the oak tree for shelter in the uncertain British weather. He should have taken charge of the situation before this and insisted on a suitable hall. Instinctively, he turned to share his indignation with Honorius. He had forgotten the sturdy monk was no longer with him.

The group of Britons was taking shape now as individuals. All their faces were turned towards the newcomers. Augustine felt a new regret, that he and his monks had not arrived first, to claim the status of hosts. It was he, after all, who had summoned the British to meet him here. Instead, he was being made to feel like a stranger.

He was dismayed to find his heart was pounding uncomfortably and he was short of breath. He had never before met a British priest, let alone a whole delegation. What would they be like? How different were they, really?

Was this how Gregory had felt, standing on the walls of Rome, watching for a Lombard army to appear? There was something not quite right with that analogy. It was the British who were on their home ground here, or very close to it, while he had travelled hundreds of miles. Was this what was making him feel uncomfortable?

He could see them clearly now. He shivered, as if in the presence of something malign. Some of their party were indeed wearing the tonsure he had described to Honorius. They had shaved their hair back from their foreheads, making their brows look immensely large. It gave an unfortunate impression of deep wisdom. The Romans, with their circular tonsure, must appear low-browed by contrast. Augustine noticed with further distaste that the locks behind, which the British let fall to their shoulders, had rarely been visited by a comb. Their tunics were strange to his eyes. There was hardly a sober black among them. They were a motley flock, mostly of creamy white, some brown, just whatever came off the sheep's back. There was no evidence of Benedictine discipline.

As he approached them, he felt the absence of Honorius keenly, his loyal companion since they had left Rome. Honorius would have walked just behind his archbishop, breaking monastic custom occasionally with his shrewd muttered comments. The younger monks he had brought maintained a proper, if unhelpful, silence.

He saw that not all the British party were monks. The British apparently had secular bishops, too. There was one there with a crozier in his hand, but untonsured.

They stood waiting for him in the open air, though benches had been set under the branches and there was a light spattering of rain on the wind. Good, thought Augustine, they know what is due to me as archbishop. I should not have liked to find them seated, in possession, and have to make my entrance into the circle as the newcomer.

In preparing for this meeting, he had asked his English hosts if they could find translators who spoke the British language. It had taken Honorius to remind him that these churchmen would surely speak Latin. 'In Wales?' Augustine had asked, using the English name for the unconquered lands west of the Severn. 'Welsh, they may be, but they're still part of the one universal Church, so they claim,' Honorius had replied.

Yet it was now a shock to hear those familiar words on the wind in Latin: 'Peace be with you.' The accent was outlandish, but the sounds recognizable. He had expected their speech would be harsh, like gulls' cries, yet this was a singing call. It carried easily over the distance between them.

All the same, when he came closer, he saw from their faces that this was not the warm welcome the words of peace implied. One of their monk-bishops stepped forward. It was more of a challenge than an introduction.

'I am Enoch, Abbot of Caerwent, this, Abbot Fracan of Llantam and this,' – indicating the secular bishop – 'is Beuno, Bishop of Llandaff.' This Enoch was clearly a bishop also, since he carried a crozier, yet he spoke as though his title of abbot were the greater honour.

There were lesser clergy behind, with more outlandish names, and some monks Enoch named as scholars, though they looked more like weather-stained vagrants from off the hills.

Bishop Beuno, by contrast, was a smiling, round-cheeked man. His tone was more conciliatory. 'Welcome to Britain, Brothers.'

He was standing on English territory, east of the Severn, yet, thought Augustine, the Welshman spoke as though the whole island were still theirs.

'Peace be with you all. I bring you the blessing of Pope Gregory, Bishop of Rome and Head of the Universal Church.'

Abbot Enoch snorted. 'And you've come all the way to the Severn to give us that message?'

'The Holy Father has made me Archbishop of all Britain. He wishes me to visit the whole of my province and see that all is as it should be.'

'In Britain, we rule our own Church.'

Augustine felt his spirit quail. It was easy for Gregory to sound so calm, so sure, sitting in Rome making his plans for this Church which he had never seen. Did he think he had only to designate Augustine head of the Church in Britain and his plan would become fact? He could feel hostility emanating from the ranks of Welsh clergy.

'Rome and Britain have been separated for a long time. It is my duty to tell you about what has been happening in the councils of Europe and Asia. It is possible that here, on the furthermost edge of the world, you have become out of touch.'

Abbot Fracan broke in. 'It is possible that here, in the land of saints, we have stayed true to the old ways, while other churches change.'

Bishop Beuno looked from one angry face to another. 'Would it not be better to sit down and hear each other in good order? Bishop Augustine requested this meeting and we agreed to hold council with him.'

Even to move into the circle of benches meant a jostling of diplomatic niceties. Augustine expected to be motioned through first, with the respect due to his seniority of rank. Instead, Abbot Enoch marched ahead, with Abbot Fracan close behind him. The chubby-faced Beuno smiled apologetically at Augustine and waved the Roman monks in front of him, a courteous host.

A few chairs had been set, among the large circle of benches. A sweeping glance told Augustine that none was grander than another. All the same, those nearest the trunk of the oak appeared to have some pre-eminence of position. He moved swiftly towards them, with a practised smoothness which gave no appearance of haste.

Enoch, Abbot of Caerwent was there before him. Augustine claimed the chair beside him. Honours were equal. He watched his younger monks seat themselves on the benches where they could, mostly opposite him with their backs to the river. He wished again that he could have kept Honorius with him. He was disadvantaged here by his lack of senior clergy. As yet, Mellitus in Essex was the only other bishop of an English kingdom. He did not count the Frank, Liudhard, who had no see. But just then, he would have welcomed even Liudhard's support. He had been told the Church was still active in the Welsh kingdoms. He had not imagined there would be so many prelates. Three bishops, even if the title of abbot seemed more important to two of them, just in this one kingdom of Gwent.

Bishop Beuno took the initiative. He invited Abbot Enoch to open with prayer. Again, Augustine felt he had been outmanoeuvred. Surely he should have chaired this meeting? He stood, as they all did, and bowed his head. It did not prevent him from seeing that most of the British church-men raised their hands to heaven in what appeared to him, who had folded his own hands circumspectly, a flamboyant attitude of prayer.

The words were extravagant too. Instead of the measured phrases of the Roman offices, honed to simplicity over the centuries, the blessing of God was invoked in a blossoming of epithets dangerously close to poetry. 'King of the Tree of Life, Blazing Jewel of the Hosts of Heaven, Darling Bridegroom of the Church.' It was almost indecent, like a love-song to God.

When they were seated again, Beuno turned to Augustine. 'Reverend Father, would you like to explain just what it is about our benighted British Church which brings you all the way from Rome to correct us?'

Was there a hint of mockery in his smile?

Augustine bowed and stood up. He wished, not for the first time, that he were taller. 'My brothers, I come in love, not as a stern teacher to repri-mand you, but as a father whose duty it is to point out where one of his family is going astray. As Paul says, "Do not look upon him as an enemy, but warn him as a brother".

'There is, firstly, the matter of Easter. It has come to our notice that you use a different calendar from Rome's for the greatest festival of the Church. In some years, your Easter falls on another Sunday from that of the rest of the Christendom. How can it be right that this day, above all days, when we celebrate Christ's Resurrection from the dead, should not be kept by us all at the same sunrise of the year?'

Abbot Enoch's voice came back angrily, 'We keep only to what our fathers learned when the faith came to Britain. We've never changed. You may play games with your calendar: we don't.'

'But if the Ecumenical Councils have seen fit to regulate Easter more exactly with the changing moons, if great Rome has agreed, and Constantinople, Antioch, Alexandria, why should you alone in the far west disagree?'

'We hold the faith, unchanged.'

'No one disputes your faith. This is not about theology. It's a matter of discipline, of good church order. If you celebrate a different Easter, then half the year is thrown out of kilter. Lent, Ascensiontide, Pentecost, Trinity. All these depend on Easter's date.'

The argument rose and raged. Rome's authority was pitted against British obstinacy. Augustine felt despairingly that he had come 200 miles across Britain to speak to men who had never meant to be persuaded. He urged the irregularity of their baptismal liturgy, the scandalous nature of their monks' tonsure, like pagan druids. That, at least, they could not claim had ever been taught them by Rome.

'Nor was your own tonsure, in those days,' the younger abbot, Fracan, spoke for the first time. 'When our monks first began to live in communities, there were no rules about the way they cut their hair. We chose to mark ourselves out as holy men, in the way our people here would understand. It was much later your kind adopted this . . .' He gestured at Augustine's head. 'What did you call it? "Crown of thorns"? You have your new fashion. Ours is older.'

'Why must we all be the same?' asked Bishop Beuno, intent, as the others were not, to make peace. 'Why can't we agree to differ? We all love and serve the same God.'

Augustine drew himself up to his full height. This was his vindication. This, at last, was what he had travelled across Britain to say. 'Because the Christian Church does not exist for itself alone. We have a mission. How can we reach out to the unbaptized heathens, unless we speak with one voice? Kent and Essex are won. I'm here to call you to join me in converting the other English kingdoms, and for that, we must first be united among ourselves.'

There was a sudden silence. A leaf drifted down into the circle. Augustine sensed the chill of shock change the heated atmosphere. He looked round at the ring of appalled British faces, and the baffled expressions of his own monks at their reaction.

Abbot Enoch rose with slow deliberation. He spat on to the grass, just in front of Augustine's feet.

'Never! Never will I open the gates of mercy to those evil heathens. I had a sister who was a nun. Those devils raped and murdered her. My family had an estate east of the Severn. This English king you've been staying with overran it and drove them out across the river. They burned our churches. They even snatched the holy crosses from the altars in their lust for gold. Thieves! Murderers! Blasphemers!'

All around Augustine voices were rising, with similar curses and condemnation. The musical tones, which had sung prayers like a love-song to God, were now harsh with grief and hate.

Augustine stood stunned by the bitterness of their antagonism. 'But, my brothers, Christ came to save sinners. I myself brought the Gospel to bloodthirsty conquerors in the kingdom of Kent. I did it for Christ. The

English are crying out for salvation.'

'What can you know of how we've suffered?'

'It wasn't your sister, your parents, your church, your home.'

Augustine grasped the arm of the chair behind him, to steady himself. Pain gripped his belly again. He was praying now. 'Lord, give me wisdom. Lord, move their hearts. Lord, what shall I say?'

Like a shaft of sunlight, there stole into his mind the reassuring memory of Canterbury. Yes, he had been successful there. Yes, he had won that kingdom for Christ. The memory sharpened, of the little church of St Martin's, a sick baby placed in his arms. In those early days, God had put into his hand a gift he had never known he had. It had worked powerfully in favour of the Church.

He lifted his head, raising his voice above the hubbub. Gradually their voices dropped to a resentful muttering. It was still some while before he could make himself heard.

'Since we cannot reach agreement, let's ask God to be the judge. Bring in some sick person and let us each lay our hands on the poor soul for healing. The one whom God answers will have truth on their side.'

The Britons were startled. Glances of questioning doubt passed between them. Augustine caught smiles on the faces of his own monks. It was reassuring to know they believed in him. He must now believe in himself. No! He caught back the thought. Not in himself, surely, but in the greater power of God.

There was some heated argument, but he had judged well. Pride would not allow the British to refuse this challenge. Augustine pursued his advantage. He sent Maurice off to find a suitable sufferer.

The young monk returned along the river-bank, after a little delay, leading by the hand a man who was obviously blind. He wore a peasant's rough tunic and threadbare leggings. He stumbled into the ring of clergymen, his other hand holding a stick, with which he probed the space around him. His unseeing face quested this way and that, like a pig snuffling for acorns, sensing people on every side.

'He says his name is Hierding, Father,' said Maurice.

There was a hissing gasp from the Britons, which made the blind man flinch.

'An Englishman?' They were backing their chairs and benches away, as if to avoid the risk of contact with him.

'A child of God, and evidently in great need,' Augustine reproved them. He turned to Bishop Beuno. 'Please, proceed, Father.'

Beuno darted glances at the British abbots. They stared back stonily. He rose himself. Maurice had let go of the man. With reluctant slowness the Welsh bishop's hands reached out to the greasy head of the English peasant. Hierding started at the touch and trembled. How much had Maurice explained to him? A stream of mellifluous Latin poured over the man. It was, Augustine thought disapprovingly, more like the poetry of a heathen charm than a plain Roman prayer.

It was done at last. Beuno's hands made the sign of the cross and fell away. The conference waited. The peasant stood, turning his face this way and that. He looked puzzled.

'Can you see, my son?' asked Augustine in English. He translated the question into Latin for the Welshmen.

The Englishman hung his head, as though the failure was his. 'No, sir.'

It was now the Welsh abbots' turn. Enoch of Caerwent seemed more angry than reluctant. He strode across the turf, as though he would have liked to cuff the peasant to the ground, not heal him. Yet he shouted his prayer in a rousing voice which would have carried above a storm.

Silence fell. Nothing happened. A slow smile curved Augustine's lips as he savoured his opponents' failure. It was several moments before he felt the intensity of everyone's stare upon him. All eyes, except the blind man's, were turned on him. A chill gripped him as he rose in his turn. When he had issued his challenge he had been so sure, remembering past marvels. Could he do it to order, in front of hostile witnesses?

'Lord, help me!'

He must concentrate on the man in front of him, a soul in need. For an Englishman, the peasant was not tall, but he stood higher than Augustine. The archbishop laid his hands on the man's shoulders, pressing him gently to his knees. He felt Hierding trembling. Did he sense the touch of power? Now Augustine could rest his hands firmly on that bowed head, ignoring the lice he saw crawling among the hairs.

How had Christ approached the infirmities of those whose friends had brought them for healing?

'Don't be afraid, my son,' he said in English. 'Christ has died to save you from your sins. Christ heals you.' Again, he repeated it in Latin for the benefit of the British. 'Peace be with you, my child.'

Silence. The man knelt there, with his eyes closed.

'Look up, my son.'

The peasant lifted his head. The slow, stiff eyelids opened. He looked baffled. Without speaking, he swivelled his head, to the left, to the right. A look of astonishment, as incomprehension brightened into understanding.

'I can see! Tall things, like trees!' He reached out fumbling hands and grasped Augustine's skirt. 'Was it you, sir? Was it you touched me? Did you give me back my sight?'

'Go in peace, my son,' said Augustine again. He felt drained.

There was a sudden hubbub, startling swans on the river. Wonder was giving way to argument, to accusation. Abbot Enoch stabbed his finger at

Maurice. 'It was him! You sent your own monk to find someone. This man was never blind. This was a trick!'

Augustine's monks raged back at the insult.

'How dare you call us liars!'

'Archbishop Augustine's healed people before.'

'He's even raised the dead!'

While the British and Roman monks yelled at each other, Bishop Beuno stood calmly. His once-friendlier face was set now in a chill dignity. He beckoned the other prelates to him. Their heads bent together. When Abbot Enoch's voice rose, Augustine caught snatches of a language which was not Latin and meant nothing to him. Beuno turned back to face him.

The archbishop had recovered something of his composure, though he felt utterly weary. He made an effort to keep his voice steady. 'Well, my brothers? You see that God has restored light to the eyes of this man. It's a token that he's offering your Church the light of truth. Will you acknowledge now that I have come as your archbishop and I bring you that light to amend the error of your ways?'

Bishop Beuno did not answer for some moments. He had difficulty forcing the words through stiff lips. 'If this . . . miracle . . . was what it seemed, it was a great mercy shown to this man. We should give God the praise, not any human. You ask a hard thing of us, Bishop Augustine. We kept the faith through centuries of invasion, war, loss of country. Here in the west, we guard the flame of Christ still, the Church's old tradition. You demand change. We cannot lightly throw away what our forebears guarded at such great cost. Allow us time to consult far more widely than just our kingdom of Gwent. We need to speak with our colleagues in all the other British kingdoms. There are famous abbeys further north, who may know nothing of your arrival in Kent. We need their wisdom. Let us meet again, say, in three months' time.'

Augustine frowned. He felt like a child cheated of a promised reward. Surely he had been fully vindicated? God be thanked, this blind man could see. But the British would not see.

'Very well then, if you insist. But you have the plain proof in front of you. God is on my side. Take care you give your colleagues a full and honest account of what happened today. I'll meet you here and lay down my same challenge to the whole Welsh Church.'

He was not prepared for the roar of rage which greeted this.

'We're not Welsh!'

'Never use that vile name in our hearing!'

'You insult us!'

Augustine's monks looked to each other for enlightenment. This word was commonly used among the English for the British they had expelled.

'Don't you know?' Beuno explained, the smile gone from his face. 'You seem to speak English well enough. Surely you realize that in that heathen tongue "Welsh" means "stranger"? They've made us strangers in our own homeland and driven us out of most of it. And you wonder that we hate the English?'

Chapter Twenty-nine

'He must be home soon.'

Middle age had scarcely slowed Bertha's long stride. She sped across the yard now to the king's hall. Everything must be ready when he came: the hearth swept, fresh rushes on the floor, the shields on the walls burnished. A palace fit to welcome a king. She had her own secret to welcome him, too.

Between the queen's hall and the king's, she cast her eyes round to see that everything outside was trim and businesslike, too. Her glance went down an alley to the stable yard. There was more than usual activity there. Horses were lined up, as if for a hunting expedition. Yet there was something strange. Mules with panniers, besides the richly caparisoned riding horses. Someone was going on a journey.

A fear she could not name clenched Bertha's stomach.

She turned her steps towards the stables. But now her feet dragged, as though they did not want to take her this way. Edith looked up questioningly into her mistress's face.

'Who is going on a journey, Edith, when the king is expected any day?' She knew the answer.

'That looks very like Prince Eadbald's horse, madam.'

'But his father is coming.'

The knot of men readying the horses turned. The grooms fell back when they saw the queen. The way led clear to the centre of the group. Eadbald, her eldest son, as tall as she was now. He flicked a falling lock of hair back from his face defiantly.

'Where are you going?'

'Good morning, Mother. I hope I see you well.'

The stilted courtesy reminded her that, young though he was, he was regent in his father's absence.

'The king is on his way home. He could be back today. I ask again, where are you going?'

'Is the heir of Kent not free to ride about his father's kingdom?'

'You didn't tell me you were going.'

'Must I be tied to your apron strings?'

'Courtesy demanded that you say goodbye to me.'

'How do you know I would not have done?'

'Where can you be going, that you wouldn't tell me your plans before-hand?'

He tossed his head, but she saw how the muscles in his neck were taut. Knowledge began to dawn.

'You didn't tell me because you knew I'd try to stop you. That's right, isn't it?'

Eadbald looked round angrily at the young companions of his body-guard, at the listening servants. She was shaming him, rebuking him publicly. Her eyes followed his round the group of travellers. A strange face in the rear, shadowed by a hood, leaped out at her. Strange, because he was not one of the court at Canterbury. Stranger still because this face was shadowed with tattoos. The fear that had been haunting her reared suddenly into focus.

'One of the priests of Thanet?' Her eyes flew back to Eadbald. 'What is he doing here? Your father banished Thurward, High Priest of Thunor, from Canterbury. Where are you going with his servant?'

Her son flushed. She thought she saw a quiver of fear.

'Thanet is part of my father's kingdom. *My* kingdom, one day.'

'Your father is coming home, and you are going to Thanet to meet that outlaw? *Why?*'

'I've had enough of questions. Since you've come to bid me goodbye, I can save myself the trouble of going to you.'

With the briefest of angry bows, he was in the saddle. The horses swung their heads towards the gate. The heathen priest's head was hidden deep in his hood as they rode away.

Bertha was left shaken. This was surely treason. In Aethelbert's absence, her son had let into his court the emissary of the most powerful priest in the cult of the thunder god, Thurward, the rebel who had defied the new Christian order and the king's wrath. Her mind flew back to the only time she had set foot on the sacred island of Thanet, when Augustine had landed. Even then, with the cross held high and forty monks singing the litany, she had felt its awe. The wood of oaks, looming round the clearing where they sat. The World Tree of the old god on its hill. The anger and the hatred of those heathen priests.

Why was Eadbald going back there? Who else knew of Thurwald's plot? Did Herman and Dirwine, those loyal servants to her and Aethelbert? Had Eadbald kept his hooded visitor a secret, before she blurted it out? What would Aethelbert say when he knew that his son had used this first little power entrusted to him to defy his orders? Would she tell him?

What might happen if she did? What if Aethelbert turned his wrath, not just on Thurward, but on her son?

Two days later, Edith's hands moved over Bertha's body, smoothing the folds of the green wool skirt. She arranged the bronze girdle from which hung the keys of the queen's household authority and a ball of rock crystal in its silver setting. Looking down, it felt to Bertha that the girl's hands were meeting a firmer resistance from her swelling abdomen.

Then she gasped. Edith, kneeling, started back on her heels too. She looked up at the queen with a laugh. 'My lady, it kicked!'

Bertha's smile was a spreading glow of joy. 'Don't they say that's when the soul enters the body, when the baby first moves?'

'It's going to be a nice surprise for the king to come home to, isn't it?'

'I hope so. And it *will* be a surprise. It's nearly twenty years since I came from Paris to marry him. Our Eadbald's almost a grown man.' Her face stiffened. 'The king may think he has sons enough to cause him trouble.'

'Perhaps this will be a girl.'

'The prince isn't back yet, is he?'

'No, madam.'

'Listen! Is that horses coming?'

They both ran to the door, scattering the women in the outer chamber of the queen's hall. Mildgith and the other court ladies sprang to their feet, almost scandalized to see their queen running eager as a young girl to meet her lover.

The men made a proud sight, riding up to the gates of the palace across the meadow. Sunlight glinted on myriad points of gold adorning Aethelbert's jacket and armour. He rode a black horse similarly caparisoned with fine leather and gold. His troops carried their spears upright, banners floating on either side. Horns sounded.

'You'd think they were coming back from war, rather than a progress through our allies' kingdoms,' Bertha laughed, with an edge of nervousness.

'Perhaps they *did* fight.' Edith was more serious.

The king had promised to take Augustine to the westernmost border of the English lands. Beyond the Severn, the British kept their still-unconquered Christian kingdoms. How long would the English spear-hosts leave them even that? Bertha saw the two halves of Edith's heritage, her English father's, her British mother's, tug at her heart.

'Aethelbert went west to arrange a meeting of churchmen,' Bertha said firmly. But she knew her husband had more warlike priorities.

They could see Archbishop Augustine and his monks now. Their black robes moved like a shadow cast by the finery of King Aethelbert and his noblemen.

'Poor Archbishop,' said Edith. 'He never really looks at home on a horse, does he? . . . Oh, madam, I'm sorry! The greeting cup!'

Edith sped back indoors, to find that Mildgith had done her job for her. With haughty disapproval, the older woman held out the goblet of wine, the silver plate of bread and salt, with which the lady of the house greeted her returning lord.

Bertha took the gifts from Edith. She straightened her back, drew herself up tall. She felt her dress moulding itself more closely against her body. Would Aethelbert notice? Would she have to break the news herself? She had begun to guess this secret, even before he set out for the west, but she had said nothing. At her age, it could be a false alarm. Now she was sure.

Would the news turn his anger away, when he found Eadbald was missing?

She stood in the foreourt to greet him as he rode in and was flattered by his look of delighted recognition. It had not been a love match, but they had made a good marriage together. The prestige Bertha brought him had helped to raise him to the rank of the greatest English king. She knew that jealousy sometimes fought with pride, when he was reminded of her Frankish ancestry, but pride usually won. She had studied her role as his queen carefully.

'My lord, I thank God you've come back to us safely.' She watched his eyes regard her over the rim of the goblet. So far, they had not left her face. She hugged both her secrets to herself a little longer, the joyful and the dark.

A sudden commotion broke the link between them. Both turned abruptly.

'The archbishop!' cried Edith.

Augustine appeared to be falling from his horse. The swift hands of grooms reached up to steady him. He was quickly surrounded by his monks. In a few seconds, he almost disappeared from Bertha's sight. She glimpsed the small, grey-faced man being supported by Honorius, before the crowd of taller figures hid him.

With a word of apology to Aethelbert, she sped towards the monks. Her hands were still holding the silver plate. Her voice, not loud, but used to command, opened a path for her.

The archbishop's face was drawn with pain. His hands clutched his abdomen. With alarm, she felt an answering tension in her own belly.

'Bring him inside.'

Honorius steered his superior towards the queen's hall. Edith ran ahead. She drew forward a chair, and threw cushions on it. She darted to the table by the wall to pour more wine.

As Bertha led the archbishop into the dim interior, she noted with satisfaction that the hospitality she would have wished for him was ready.

They lowered Augustine into the chair. He seemed embarrassed.

'I'm sorry, your majesty. A foolish weakness. I'm not used to riding such distances, and the wind was cold.'

The skin around his lips was yellowish-white. It struck her that he had lapsed into Latin, though after his first year in Kent, they had used English to each other in public. It was a measure of how much the pain was making him forget all but his immediate surroundings. Yet still he was struggling to salvage his dignity.

'Hush. Don't try to talk. Drink this wine.' As if she stood over the sickbed of one of her children.

He obeyed, and a little colour crept back into his face. He was never, Bertha told herself, a rosy-faced man, unlike the ruddier complexions of the English.

She observed his cramped muscles begin to relax. With relief, she felt her own taut body ease in sympathy. For a brief while, she had feared for the baby.

She felt strangely betrayed, looking down at the little archbishop. Wasn't this the great Augustine of Canterbury, the healer, who had even raised the dead? It alarmed her to see him helpless and in pain.

She looked around for her chaplain, Liudhard. As so often now, he was a tall shadow on the outskirts of her circle. 'Bishop, will you lead a prayer for Archbishop Augustine?'

The Frank looked startled. But he came forward. His long hands rested on the Roman's head. He said a formal Latin prayer. She felt no thrill of grace from it. She doubted if Augustine did.

'Have you suffered anything of this sort before?'

'A twinge or two. Not like this.' Was he being brave?

'I'll get the king's physician to attend you.'

Augustine lifted his hand to stay her. His voice was weak. 'Forgive me, your majesty. Father Laurence was our abbey's doctor. He holds the rank of prior now, but he was for years our infirmarian. He'll know what to do . . . I should like to go back to the abbey.'

She recognized that plea: the hurt child, the frightened bride before her first childbirth, the longing in a crisis to run home to the familiar.

'Of course. I'll have a litter brought. You shouldn't walk just yet.'

He closed his eyes and did not argue. His very meekness frightened her more. Augustine's coming to Kent had changed everything for her. Was she about to lose him?

She found Aethelbert in his own hall, surrounded by the noblemen and counsellors who had not accompanied him, as well as by his own retinue. This was men's talk. She heard the loud masculine voices, not quarrelling, but demanding the right to be heard, to be the one proffering sound

201

advice. She caught the names of Mercia, Wessex, the Hwicce. Augustine's meeting with the British Church had only been a sideshow to the king's political progress through the English kingdoms.

Eadbald should have been there. Had the king asked about him? What had he been told?

Yet Aethelbert turned from the centre of this political discussion at her entrance. 'Is Father Augustine well?'

The concern in his face seemed genuine. The Roman archbishop was, after all, one of his prized possessions. Aethelbert would care about Augustine as he would for a valuable horse.

'He's a little recovered, with wine and rest. I've sent him back to the abbey in a litter. But I'm afraid this may be more than a passing weakness. When he clutched his belly he looked truly ill, and it's not the flux.'

'He doesn't eat enough. What do these monks expect, picking at bread and greens? Don't they know you need red meat to put muscle on bone?' He laughed, flexing his own sinewed biceps for all to see. His warriors cheered him.

'Indeed, my lord, it's made you as fine a man as England has ever seen.'

It was not far from the truth. Kings expected flattery from their wives. It was her joy that, with Aethelbert, this was hardly necessary.

'Where's my son?'

It was the question she had been dreading, yet it came with a sudden directness that caught her off guard.

'He rode off to . . . to the coast with his companions two days since. We expect him back soon.'

'Touring the ports, is he? That's good. I'm glad he's not idle in my absence.'

No one contradicted her. No one said that Eadbald, heir to Christian Kent, was on the island of the thunder god with its banished priest. Did these men around the king know?

She waited until the tide of politics and strategy ebbed. Aethelbert, it seemed, had fought in a skirmish with some Mercian troops, to impress upon the midlanders the limits of their border with his client king of the Hwicce.

Her heart turned over, imagining it. It happened all the time. This was a warrior king. Yet one unguarded moment in some minor fight in an obscure outpost could bring the greatest king in England down, and leave her a widow. Was it the danger of a late childbirth which made all their lives seem suddenly so fragile?

What would happen to Kent if Eadbald survived to become its king?

The crowd around the king thinned as the day drew on towards supper. Bertha took Aethelbert's hand with a little laugh. 'Come, my lord, let's walk outside for a few moments.'

If he looked surprised, his laugh answered hers. He let her lead him out into the last of the daylight. A purple and gold sunset was painting the underside of black clouds with drama.

At the back of the king's hall was a garth of apple trees. They leaned at erratic angles, bent down by the heavy crops of many years. She led him among their trunks, dipping her head to avoid low branches. Her free hand caressed the swelling apples as she passed. She pulled one from its stem and handed it to him.

'It's not ripe yet. It'll be sour,' he objected.

'But in a few months, it will be sweet and ready.' Her eyes smiled up into his. She watched the puzzled rejection give way to questioning, and then to realization.

'Another son! At our age?' He threw back his head with a triumphant laugh.

'Yes.' She laughed with him, as his arms swept round her. 'Or a daughter. Don't you have sons enough?'

She had given him, yet again, what he wanted. The proof that Aethelbert, King of Kent, overlord of Britain, was a man at the peak of his powers. Still virile enough to sire a warrior son.

The green apple dropped, unheeded, into the grass.

As the pain retreated, it was the worried faces of the monks around him which alarmed Augustine. A wry smile twisted the corners of his exhausted mouth. Could it be that the brothers who had mutinied against him on the journey, and sent him back to Rome, now trusted him so much they were appalled at the thought of losing him? He lay back on the narrow mattress in his cell. He had not been a total failure, after all.

Laurence came hurrying in, with the new infirmarian, Fastidius.

'What's this, Father? You've been overdoing it?'

Augustine consented to Laurence's hands probing his body. With all his years of experience in the sick room, the prior was clearly not going to trust this to his junior. His sensitive fingers pressed and squeezed. Augustine winced.

'That hurts?'

The archbishop nodded, unable for the moment to speak.

Laurence's eyes grew grave. 'I can give you something for the pain.' He nodded to Fastidius, who left quickly and silently.

When they were alone, Laurence folded his arms. 'Father, you'll have to take care of yourself. There must be no more of this gadding about to the far reaches of this island. You're a sick man. You must ration your strength carefully, to make the most of your days.'

'You think I'm dying? Tell me the truth.'

'Death and life are in God's hands. We are all going to die.'

Augustine managed a half-smile. 'I am well rebuked.'

He saw Laurence's face soften with old friendship, touched with sadness. 'But, yes, I'll be honest with you. What I felt was not good.'

Augustine thought, meeting his eyes, that part of Laurence's own gift of healing lay not just in prayer and medicine, but in the loving sympathy he offered his patients. When the end draws near, he thought, it will be good to be nursed by Laurence.

Fastidius was back, with a glass flask. The reddish liquid it contained was faintly steaming.

'Drink this.' Laurence's arms lifted Augustine to sit up. When he had drunk, the prior laid him down again tenderly.

Augustine's mind began to drift away. He said drowsily, 'I made a blind man see.'

'Did you, indeed? I don't have your gift. I just know about medicines.'

'But I can't remove this canker from my own body.'

' "Physician, heal thyself." We usually can't, can we? It's good to realize our limitations.'

Augustine caught Laurence's hand. 'Sometimes I think we've done so much. Kings converted. Kent and Essex Christian. I may, with God's grace, bring the British Church back to Rome. Then I wake in the night, and I know this could all pass away. The next generation could overthrow it. Prince Eadbald, king here. And Sabert's sons in Essex. I see a dark pit opening in front of us.'

Laurence laid a soothing hand on the archbishop's forehead. 'The middle of the night is never a good time for hope. Sleep now. You'll feel better in the morning.'

But Augustine retained his hand. 'Laurence, when I go, it's important that Canterbury has wise leadership. I fear for the succession of the crowns of Kent and Essex. I must be sure of the right succession in the Church. I want you to be the next archbishop.'

'I?' Laurence was genuinely shocked. 'I know you spoke of this before, but now Mellitus is Bishop of London. And you talk of consecrating Justus to Rochester. I'm only prior of the abbey here.'

'You've been my companion all the way. At St Andrew's in Rome. On that long journey across Europe, when none of us knew what to expect. Here in Canterbury, while it was still heathen, and Titus died. Mellitus came after Kent was won, when the fear of those dark gods and their servants was behind us. When Essex was a cornfield ready for the scythe. Only you know how hard it was then, how hard it could be again. Please.'

'It doesn't sound right to me. Is it usual for an archbishop to appoint his own successor, Father?'

'I'll write to Gregory.' The words blurred. His consciousness was slipping away. 'I want to consecrate you myself, in Christ Church cathedral.'

'But you can't! Not after you're . . . dead.'

The last word fell softly. Augustine was asleep.

A figure towered over Bertha's bed. A powerful hand seized her shoulder and pulled her upright. A voice shouted in her face.

'You bitch! You lied to me!'

'My lord?'

Aethelbert's other hand struck her across the cheek. Her own hands went instinctively to protect her swelling abdomen.

'Eadbald! They say that Thurward's priest was here. That my son has ridden to Thanet to meet with him. That you knew!'

'My lord, I tried to stop him. I told him you'd be angry, that you'd banished the high priest. But he's young, my lord. His judgement isn't mature yet. You know how he grieved when you abandoned your old gods. Forgive him; he means no harm to you.'

'No harm!' He threw her back on the pillows. She looked helplessly into his angry face. She was aware, on the edge of the lamplight, of the scared face of Edith, crouched in a corner. Her own face must look just as terrified. 'No harm? When the son conspires against the father? When he countermands my express orders? When he takes himself and his friends off to that nest of traitors the moment my back's turned?'

'He's young,' she pleaded again. 'He still has to learn statecraft.'

'I'll horsewhip it into him when he gets back. It'll be a long time before I give him responsibility again.'

'Perhaps that's what he needs. If you trusted him with more—'

'You'd teach me how to be a king? By God, madam, I should whip you too!'

His hands were reaching out again for her, powerful warrior's hands. Hands that had killed strong men. She pulled herself up to meet his face, and tried to still her quivering lips. His blue eyes blazed at her.

She felt the baby kick. Her look went down to the shield of her protecting hands.

Aethelbert's grip shifted abruptly. 'That was my son, was it? A more loyal one than your eldest, I hope.'

Her eyes lifted again. A possessive grin had transformed her husband's furious face. His arms went round her. 'I should whip you,' he said, more softly. 'You always did have a mind of your own.'

Her moment of danger had passed, like his in that skirmish by the Severn. For how much longer would either of them be here?

Chapter Thirty

Placing his hands on Justus's untonsured head, Augustine felt the glow of achievement. This was more as the consecration of a bishop of the Roman Church should be. Mellitus, Bishop of London, stood beside him, lending the authority of his own hands to his archbishop's. Augustine was no longer the solitary prelate in a far-flung mission. He had never really counted the Frankish Liudhard. Now there were three of them. He had taken Justus, the secular priest, and consecrated him bishop of the thriving port of Rochester on the Medway. King Aethelbert had again paid for this new church for the purpose.

He looked down the lofty wooden nave, over the ranks of king, queen and nobles, warrior leaders, grey-bearded councillors. This congregation was overwhelming evidence of an established Church.

Afterwards, King Aethelbert and Queen Bertha entertained them at a feast. Augustine studied Justus, in the place of honour at Aethelbert's right hand. The new bishop was in laughing conversation with the king, despite his still-imperfect grasp of English. Augustine noted that Aethelbert seemed easier in Justus's company than he did in his own. The secular priest was of a different stamp from the monks. Their rule of gravity was not so ingrained in him. He could be circumspect in monastic company. He had been careful to give no offence when he lodged in the abbey at Canterbury. Yet he could be all things to all men. He chatted to the poor like a family friend, or bellowed with laughter at the lewd jokes at the king's table. Augustine, as so often, had an obscure sense of his own inadequacy, and yet he felt relief.

He was rid of Justus. It had been a wise move to give him Rochester. Now Canterbury could return to what it had been from the start, his monastic centre. There was no Roman now to overshadow Augustine and make him feel inferior. The suave Mellitus was busy in Essex, as the jovial Justus would be in Rochester. The archbishop's authority in the royal capital of Canterbury would once more be undisputed.

Except . . . his eye travelled down the long tables. It was some distance, for this younger monk had yet little seniority. Yet something in Paulinus's bearing drew the eye inexorably to him. He was very tall, for a Roman.

Even at this noisy feast, where the monks were conspicuous by their silence and gravity, Paulinus's intensity of stillness sent a shiver down Augustine's spine. The hooded eyes were cast down at his plate. Yet Augustine knew that if Paulinus lifted their gaze to his, he, the Archbishop of Britain, would feel the shock of authority.

Paulinus was too young to be made a bishop, yet Augustine wished fervently there were somewhere he could send him, further than Essex. If the swelling tide of Christianity reached the north of England. . . ?

'You can't go.' Laurence was blunt. 'Another journey to the west could be the death of you.'

'I'm going to die, anyway,' said Augustine, with a ghost of a smile. 'We both know that, don't we? Better that I do it in a noble cause, than shrivel away here in Canterbury with my mission unfinished.'

'Does it matter so much to you, to bring the British to heel?'

A spasm crossed Augustine's face. He hardly knew himself whether the pain was in his belly or his soul. 'Gregory made me Archbishop of Britain. He's trusting me.'

Their eyes met in sympathetic remembrance. St Andrew's, Gregory's beloved monastery in Rome, which had once been the Pope's ancestral home. The well of shared experience as his monks, Augustine and Laurence had trained under him, before Gregory took the papal tiara. Both men loved him with a warmth it was hardly proper to acknowledge.

Augustine swallowed his nostalgia. His eyes pricked with tears. 'Gregory asked two things of me: that I should bring the English to the light of Christ, and that I should end the divisions of the British Church and bring them back into the Roman fold. And with my dying strength, I mean to do this.'

Laurence gave his former abbot a long and loving look. 'I honour you for it, Father. I'll give you some medicine to take with you for the pain. That's all I can do . . . unless you'd like me to come with you?'

Augustine shook his head. 'You know my plans for you. No, don't argue. I need you here in Canterbury, in my place. I wonder . . . You know I spoke of consecrating you the next archbishop before—'

Laurence held up his hand in shock. 'Please, Father!'

'If I don't come back, I shouldn't want Mellitus to take precedence over you.'

'Isn't that for the Church to decide?'

'I'm the Archbishop of all Britain. Gregory put supreme authority over this Church into my hands alone.'

'Until the north is converted and you can have a brother archbishop in York. And, forgive me, Father, didn't he speak of York and London, not Canterbury? After your death, of course. Mellitus—'

'I shall write my will before I go, naming you my heir. And I shall make it public.'

Augustine rode west again, this time without the protection of the king's presence. Nevertheless, Aethelbert sent a stout body of spearmen to escort his archbishop. Queen Bertha had released Gosfraeg to ride with them. The Anglo-Frankish lad sat tall and proud on his mount. Augustine noticed that he had exchanged the frisky pony, on which he had ridden with Augustine into Werburh's ambush, for a larger strawberry roan. Gosfraeg had blooded his sword that day, daring the curse of his father's gods. He was growing into a more serious young man.

The chalk uplands of the English kingdoms seemed, if anything, more wearisome the second time. There was no longer the thrill of newness. Augustine was burdened with greater knowledge of what lay in front of him. The thought of those passionate Welshmen daunted him.

'You should be confident. God favoured you last time,' Honorius assured him.

The archbishop did not feel confident.

Orders from the King of Kent secured him hospitality in the courts of heathen rulers, whose kingdoms they passed through. Aethelbert's power was palpable, even here.

They reached the broad mud-banks of the lower Severn, and were safely installed again in the royal fortress at Aust. There were three days yet to the meeting. Though Augustine had ridden through pain, he had not been so ill that they had lost travelling time.

He went to King Tondbert. 'Your majesty, it is not fitting that the Archbishop of Canterbury should meet the British again under an oak tree, as pagans do. Do you not have some hall near the river which we could use for a council chamber?'

He flinched at the frown which crossed the heathen king's face. 'The Council Oak is good enough for me. Is a Roman priest too delicate for the fresh air?'

Augustine bowed his head. Tondbert's manner was more scornful without the charismatic presence of Aethelbert. 'As you say, your majesty, I am not a well man. And your British weather is changeable.'

Gosfraeg stepped forward from Augustine's party. His bow to the Hwiccan king, from his taller height, was no more than polite. 'Your majesty, forgive me, but did I not read out to you King Aethelbert's command, that you should give Archbishop Augustine every assistance?'

An expression of anger twisted the Hwiccan king's face. It was swiftly replaced by his usual bland smile. Augustine was not sure how to interpret the dismissive wave of the king's hand.

'This time,' he informed his monks, as they left the royal presence, 'we must be at the meeting place early.' He tried to sound more authoritative than he felt. 'Lesser bishops should come to my ecclesiastical court, not I to theirs. As Archbishop of Britain, I must be seen to be the one in possession.'

More than a hundred miles north, forest sprawled around the River Dee as it slipped its way northwards to the Irish Sea. British kings built fortresses, ringed with earthworks, on the hilltops, yet the great abbey of Bangor in the Woods needed no such guard. A bank of earth and a ditch were enough to delineate sacred land.

Hundreds of trees had been felled to make clearings. Between the yellowing foliage of oaks had sprung up churches, schoolrooms, work-shops for scribes, smithies, studios for jewellers and silversmiths, refectories, a chapter house, an infirmary, and a myriad scattered cells for monks. It was a monastic city.

Out of its gate came now four of the finest scholars in Britain, The most commanding of them was Bangor's own tall abbot, Dinooth. His grey hair, still streaked with red, fell to his shoulders behind the shaved dome of his forehead, like a waterfall caught in a stormy sunset. The anxious figure of Abbot Enoch from Caerwent in the south followed him. The look he cast around him as he walked was still overawed by his first sight of this north-ern citadel of learning, to which he had brought the news of Augustine's challenge. Two other abbots accompanied them, from Penmon and Llanrhaiader. Together they represented the length and breadth of the still-unconquered British lands. Their faces were sober. The step they were about to take was a great risk. The way of faith their ancestors had preserved for centuries trembled on its outcome.

They needed their staffs on the steep climb. The rocky path was slip-pery with fallen leaves. Water laughed unseen, leaping down a succession of waterfalls through the forest.

'This path's well-trodden, for such a mountain,' observed the Abbot of Penmon, panting.

'A hermit doesn't always enjoy the seclusion he hopes for. Piro chose this place so that could live closer to God. But the holier he becomes, the more he attracts the sinful world to him. However far into the wilderness he tries to escape, they pursue him.'

Enoch put out his hand to still the others. 'Listen!'

A voice was singing above them. It sounded cracked, but oddly cheer-ful.

'I will awake the dawn!
I will give thanks to you, O Lord, among the peoples,
I will sing praises to you among the nations.'

The abbots looked at each other and set their aching muscles to the last steep haul.

They came out on a wide ledge above the treetops, fringed with rocks and bilberry bushes. Short turf carpeted it. The stream, which had thrown its waterfalls down through the wood, here trickled sedately across a lawn. At the back of this terrace reared a wall of rock, with a shadowed cave mouth.

Their eyes could not immediately find the hermit, though they could still hear his psalm.

Dinooth swung round slowly, then pointed. The others followed his silent gesture.

Piro was perched on the lip of a precipice. He was a small man, thin to the point of goblin sharpness. His tunic was short and his scrawny legs were caked with dirt. His tangled hair blew in the wind. Beyond him they saw nothing but huge blue space.

When Enoch narrowed his eyes against the dazzle of light, he could make out gradations of sky and scenery. The myriad glistening channels of the Dee snaked among the sands. The smothering foliage around Bangor ran out into the level cornfields of the coastal plain. Across the sparkle of the Solway Firth, the colour softened into purple mountains, which dissolved into clouds far above Scotland.

Much nearer, a sparrowhawk hung in the air, dizzyingly far below Piro.

Seemingly oblivious of his visitors, the hermit shouted his way to the end of the psalm.

'*Glory be to God, and to his Son, and to the Holy Spirit.*'

He looked round on the last word and stared straight at them. Their voices automatically responded.

'*As it was in the beginning, is now and ever shall be, world without end.*'

'*Amen!*' he crowed, and sprang off his perch on the rock.

For a sickening moment, he seemed to disappear into that enormous drop. Then his head emerged a little distance to the right, as he hauled himself up from an unseen ledge to the terrace where they stood. From his shorter height, he looked them up and down.

'Your feet made no sound on the leaves as you came, but your tread was heavy with wrath. You carry those pilgrim staves like weapons . . . It's grand weather for singing out of doors, isn't it?'

Dinooth bowed, as to a king. After a moment, the other abbots did the same. Dinooth took the small satchel he had been carrying and held it out to Piro. 'Some eggs and new-baked bread from Bangor's kitchens, Brother.'

The hermit's eyes lit up. He scrambled across the stream to them, emerging on to the grass with his legs streaked with wet mud.

'Praise God!' He took the satchel from Dinooth and sniffed the contents. His brilliant eyes shot up to the abbot. 'Fine gentlemen like you don't climb this mountain to give me dinner for nothing. The one who is both a brother and a stranger has made you angry.' It was a statement, not a question.

'Brother? Augustine of Canterbury!' From behind Dinooth, the Abbot of Llanrhaiader hissed the name, like a shower of raindrops among the leaves.

'You read us too well, and you've heard more than we thought,' Dinooth acknowledged. 'Can you read this foreigner as clearly? A man you've never met?'

'Scholars! You're poor foolish men, because you haven't the wit to ask for wisdom where it can be found. What do you think I do all day, by waterfalls in the wild woods? Just listen to the birds? I'm listening to God, man, till I can't hold up my arms to Heaven any more and my legs turn to ice in the water. So should you.'

Dinooth bit his lip. The pale oatmeal of the abbots' gowns was muddied as they knelt in prayer. The hermit's own knees showed bare, grotesquely calloused. The original brown of his ragged short tunic had collected many more dubious shades of the same hue.

'Lord, forgive us. Grant us your Spirit of wisdom in our hour of need.'

'That's more like it.'

'For generations, our Church has battled against the pagans amongst us and heathen invaders. Now this churchman comes from Rome to attack us.'

'What was it Paul enjoined? Faith, hope . . . and charity?'

'Charity!'

'So you haven't heard what that man Augustine demanded of us,' Enoch burst out, 'That we change the date of the holiest feast of the Christian year. Our Saviour's Resurrection! That we alter our manner of baptism, as if we'd never truly washed anyone of their sins. That we recognize his supremity, not just over his English cronies, but all of Britain. Bangor, the sacred islands of Iona and Bardsey. Even Glastonbury, where the Holy Child himself once walked!'

'And. . . ?' The hermit's eyes held Enoch's, sharp as a stoat's.

'That we join him in preaching Christ to the English!'

The last word broke from his tight lips so bitterly that it frightened a red squirrel on the branch behind him and sent it scampering into the oak trees in a burst of flame.

'Who sends this Augustine to bring you such a hard message?'

'Gregory, Bishop of Rome.'

Rome. Such a small, remote sound, in the mountain wilderness of Powys. Its echo of an imperial past was almost lost in the rush of falling water.

'Did his ambassador give you no sign?'

'It was a trick! He challenged us to heal someone. The man they produced was English! They claimed he was blind, but how could we know the truth?'

'Did he expect us to speak English?'

Piro held up his hand against their wrath. Small, dirty and impoverished though he was, the greatest princes of the British Church fell silent. Suddenly he subsided cross-legged on the banks of the stream, as though his spindly legs had given way. He grinned up at them, through the streaks of mud on his face.

'Look to your Master, who gave us the Spirit of wisdom. Set your own test. Come late to the meeting by the Severn. Let the man be seated in his chair, waiting for you. What would Christ do? Remember his story of the father with the prodigal son? When he saw him coming at last, he didn't wait, did he? He ran down the road with his arms outstretched to embrace him. He didn't care about judgement.

'Will a true servant of Christ remain seated when you approach, like a proud lord on his throne? Won't he fall on his knees and wash the dust from your feet, as Jesus himself did to his unworthy disciples at the Last Supper? If Augustine is such a man as Christ, then he may truly speak to you for our Master. He may be bringing you the truth, even though it's a truth you don't want to hear. You may have to offer the Gospel to your enemies.'

'To the *English*?'

Piro peered into the satchel. 'Did you say fresh bread? And eggs? I've some lovely watercress growing here that will go down a treat with this. I might even find a bit of honeycomb. Isn't God good? Won't you stay and share it with me?'

The Abbot of Bangor rose from his knees. The others followed, brushing the mud from their skirts furtively. Echoes of doubt and anger still showed in the glances they gave each other. Then a difficult smile edged across Dinooth's severe face.

'Thank you, no. The gift is yours to enjoy, Brother. Yet you drive a hard bargain for it. If this Augustine welcomes us, we should have to forfeit what we've guarded all our lives at such great cost.'

'Why did you come all this way up the mountain, then?'

'To seek your wisdom . . . Yes, I am rebuked, Brother.'

'Go in peace, Brothers.' The hermit grinned.

The woods closed around them. Piro was chanting again before they were out of earshot. A new psalm floated out over the plains of the Dee. As the wind bore it towards the English settlements across the river, they could not hear whether it was a benediction or a curse.

Chapter Thirty-one

The great oak was shedding its foliage. Yellow leaves, crooked twigs, ripe acorns, littered the ground.

'A golden carpet to welcome us,' murmured Augustine, shuffling his sandalled feet through the drifts.

As a monk, he had disciplined his mind to dwell on the higher themes of devotion and theology. The physical world was sinful, fallen, a snare to the senses. Yet since his illness had become undeniable, the world around him had broken through that habitual barrier. It ambushed him with visions of loveliness he had never valued before. So late discovered, so soon to be lost. He concentrated on the leaves in front of his feet. The subtle varieties of colour: soft yellow, brittle brown, decaying black. The polished sheen of an acorn, still tinged with green in its grey knobbed cup. The hand of the Creator had, after all, shaped these miniature miracles.

The more fiercely he fixed his attention on these freely found jewels, the less of his mind there was left to attend to the sharp pain in his guts.

'That must be the hall, through those trees,' muttered Honorius. 'It's a pity King Tondbert couldn't have offered it to us before. We're in time, though. Not a sign of those Welshmen.'

The path wound along the riverbank. The wooden building in front of them was not large, perhaps a royal hunting lodge. A figure who stepped out to greet them wore a tunic embroidered at neck and wrists, though not so showily as to suggest a nobleman. He scanned the group of Roman monks and Aethelbert's spearmen escorting them, and bowed.

'The king has commanded this hall be made ready for your meeting with the Welshmen. Let me know if there's anything more you need.'

'The Lord Archbishop would be glad of a cup of wine.'

'So, I'm sure, would our guests when they arrive,' Augustine added.

An expression of disgust wiped the smile from the steward's face. 'Wine? I've yet to meet a Briton who'd take so much as a cup of water from English hands, even if he were dying of thirst. We're worse than dogs to them.'

He strode before them into the hall. A ring of benches and chairs stood ready, as they had before under the great oak. Augustine studied the arrangement.

'Should we have my chair moved up to the dais, do you think?' he asked Honorius.

'As the steward says, they're a touchy lot, these British. Mightn't they find that a shade provocative? You don't want to give them any excuse to walk out this time.'

'You're right. I shall show humility. I'll meet them at their own level.'

All the same, there came into Augustine's mind the memory of the papal audience chamber in Rome. Gregory sat on a dais, which both ambassadors and petitioners approached. It was a mark of favour to be invited to come up and sit beside him to talk.

Was Gregory still alive? It had been a while since his last letter. Augustine recalled how even a man with Gregory's strength and energy had been brought low by physical weakness. For far longer than Augustine, he had fought a constant struggle against pain. The burden of responsibility for both the universal Church and the secular city of empire were borne by a body racked with suffering.

Watching his friend's anguish as closely as he did, Augustine had always assumed that Gregory would die before him. Now, in these last few months, he could not be sure. Especially not *now*, this moment, as his own pain gripped him.

'Sit down, Father!'

He must have staggered. Honorius had caught his elbow and was supporting him. There was a chair, into which he sank gratefully. He leaned his head over his knees, gasping.

Honorius signed to Maurice, who drew a leather flask from his satchel and passed it to the older monk. Augustine took it obediently. But he allowed himself only a few sips before he handed it back.

'Too much of this makes me sleepy. I need a clear head today, above all days.'

He would give anything to be back in Canterbury, lying on the mattress in his private cell. Not to have to do battle with the recalcitrant British, to have to assert his authority as archbishop, the authority of Rome, of Pope Gregory, over men who thought themselves the equal of even the most senior churchman. How was it possible to be so arrogant? This was a church of semi-barbarians from mountain fastnesses, of defeated refugees. A people on the edge of the known world, out of touch with Rome. Yet with total obstinacy they could believe they held the oldest traditions of the Church intact. His head reeled with dismay at the thought of the coming conflict.

If the Romans were early, the British came late. The sun shifted across the brilliant blue sky, glimpsed in fragments of lapis lazuli between the bare twigs of the oaks The steward brought food and ale to the waiting monks.

The pain had ebbed somewhat, but Augustine sat on in a kind of stupor. He found himself unwilling to move, in case the shift of his body caused it to flare up again.

'Do you think they're really coming?' Honorius asked. 'Is this our answer? They've turned their backs on us?'

'It's in God's hands. I'll stay here till sunset, if necessary. This must be settled. This reconciliation is the gift I want to give to Gregory, before. . . .'

Before whose death?

Maurice's young ears were sharper than most. He started up from the chair where he had been resting. Now all the monks were on their feet, their eyes on the door. It stood wide open to where the afternoon sunshine glistened on grey mudbanks as the tide dropped. Only Augustine still sat, leaning forward. His hands gripped the arms of his chair.

Now there was movement under the branches. He had not expected so many of them. Too late, he wished he had brought more senior men for the Roman party. Another bishop, certainly. He could not have separated Liudhard from the queen, and he would have felt threatened by the very presence of Mellitus. But the new Bishop of Rochester? Justus was suitably deferential to his monastic archbishop, even though his detached urbanity suggested he was observing the rules of ecclesiastical etiquette, rather than any deep humility. Still, Justus had spoken strongly against the vagaries of the British Church. He would have given Augustine firm support.

All this time, they were coming nearer. He recognized the craggy jawed Enoch from Caerwent, and the grim lines of that face made his stomach drop. The Welsh abbot was taller, too, than Augustine remembered. If he hauled himself to his feet now, he would still have to look up to his adversary. Too late to wish he had moved his chair up to the dais.

Behind him, the secular Bishop Beuno seemed almost a friendly face. He, at least, had attempted to be more conciliatory. But today he was well to the rear of this larger party. The British Church held their abbots preeminent. To free himself for his archiepiscopal duties, Augustine, by contrast, had handed over the new abbey of St Peter and St Paul to another.

'*Ah!*' Pain stabbed him as he moved. For agonizing moments, it slammed a shutter down on his vision. He could no longer see the delegation approaching through the dappled shadows of the oak tree, nor cast his imagination back to Canterbury. All the reality in the world was here in his belly, in the vicious fist which was seizing, wrenching him.

The agony ebbed. His face was cold with sweat. He was shaking. He glanced round at his monks. None of them had noticed, not even Honorius beside him. They were all intent on the impressive entry of the British.

215

Augustine fought back a wave of sickness and forced himself to concentrate on the newcomers striding into the hall.

There were so many he had not seen before. These must be the northerners Beuno had told him about. The Abbot of Bangor-in-the-Woods would be foremost among them. Yes, there in the forefront beside Enoch, with flames of red in his ragged grey hair, surely distinguishable by his authoritative bearing, as much as by his crozier and outlandish tonsure. There were other abbot-bishops, and twenty or more monks and clergy at their heels. Augustine noticed with a shock two women in white nun's clothing. Did they include abbesses, in the councils of their Church?

The Abbot of Bangor stood over Augustine, as Beuno made the introductions. He was clearly furious, before any word had been spoken. The look on all the faces behind him was close to hatred. Why? Augustine had not said a word of rebuke to them yet. What was so upsetting them?

Abbot Dinooth turned to his followers. The British tonsure made his head look so large, with that immense shaved forehead. His voice rang out, his Latin even more heavily accented than the southern Welsh.

'You see? Look at him! Piro was wise to warn us. This foreigner hadn't even the courtesy to rise to his feet and greet us. We're no brothers to him. He's only come here like a little emperor, to order the British to obey him.'

Roars greeted this, some in Latin, more in the British tongue. It was the shout of warriors hailing their leader on the eve of battle.

Augustine gripped his chair harder. Could he, should he, have risen at their entrance? Acknowledged these British bishops as his equals? Did the Pope rise for lesser prelates who came to his audience? How could he assert the authority he needed, if they refused to recognize his supremacy as their archbishop?

He remained resolutely seated, trying to control his trembling. He was not sure, in any case, if he could have stood just then. The network of sunlit sky and branches beyond the door was dazzling him. If he stood, that dizziness might tip him over from light into darkness. Whatever happened, he must not faint in front of them and reveal his weakness.

'You are welcome, Brothers and Sisters,' he said, in a voice he could not entirely prevent from quivering. 'Peace be with you.'

'And with you.' A reluctant, belated growl, from some, but by no means all of them.

He motioned to them to take their seats around the circle. Some lesser clergy moved towards the benches. Abbot Dinooth stood his ground. The others halted.

'Be seated, please.'

'We're not yours to command, little Roman. We've come. Have your say, and be done with it.'

216

Augustine signed to Honorius, who unrolled the scroll of Rome's demands. The British must accept the Roman calendar for the date of Easter, they must conform to the Roman rite of baptism, they must abandon their tonsure with its heretical pagan history and adopt the circular 'crown of thorns'.

Honorius struggled to make himself heard above the outbursts of anger. Augustine had almost ceased listening to the words he himself had written. He fixed his eyes on a ladybird staggering across the dusty floor in a shaft of sunlight. The shell encasing its folded wings was brilliant scarlet, peppered with black. Its journey from here out to the meadow flowers would be immense. Would it ever achieve it?

Honorius battled on. No one was asking the British to change their faith. The archbishop's injunctions were simple matters of Church discipline, a necessary proof of unity. Unity was the essential condition for what must follow. Above all, the British Church, from Cornwall in the far south-west to the islands of the Scots, must join Archbishop Augustine and the Church of Canterbury in the great mission which had brought them here from Rome. They must not rest until every English kingdom had been won for Christ.

A louder howl than ever cut him short. Honorius took a step backwards. The rage on every side was frightening. Now the other Roman monks were on their feet, braced for physical violence. Honorius looked in alarm to Augustine.

The frail archbishop got to his feet with difficulty. The pain had spread to every joint. It would have been easier if they had been seated around the circle. Standing as they were, he could hardly see beyond their front ranks. Abbots Dinooth and Enoch glowered over him.

Augustine sent up a silent prayer. His mind flew back to the slave market in the forum at Rome, to the two fair-haired boys who had seemed more angels than Angles, to the compassionate hope sweeping across Gregory's face.

He held up his hand. The baying of these churchmen, that they would never offer Christ's forgiveness to their English enemies, gradually subsided. He found his voice. It was not as loud as theirs, but he had it under control now. It was clear, precise.

'Very well. If that is your decision, then hear the doom you are bringing upon yourselves. If you refuse to make peace with your fellow Christians, the only alternative is war from your enemies. If you refuse to carry eternal life to the English, they will bring death to you.'

His brief strength failed. He sat down abruptly. In one stride, Honorius was leaning over him. The hall was an ocean wild with storm. It battered the walls of Augustine's mind, but did not break in. His world had contracted to the circle of floor at his feet. The ladybird took off in a dazzle of spotted wings towards the sunlight.

Augustine released his breath in a shuddering gasp. 'I spoke no more than the truth. But I think I may see my death before they meet theirs.'

Chapter Thirty-two

Ahead of me soars the thatched roof of the Church of the Saviour in Canterbury. I'm back where it began. The King of Kent ordered this church to be built for his own baptism. This is where it must end, with my successor's consecration.

Poor Laurence. I saw the grey stubble on his chin quiver as he tried to argue with me. He fears I'm acting against ecclesiastical custom. He's remained more of a monk than I am now, prior of our growing community at St Peter and St Paul in the meadows. Benedict ruled that when an abbot dies, the brothers choose his successor. But need it be so with an archbishop? Didn't St Peter himself ordain Clement to follow him as Bishop of Rome? Gregory told me to make my own Rules for this English Church, and gather the most suitable customs I found in Rome or Gaul into a single new sheaf. I've told—

Pain again, like a lightning bolt. Have I left it too late? Will I reach the cathedral before I collapse for ever?

Fix my eyes on that goal ahead. The thatch has weathered from gold over six years, to a pale brown. Like Gosfraeg's hair.

Why am I suddenly thinking of those two English boys, Gosfraeg and Tyrri? Because they were our first bright-eyed converts at the palace. Because they are to me, what those fair-haired boys in the slave-market were to Gregory.

I couldn't have walked this far. I must turn my mind to anything but the pain gnawing me.

These streets are crowded. English men, women and children are staring at me. Their skin still looks pale to me, their hair strangely lank and colourless. But they have blue eyes like jewels, bright and disturbing. What are they thinking of me, carried in this chair in my white and gold mitre and cope, my rubied crozier in my hand? Do they see me lifted above them, too proud to walk their streets?

Would I have walked, if I were stronger? Of course I wouldn't. It's not from personal pride. The man beneath the mitre is nothing. I never have been. It's the honour of the Church I'm upholding. I'm Rome made visible. I am Gregory's representative to the English, and so Christ's.

That stab of anguish? Was it wholly physical this time? I flinch every time I remember that meeting with the British churchmen beside the Severn. Did I fail? Was it my fault? They called me proud. If only they knew how fearful I was then, have always been. Even now, I still wince when I think how I ran back to Rome, only a few days into our journey to Britain. I wasn't proud enough then to go on. But I stood my ground by the oak tree at the Severn. What would Gregory have done?

I wish Gregory were here.

The cloisters of St Andrew's in Rome, with sunlight making barred shadows along the pillared cloisters. The trickle of a fountain. The eager slap of Gregory's sandals approaching.

Would he have rushed to meet those Welshmen, arms outstretched in brotherhood?

More pain.

The streets of Canterbury are too narrow. The crowds are pressing close. Gaping mouths, a reek of onion breath.

They are my flock, the English Church. My success.

Not even Gregory's warmth could have swayed the stiff-necked British, could it? They are determined to cling to their hatred of the English, whatever I say. My failure.

And theirs.

The little hands of English children are reaching up to touch my chair. Strange that they should think the wood which carries me can give them a blessing, when it cannot cure the man who sits on it.

Is it little hands like these which will pick up the spear and aim it against the British? Will these sweet blue eyes laugh when the white robes of the monks of Bangor are dyed scarlet with blood?

Did I prophesy truly when I spoke their doom?

I am almost at the end of my journey. The doors of the cathedral are open before me. The carving around them is still brilliant with colour. Green-painted leaves, red berries, blue and gold birds. Less beautiful faces peer out from among them. They show the world of sinful nature we must leave behind us, to find the purity of Paradise within.

Laurence is a small, blurred figure at the end of the nave, through the candle-smoke. My friend, my doctor, my successor. Is he as fearful of his new destiny as I was of mine?

Mellitus looks angry. I should have expected that. A knot of pain every time I look at him. Mellitus despises me. He knows I'm risking this ceremony so that he can't succeed me. Here, at least, I've outmanoeuvred him.

Justus seems amused. Rochester is enough for him, for the moment. I can't tell how ambitious he is.

Concentrate on the little things to block out the pain. *Now. Hard.*

That beam of sunlight from a high window is catching the crystal ball which the queen wears on her girdle. What does it mean? Is it a sign of some old Frankish goddess? It shines more brightly than her crucifix. Yet she's a devout lady.

Her body is swelling close to childbirth. Will I be alive to baptize her baby?

My hands are over Laurence's shaved head. I don't remember how we got here. But the singing continues undisturbed, those ravishing chants Gregory taught us. I must have done what was necessary.

His scalp bears the brown mottling of age. I can't remember if Laurence is younger than me.

Six years here. Seven, since we left Rome. Has it aged us both so much?

Tens of thousands baptized, in Kent and Essex. Two kings Christian.

Two boys in a slave market led to this. What happened to Edmer, after he ran from St Andrew's? Did he ever find his way back?

A face staring at me, at the moment I say the words which will make Father Laurence the next Archbishop of Canterbury. How can eyes so black burn like a furnace? How can a mind so intense serve under me, or under Laurence?

Paulinus. Where will his destiny be in Britain?

I move to raise Laurence, but he's supporting me.

He mutters, under cover of the kiss we exchange, 'Did you take the cordial I gave you?'

'A little. I mustn't sleep yet.'

But sleep is all I crave, to obliterate the pain.

It is done. Laurence is consecrated as my heir. I didn't write to ask Gregory's permission first. When I've slept, I must compose a letter to tell him what I've done.

'He should be in bed, your majesty.'

Was that condemnation in Archbishop Laurence's eyes? Was it right for her to call him 'Archbishop' while Augustine was still alive? Could there be two of them? Today, he was more of the doctor than a prince of the Church. Or like a loyal hound growling at someone who has intruded on his master.

It would not have been seemly for Augustine to receive a woman in his celibate monk's cell, even his queen. Never mind that Bertha had bent over many sickbeds, with her growing family. Even closed the eyes of little Eanswythe in death.

Augustine was her spiritual father, not her child. Yet his weakness tugged at the strings of her maternity. He looked so shrunken, trying to hold himself upright on this hard chair in the abbey's parlour. In his illness, they had taken him from the narrow and noisy lodgings of his old community in the city, to the new abbey of St Peter and St Paul outside the walls. But even here was the clamour of builders outside, raising the new church. His monks would bury him there.

Poor Augustine. How much she wanted to reach out her hand and stroke the frown from that lined brow. He was tense with pain and duty. Was she wrong to have come, to place this extra burden on him, when he should have been in bed?

She knelt before him, as a daughter, not a mother. It was his hand which rested in blessing on her head, not hers on his. He had come to Britain to give, not to receive. She would be everlastingly grateful.

'Father. I've brought something . . . someone . . . to show you.'

The delighted smile of a mother with her first baby, though she was well into her middle years and had given the king princes and princesses in plenty. She motioned to Edith behind her.

'Our newest daughter, Aethelberg.'

The young woman stepped forward, proud and shy. In her arms she carried the precious bundle. The baby was wrapped in the softest white wool on the outside, and with the finest linen inside touching her tender, rosy skin. Augustine reached out a trembling hand towards her. This little northern child glowed with warmth and health. Against her, his southerner's hand looked greyish-yellow, cold, sickly. For a moment, Bertha felt fear that his illness might communicate itself to her baby, though she knew it was not contagious.

'The grace of the Father, the Son, and the Holy Spirit be with her.' His voice faint but steady.

'I hoped that you would baptize her. This is the first time I've been able to offer a newborn baby to Christ. Before you converted Aethelbert, it was never possible.'

She laid down the grief which this had cost her at the archbishop's feet. His hand moved back to her. His touch was light as an autumn leaf falling.

'God saw your intention, not the deed. All is well now. Your children are baptized.'

'All except Eadbald. He refused. I fear. . . .'

Pain crossed Augustine's face. 'We must keep praying, my daughter. It may be, before the king dies. . . .'

'I'm sorry, Father! I didn't come here to burden you with my fears of the future. I wanted to share my joy with you. Since you couldn't perform the baby's christening, I thought I'd tell you about our plans for her.'

He managed a small, weary smile. 'She is very small. I think it is Archbishop Laurence who needs to hear your plans for her future. They will not concern me much longer.'

'God keep you, Father! But Aethelberg is part of your vision. The vision Pope Gregory wrote to us of. Of the heathen court of Deira, where those boys in the slave market came from.'

'The north of Britain is a long way from Kent. I fear even King Aethelbert's authority hardly reaches that far.'

'Where armies cannot go, a Christian princess may, as I did.'

Augustine opened his eyes wide. He was suddenly alert. Laurence offered the queen a chair. Bertha sat back into it and smiled. She held out her arms to Edith, who placed the baby in her lap. For a moment, the queen looked down tenderly. Then her eyes met Augustine's again. This time there was anxiety in them.

'Already Aethelbert is talking about how he can make alliances. The old king of Deira had sons. We had hoped that one of them . . . but now that's all been overturned in bloodshed. They call the man who seized his kingdom "Aethelfrith the Ferocious".' She rocked the baby in agitation. 'I should be sorry to see her wedded to the heathen son of such a man. But I know that such political marriages can also open the gates to Paradise. Mine did. Kent is now a Christian country.'

She looked at him straight, then. She saw him flinch, and felt a moment's guilt. Had her thoughtless words snatched his triumph away from him, in his last hours? She had a sharp-edged memory of that frightened but brave group of monks, marching out of the forest on the Isle of Thanet. Titus carrying the silver cross. Maurice with the board painted with Christ's face. Augustine heading the rest, as they sang their litany. When he preached his first sermon to the king and queen, under Thunor's Oak, his voice had shaken on the opening words. She must not belittle him.

Her face softened into a consoling smile. 'I came here as a Christian princess, to marry the heathen King of Kent. I brought my bishop as chaplain, but he spoke little English. Aethelbert despised him. For years, I wondered what more I could do. And then my family wrote that Pope Gregory himself had dreamed of coming to Britain to bring them Christ's Gospel of love. I couldn't open the ports of Deira to him, where your slave boys came from, but I could offer Kent. I knew that Aethelbert might be flattered to be approached by Rome. He's the nearest thing the English have to an emperor.'

She saw Augustine's dark eyes fill with tears. Had all that fearful journey across Europe, that turning back to Rome, the slow agony of their detention on Thanet, his facing of the heathen king under the oak, come down to this? The door to Kent had already been unlocked for him, by a woman.

'God was generous to us,' he said with difficulty.

'But *you* were the man I needed, when the moment was ripe,' she assured him eagerly. 'You fulfilled all my hopes, and more. You persuaded the king, as Liudhard and I never could. You've baptized thousands of Kentish folk. You spread the Gospel to Essex. You even tried to offer new hope to the British in the west.' She reached out her hand across the sleeping baby to him. 'Father, the name of Augustine of Canterbury will live in history, wherever the English tell their story.'

The slow smile that answered hers was deep relief. His shoulders straightened with renewed confidence, then slumped, as though a great burden had been lifted from them. Hastily Laurence moved towards him.

'Because my own hope has been so richly fulfilled,' Bertha went on. 'I dare to hope that this little girl of ours may do still more for the English in the north. . . .'

'Your majesty!' whispered Laurence. One arm supported Augustine's sagging frame. The other reached out to her in appeal. 'He can't hear you now. He's gone.'

Bertha rose in distress. Edith moved swiftly to the door and whispered to a monk outside. The queen and the new archbishop stood mutely facing each other. Laurence cradled his dead leader and friend in his arms, Bertha her newborn baby.

The bell of St Peter and St Paul's began to toll across the meadows, breaking the news to Canterbury. It told of a traveller who had left behind the glory of Rome, had sailed beyond the limits of the known world and come safe at last to harbour.